Praise for Emma Kavanagh

'A thrill a minute - I loved it' **Clare Mackintosh**

'One of my favourite books of the year. The intricate, clever story is told well, and the characters are brilliantly drawn' **Rachel Abbott**

'Fast-moving. Unexpected twists. Punchy writing. This author has teeth! A perfect thriller for winter nights' **Jane Corry**

'Wow. Whether you like fast-paced thrillers or in-depth (spot-on) character-led mysteries, you're going to love *To Catch a Killer* by Emma Kavanagh. LOVED it' **Caz Frear**

'A real white-knuckle ride of a thriller that packs a big emotional punch. This is top-class crime writing' **Tammy Cohen**

'I absolutely raced through it and loved every minute of the heart-pounding cat-and-mouse chase. DS Alice Parr is brilliant, three-dimensional, and utterly memorable, and I can't wait to see more of her soon' **Elle Croft**

'This transatlantic thriller has elements of Bourne and Lee Child while remaining true to its British police procedural roots. Beautifully written, expertly paced and highly entertaining' **Sinéad Crowley**

'*To Catch a Killer* is a pacy cat-and-mouse thriller with real depth and a protagonist I want to go for a drink with. A brilliant character-driven story perfect for anyone who adores a twisting, turning read. I loved it' **Amanda Jennings**

Emma Kavanagh was born in Wales in 1978 and currently lives in South Wales with her husband and two young sons. She trained as a psychologist and, after leaving university, started her own business as a psychology consultant, specialising in human performance in extreme situations. For seven years she provided training and consultation for police forces and NATO and military personnel throughout the UK and Europe.

For more information, tweet Emma @EmmaLK

Also by Emma Kavanagh

To Catch a Killer
The Killer on the Wall
The Missing Hours
Case 48: The Kidnapping of Isaiah Rae (*short story*)
Hidden
The Affair (*short story*)
Falling

the devil you know

EMMA KAVANAGH

ORION

First published in Great Britain 2020 by Orion Fiction,
an imprint of The Orion Publishing Group Ltd.,
Carmelite House, 50 Victoria Embankment
London EC4Y 0DZ

An Hachette UK Company

5 7 9 10 8 6

A CIP catalogue record for this book is
available from the British Library.

ISBN (Paperback) 978 1 4091 7503 2
ISBN (eBook) 978 1 4091 7504 9

Typeset by Deltatype Ltd, Birkenhead, Merseyside

Printed in Great Britain by Clays Ltd, Elcograf S.p.A.

www.orionbooks.co.uk

For my sister, Jessica.

For being my safe harbour in stormy seas.

Prologue

There was a chill to the air, on the day that her story began. The fallen leaves had taken on a furled-up crispness that spoke of winter to come. And back then, with a new wife, the ring still a luminous glow on my alien finger, life was potent with possibility. I was thirty years old, Laurence McCabe, although everyone always called me Laurie.

I drove through the still sleeping city, watching the comforting homeliness of it slip by. Madison was my wife's home by rights, not mine. And yet the past five years, it had taken root in me. It pulled me in until it felt like I had always been here, like my childhood on an Idaho plain was all just a story I had heard once. On that morning, I was headed out to Monona Terrace, an early-morning run along the footpath that ringed the lake. I was trying to lay it all down, set it in my memory before we left. I had accepted a new job, a firefighter out in Bloomington, Indiana, starting a week from that day.

I rounded the corner onto South Carroll Street, the dome of the Capitol building purple in the early rising sun. And I was looking at it, and thinking how much I would miss it once I was gone, and so I was distracted, lost in my thought. It took me longer than it should have to notice him.

Or then, was it a her? A person, made thick with a dense winter coat, too warm for the season, even with this chill that had sprung from nowhere. The figure hunkered down beside the Capitol, its shape dark against the light of the walls.

It shouldn't have meant much to me. My mind should have gone to some poor soul, sleeping rough, trying to catch some shelter in the arms of the great white dome.

But my foot eased off the gas, and my heart rate began to climb and the little hairs across the backs of my arms stood up proud.

I have thought about this often in the years since, about what it was that made me stop that day. And the best I can come up with is a stirring in my gut, some deep-down notion of something being wrong here.

They say that the battlefield never really leaves you, that once you have fought, a part of your mind will live forever on burning-hot sands. They're right.

I drove on a little ways, swinging a right onto South Hamilton, and then eased the truck to a stop, parking up on the still empty street. I remember sitting there, my fingers hesitating on the ignition key, wondering just what in God's name I was doing. And then I turned it, the engine falling silent. I opened the door and slid myself out into the cool morning air. I turned, moving back towards the Capitol building.

My insides twisted, thinking of Oklahoma, only

the year before, of a truck parked outside the Alfred P. Murrah Federal Building, an explosion that ripped it near in two. More people than I could even imagine dead, and that was before you even started thinking about the kiddies. I slowed to a walk as I approached the Capitol, slipping into the shadows of the trees, and peered towards the building.

For a moment I thought that he – or she – had gone. Then I saw a movement, a shape shifting from the shadows, and I felt my body tighten up, a spring now, just getting ready to fly.

See, that's the thing. Once you've seen combat, once you've served, and seen bombs blow and men who were once your friends shredded into little pieces of meat before you, it changes the very body of you. After, your brain is always waiting, for the next gunshot, for the next blast.

I could feel it, how shallow my breath had become, the way my eyesight had narrowed itself down so it seemed like I was looking through a dark tunnel. My body had done the math, had flung me five years back in time onto a god-forsaken spit of Iraqi land, where it seems that even the heat wants to kill you.

The figure, it just stood there, twisted around the corner of the building, its gaze hooked on something I couldn't see. I moved closer, keeping low to the ground, fighting my brain to keep my vision clear, my thinking in check. The figure, its movements small, careful. And something else, some ill-defined shape propped up against the wall of the Capitol building, discernible only by the deepening of the shadows surrounding it. The figure fussed over it with delicate movements.

It was clear to me. Undeniable.

The figure had stepped back now, the darkness of it melting into the building's outline. And I flexed my fingers, testing the grip of them. I would have to be fast. Seemed to me like my brain had shifted down a gear, settling to autopilot, the memory embedded in my muscles saying to me, *It's okay, we'll take it from here.*

I'm sorry. You probably don't want to hear all this.

It's just important to me that you understand. That you see the world the way I saw it on that day. I feel like you deserve to know the full and unadulterated truth.

And so for me, the sounds of the birds vanished and the rustling of leaves stopped, and all that remained was my breath, the figure and the shadowed shape pressed up against the side of the building. I moved about the tree, slow, steady steps, thighs burning with the crouching lope, and then I was running. It seemed to me later that the good Lord had infused my legs with a little extra something, a touch more fizz. The world fell away behind me, sidewalk, kerb, until I launched myself out into the open roadway, legs reaching for the grassy bank beyond. My entire body all twisted up in anticipation of the blast that would surely come now, of the lancing pain that would fell me.

I dove into the shadowed shape of the Capitol, willing my eyes to move faster, to adapt to the sudden darkness, flinging out my arms, coming up on …

Nothing but empty air.

I stopped, twisting in space. My vision clearing, the shadows spilling their secrets. Just a whitewashed wall, and a couple of fallen branches and me, breathing like I had just run a marathon. I forced myself to still, to listen. Because there would be footsteps, yeah? The sound of running, of soles hitting autumn-crisp leaves.

But all I could hear was my own breathing.

I stood there for a moment, and then a moment more, one hand resting against the smooth expanse of wall, the other propped against my thigh. And I parsed it all out, tried to think. I had seen it, right? Someone standing here, waiting and watching. I had ... and then my mind shifted away, spinning in doubt. Because they said this. About guys like me, who'd seen the stuff I'd seen. That sometimes it breaks you, twists your mind so that you just can't trust your own senses any more. And me ... but I was fine. The odd nightmare, sure. Sometimes I'd jump, at the slamming of a car door, the popping of a cork, but that, that wasn't this.

I felt a bitterness rise up through my gullet. What the hell was happening to me?

I sucked in breath, thought briefly about just giving it all up as a bad job, just turning around, heading back home to the divot in my mattress and my wife and her soft skin, that gentle smell of apple from her shampoo. Then I shook myself. Because you couldn't, could you? Just go giving up like that. Life was so stuffed full of opportunities to quit, if you took every last one of them you'd be dead before the clock struck noon.

5

So I pulled in another deep breath, this one tasting of autumn mulch and a tangy cold wind, and I straightened my shoulders and began to turn, back towards the way I had come.

And that is when I remembered the shape, the one hidden low down in the pool of darkness where the wall met the ground.

I stepped closer, and it grew in me, that confidence, that, no, it wasn't my mind, splintering the way so many others had. That I hadn't imagined anything at all. Because there it was, that patch of darker darkness, just waiting for me.

I stepped towards it. Each step a careful one, like I was treading on a crystal floor, instinct trying to pick out the shape of it from in amongst all the plunging shadows. My senses looking for wires, listening for the sound of a ticking clock, time running out.

I was listening so hard, that when the sound came it all but knocked me from my feet.

It was a wail, loud enough that it pierced the dawn sky, sending a flock of starlings spiralling from the trees.

For a dizzy moment, it seemed to me that it was a siren.

Then the wail descended, faltering out into a barking series of sputtering coughs, before climbing back up again, a shriek now, angry and hoarse.

'Holy shit!' I muttered.

I apologise for the profanity, but that's the truth of it.

I ducked down into the shadows, pulled the shape towards me, hard edges, all covered in a soft downy

6

blanket. But I wasn't afraid any more. I knew exactly what it was.

I eased the blanket away, rolling down the trimmed edge of it.

The baby within didn't look at me. It – because the he or she of it all remained a mystery – was too caught up in the indignity of the whole thing. It had screwed shut its eyes, its apple-red cheeks flushed with fury. Small hands waved wildly beneath the blanket, shoving at the knit hat pulled low on its brow, pushing it lower, so that one eye was covered. A breathless silence, a moment of infantile disbelief, then a howl of fury, waves of sound growing louder and louder so that in the end it seemed that the whole world must know what I had found here.

'Hey,' I said.

Shaking like a leaf, I reached out, hooking the knit cap back up from the baby's eye. The howl stopped then, as if cut with a knife, and the child froze, easing open sky-blue eyes and peering out at me, its forehead creased up into a furious frown.

'I ...' I never had been good with kids. I struggled, casting about for the right words. 'It's okay, little one. It's going to be okay. You're safe now.'

Book One

Book One

Chapter 1

Now

'She can't expect you to stay a baby forever.'

I grunted, not turning away from the computer screen. 'What my mother expects and what reality dictates are two very different things.'

'Well, sure.' From behind me came the sound of Eve setting her soda can down on the desk. 'But, dude, you're twenty-five years old. You have a master's behind you, a PhD on the way. You, Rosa Fisher, are officially a grown-up. I mean, surely even your mother gets that you're going to have to move out at some point.'

I glanced over my shoulder at my best friend, her magenta lips stark against mahogany skin. The lips were currently pouting. 'This is the same woman who still buys me string cheese because I said I liked it when I was twelve. My mom is not going down without a fight. I mean, look, Drew and Addie, they're up, they're out of the house ...'

Eve snorted.

'Okay, well, Drew is mostly out of the house,' I conceded. 'Mom, she's just trying to cling on to that last little piece of my childhood.' I sighed, swivelled about in my chair to face her. 'I'll tell her. I promise. I just, I have to pick the right moment, is all. Like when she's unconscious.'

'You ever get sick of it?' asked Eve. 'Being the baby for them, I mean.'

And I took my time, considered my answer. And in the end shrugged. 'I guess we all play a role, one way or another.'

My older sister, Addison, the wife of a cop and mom to two little girls and anyone else who happened to find themselves in her orbit. Andrew, two years younger than Addie, four years older than me, the wild child, a new job every two weeks, who can never quite seem to make a relationship stick and has a frankly unhealthy fixation with Michelob Ultra. And me. Rosa the baby. Rosa the good girl.

Eve frowned at me. 'It's just you're so ... not like that ... not with me, at least.'

And I pursed my lips, and failed to point out that maybe I was playing a role for her too. The PhD student, the psychologist taking a deep dive into the minds of the con artist. Calm. In control.

Was that any more me than what my family saw?

Eve folded her arms beneath her ample bosom, giving me a long look. 'Whatever. But my lease is up in January. And I am not signing up for another year with Charlie and Rhi, the dope-smoking dummies.' She shook her head. 'I swear, I've gotten stupider since living with them.'

I grinned. 'Good. Give the rest of us a chance to catch up.'

I twisted back towards the computer screen. And tried to concentrate on the article I was editing, to not think of my mother, her sing-song voice saying, What would I do without you, Rosa-bel? I guess it was the way of it, when you were the youngest of three. Your mother, she watches her older children grow up and fly the nest – even if some of them don't fly too far, and insist on returning to the nest every time they run out of fresh underpants – and with each one that leaves, she loses a little piece of who she was. Until, in the end, all that is left is the baby, and suddenly that baby becomes your whole world.

Yet the truth of it was, my mother's embrace had begun to feel like a stranglehold, what had once been affection mutating into a straitjacket.

'What time are you leaving for Chicago?' asked Eve.

'Three. Addie has to wait for Gray to take care of the kids.'

'Should be fun,' Eve offered.

I sniffed in response. 'Girls' trip', my mother kept calling it. A belated birthday present from my sister and me, a two-day trip to Chi-town. With *Hamilton* tickets. So ... yay. Only the truth of it was, most of me was bracing for it, preparing to pack myself away, tuck the real Rosa up tight in some closet, stepping into character. Rosa-bel.

The path had been laid out early, you couldn't say we weren't warned. Grow up, stay out of trouble, marry, punch out a couple of kids. Stay close. And Addison, the eldest of us all, she was the poster child, the shining light of what a good daughter could be. She had checked all the boxes, the husband and kids all coming right on time and in precisely the right order. Drew ... well, he'd married. Had lasted a year before the whole thing had collapsed in on itself like a dying star. Had mostly stayed out of trouble, the odd DUI notwithstanding. He had stayed close, his trailer park only a mile or so down the road from the family farm, although, truth be told, he spent more time in his childhood bedroom now than he did when he was an actual child.

And then me.

First one to go to university. A degree. Then a master's. Then, just about the time when everyone is muttering about me being a perpetual student, embarking on a PhD, a course which pretty much confirmed all their worst fears about me. Maybe, my mother had offered, you could do something, you know, normal instead? What about teaching kindergarten?

I had reached the end of my first year, there or thereabouts, the prep work done, the subject well beneath my belt. White-collar crime. Like somehow it's cleaner than the other types.

The goal, my goal, was to develop an understanding of what has to happen in life before someone with no criminal history, someone who is ostensibly a good sort, turns, biting the hand that feeds them. What has to happen to allow someone who thinks of themselves as an innocent to bilk their company for thousands, hundreds of thousands.

It was the quintessential slippery slope, minor missteps paving the way for massive crimes, until in the end, the unthinkable twists into the inevitable.

It was the kind of crime that seemed to evolve from a heartfelt intention to be honest and good, until, somewhere along the way, something changed. Until eventually you are weighted down by opportunity and by pressure and by the ability to rationalise what you are doing, and before you know it, you're a criminal.

It felt like a calling, although it seems hyperbolic to call it that. But, throughout my life, I had always been fascinated by the bad guys. When we were kids, Drew and Addie would insist on being the superheroes, with towels knotted about their shoulders as capes, their underwear tugged outside their pants, much to Mom's consternation. But me, I always wanted to be not Superman or Batman, but rather Lex Luther, the Joker. They were, I would say, just more interesting.

I had fought hard, and yet had also been luckier than most. At the eleventh hour, a finance company out of New York had come forward with a scholarship, a full funding of my research, a stipend to live off. It is important to us, the letter had read, to reach an understanding of how an employee might justify to him or herself the committing of a financial crime against our company, and to develop a strategy for identifying vulnerabilities in such people.

I blew out a heavy sigh, focusing back on the screen.

'What turns white-collar criminals red? An examination of violent index offences'. By Rosa Fisher and William Beddows.

The journal article was written, albeit in rough form. I shouldn't forget, my PhD supervisor had said, that it was early days. That the study was still in its infancy, okay not to already have publications rolling in. Only it wasn't okay, was it? I felt a familiar burn creep across my cheeks. I had been lucky, the scholarship was generous. Eve, on the other hand, had been less so. She was struggling on with help from the Bank of Mom and Dad, together with as many part-time jobs as she could cobble together. And luck like mine, it brought with it pressure, to prove that you are worthy. And no small measure of guilt.

The knock on the door came sharp, and I twisted to look over my shoulder, as Will stuck his head in. My PhD supervisor was in his late thirties and better-looking than he had any right to be. I half glanced at Eve, her head tipped coquettishly, suddenly looking far more enthusiastic about life, and I pushed down a laugh. She had a nuclear-level crush on Will. I like older men, she'd protested. Older, bearded men, who look like they know a thing or two about what a woman wants. I'd stopped listening at that point, in the interest of self-preservation. Tragically for Eve, Will was firmly married, and what time wasn't swallowed up by marriage and 2.4 kids was devoted to his research. Also, I'm pretty sure Eve terrified him.

'Hey. How's it coming?'

'Nearly there. I just want to run through it a couple more times before I submit,' I said.

Will leaned around the door, handing me an envelope. 'This came for you.' He grinned. 'Looks like you made a friend.'

I sighed. 'Another one? God!'

He gave a brief laugh. 'Just don't reply, keep any interactions you have to have clinical, and if you have to have any face-to-face, don't go alone. You'll be fine.' His eyes sparkled. 'When you work with psychopaths, you haven't really made it until you have your first death threat.' His voice got wistful. 'I remember my first death threat …'

'You guys are weird.' Eve looked from me to Will, shaking her head. 'These criminals of yours, they creep me out.'

I laughed. 'It's great. Seriously, these guys, they spin a great line of bullshit. It's hugely entertaining.'

Eve gave me a look. 'Yeah, well, you creep me out too.'

'And on that note …' Will retreated back out of the office. 'Rosa, have a good trip, yes? And give yourself a break, okay? You're doing great.'

My stomach did a little flip-flop. 'Thanks, Will.'

I slid open the envelope, pulling out a card from inside. It had butterflies on it, 'Thank You' embossed in gold across the front. I flipped it open, inside, in large looping letters, the words 'Thanks for listening. Carl.'

'Boyfriend?' asked Eve, wryly.

17

I waved the card at her. 'Sixty-three-year-old pastor. Married. Four children. Caught defrauding his church of somewhere in the region of fifty thousand dollars.' I pursed my lips. 'Not entirely sure he's my type.'

'Sounds like mine,' muttered Eve, ruefully.

My desk phone rang, and I reached for it, gaze still on the card, thinking not of the call, but of Carl in that studio apartment he was renting on the outskirts of Pittsburgh, of the wedding ring he still wore in blatant defiance of reality and all his soon-to-be ex-wife's pronouncements. Poor Carl. Poor, stupid Carl.

'Hello, Rosa Fisher.'

'Rosa?' My sister's voice sounded different, all high-pitched and sharp-edged. 'It's Mom. Something happened. She's on her way to the hospital.'

Chapter 2

The dog was barking.

It was a hard awakening, pulled up through layers of sleep, and I lay in my bed, blinking into the black night, thoroughly disoriented, the sounds of Fleck's agitation mingling with the smoky remains of a dream.

The clock read 3.12 a.m. As my senses slowly began to rouse, I remembered that I was alone, the big old house empty apart from me. The recollection brought with it wakefulness, the room coalescing into dark shapes and shadowed corners.

A heart attack. That was the only explanation for the pains in her chest, for the ache in her back, the shortness of breath, the sense of a faint only moments away. No, don't call an ambulance, my mother had said. I don't want to be a bother.

By the time I had arrived at the hospital, it was all but done.

It hadn't been a heart attack, or so the doctors had said. They had delivered that news, grave, like they were informing her of her imminent demise, and my mother, she had taken it as such, her face falling with the devastating news of her perfect health. One more night in hospital, for observation. It had been offered as a balm to ease her disappointment; a balm covered by our more than generous family health insurance.

'I don't want you to worry about me,' my mother had said, my hands gripped between hers, shockingly tight for a woman at the doorway to death. 'I'll be okay.'

And I had forced my face into a look of concern. 'I'm not sure you will, Mom. I mean ... you look AWFUL.'

And Addie had slapped my thigh, her movement hidden by the height of the mechanical bed, a low mutter, 'Would you stop encouraging her!'

My mother, looking gratified and appropriately weary. 'I know, my poor little one. You're such a Mommy's girl.'

Drew, on the other side of the bed, had stifled a laugh.

It was not the first time we had done this dance of death. Likely it would also not be the last.

I listened to the German shepherd's barks and thought of the empty expanse of house, of the stretched-out fields beyond its four walls, of the perfect isolation. And I let out a slow breath. Isolation is a rare thing when your role as the baby has so far guaranteed you a constant string of protectors, even though you are twenty-five and an adult and have about as much use for a babysitter as a fish has for a bicycle. My heart beat a little faster, in tune with Fleck's yips. Perhaps, I reasoned, he was uneasy, unsettled by life's changes. He had, after all, fussed and growled and whined when I had finally re-turned home, a little past ten, the darkness in the house and its surrounding fields so perfect that his barks had seemed exaggerated, piercing.

I had come in, had been unable to settle, had made myself a cup of sleepy-time tea, settled at the dining table to continue work, my papers spread out across it, had sat there until the words had begun to shimmy and dance on the page before me.

Fleck had begun to growl now, low and deep-throated. So I levered myself up in the bed, half hitched the low-slung blind to peer out into the darkness at the squared-off shape of the dog run. What the hell had gotten him so riled up? He was a good dog. A German shepherd who fancied himself as a spaniel, all perk and bounce where he should be serious and teeth. But he didn't sound like that tonight. Tonight he was a dog of fury. I shifted, going for a better view of the yard, but there was only the plunging shapes of shadows, flashes of movements that were Fleck racing about in his enclosure.

A ripple of unease ran through me.

Then Fleck let out a low whine and the incessant movement stilled and then ... nothing.

I watched still, waiting for something to emerge from the shadows, for shapes to begin to make sense for me. But it was just the curving arc of the hill behind us and the overreaching arms of trees and the darkness. I let the blind drop back down, sighed a little. It was probably just a coyote who had gotten too close, gotten Fleck all riled up, setting my adrenaline pumping for good measure.

Damn dog.

I didn't mean it. I loved that damn dog. Stinking gas and all.

I scooted back down beneath the comforter, pulling it up to my chin. It wasn't cold out, not by a long stretch, autumn turning into an Indian summer, where your skin puckers with sweat and you begin to think with longing of the first snow. But still I pulled the comforter high. Because every child knows there has never been a monster that cannot be defeated by the safety of your duvet.

And then I rolled my eyes. That was the trouble with playing a role, no matter who you played it for. Sooner or later, you started to believe it.

'Go to sleep,' I muttered. 'You are a grown-ass woman.'

I forced my eyes to close, my heartbeat gradually slowing, drifting in the sudden silence. Addie had suggested I stay with her and Gray and the girls. Although suggested might perhaps be too loose-limbed a word. Had bumped right up against insisting. And then, when that had failed, my brother Drew had made some noises, muttering something about staying over at the big house, because, after all, didn't he have work he'd promised Mom he'd do in the yard, so staying over, well, it only made logical sense. Nothing to do with the cable TV at the big house, or our fully stocked fridge.

I had begun with gentle dissuasion, had ended with flat refusal. You guys, I'm a grown-up. You gotta let me be a grown-up. I'll be fine.

22

And I had mostly believed it.

Did I sleep then? I don't remember. Perhaps safest to say that my mind had begun to drift. First to the hospital, Mom's large frame clinging to that too-narrow bed, her forehead furrowed in that permanent frown of sleep. Then to the university, to my study, the intricacies of qualitative analysis. Then that steady drift, my mind loosing itself from the shore, my limbs beginning to sink beneath the waves.

Then the sound of breaking glass.

There was no easy wakening this time, no gentle climb from sleep. I started awake, sitting upright in the same movement, so it seemed, my heart thumping in my chest. Was it . . .

That brief moment where you allow yourself the luxury of denial, telling yourself that you can't have heard what you so plainly did. Then the next sound, coming as if it were lines in a book I had already read. The low squeak of footsteps on tiled floor.

I froze, my breath stilling in my chest. It would be Addie, coming to check on me. But no, it wasn't Addie. Because it was 3 a.m. and Gray, when it became apparent we weren't actually Chicago-bound, had ended up pulling an all-nighter on some stabbing out in Greentree, and no way could she leave the kids alone. Drew then. But no, not Drew. Because Drew was going to some poker game out at his buddy's trailer and likely would be so intoxicated by now that he no longer remembered where the big house was.

I strained to listen, was aware of a tremble in my fingers. Silence. And then more silence.

I let out a slow breath, closing my eyes with relief.

I had dreamt it, the edge of a dream spilling over into wakefulness, scaring the ever-loving shit out of me. Eve was right. I really needed to stop this, stop playing the part of the baby. It was starting to get to me, to creep beneath my skin.

Then came another sound. Heavy soles on a hard tiled floor. One. Two. A pause. Three.

It should have been fear. Bitter terror should have frozen me in place. Instead, something else, a stilling, my mind going quiet and cold, all thoughts lining up behind one another to reach an inescapable conclusion. Someone was in the house.

Think. I breathed deeply, slowly, a creditable attempt at forcing blood flow back into the frontal cortex, to find my knowledge of the world, and of the bad people that inhabit it.

Burglary. A rational choice from someone who has a need for money, has chosen burglary as a reasonable route to that money. They look for signs of occupancy.

I had turned all the lights out. I had put my car in the garage. Did he think no one was home?

A floorboard creaked directly beneath me. The same floorboard that creaked each night as my mother made her way to bed. He was in Mom's bedroom, the room underneath mine.

Burglars, they look to the master bedroom first, knowing that's where most people keep their valuables.

I held my breath, weighing between options, blind panic waiting just on the horizon. I should shout, scream. Scare him away. Only ... if it didn't, then I had revealed myself, had made a bad situation a whole hell of a lot worse. My body began to ache from enforced stillness. Perhaps he would take what he wanted, would flee. That would ... it would be logical, wouldn't it?

Beneath me, I could hear drawers being pulled open, a clatter of something spilling.

They, whoever they were, were making little effort to remain quiet. Perhaps then that did mean he thought the house was empty. And I felt the faintest flush of relief, that they would steal but then would leave. And bad would not become worse.

Then movement, steady, unhurried, from my mother's room out into the living room. The strained wheeze of weight on floorboards, low, distant, and I could see it, a figure standing before the elongated windows, looking up towards where the cathedral ceiling curved down, an internal veranda jutting out above the open expanse of the living room. On the veranda, a pair of overstuffed armchairs, a pouffe between them, the walls of the alcove densely packed with bookcases. And then, visible in amongst them, a solitary door. My door.

Leave. I lay, unmoving, barely breathing. Told myself to remain calm. Please leave.

The distant floorboard creaked and it seemed to me that I had my own private sonar, each sound corresponding to a movement. Now standing in the centre of the living room, near the dining table, now moving closer to the stairs.

An off-centre creak, deep and timorous. The bottom stair.

He wasn't looking for valuables. He was looking for me.

I was in trouble.

Do something.

I shoved back the comforter, all faith in its protective power gone now, clambered from the bed, bare feet on wooden boards. My breath came in short, sharp bursts. The dark room seeming to come into focus all at once, the shapes that had been murky now becoming clear. My cellphone, plugged into the socket, sitting at the other side of it.

I listened. Another footstep. Then I moved, quick, fairy-light steps across the room, tugging my cell from its charging cable, fingers awkward.

9-1-1.

'What is your emergency?'

'Help me.' It wasn't words, rather a breath. I sank into the corner, folding myself up beside the heavy wood chest of drawers, tucking the phone close to me. 'Someone is here. Someone is in my house.'

The air was thick.

'Ma'am? I'm going to need you to speak up, Ma'am.'

My breath caught in my chest and I strained, listening not to the voice, but for sounds beyond my bedroom door. The movement, it had stopped. The house silent.

Heat rolled over me. Had I made a mistake? Was it simply my imagination?

'Ma'am? Can you hear me?'

Then it came again, the creak of weight on a stair, closer than it had been before.

'Someone is in my house. I'm alone. Help me.' The words hissed from gritted teeth.

Had the steps slowed? I tried to still my breathing, to listen. Had they heard me?

'What's your address?' The woman's voice was clipped. 'Ma'am? You there?'

'123 River Hill Drive,' I breathed, fought between competing desires, to be heard, to be silent.

'A unit is on its way, Ma'am. Can you get out of the house?'

I thought of weight on stairs. Of the wide landing beyond my door, at its limit only a narrow spindled rail separating it from the living room below. No escape that way without a fifteen-foot drop. Along the landing, past my brother's room, and you would find yourself on the staircase, face-to-face with whoever stood on it. I thought of my sliding window, another precipitous drop beneath. Every door leading to a death of one kind or another.

'I can't.' A ripple of panic flexed through me. 'I'm trapped.'

'Do you have somewhere you can hide?'

I peered around the edge of the chest of drawers into the undeniable expanse of my bedroom, with closets and a bed and nowhere I could hide that I wouldn't be found.

'I …'

The footsteps were steady, constant, closer now. I was a deer on a country road, the headlights of a semi capturing me in their glare. Future is already written. You lose.

'Ma'am? Are you there?'

I looked down at myself. At my short shorts, tank top with the spaghetti straps. And, God help me, I wondered what rape would feel like. I wondered if I could survive it. And then I wondered if I would be given the option.

A higher-pitched groan. The top step. My heart racing and my ears ringing and then a random thought hitting me. Why did the dog stop barking?

'The unit is five minutes away, okay? Help is coming.'

But I wasn't listening now, was instead replaying the low growl, the following silence. Was there something in there, a yelp of pain, some sound I should have heard? What did they do to Fleck?

And that was the moment of change. I felt a wash of stark cold horror, at the thought of my big, dumbass German shepherd, a hole sliced across his gullet. And some other feeling following hard behind it, a white-hot fury.

'Tell them to hurry,' I muttered into the phone.

Then I set my cell on the ground, crawled forward, reaching beneath my bed, looking for something, anything. An abandoned doll, the inline skates that I had worn twice, breaking my left wrist on the second go, and then a wooden shape I had all but forgotten. I tugged the baseball bat free, weighed it in my hands, a silent war cry.

28

Dim from the phone: 'Ma'am? Ma'am? I think I lost her.'

Another creak. This one on the balcony, that loose floorboard before the bookcase that held all the Jane Austen and John Steinbeck and Ernest Hemingway. The one to the left of my bedroom door.

I thought of a gloved hand reaching for my handle, of a dark-masked man, a knife throwing light into the darkness.

I raised the bat, and now thought only of Fleck.

I do not know how the door opened, only that it did. And then I was gone, was not Rosa-bel, but now was someone else entirely. I flew from the bedroom door, towards the amorphous shape, all darkness and shadow. I brought the bat down over my head, aiming for head or heart or anywhere on the demon before me.

And then ...

Then the wood of the bat was hitting the shape of the shadow, and then I was flying, my feet lifted from the ground and up and up and knowing without seeing that the landing's limit with its wood-slat railing was coming closer, the living-room floor, so very far below. Knowing that I was powerless to stop. And in spite of that, my fingers reaching out, trying to grab the railing, trying to save myself, and grasping only at empty air, and suddenly I am beyond the railing, nothing beneath me now but open space. And falling, falling.

Chapter 3

It was darkness, followed by breaks of light, round and sharp, a dislocating feeling coming to me that I was on a stage, was the main attraction. Voices, low, urgent. Were they talking to me? It was so hard to tell. It was pain, a breathtaking arc of it that wrapped its way up my arm, around my shoulder. A sensation of having fallen face down into a puddle, only the water was thick, viscous, working its way into my nostrils, my mouth, the heady taste of iron.

I wasn't afraid then. It wasn't courage or resignation. Just that in amongst this scattering of sensations, I couldn't seem to find any room for fear. I would die. That seemed to me to be obvious. A little voice in my head, Ah well, what can you do?

The floorboards rolling beneath my head, a heavy crunching footfall, hands on me. The distant thought, This is it, here we go.

'Ma'am? Can you hear me?'

Saying yes, and only then realising that I hadn't said yes at all. That my mouth had opened and in the place of a solid, recognisable word had oozed a low moan.

'She's alive. What's the ETA on the ambulance?'

She. Did he mean me? Oh good. That was good news.

I shifted, tried to lift my head from the inconvenient puddle, and the pain bucked and roared, racing across my chest, down my back.

'No, no, it's okay. You stay where you are. We got you.'

It annoyed me that I couldn't see the face that accompanied the voice. Annoyed. How absurd is that? True though. But when I shifted my gaze, the rough shapes of the living room shimmied, and everything was painted in a red haze. I felt a hand, encasing mine, could hear the quiet muttered reassurances, the meaning reaching my brain without first doing me the courtesy of passing through my ears.

'Am ...'

It was too far. The entirety of the syllable more than I could manage. It was, it seemed, enough.

'You're going to be just fine. We're Madison PD. You're safe.'

Then more sounds, of a door opening, of wheels scraping against wood, new voices, a wave of cool air. The hand slipping from mine, my fingers questing in its absence. Then a pinprick of light, the ripple of plastic fingers touching me.

'Hi, can you hear me? I'm Colette. What's your name, honey?'

I sighed internally, took a long run-up to it. 'R ... Rosa.'

'Okay, Rosa. We got you now.'

And then ...

Kaleidoscope memories. Of being borne aloft, of cool night air, of a rumbling road, the distant whirr of sirens. Thinking that sleep was what was needed, that sleep would help everything, but Colette talking and talking in that loud, insistent burr, chattering about everything and nothing at all, wanting to tell her to shut the hell up so that I could nap, but of course I didn't do that. That would be rude. Then the emergency room. The smell of people packed tight together, of bleach and blood, sailing past curtained boxes, the movement sending my brain tipping, a swell of nausea that came up from my feet. And more hands and more voices and questions, so many damn questions, and struggling to force my mouth to form the words, and when it did, struggling to make my voice heard across the din.

'Did they catch him?'

Only they didn't hear me, or if they did, chose to ignore me.

'Rosa?' A male doctor, starvation-thin with a hawk-ish face, his mouth set into the kind of line you could underline homework with. 'You have a head injury. You've lost a lot of blood. We're going to scan you, check for any underlying damage, okay?'

'Fleck?'

The hawk pulled back, looking about the room. 'Is she ...'

'Fleck,' I forced out. 'Dog. Okay?'

The man stared at me, seemed to be having trouble getting sound and meaning to work as one. 'I ... I don't know, I'm sorry, Rosa.' He shook his head, as though to clear it. 'Providing the scan comes back clear, we're going to need to stitch you up, so we'll be taking you straight in for surgery. It also looks like you've fractured your shoulder.' Then, his voice dimmer, like he had turned from me, had already forgotten I was there, 'She's B negative. Going to need about fifteen hundred millilitres.'

What was there to say? I closed my eyes, in my damaged head seeing dark shadows, feeling the hit of the bat, my feet leaving the floor, my body arcing through the air, falling from the balcony down towards the looming darkness of the living-room floor. And once I had fallen, what then? Had he come to me? Had he knelt down beside me? Had he touched me? I tried to remember, picking out from in amongst the collage of images the feeling of palms running over my hips, my back. But no, that had been the paramedic. Hadn't it? Why didn't they kill me? He could have killed me. But then, maybe he thought I was dead. I thought I was dead. Why not him too? I would need to remember. The police, they would need something, some flickers of information to go on. But all that I had was the sound of weight on a staircase, a dark shape, the sensation of hitting a brick wall. It wasn't much, was it?

Then another thought, worming its way up out of the heavy-lying fog. It could be anyone. And wanting to panic then, feeling this pressure rising up through my chest, and wanting to twist away from the skeletal doctor with his hook nose, but the pain racing along my

33

shoulder, the dense thundercloud resting over my head, all pinned me down.

I couldn't move if I wanted to.

And then ...

I remember a tunnel, a series of loud bangs. The hawk smiling, or grimacing at the very least. Scan was clear. The damage to your head was superficial, looks like your shoulder absorbed most of the impact. You were lucky.

Lucky.

Good one.

Then an operating theatre. Count backwards from ten.

And then ...

'We shouldn't have left her at home alone.'

'Addie ...'

'I should have made her come stay with me. Why didn't I make her stay?'

'Ads, she didn't want to. It was one night. And it's not like she's a child ...'

A snort. 'It's not like she's an adult.'

I forced my eyes open, lashes sticking together under the weight of all the sleep, tried to focus on the too-bright room. A mistiness blanketed my left eye. My right focusing on my fretful sister, her dark blonde hair tucked back behind her ears. Her face was free from make-up, her already pale features paler still.

'I can hear you, you know.' It came out as a whisper, but at least it came out.

Addie let out a little gasp, all but flew across the room,

her hand plucking my limp one from the starch-stiff bed, drowning me in the smell of coconut and sun cream. 'Oh Rosie, I'm so sorry, honey. Oh my goodness, it was all my fault. I told Drew. If only you'd stayed with us ...' She leaned in close to me, but it was like I had been coated in grease, that her focus just couldn't land on me, her gaze slip sliding away no matter how hard she tried to hold it there.

A waft of stale cigarettes and I turned my good eye to the lumbering shape of my brother. I could feel the tension rolling off him in waves, in the tightness of his broad shoulders, the set of his jaw.

'You okay, kid?'

I grunted, shifting my weight, a wild, vain attempt to sit up, given up in poor grace. 'Never better. What happened to Fleck?'

Addison pulled back a little, grey eyes scouring mine. 'What?' The word guarded, wary, like she had decided she was a better gauge of brain damage than any MRI.

'The dog,' I whispered. 'Did he kill the dog?'

Drew let out a quick bark of a laugh. 'Did he hell.'

'Drew!' said Addison. 'Language.'

My brother rolled his eyes. 'Your damn guard dog should be ashamed to call himself that. You want to know what happened to Fleck? Fleck got himself a little bit of a midnight feast is what. Bastard brought meat with him, stuck it through the fencing to shut the dog up. And Fleck, being the loyal protector that he is, he just chowed down, and damn the rest of the world.'

Addison scowled at him. 'Would you stop?'

35

'No, I'm just saying, is all, what the hell's the point of a damn German shepherd if it'll give up at the first sign of sirloin? Should've got you one of those stupid little chihuahua things, for all the good Fleck did.'

'So …' I struggled to focus on my sister. 'He's not dead?'

Drew snorted.

'No!' Addie glanced back at him, warning in her voice. 'He's not dead, honey. Just very much in the doghouse. So to speak.' She stroked my arm. 'How are you feeling?'

I really wished she hadn't asked me that. The taking stock then. The internal reality check, bringing with it the realisation of a low thunderstorm of a headache, of a mistiness in my left eye, a dull throb of pain lancing across my shoulder, that sense of distance from myself that spoke of painkillers, and strong ones too. 'I don't know. Sore.'

Addie pursed her lips. 'They stitched up your head wound. Said it'll heal just fine.' Her gaze flicked up to my face, lingering there, just a moment too long.

I sighed heavily. 'It's bad, isn't it?' I raised my right hand, fingers grazing padding, skin that started far above where mine should have been, taut and alien.

'It's … There's swelling, honey. That's all. Doctor says it'll be gone in a week or so.' She took my hand in hers. 'Don't touch it, sweets. And maybe … maybe best you stay away from a mirror for a day or two? Just until you're ready.'

'Jesus, Ads, scare the kid a bit more,' muttered Drew.

'I'm not trying to scare her,' snapped Addie. 'I'm trying to protect her.' Her voice shimmied. 'Like I should have last night.'

'It wasn't your fault,' I offered.

My sister looked away from me, a tear catching the sunlight as it rolled down her cheek.

'Did they get him?' I asked, quietly.

Addison didn't look at me.

I looked, one-eyed, from her to my brother. 'What?'

Drew sat down heavily on the bed, the creak of it weaving its way into his sigh. He'd put weight on recently, blamed it on losing the job at the sawmill, the break-up with whatever this last one's name was, and rolls of fat bunched over the neck of his T-shirt. He glanced up at me, then quickly away. All recoil from the monster.

'Bastard had bolted by the time the police got there.' He patted me limply on the leg before whipping back his hand like he'd been burned. 'Lucky too. If I'd got my hands on him, I'd have made sure he got friendly with my Glock.'

'Let's not talk about this now,' said Addie, warningly.

'No.' My voice came out firmer than I had expected. 'I need to know.'

Drew sighed. 'Cops say he smashed a hole in the back door, let himself in that way. They've gone through the area, but everyone was asleep, no one saw anything. That Jenkins guy, further up the road, he said he heard the dog barking, but just assumed it'd gotten a scent of coyote, something like that.'

As sleep receded, I was aware of a new sensation replacing it. A bubbling anger. 'Did they take anything?'

Because there would have to be a reason, a justification. All things can be justified, one way or another. Did he need money? Maybe a drug craving had taken hold of his system, so that breaking into a person's home, that suddenly becomes small fry next to the horrors of going cold turkey?

'Gray had me meet him out at the house, see if I could spot anything missing,' Drew said, his voice guarded. 'I couldn't see anything ... Laptop was still there, TV ... They turned over Mom's room pretty good, took the money she keeps in her dresser, went through her drawers, but far as I could tell, they didn't get much else.' He snorted. 'I don't know, maybe the guy had a thing for big panties.'

'Andrew Taylor Fisher, I swear to our Lord, Jesus Christ ...' snapped Addie. 'Would you just—'

'If it wasn't about getting valuables, maybe ... maybe it was about something else,' I interrupted quietly.

Addie looked at me, face heavy with a frown. 'Like what?'

I twisted my head to look at her through my good eye. 'Maybe he wasn't there to steal. Maybe he was there for me.' When no one spoke, I clarified my position. 'Rape. Perhaps he was planning to rape me.' I looked from one to the other. 'Mom wasn't home. Mom is always home. What are the odds that was a coincidence?'

It seemed that the air got sucked from the room, and

Addie quickly traced the sign of the cross about her shoulders. Drew shifted, uncomfortable.

My head was throbbing, and I closed my eyes briefly, hoping to quell the pain. 'Why come upstairs? Unless his motive was sexual.'

'Christ, Rosa, take a day off, eh?' muttered Drew.

'I'm just saying ...'

My sister let out a low moan, gripping my hand tight. 'Look, Gray is on it. No need to go getting yourself upset ...'

'Why did they bring the meat?' I asked.

'What?' Drew looked startled.

'The meat. Why bring it?'

'For the dog.' He said it like he was talking to a three-year-old who had asked why rain doesn't fall upwards.

'The run,' I said, voice hoarse with the strain. 'It's behind the house. You can't see it from the road. You have to come into the yard and round on into the back before you know it's there.'

'Okay?'

'So,' I said, faintly, 'if they were just looking for a random house to burgle, he wouldn't have known to bring meat.' There was a long and heavy silence. 'He must have been watching.'

'Rosa! How can you talk like that? It's not ... Please, stop it.' My sister looked close to tears. 'Gray, he said it's likely whoever it was didn't know anyone was home, thought they'd make some easy money. You're safe. It's all over now. That research of yours probably isn't helping,' said Addie, on safer ground now, singing a familiar refrain. She smoothed the hair from my face. 'No wonder your head is full of all the worst things that can happen, obsessed like you are with all these psychos.'

I didn't answer, dropped my gaze to the white sheet pulled taut across my lap, the sheen across my left eye morphing it to grey. And I tried to remember it, to see the opening of the bedroom door, the crossing of the landing. Trying to grab hold of some image of who had stood beyond the bedroom door. But there was nothing, only a black hole where a memory should be.

'I ...' I looked at Addie. 'I can't remember.'

'Of course you can't.' My sister squeezed my fingers tight. 'Don't worry. It'll come back.'

Only it wouldn't, would it? Because the image, whatever it was I had seen waiting for me on that balcony, had been swept away in a deluge of stress hormones that had left my memory a barren flood plain. And so all that was left was the evidence. A smashed-out window. Pulled-out dresser drawers. Footsteps on the stairs.

A single tear fell, unbidden.

Addie looked from me to Drew, the silent communication, the how do we divert her from this, what do we say?

Fortunately, my mother had always been a great one for diverting attention.

The door flung open as if blown by a great gust of wind.

'Oh my sweet baby Jesus, look at the sight of you.' My mother trundled into the hospital room, a force of nature, her face a rictus of horror. She flapped at Drew, shifting him from his perch beside me, leaned in close, smelling of lilac and simply Mom. She studied me, her gaze hooking on my swollen eye. 'Oh my little girl.' Then came the tears, as inevitable as worms after rain, her face crumbling, her hand gripping mine tight. 'How could they? How could anyone do this to you?'

'Mom ...'

'They said I couldn't come. That I needed to wait for that doctor to release me and I said to them, my baby girl is upstairs after having gone through the Lord only knows what, so you'd best be getting out of my way because I am leaving, come hell or high water.' She cinched her grey robe tighter beneath the mound of her bosom, the sides of it falling open at what should have been her waist, to reveal a lavender check nightgown beneath. In spite of the nightclothes, her make-up had been carefully and generously applied, her bottle-red hair twisted up into a tight chignon. She spun round, gaze swinging between my siblings. 'Did he ... I mean, was she ... you know, violated?' She breathed the last word, apparently under the impression that my head injury had left me deaf.

'Holy shit,' muttered Drew.

'No, Mom. She's fine. Aren't you, Rosa? Just a bump to the head, a broken shoulder ...'

'And that's fine, is it, Addison? She doesn't look fine to me. I mean, look at her! Look at her face!'

'I'm feeling great about myself now, FYI,' I murmured, mostly to myself.

'Who in the hell would do something like this?' She turned on Drew now. 'Have they got him? That son of a bitch who did this?'

'Not yet, Mom,' said Drew with a sigh. 'I'm sure they will. Gray is dealing with it.'

My mother harrumphed. 'Oh, well then, I'm sure we can all sleep well at night.'

Perhaps if I closed my eyes, I could slip into a coma. That would be nice.

'They'd best hope they get him before I get him, because that asshole will be in for a world of pain ...' She sank back onto the bed, head of steam almost spent. 'Bastard,' she muttered. Then she shifted again, facing me full on in a way my siblings had not, studying me.

I felt my hand twitch, itching to raise itself to my swollen face, to trace the outline of it.

'This will be fine, Rosa,' she said, firmly. 'It looks bad, yes, it does. But this swelling, it will go down. The shoulder, that will heal too.' She leaned in, speaking soft and hard both, 'These wounds, they will heal. And we need to thank the good Lord that it wasn't anything else, anything worse.' She squeezed my hand. 'We will get through this, Rosa-bel, and then life will go back to normal. Everything is going to be absolutely fine.'

How tempting to sink beneath the waves of her reassurances, to let the steady tempo of her voice lull me into safety. I told myself that she was right. That this would pass, and then life would be exactly as it was before.

Mom studied me for a moment longer, then finally released her hold on me, a sigh like the air being released from a balloon. 'If only you'd gone and stayed with Addie and the girls like I told you to.'

'And Gray,' offered Addie, pointedly.

Mom sniffed, her gaze hovering over me. 'This damage to her head ...' Looking at me, talking to Addison. 'Is it bad? Will she be ...?'

'No, Mom. There's no brain damage.' The sigh was implicit in Addie's words. She glanced at me, gave me a swift wink and then smoothed her expression out, looking back to our mother, her tone parental. 'She's going to be just fine.'

'But the blood. Did she lose much blood?' Mom's gaze still roved over me. A piece of cattle up for auction.

'They gave her a transfusion. She's doing good.'

It seemed to me then that my mother paled. But I was working with one good eye and a storming headache, so what did I know? Nonetheless, the room fell mercifully quiet for long seconds that seemed to stretch out into an eternity.

Sometimes just the absence of conversation can feel like a spa day.

Then my mother sat up straight, shifting. Her nightgown had ridden up on her thighs, exposing sausage legs stuffed into a casing of surgical socks. She placed a hand to her chest, closed her eyes briefly in what Drew had come to refer to as her martyr pose.

The three of us looked at each other, sibling code. You say it. No, it's your turn. I gestured with my good arm towards my swollen shut eye, my shoulder in the sling. I'm injured. You deal with her.

43

Addie narrowed her eyes at Drew and me, then, working hard to sound patient, 'You okay, Mom?'

Our mother kept her eyes closed, hand hovering over her heart, like she was fighting to keep her composure. 'It's been a terrible shock, is all. Seeing my baby girl like this. And on top of my problems ...'

'But the doctors, they said your heart is fine, right?' said Addie, delicately.

Mom's eyes snapped open. 'That's what they say. Seems to me they're just too busy to bother with the likes of me. Now, if I was one of those immigrants ...'

'Oh Jesus,' muttered Drew.

She held up her hand. 'All right, I'm just saying, is all.' She looked up at my brother. 'Be a good boy, Andrew. You pop on down to that coffee shop in the lobby, that one that does those good doughnuts. Get us all a nice cup of coffee and a couple of those doughnuts. Chocolate-covered for me.'

My brother looked from me to my sister. 'I ...'

'Go on, Drew, there's a lamb. You bring your sister with you to help out. Rosa could use some rest, I'll bet. Go on. Rosa, you close your eyes and get some sleep. Mommy will stay right here.'

You might as well try to hold back a hurricane.

My eyelids closed, happier to obey than I had expected, and I heard the mumbled voices, steadily retreating footsteps, sinking into that half world, neither quite asleep nor quite awake. And I would have stayed there, had it not been for a feeling, settling into the pit of my stomach, that sensation of something being not quite right.

44

The sound of paper rustling.

I eased my good eye open, only a very small amount, the room blurry and indistinct. And yet it was enough to see that my mother had moved, that she no longer sat by me, but stood now, at the base of my bed, flicking through the sheaf of my medical notes. And it was enough to see that her hand was over her mouth, that silent tears had begun to roll down her cheeks.

I allowed my eyes to close again, one question rolling through my mind. What was it they had not told me?

I must have truly slept then, for when I awoke, I was alone, the room settled into darkness. Beyond the window, pinprick lights of stars punctured the sleeping sky. I lay in the narrow bed, thinking that I could hear it again, the weight of footfall on stairs. Then came a different sound, laughter, and I told myself that I was safe, that it was merely the nurses' station beyond my door, my imagination once again, leading me astray. That it was all okay.

But I couldn't dislodge it, that sense of wrongness, of a warning, just out of sight. And I thought of my mother, of her face as she studied my medical notes. What had she seen?

I lay there for a while, looking out at the night sky, made cloudy by my murky vision. Trying to steer my thoughts clear of my mother's face, trying to tell myself that it had all simply been too much, that it was natural for me to be looking for danger when there was none, that my senses were heightened, my amygdala firing with wild abandon. It would be nothing.

I closed my eyes again, aiming to drift back to sleep, but the darkness brought with it memories, of voices and sounds and bright lights and sharp pain. And I thought of the hawk-nosed doctor and the feel of his brisk fingers on my skin. And his words. She's B negative.

And my spinning thoughts ground to a screeching halt there, and I opened my eyes.

Because I wasn't. A flower of fear blossomed in my stomach. That they had done something wrong. That they had given me the wrong blood.

Only . . .

My father had joked, after the accident that ultimately killed him, when he was here, in this same hospital, as they fought to save his life, had looked me square on and said, 'See, Rosie, I'm an A+ kind of guy. And your mom there, she's just as A+ as I am. An A+ pair, that's what we are. Isn't that right, Nora?' And she had shushed him, had looked close to tears, but then, of course, she was. A tractor had just rolled over her husband, and the life that she had known hung right there in the balance.

I levered myself up, a lance of pain barging its way along my spine, nausea swelling up. I slid bare feet to the cold tiled floor, tentatively reaching my good arm towards the paperwork. Dizziness swamped me. I should stop. I should go back to bed. I should. I should. I should.

I flipped open the notes, struggling to pick out words in the dim light. And those that I did pick out, I could not understand. I turned the pages, thinking that it had merely been my mind playing tricks on me, words taken out of context, perhaps meant to apply to someone other than me. That my mother's tears, they had simply been her way of coping, overwhelmed with the sight of her youngest child injured. That the correspondence of the notes and the tears, that they had simply been two things occurring at the same time, unrelated to one another.

And then I saw it.

Because the light was dim and my mind was slow, but together they were enough to be able to pick out a single letter in amongst so many others.

B-.

I sank onto the bed, notes held tight in my hands. That feeling settling over me of finally learning the words to a long familiar melody.

Because two A+ parents cannot produce a B- daughter.

47

Chapter 4

Five days. Five days of hospital food, of the caustic stench of bleach. Five days of half-slept nights and half-woken days. Five days of that equation running through my mind, $A+ + A+ = B-$. Twisting it and turning it, trying to get the sum to fit the variables.

I made it until day three before I saw a mirror, one of those happy-accident things that aren't an accident at all. Stared at the alien face in it, clinging to the sink edge until my fingers lost all feeling, my ears full of a low ringing. The line of stitches ran in a diagonal slant, clear across the right side of my forehead, the skin around it swollen up, a burnished blue bruise, taut and slick-looking, like at any moment it would erupt right there on my forehead. Remember those aliens in *Star Trek*, the ones with their messed-up heads? Yeah? Yeah. Beneath the mountain of my forehead, my eye had swollen itself almost shut, a swathe of bruising that reached right down to my cheekbone.

I try not to be too fussed about my appearance, that's the honest truth. Try to tell myself that the world will put more stock in you if you have a good mind and decent intentions, rather than the perfect boobs and puckered lips. But I'm not ashamed to say that I cried that day, looking at this formless shape in the mirror before me.

The irony of not being able to recognise myself was not lost on me. I guess that's normal when you suddenly realise you have no idea who you are.

I had lain awake, on that first night, horror fighting against the soporific effects of the drugs. Had lain in bed, the medical notes laid out beside me so that my good arm rested on top of them, like I thought that if I let go, they would disappear. I had stared at the crookedly fit tiles of the ceiling, my gaze tracing the pattern of them until in the end I would convince myself that it was not true, it had been my imagination playing tricks on me. And so I would reach out with my good arm and flick the light on and I would flip through the notes again, willing it not to be there, willing the world to remain what I had always believed it to be. But each time, there it was, a 'B' where there should have been an 'A'. One little letter, a world of difference.

At about 4 a.m. on that first night, I had given up all notion of sleep, had clambered out of the hospital bed and inched my way, still clutching the medical notes, towards the stiff upright chair pushed up against the stretched-out windows. I had watched the Madison lights sparkle against the waters of Lake Monona, and had wished and wished to go backwards, to yesterday, or maybe even just to those moments when my eyes had opened and I had seen my mother peering at my notes. Seemed to me like that was when everything had spilled

49

from bad to catastrophically bad. I sat there in that chair and I ran my good hand across the swollen, pulsing skin straining from my right eye and felt this wrongness, this overwhelming sense of everything sliding out of whack. What did it mean? Rolled it around in my head, trying to find a way to make the pieces fit, to make an A+ and an A+ equal a B-, but every way I turned it, I stuck out at an odd angle. There had been a mistake in the lab. That would be it. They had gotten my blood type wrong.

I had stared at the distant water, had tried to let that thought settle, allow it to be enough. But both me and the lake knew that I was lying. If the lab had got it wrong, well, odds are I wouldn't be sitting here now having this little conversation with myself. They had transfused me. They had gotten it right.

Then memories coming in a jagged-edged rockfall. That family tree thing they tried to get us to do in high school, the mention of swabbing our DNA to find out if we were 60 per cent Irish or 20 per cent Spanish or 2 per cent Latvian or whatever, and Mom losing it, a hot and spiralling rage about invasion of privacy, government overreach, schools intruding where they didn't belong. And me, folding in the face of her anger, and telling myself that privacy mattered to her, that it was nothing more than that. And then the time, after Poppa's accident, when I wanted to donate blood, when I told her that after all they had done to try and save him, that it was the least I could do, and her weeping this time, about how I just didn't understand, how I needed to just be a good girl and stop trying to make it all about myself. And me, folding this time in the face of her sadness.

I had watched the lights on the water and the realisation had settled, with a crystal-clear clarity, that my life had been one extended series of lies.

My mother (was that who she was now?) had come in on the following morning, fully dressed, the eternally patient doctors finally reaching the end of their rope and levering her from her hospital bed, consigning her to the harsh wilderness of the heart-healthy world. And she had fussed and frowned and talked to me about God only knows what, and I had watched her, a feeling of being a million miles away. Searching her face, with its well-padded cheeks and too much rouge, the chin that vanished into neck, the grey-green eyes, the button nose. And I searched for myself in her. But there was no seeing her anew. I had seen this woman on every day of my life thus far. How now could I look at her as if for the first time?

On day five, the hospital finally called it quits, sending me on my way with well wishes and a bag full of high-powered drugs. Drew loaded me into Mom's Prius, the outside air sluggish and hot, autumn remaining elusively out of reach. I eased myself into the passenger side, wincing as my brother – my brother? – slid the seat belt over my wounded arm, my mother hovering at his elbow. Don't do it like that, careful with her now, you put that seat belt on, missy.

'Mom. It's fine. I'll make sure she's buckled in.'

Drew ducked in beside me, nostrils flared wide, sparing a moment for a quick eye roll, a mutter of 'pretty sure I know how a seat belt works' that we both hoped Mom missed.

Drew paused, his face just inches away from mine, and I could smell the cigarettes that he swore he didn't smoke hanging over him, 'It's going to be all right, you know. We replaced the glass, checked the whole place over. Gray even added a new security system, just so, you know, you feel better.'

'He won't be back.' My mother's voice rolled from the back seat. 'He wouldn't dare.'

Drew gave me a quick half-smile and then pulled back, easing the door carefully closed, like any sudden movement of it would break me. I stared out the windshield at the parking lot beyond, the heat sending shimmering lines up from the tarmac.

I could hear the wheeze of my mother's breath, the scrape as she shifted the seat belt over the mound of her belly. See, thing was, since that night and those notes and that B- of mine, every move of hers sounded to me like those footsteps on the staircase, a motion that didn't belong where it was, that was suddenly inexplicable.

Could it have been an affair? I kept my eyes on the road ahead as we slid up to a Stop sign. Mom today … I mean, you don't really look at her and think affair, but I guess, back then … I mean, I've seen the pictures, of a round-cheeked young woman with her mass of bottle-red hair, the dark lipstick and kohl eyes. And Poppa, he was always kind of like this moon orbiting a planet, each of his movements dictated by hers, her quirks, her inconsistencies, never commented on apart from perhaps the slightest hint of a raised eyebrow. I listened to the weight of her breath behind me as we took a right on the 151, heading south. Could it be that? Could that explain this imbalance between them, the sense of almost losing her once, the second chance being flimsier somehow?

I glanced sideways at Drew, his forehead puckered in concentration, grip tight on the steering wheel. Would he know? Would Addie? Was it a truth universally acknowledged by everyone but me?

I gazed out the window at the fleeting forms of the Pick 'n' Save, the Arby's, my stomach twisting up into knots. Or was the truth something else? Had I come from neither one of them?

As we picked up the interstate, my gaze shifted, settling on the face in the passenger side mirror, with its bulbous head, its nickel-plate eye. Who the hell are you?

The drive passed by in bunches, speckled with conversation, Mom driving from the back seat, Drew's knuckles growing whiter against the wheel. I had begun to feel nauseated, eyes weighted with sleep, when we finally turned onto the long gravel drive, the trees arching across it to meet in the middle so that, as a child, I always imagined we were sliding into a tunnel, home existing somehow a world away from everything else in life. Through the tree tunnel and then out the other side, edged by lurid green lawns, Drew pulling the car to a stop outside the garage door. I looked up at the house, a feeling of being outside myself, like I was seeing it for the first time, with its overlarge windows, reaching up to the triangle of the roof, a pyramid with a growth on its side, a stretched-out tumour of narrow sash windows balancing above a paint-chipped garage door.

'Hey! Welcome home.' My sister hurried down the steps, a pair of girls twittering behind her, pushing and shoving until the air was thick with flung-out ponytails and 'Mommeeee'.

Addison pulled at the passenger side door, was hugging me before I could release the seat belt. 'You okay? You look better.'

My sister. A genuine believer in a solid lie for the right cause.

'Uh-huh.' I clambered carefully from the car, weighting my right shoulder in its sling. 'Like a supermodel, I'm sure.'

'Girls! Now be careful with Auntie Rosa, okay? She's been sick.'

But she needn't have worried. My nieces, Mason and Gabriella, six and four respectively, clustering about her legs, peering up at me like I was an alien dropped off in their midst. I was inclined to agree.

I looked up at the house, a shiver darting across my spine. The sound of floorboards creaking, the floor on which I had bled.

'Rosa?' Gray's gravel voice cut across my thoughts, and I snapped back, enmeshed suddenly in my brother-in-law's embrace. 'Kid, you scared the hell out of us.'

I stood on tiptoes, hugging him back, the familiar scent of him making me want to cry suddenly. And then a second thought, hard on the heels of the first. Did he know about my B minus?

I watched as Addie shooed the rest of the clan inside, our mother complaining loudly about the heat, how I needed to come in, how I needed to lay down, that she wasn't going to bring her child home only to have her die of heat exhaustion right there on the porch. The girls bouncing around her, ponytails flying, Gabriella protesting that no one, not no one, had noticed her party dress. My sister tucked her arm through Mom's and pulled her towards the house, looking back at us, a quick wink, mouthed 'take a minute', before leading her inside,

'You okay?' asked Gray.

I snorted. 'Fan-fucking-tastic.' I glanced at him, grimaced. 'Sorry.'

Gray grinned. 'No apologies necessary, sis. I'd say that pretty much sums it up.'

I looked back to the house, where the girls had now taken up position on the deck, their high voices tumbling down towards us as they ran, backwards and forwards.

'Those girls of mine,' Gray muttered. 'Where the hell they get that energy ...' Then he grinned, pointing towards the side of the house, where sat a dark-coated German shepherd with liquid eyes, his gaze hooked on me, his head hung low. 'That's one guilty dog,' muttered my brother-in-law.

I studied Fleck, sighed. 'You know, you? You are a rubbish German shepherd. You know that, right?'

The dog let out a low whine, and I sighed, patting my thigh with my good arm. 'Come on, dozy.' Fleck leapt up, trotting towards me, his tail wagging hopefully. 'Dumb dog,' I said, fussing him behind the ears. 'I'm glad you're not dead.'

Gray shook his head. 'That animal needs some aggression training.'

'Did you find anything?' I asked. 'Did you catch him?'

Gray didn't answer for long moments, seemed like he was building himself up for what came next. 'Look, me and the guys, we've been over the place with a fine-toothed comb. Seems to me like nothing's missing, just some cash from your mom's room. Made a good enough mess in there, but other than that ... Our best guess, whoever it was, they figured the house was empty, took their chances on it, then you disturbed them and they ran.'

Fleck leaned against my leg, the weight of him heavy. 'Why come upstairs?'

Gray considered me, 'Addie told me what you were thinking. Look, I know, coming from your background, your research and all, you see bad guys everywhere. And I get that things like that, they make your mind go to dark corners. But I think, in this case, it's really important that we go off the evidence. I mean, if it was sexually motivated,' my brother-in-law flushed, using the 's' word with his little sister. 'Look, I don't want to freak you out any, but whoever it was, they would have had time enough for that after you fell. Took patrol a little while to get out here. The fact that they didn't, suggests to me that's not why they were there.' He looked sympathetic. 'I know this is tough. But I think evidence suggests this was an attempted burglary, that you interrupted them, and after you fell, they fled.'

The heat pressed down on me, and I looked up at the house. Did you stand here, in this spot, looking up at the sleeping house, anticipating what you would do next? Then I turned, could feel Fleck turning with me, his breath warm against my leg. It would have been dark, on that night, no street lights this far out in the wilderness. A sleeping house. Who's to say not an empty house?

'Maybe you're right,' I murmured.

'We did a sweep. Looking for forensics, blood, fibres, prints. Came up empty.' He shrugged, sympathetic rather than nonchalant. 'It's not that unusual, no matter what TV would have you believe. And if it's a savvy burglar, someone who's forensically aware, it's even more common.' Gray turned towards me, taking in my battered face without flinching. 'I know you're not going to feel safe. And I know this has been one hell of an experience for you. But in my honest opinion, whoever was here, they're gone. We've put visible security in place. It's not likely they'll try again.'

I nodded slowly. 'Thanks, Gray.'

'Look, if there's anything, anything at all, you just call, yes? I'll be here faster than my kids can give you a migraine.'

I smiled at that, looking back towards the house. 'I guess we'd better …'

Gray sighed. 'Better had.'

The dog let out a low whine, and I patted my thigh again. 'Come on, you.' Fleck leapt up, tail wagging.

We made our way into the house, the air smelling meaty and rich, the distant chatter of my nieces, Taylor Swift crooning on the radio in the kitchen. Gray peeled off towards the children, and we walked, Fleck and I, along the rear corridor, taking a turn into the living room, then up the stairs, the creak of them sending my heart rate spiking. I paused on the landing, a sudden sense of vertigo, my body fearing the plunge. I let my fingers trace across the top of Fleck's head, and focused on the bookshelves, trying to centre myself.

That was when I noticed.

Family pictures stood in frames, tucked in the gaps between Gillian Flynn and JK Rowling. Only one was missing. It was a chestnut-framed photograph, taken on my graduation from my master's, showing me in cap and gown, my dark hair piled up beneath the mortar board, smile lipstick-red and anxious. I scanned the shelves, thinking that I had merely missed it, that I was looking for trouble. But the photograph remained resolutely gone.

'Mom?'

'Yeah?'

'Hey, you move that photo of me in my graduation?'

'Why yes, Rosa. In between hospital appointments and my youngest daughter's near-death experience

I decided to do some rearranging of the decor in this house.'

I guessed that was a no. Fleck let out a low whine. I turned about on the landing, my gaze hooked on the shelves. It was gone.

I stood for long moments, staring at the shelf, at the empty space. My brain nothing but the densest of fogs, and then, having resolved nothing, my body turned, began to walk slowly down the stairs, into the bustle of the kitchen.

'That girl called.' My mom was sitting on a stool at the kitchen counter, watching as Addie loaded a plate with dinner rolls.

'What girl?' My voice sounded unreal to me.

'You know, that girl. The big one.' She lowered her voice to a theatrical whisper, a quick glance at the children still out on the deck. 'The black one.' Emphasis heavy on the black.

Addie looked back at me, rolled her eyes.

Heat clambered up my cheeks. 'Her name is Eve, Mom. You know, my best friend?'

'Well, whatever, she called. Wanted to stop by. I said no. I told her you weren't up to visitors yet, that this was family time.'

I gripped onto the kitchen counter, fingers attempting to dig into granite, and mentally counted to a billion.

'Come on,' said Addie, firmly. 'Dinner.'

I followed the sound of voices out onto the deck and suddenly felt a wash of exhaustion. I wanted silence. I wanted sleep. Yet my nieces, finally subtracting one black eye, one bulging forehead and coming up with Aunt Rosa, now swept up against me, small hands slipping into mine, a rising tide of conversation. And then my mother was loudly informing us that she would surely collapse if she did not eat soon, and so we were eating, on the long wood table set out on the decking that overlooked the spreading valley. The sun began to sink, spilling out fingers of orange and lavender, air rich with honeysuckle and brisket. The world seemed to have sped up now, the swim of it threatening to leave me behind as Addison loaded my plate with meat and spice-flecked rice and bulbous tomatoes and smooth-skinned rolls. The chatter of conversation that seemed to me to be the song of crickets, me holding my fork awkwardly in my left hand, carefully moving a dozen grains of rice, backwards and forwards, and thinking that if this didn't end soon, then I would be sick. Then finally Gray noticing my silence and shushing the adults and the children alike, she's exhausted, look at her, and then Addie ushering me up to my bed, the comforter all clean, sheets freshly laid, the room smelling of the flesh-coloured lily stocks that stood proud in a clear glass vase.

In my head, I told my sister that I didn't want to sleep, that it was all drowning me, that I needed to speak to Mom, that I needed to ask her who I was, where I came from. But my mouth, it had other ideas, staying firmly clamped shut, and my limbs folding beneath the dense comforter and sleep crowding in fast behind.

Only the sleep, it was full of running and chasing and

never quite catching, and so I flicked awake, once the sun had sunk way down low, leaving the world coated in a twilight gloom. The house was silent.

I reached across, flicking the switch on my bedside lamp, a warm orange glow bathing the room. And lying there in that muted softness, I allowed myself a moment to think that maybe it was all going to be okay, that the break-in had been a one-off, just one of those things that come and then go again and are soon forgotten. That the hospital had made some kind of mistake and that the evidence I had corralled in favour of my origin mystery was all just life, viewed from a slightly wrong angle.

I allowed myself a moment to just be the Rosa I had always been.

Then my attention drifted to the sickly-sweet smell of lilies, and with one hand, I pushed myself up in bed, reaching for the miniature bright-white envelope tucked in amongst the green of them. I slipped the flap open, sliding out a small folded card, inside of it written a solitary word.

Sorry.

Chapter 5

I stared at the single word. There were no sounds now, few sensations, the world narrowing itself down to the putrid scent of the lilies and the dark blue script. I turned the card over in my hands. There was no name, nothing to indicate where the flowers had come from. I experimented with telling myself that it was innocent, a gift from a friend, a poor choice of wording, an uneasy feeling that I was lying.

I eased my way out of bed, framed now before my bedroom window and the plunging blackness beyond it, and my heart sputtered with the realisation that I was highlighted, caught in the light of the lamp. I snapped the light off, standing in the dark and waiting as my eyes adjusted. Was someone out there?

I strained, listening, but just the distant sound of a car off on the main road, the chirrup of crickets.

My gaze shifted, back to the dark outline of the flowers.

Who are you?

Ah, that question.

I walked barefooted across the bedroom floor, the creak of the boards beneath my feet making my heart race, and eased open the door, stepping out onto the landing. The living room beneath was lit with the glow of an orange lamp, and I could hear the pages of a book turning, the heavy harrumph of my mother's breath. Fleck lay at her feet, his head resting on his front paws, the low rumble of a snore coming from him.

I took the steps quietly, staying close to the wall, pausing at the dining room, my papers still laid out across it as I had left them that night. I hovered there, the sense of how different life had become in the days since overwhelming. Then my attention shifted, inward to outward, and I realised something was missing. I shifted the papers, left to right, trying to find the journal article I had been editing, searching for the words 'What turns white-collar criminals red?' amongst the strewn papers. I reached the bottom of the pile, began again. Where the hell was that? I had left it here. Or ... maybe I didn't leave it here. Or maybe I did and someone had moved it in the days that intervened. It would be the children, Gabriella looking for a canvas for her latest glitter-soaked project. Or Mason. Or Gray. Or Addie.

I stood there, reminded myself to breathe. After all, what was this but a tactic to stall, the putting off of a conversation I did not want to have. And stalling time was just about up.

I sighed, turned from the dining room, along the corridor to the living room, bare feet light on the floorboards, so that when I reached the doorway and my mother sensed the presence of me, she looked up with a start. Fleck gave a small yip, then settled back down into sleep.

'Rosa,' my mother said, looking at me from over her reading glasses. 'My good grief, you just about scared me into a heart attack. Lord knows, I don't need another one of those. What on earth are you doing up? You need sleep.' She shooed me away with a flick of her hand. 'Go on, back to bed.'

I stood, stock-still. 'Everyone gone?' I asked, my voice surprising me with the lightness of it.

She nodded, an ostentatious roll of her eyes. 'Lot of fussing. Drew was going to stay, but then some friend of his called to see if he wanted to go down State Street.' Her lips compressed together into the thinnest of lines. 'Gray said he's going to come back tomorrow and talk you through how those security cameras work. It's going to be like we're living in *The Truman Show*.' She looked me up and down. 'You need to get back to bed, missy.'

I breathed out, slow. 'Mom, the flowers in my room, the lilies ...'

She looked back at her book again, a slow shake of her head. 'They were waiting on the front porch when I woke up this morning. Whoever sent them, they were up and about early delivering flowers. I thought they'd brighten your room up a bit.' She glanced up. 'From the university, was it?' She brightened. 'That PhD supervisor of yours?'

'I'm not sure,' I murmured. 'Maybe Eve?'

Did I sound hopeful? My mother pursed her lips again, her gaze locked on the book before her.

I tested the theory. That the flowers were entirely innocuous, poor phrasing alone making them appear

64

sinister. I'm sorry. I'm sorry you got hurt? I'm sorry for all you've been through?

Or I'm sorry for what I did?

I glanced up at the dark square of the picture window and, on instinct, sank down onto the sofa, hiding myself from the outside view. Seemed that I just couldn't shake the sense of being a rabbit on the run from a pack of hounds.

'And ... that picture. My graduation. Is there any way you could have moved it, and, I don't know, forgotten?'

Mom looked up, 'Rosa, I don't know! I've had a lot on my mind lately. Maybe I moved it when I was cleaning.'

Maybe it was nothing. My fearful brain taking two plus two and making twenty-six.

I watched my mother, deliberately not watching me. Perhaps I should let it go, just for now. Until I got my strength back, until I was ready to cope.

Perhaps not.

'I know, Mom.' The words slid out like they had been greased, rolling onwards with an inevitability. Because being a rabbit, that was one thing. Being a rabbit but thinking you're a fox, that's quite another.

Did her colour change or was that just my imagination? Did her breath quicken? 'Know what?' She did not look at me, her gaze resting back on her book. But there was a tremble to her fingers, the pages fluttering as though they had been caught in a breeze.

'I saw my medical notes. I saw my blood type. I know that you've been lying to me.'

Time froze then, elongating and twisting.

'Rosa . . .'

'I know that Poppa was A positive. Remember him saying? That A plus joke?' I leaned closer. 'I know you are too.'

She shifted, looking for a moment like she would interrupt me, but I ploughed on.

'I know I'm B negative. And I remember my high-school science well enough to know that you can't get a B-negative child from A-positive parents.'

Fleck let loose the lowest of whines.

'Did you cheat on him? Poppa. Did you cheat on Poppa?'

My mother continued to stare at me, the book that she held sagged open in her lap, thumb and finger holding her page, like at any moment I would give this up, allow her to go back to her reading. 'Rosa . . .' She sounded old suddenly, wounded, choosing her words with care. 'Sweetheart, you've had a nasty fright. The burglary, then the fall . . . all this, it's upended every-thing. And that's what we need to be thinking about right now. Getting you well. Taking care of you.' She looked down at her book, and I could have sworn that in her voice was the slightest of shakes. 'Don't worry about some silly blood test.' A deep breath in. 'I'll bet the hospital just screwed it up.'

I sat there and I watched her. And a sense of certainty settled over me. That that B minus was an answer to a question I had never thought to ask. Why I had always seemed to be a round peg in a square hole, always just that little bit different from everyone else around me. More curious. More driven. That suddenly the answer I had grown up with, 'That's just Rosa', no longer seemed to be enough. That it wasn't enough to hear that I jutted out from my family at an odd angle, that suddenly it mattered more than anything else to know why.

'Mom,' I said, 'I need to know.'

My mother still was not looking at me, her gaze hooked on her book, eyes unseeing. A single tear snaked its way down her cheek. 'Rosa,' she said quietly, 'you are my baby. You have always been my baby.' In the words were an unspoken plea, to stop pushing, to just let it go.

I couldn't.

'Mom.' I leaned forward, my fingers trailing along the soft wool throw slung across the arm of the chair, as if I was reaching out to her, was pleading, thinking that if I could make her listen, if I could make her understand, then she would hear in my voice how very much I needed this.

She looked up at me, face etched with consternation. Then, with a soft sigh, she picked up a silver bookmark and slid it into the pages of her book. She slowly closed the cover, allowing her fingertips to trace across it, like she was buying some time. Marian Keyes. *Watermelon*. Then she set the book down.

'Listen.' Her voice sounded weary, careful, very un-Mom-like. 'You need to understand. No matter what, you are my baby.' She trailed off.

I watched her, waiting.

She looked at me, for long moments, and then, wiping her hand across her cheek, she steepled her fingers on her lap. 'Your father, he always said that we should have told you, said that no good can come from secrets, but I just thought ... I wanted to protect you, Rosa. Didn't want to cause you hurt. But even I knew that couldn't last forever, that sooner or later you would need to know. Guess you never expect tomorrow to become today. I've been thinking on it a lot, the older you got. Been trying to find the right words to say it. But I just never could seem to.'

I leaned closer to her, so that my gaze caught up hers and held it tight. 'Mom?'

She sighed again and tugged the thin-framed glasses from her face.

'You have to understand, things, they were different back then. I mean, now, people, they talk about everything. Back then, we valued privacy and dignity ...'

'Mom.'

She waved her hand at me. 'I'm coming to it. Your sister and your brother, well, they were the heart of me. I mean, you know how it is, for me and your Poppa, that we came from big families, six of us on my side, eight on his, so I just, I guess I always thought that's how it would be for us, that we'd have this big circus of a family, enough kids to fill up all these acres. But Addie ...' She shook her head, her voice hooking at the inside of her throat. 'She struggled on her way out. Rosa, it was a terrible thing. A horrible birth. It went on

68

for days and days and then she got stuck, that shoulder dystocia, and it was touch-and-go for a while if she and I would make it. Well, I mean, they saved her, but me? I was so badly damaged down there, they just couldn't stop the bleeding, and I'll tell you now, I believed that I was dying. All these doctors rushing about, and your Poppa, his face the colour of chalk, and I can hear the baby crying and I'm thinking, Well, at least she's okay. So, they knock me out and when I come to again, my uterus is gone. Partial hysterectomy. They told me that it was the only way they could stop the bleeding. Oh, I cried. For weeks and weeks, I cried. When something like that happens, you mourn for the family you thought you would have, you know? The life you imagined for yourself.'

I nodded, lining up her words with the ones I'd heard before. About the hysterectomy, the shoulder dystocia. Only those were me. At my birth. I listed them in my account sheets, labelling them as lies one and two.

'See,' said my mother, folding her hands over her belly, 'I wasn't done then. It wasn't my time. But we don't get to determine things like that, and there was a higher power that disagreed, so there we were.'

'And me?' I asked, quietly.

She nodded. 'I'm getting there.' She looked down at her hands, her fingers picking at one another. 'When I saw you, I knew that you were meant to be mine. It was like God himself was telling me, Nora, this is why it happened, this is why you had to suffer so, so that you had room in your heart for this child.'

'When you saw me?' I asked. 'I don't understand.'

She sucked a deep breath in. 'It was ... you were on the news. I remember it like it was yesterday, that I had taken Drew and Addie to school and I came home to start my cleaning and flipped on the television and there you were, this chubby little poppet of a thing in this bright yellow onesie, just stuffing your little fists in your mouth, and I tell you, Rosa, my heart, it just stopped right there, and I ran outside and went and found your Poppa and I told him that I had found our daughter.' She shook her head. 'He thought I'd lost my mind.'

'So ... I'm adopted.' It was a question and an answer both, the pronouncement sliding in, a ready understanding of my dark hair against their fair, my wide mouth against their thin lips, my quietness and seriousness and studiousness and the way that they always looked at me, that look that made me uneasy, of sympathy almost.

She did not look at me, was focusing down, short, shorn nails plucking at the fibres of her bathrobe. 'We never thought of it that way. You were just ours.'

I felt dizzy and sick and like I had just been dropped into a foreign landscape and that the language around me had twisted, becoming one I couldn't understand.

'But ... then, who am I?'

My mother shoved herself upright, lips compressing, a deep crack snaking through the peppered-on foundation across her forehead. 'You are Rosa Fisher. You are my daughter.' It was a declaration, as if with the force of will alone, she could make it so.

I looked at her, felt my mouth moving, the words

lining up behind it. Wanting to say that, no, Rosa Fisher, it turns out, is a fiction. Rosa Fisher was born to Nora and Jim Fisher, the youngest of their three children. Rosa Fisher knows who she is, she understands her place in the world.

Rosa Fisher disappeared on that B-minus day.

'And the others, Drew and Adds, they knew?'

She sighed, like the question irritated her. 'Yes, they knew. Of course they did. But they just, they loved you so much, just as soon as they met you. You were their little sister, no questions asked.'

I thought of my grandmother, with her arthritis-twisted hands, her love of jazz, of the books she would gather for me, presenting them and then watching my face, like she was waiting to see if she had won an award. Of my aunts and uncles and cousins and neighbours and friends.

'And everyone else?' I asked. 'Everyone else knew too?'

She nodded slowly. 'They knew.'

I sat, pulled my knees up towards me, my head spinning. An entire world surrounding me, all of it knowing that the person I believed myself to be, that she didn't exist at all, each one of them watching me live out this fiction.

'Rosa,' said my mother, 'you may think that we did what we did out of spite, not telling you, keeping it all to ourselves, but we were thinking of you, all of us. To us, you were our little Rosa-bel. What would be the point in raking things over, making you feel differently?'

'I ...' My mind swirled. Was it the painkillers? The drugs lingering over me, stilling my thoughts. Or the pain itself, that spiking, severing reach that stretched beyond what the drugs could do. 'I'm not following, Mom. You said you saw me on the news? Why would I have been on the news?'

She looked down then, for all the world like she was returning to her reading, fingers bothering the edges of the book. 'It's ...' A sound like a moan. 'Why do you need to know this, Rosa? You know the truth now, isn't that enough?' She looked up at me, pleading.

And I wanted to say yes. Because I was the baby, and she was my mother, and I was so so tired and scared, and if it was enough, then I could go back to bed and I could cry and try to reshape my life to accommodate all that I had not known. And my mouth opened, entirely on its own, prepared to do it, the right thing. But the words, they rebelled, sticking themselves against my tonsils.

My mother studied me, then allowed her head to drop. 'You were found, Rosa. A little itty speck of a thing. Your parents, whoever they were, they put you in a box and they took you to the Capitol building. And they abandoned you there.'

Chapter 6

I watched him, all the while trying to pretend that I wasn't, that my attention was absorbed in my lemonade, the dogs at play on his wide, sprawling lawn. Laurie McCabe stood to the side of the porch swing, hands planted firmly on his hips, legs spread wide apart in the way that big men stand, as if they are trying to appear bigger still. He watched as the dogs, Fleck and his biscuit-coloured golden retriever – Archer, I think he called him – bounced before him, taut with anticipation, mouth stretched into a broad grin. Fleck ducked down low, his rear end waggling to the sky, suddenly a puppy again, and Laurie laughed and I felt myself smile along with him. It was a good laugh, reminded me of maple syrup.

Laurie plucked the once yellow ball from between blades of grass, weighed it in his hands, one eyebrow raised as the dogs yipped in unbridled joy. Then, in one quick arc, Laurie flung the ball out towards the treeline. The dogs took off, tumbling over one another in their haste.

'You know,' offered Laurie, 'I've waited for this day for a long time. Always knew that somehow you'd find your way back here.'

Those words nuzzled their way beneath my breastbone. Always knew. How many times had I heard them in the last two weeks? I always knew I would have to tell you some day. I always knew you would start asking questions eventually. I always knew you were meant to be my sister. Always. Always. It was like the rest of the world had known this staggering secret that had shaped my existence, and there was I, right in the middle of it, bumbling along blind.

Fleck had won the prize, came trotting back towards the porch, mouth full of tennis ball, his tail held at a jaunty angle. I watched Laurie as he ducked down to fuss over him.

He had the look about him of a once fit man gone slightly to seed, the suggestion of the beginnings of a gut that hung over the leather loop of his belt. His hair had greyed, was cut short to his head. A full beard swathing his face, the faintest hint of red peppering the grey of it. His eyes squinted behind wire-framed glasses, as if he was always trying to remember something.

He had opened the door to me before I had gotten past the front gate, a big man with a large smile, tears in his eyes as he watched me draw closer.

'Can I hug you?'

They were his first words to me. Pretty good as an opening line.

I had nodded, mute suddenly, had allowed myself to be folded into his arms, a feeling of relief, of finding some kind of home. And then my body had expelled a sob I hadn't known was inside me, my brain flying between mortification and the sense of no longer giving a shit, and Laurie had hugged me tighter.

'It's okay, little girl. You're safe now.'

He had drawn back, had studied my face, glasses slipping down his nose as he peered over the top of them, tracing the shape of my eyes, the arc of my nose, the curve of my lips. My face had for the most part recovered now, all of my features sliding back into their traditional alignment, just the faintest hint of purple left across my temple to suggest what had been.

'Sorry,' he'd said, grinning. 'I just ... in my mind you're still this teeny-tiny baby wrapped in a blanket. I can't believe that you're here now. That you're all grown up.'

I'd nodded, wiped the tears from my face with the back of my hand. 'Well, I guess that does tend to happen.'

He'd laughed again, a rumbling thunder of sound. 'Yes, it does.' And then he'd looked beyond me to the car. 'That your dog in there? Bring him in. Archer'd love to meet him.'

Archer and Fleck waited, bouncing impatiently on the pads of their feet as Laurie drew back his arm, flinging the ball towards the farthest reaches of his lot, and both dogs twisted on the spot, darting after it, bullets from a gun.

'So,' I said, settling my tone somewhere between polite and casual, 'you're still a firefighter?'

Laurie shook his head, looking not at me but out at the mad tumble of fur and grass. 'Retired a year or two ago. My wife informed me I wasn't getting any younger, which, let me tell you, came as a bit of a shock to me. So I called it a day, we packed up ourselves and Archer over there and headed back to Madison. She still has family here, y'know. Thought it'd be a nice place to settle. Lead a slower pace.'

I nodded. 'Your wife – sorry, I don't know her name?'

He didn't answer for a moment, stooping down and wrestling the ball from Archer's unrelenting jaws. He pulled it free, sending it flying once again.

'Sorry ... oh, it's Beth. Betsy if I'm trying to annoy her.'

'Is she here? I'd love to meet her.'

He turned to give me a grin, eyes twinkling. 'She's gone to Florida to take care of her sister for a week or so. St Pete's. Sister's just had an op.'

'Oh, I'm sorry.'

He laughed again. 'Don't be. It was a nose job. Pity her health plan didn't offer personality transplants, but there you go.'

I laughed with him.

'How's your mom?' He pronounced the word mom carefully, a bomb close to going off, a quick glance back at me to gauge my reaction.

I hesitated. What was the right answer? She was sick. She was sad. She was angry. She was watching me, waiting for my anger to fly. She was my world and my safety net. She was a stranger. 'She's fine.'

I thought back to that night. The night everything changed. I don't know how long we had sat there, on the sofa, that book still waiting on the arm of the chair, like at any point I would give up on this, would walk away and let her return to her reading.

'It took months to adopt you, for the checks, the visits,' my mother had said, quietly. 'But we knew it was worth it. Knew it was the right thing to do.'

'Why didn't you tell me?'

'I ...' and here, I could see her parsing answers, shuffling words around in her mind, trying to find the ones that would suit me best. 'I considered it. And before your Poppa died, we had it all planned out, how we would show you the newspaper cuttings, the things we kept for you. Only then the accident happened and everything else just fell by the wayside. I have been thinking on it,' she'd said, the faintest edge of defiance in her voice. 'More of late. Been thinking how I would say it to you. What you would want to know.'

'I wish you had,' I'd said, quietly.

Then her nostrils had flared, lips pursing, the well-trodden sign of a tempest approaching. 'Thing is, Rosa, you've always been such a sensitive girl, so quick to take on all the world's troubles. Didn't know that you'd cope, not if you knew the truth. But you can ask Laurie, that firefighter that found you. We've been talking on it, about how I could break it to you. He's a good man, he keeps in touch. Always has.'

A sudden recollection of a doll's house beneath the Christmas tree when I was, what, six, seven maybe? Of a name I did not recognise on the label. Uncle Laurie. And asking my mother, and my mother flipping the question away with a quick, 'Just an old family friend.

77

Look at those lights. And the itty-bitty furniture as well. Now, aren't you a lucky girl?'

I had sat there on that sofa, and had breathed, had tried to find the middle ground between the me I was today, the me I had been only hours before. Had tried to twist what I knew now, to find a place where it could sit within my brain, that my family had abandoned me, had left me with no assurance of my safety. A bubbling anger had risen up, at my mom, at the mysterious parents, and the still more mysterious me, just so much anger that it seemed my small frame could not possibly contain it. I had wanted to run, to fling open the front door and take off, up the steep hill, into the trees, lose myself in the forest behind us. But my body had refused to comply, had been frozen in place, a quiet whispering that I could run, but that I would bring all of my horrors with me wherever I went.

And then my mother had stood, her movements marked with a greater alacrity than I had seen in her in years. 'Well, I'm going to bed.' She had paused before me, one hand resting heavy on my shoulder, and had said, 'You know now. I'm sure it's for the best. And now we can go back, and things can be just like they were before.'

I didn't throw anything at her. I remain pretty proud of that.

Then, in the days that followed, all went dark. She had told Addie and Drew about it. Not that she said that to me, but I could read it in their faces, in the way that they watched me as I walked by, in the tightness of my sister's hug, the way that they looked at me, like I was an unexploded bomb, like at any second I would detonate. And me, I went dark too. It's strange to me, how it was. How I was. All my life, I have needed to know, have never been able to bear a question without an answer. Hence psychology, hence research, all of it fuelled by this desperate need to know, to understand the world around me. And yet here I was, my entire life behind me and ahead, a complete mystery, and for one day, for two, for three, I simply let it sit.

The honest truth is, I think I had learned about all I could bear. That the enormity had to be broken down, digested in bite-sized pieces. I spent a lot of time on the phone to Eve during those days, turning my story over and over again, until by the end my brain finally came to accept it as mine.

And then day four.

I came downstairs early, already dressed, my arm still held awkwardly in its sling, face still twisted and dis-tended. My mother was up, moving about the kitchen in her oversized nightgown, grinding beans and ladling grounds into the coffee machine.

'Hi.'

'Morning honey. Oh, your face looks better. Well, better than it did. Why don't we head into the farmers' market today? We could pick up some curds. You love those.'

'Mom. You said you had kept things for me. News-papers and stuff. From when I was found?' I heard the quaver in my voice. 'Can I see them?'

She had frozen in place, the coffee pot held useless in her hand. 'I ... thought everything was okay now. I thought you were done.'

And I had almost wanted to laugh at the goddam absurdity of it all. Sure. You aren't really ours. You were dumped outside a city landmark. All good? Excellent. And I hadn't answered, had simply stood there, knowing that there were no words that could make sense of nonsense. So I waited and waited, until finally my mother had set the coffee pot down with a clunk, had bustled into her bedroom, tugging open drawers more loudly than was truly necessary. Finally she had re-emerged, a large Manila envelope in her hands, the edges of it roughed with age.

She marched to the kitchen counter, spilling the contents out. A dozen different textures and colours. 'It's just ... stuff we thought you'd want to see some day. When we told you,' she said, defensive, proof positive that her lie had been finite. 'Newspaper articles, letters, things like that. There's some photographs too.'

She handed me the empty envelope and picked up her coffee cup. 'Now, if you'll excuse me, I'm going to head out to the farmers' market.' She glanced down at the counter, back up to me. 'I'm assuming you're not coming.'

I stared down at the scattered sheets. No, I wouldn't be going with her.

A newspaper page, the main photograph a baby staring down the lens of a camera, her eyes wide, expression astonished. **How could you leave me?**

Baby Abandoned at Fire Station. I read through the text of it, mottled with age, of Laurie McCabe, the firefighter who had found me, of the search for parents who seemed to have vanished into thin air.

I flipped through to the next sheet, with its glossy finish, a magazine article, the story of the West Middleton baby, my gaze landing on a line towards the bottom of the page:

Despite extensive police investigations, no trace of the baby's parents was ever found. Baby Middleton has now been adopted.

A single photograph, thick-edged Polaroid, blurry with age. Of Mom, as she used to be, holding the baby in her arms and looking down on it with an expression of hallowed awe.

Heat sprang to my eyes, and I blew out a slow breath.

I shifted through the detritus, then, voice less steady than I would have liked, called, 'Mom? You said there were photographs? I only see one.'

A long silence, then my mother re-emerged from the bedroom, an expression of reluctance on her face. 'There should be a bunch of them in there. Those old Polaroids.'

I moved the papers about, tipped the envelope upside down, empty. 'No,' I said. 'Just this one of me and you.'

My mother came closer, plucked the photograph from my fingers and studied it, quietly, her face flushing, eyes filling. 'Well ...' she cleared her throat, 'I don't know,

Rosa, I really don't. I guess, maybe they got spilled out in the break-in and they didn't get put back in the right place. I've not looked at them in years.' She handed me the photograph, slowly, reluctant almost.

'Mom? Where did you keep this stuff?'

She wiped at her eyes, like she was brushing away a stray hair, 'My bedroom. In the dresser.'

My stomach clenched. 'Did anyone know that?'

She frowned at me. 'Did anyone ... I don't know. I mean, obviously your father knew. Drew and Addie probably.' She looked at me, suddenly suspicious, 'Why? Why are you asking this?'

I thought of footsteps on the stairs, of hands searching through dresser drawers, and then I lied. 'No reason. Just curious. Could you ... Here, just look at this for me, make sure everything else is here.'

My mother leaned over the counter, studied the papers. 'I think so. Not that I look at it often enough to have it all memorised.' She sighed. 'I have to go. Else all the good tomatoes will be gone.'

I nodded, although her words barely penetrated my tangle of thoughts. A break-in. All that was taken, a graduation photograph of me and a handful of old Polaroids, evidence of a long-kept secret. The flowers. The Sorry. A sudden feeling like all of it wound together, the secret, the fall, that somehow one led to another in ways that I just couldn't see yet.

I let out a slow breath. Focus.

Buried within the sheaf of papers, another envelope, smaller this time, containing Christmas cards, one from every year that had passed, from firefighter Laurie McCabe. And a letter, handwritten in a jagged script.

Dear Nora,
I'm glad to see that the baby – Rosa – is settling in
well. Thank you for the pictures. I think of her often.
My wife and I were talking and we thought that maybe
it would be good for Rosa if she had something to
keep, if I wrote down my version of her story, so that
when she's older, she'll understand. I hope that's okay.
Obviously, I leave it to your judgement as her mother
if and when you feel it's appropriate to give it to her.
Whatever you think is best.
    There was a chill to the air, on the day that her story
began.

And on the rear of it, an email address, a scribbled note:

Don't forget, if Rosa ever needs me, all
she needs to do is ask

And so I'm here. Asking.

Laurie gave a low whistle and Archer bounded closer. Fleck, delirious with excitement, followed suit. He held the ball up high, waiting as the dogs settled into a seated position, two muscular balls of coiled energy. And I watched him, trying to imagine it, that morning, trying to take him back twenty years in time, to turn his grey hair dark, slim down the age spread. And I tried to imagine how he would have seemed to me, a giant against my six-month-old form. Was I frightened? Did I cry? My mouth opened to ask, then snapped shut again. Some things I just didn't want to know.

'Can I ask you something?'

He flung the ball, watching the arc of it. 'Dare say you can.'

'Why did you stay in touch? Every year you sent a Christmas card. Why?'

Laurie looked back at me, appeared to be considering. Then he sighed, lowering his wide frame back into the wood-slat seat. 'That day ... it changed things for me. You know? I mean, as a firefighter, you prepare yourself, you go into work and you grit yourself for what you're going to see. But you ... I wasn't prepared for you. Who could have anticipated a little-bitty thing like yourself left out on the street?' He shook his head. 'We hadn't been married long. And, the thing is, I wanted to have some fun still, travel, enjoy ourselves a bit before we started thinking about a family. Only, finding you, it felt like a sign.' He looked out over the garden. The dogs were chasing each other now, had become firm friends in their short time together. 'I don't know if I should tell you this.' He glanced back at me. 'I wanted to adopt you. The wife and I ... we spent a lot of time talking about it, even started filling out the application.'

'And then?'

'And then she found out she was pregnant. That's Abbie. Our eldest.' He shrugged. 'I don't know, I guess I always did feel like God had put me there for a reason, that it was my role in life to be there for you.' He studied me, gaze examining my arm, the sling I wore.

'I didn't like to ask before, but what happened? Your arm. You okay?'

Tears sprang to my eyes suddenly and I looked down, steadying myself. 'Yeah, broken shoulder.'

He frowned. 'You sure you should be driving?'

'Doctor says it's fine,' I lied. See, I wasn't here. Everyone thought I was at home, just needed some time to myself, to process, lick my wounds. And Mom, she had that standing lunch date, once a month, regular as clockwork, with the women from the church, and she had hovered over me, already dressed in her pink polyester dress. I can cancel. I can stay. I shook my head, hadn't thought it through then, wasn't that organised, just knew that I needed her not to be there, watching me like a fissure about to crack open. No, I'd said. You go. I'm fine.

And so she had walked out the door, muttering that Drew needed to hold his horses, that he needed to stop that honking if he knew what was good for him. And as the door closed behind her, I knew what I would do next, where I would go.

'There was ... We had a break-in.' The words came out without any intention. Only Laurie, he was looking at me in that fatherly way, his face heavy with concern, and his expression, it just tugged the words right out of me. 'Someone came into my house.' I looked down at the sling, my hand hanging useless from the end of it. 'I fell.' My voice cracked.

Laurie sat up straighter, frowning heavily. 'Police catch him?'

85

I shook my head. 'There's no evidence.'

He studied me, lips pursed. 'I'm sorry, kid. It's never easy. Happened to us, once, maybe fifteen years ago now. Some piece of shit wormed his way in here, turned the living room upside down. Your home don't feel like your home after that.'

And there it was, my world encapsulated. A home that wasn't a home. A Rosa that was no longer a Rosa.

I took a sip of my lemonade, felt the first sheen of tears prickling across my eyes. 'I don't feel safe,' I murmured into the glass. 'I keep thinking ... I don't know, that the burglary, my abandonment, that it's all connected somehow.' My voice cracked, and I took another swallow as cover.

Laurie looked down at his hands, his head bobbing up and down slowly. 'I hear you. What you've been through, it's a lot. Like as not, you've got a little bit of post-traumatic stress going on there.'

I glanced up and he pulled a face. 'Firefighter. Believe me when I say I've done the post-trauma dance more than once. I'm guessing your adrenaline is still running pretty high right now. Hard to feel safe when it gets like that.'

Fleck flopped himself down on my feet, panting, and I leaned down, absent-minded, to ruffle his ears. The burglary. The fall. Finding out the truth about my origins. Each of those things would come with a psychological cost, would leave my system primed, the thought of 'what the hell next' sending my amygdala scouring for danger. And, when you thought about it, if you could split your mind apart from wild emotion into cool logic, there was little evidence of anything other than a failed burglary, just like Gray had said. Little evidence of a connection between that and the unravelling story of me. Perhaps I was just jumping at shadows.

'Give yourself some time, kiddo,' offered Laurie. 'Let things settle down. All that's happened, it's enough for anyone to deal with.' He gave me a long look. 'Just let yourself have a chance to heal.'

I didn't answer, not immediately. Then, 'Thing is, I just keep thinking that I have no idea who I am any more.'

Laurie smiled. 'Rosa, you are who you have always been. So your story begins on a city street instead of inside a hospital like most folks. Doesn't change the truth of you.' He shook his head slowly. 'Kid, I would do anything to help you out, tell you what you need to know. Truth is, everything I know is what I told you in my letter. I found you. Damn near scared the bejesus out of me.' He gave a soft laugh. 'I scooped you on up, ran you straight over to the police department. They just about had to pry you out of my fingers. Guess I sat there for hours, you all curled up and asleep on my lap. I wouldn't leave. Not until I knew you were going to be okay.' He shook his head. 'One of the captains from that day, still one of my closest friends. He had a baby of his own about that time. Hits you harder then, when you're a father. We still talk about you.' He grinned. 'Guess I'll have something new to tell him next time we speak.'

'And there was nothing that might have given you any clue about where I came from?'

He shook his head. 'Nothing at all. Just you, all bundled up against the cold.'

Then a noise, my phone ringing on the chair beside me. I glanced down at it. Mom. I hesitated, then pushed the button sending the call to voicemail.

I glanced up to see Laurie watching me. 'My mom,' I said, 'she doesn't know I came.'

He pursed his lips. 'You're angry your mom lied to you.' It wasn't a question, rather a statement.

I considered, probing the feeling. 'No ... It's not the lie ...' The lie, that felt like a choice in the service of the greater good, ends justifying means. What stuck beneath my skin like a splinter was that sense of wrongness, that feeling of looking in a mirror and not recognising the face looking back. 'My mom, she wants me to be okay. She's told me now. I know the truth. And that's it. Now I'm just supposed to forget, go back to being the person I always was with her.'

'Who's that?'

I thought of all of the many Rosas: the baby, the academic, the friend, the sister. And the Rosa who flew from the bedroom door, a baseball bat raised above her head. 'I was who everyone wanted me to be.'

Laurie nodded, slowly. 'Thing is, kid, none of us are easy to figure out. We've all got dark sides, hidden bits to us. You say you don't know who you are now. Sounds to me like you've always had a better notion of yourself than your family has. This, it hasn't changed anything. You're still you. Sure, your story isn't what you thought it was. I get that. But don't go letting it get in your head, fooling you that you're somehow magically different. You ain't.'

I nodded slowly. 'I should go. I want to be there by the time she gets back.'

Laurie let out a whistle, summoning the dogs to heel. 'You need me, all you got to do is reach out. I'm always here.'

I followed him through the sliding glass doors, into the tucked-away family room, and felt a warmth settle over me. 'Thank you. You have no idea how much this means to me.'

Laurie gave me a smile, shy almost. 'Little girl, you have no idea how much this means to me.'

Tears had sprung up again, threatening, and I turned away, my gaze falling on a sideboard, an array of photographs. Children playing on a nameless beach. Laurie, his arm wrapped around a woman with fair skin, copper-red hair. Behind them, in the distance, trees sputtered away down to a glass lake, framed with a wall of mountains, green giving way to jagged-edged white snowcaps. Fleck bumped up against the back of my leg, and I stared at the pictures, of a normal life, a normal family. And, God, I wished for that. I wished for that so much.

'Rosa,' said Laurie, choosing his words carefully, 'look, I gotta say this to you. Your folks, whoever they are, they left you out in the cold. In my book, that's just not what a person does. Just be real careful about what

89

you do next, okay. You have a family that loves you. You have a good life. Be careful that if you go asking questions, you're real sure you want the answers.'

Chapter 7

To go in to work would be ludicrous, all things considered. To drive myself to the university, in blatant
defiance of the doctors' orders, to sit at my desk in the
shoebox office I share with Eve, it would be lunacy
of the highest order. That was how my mother had
described it anyway.

I leaned back in my chair and let my gaze fall upon
the rows of box files that lined the shelves above my
desk. The case files of myriad white-collar crimes. What
had it come to that it was better to be here, lost in a
world of fraudsters and psychological hunters, than at
home with the family that loved me?

But then, it made sense, when you really thought
about it, this mission to plunge right past the surface of
who people appear to be, down into the depths of who
they truly are. I studied the dark-edged box files and
wondered now if it had in fact been part of some grand
cosmic design. If, deep down, I had always known I was
not who I appeared to be. If this quest to understand
what lay beneath the veneer of people was in fact a way
of trying to understand myself.

My phone buzzed with a Facebook notification, and I

started, knocking my pen to the floor. 'Shit.' Exaggerated startle reflex. Right now, the slightest of sounds was enough to send me spiralling like a chihuahua after a triple espresso. Ah, post-trauma stress reactions, how I love you.

I slid the tab across on my phone, opening the message, and my breath caught in my throat. A reply to my post on the Foundling group I had found last night on Facebook, a random collection of people, all of whom had been dumped at birth, all trying to make sense of it in whatever way they could. I was one of those people now, reaching out to strangers across the anonymous gulf of the internet because it seemed somehow safer than talking to people I actually knew.

Hi there, I was touched to read your story on the Foundling group. I too was a foundling. I was left behind a dumpster in Oakland thirty-five years ago and learned about my story just last year. I am currently trying to track down my birth family but have so far met dead end after dead end using traditional research. I have now decided to enter my DNA onto a genetic database in the hope that will turn up something. May be worth thinking about? I'll be praying for you.

DNA. It spoke to the scientist in me, so had that going for it. But it was so clear-cut, so decisive. Answers playing ready or not, here I come. Was I ready?

It had been a little after 9 p.m. when Addie had

come to my room, her soft knock almost lost in the low-playing Rachmaninov. She had slipped inside, the open door bringing with it the sounds of my nieces, high-pitched voices engaged in a sibling war, the words poopy pants distinct. Addie had grimaced at me.

'They're tired.'

Tired. Such a generous word.

My sister had delicately smoothed down the comforter, had perched at the foot of my bed, studying me, my knees drawn up close to my chest, *Persuasion* open beside me.

'How are you doing, sweetie?' There was a careful edge to her words.

'I'm okay.' Careful in return.

'And your arm? You still in a lot of pain?'

'Some,' I murmured.

Addie picked at a loose thread on an oversized stitched poppy. 'Rosa, did you go and see him yesterday?'

I hesitated, arranging my face into a pokerish one. 'Him who?'

My sister unfortunately was a mother of two small children and therefore well-trained in the art of spotting bullshit. 'You know who. That guy. That firefighter.' She gave me a steady look. 'We came by here, me and the girls, yesterday when Mom was out. Thought we'd see if you wanted to come to Culver's with us. You know how Mason is for her frozen custard. Only you weren't here.'

I could have lied. I planned to lie. Only, when it came time to lie, I just didn't have the energy.

'Yes,' I said, challenging. 'I went to see that firefighter guy.'

My sister nodded, dropping her gaze to the quilt, that poppy again, did not respond right away. 'Rosa, honey, I know this has been hard. Of course it has. But, I just, I think you've gotten it into your head that this is going to work out, that it will end up in some kind of fairy-tale reunion.'

I shifted on the bed, sliding my iPad further underneath Jane Austen's skirts, the screen open onto Google Scholar, the journal article 'Birthparent romances and identity formation in adopted children'. I tried to look innocent.

'I mean,' said Addie, 'I get that you want them to be these amazing people . . .'

'Got to keep my ego from crumbling somehow,' I muttered.

She gave me a long look. 'Okay . . . but the thing is, they left you on the street. They put you in a cardboard box and left you out in the cold. Anything could have happened to you.' Addie sighed heavily. 'Look, maybe it's not my place, but I just feel someone's got to warn you.'

'I know.'

'So . . . what are you going to do?'

She might as well have asked me the correct procedure for walking through walls.

'I don't know, Addie.'

'Maybe . . . Look, will you just give yourself some time? Allow yourself the chance to process this. To

94

get over your fall and, you know, come to terms with everything? Just, promise me you won't do anything yet, okay?'

'Okay.' My mouth moved, all on its own.

A flurry of voices came from beyond my office door, the burble of laughter, and I started again, my heart beating far too wildly for the occasion. I blew out a breath, pushed my chair back from my desk, Addie's words from last night looping about in my head. I had promised. I had told her I would wait, would allow the dust to settle. And yet in the dust were so many questions, and here, perhaps, would be an answer. I gazed at the screen of my phone, at the stranger's sad, sad story, long enough that the words had begun to dance and spin before me. DNA.

And yet, I had promised.

I blew out a slow breath, tried to bring my mind back to where it was meant to be, here, now. Work. I was here to work. What had I been doing? What was it that the burglary, the fall, had interrupted? The paper 'What turns white-collar criminals red?'. Perhaps I had left it here, on that night, the recollection of editing at my dining table the right memory on the wrong day. I eased myself up to standing, an arc of pain shooting across my shoulder, and moved awkwardly to the paper tray that sat on the windowsill, riffling through the sheets with my good arm. But there was nothing, just a collection of half-finished words, of memos I had yet to pay attention to. I stood, considering. It must have been one of the children then ... I should ask them ...

The office door opened, and I started again, knocking my phone to the floor. 'Dammit.'

'Woah!' said Eve. 'What a welcome.'

'It's not you,' I muttered, awkwardly twisting to retrieve the phone. 'My stupid nerves are shot.'

'Well yeah,' she said, closing the door behind her, 'of course they are. And what the hell are you doing in work, missy? This stuff, it can wait. You got more important things to be doing. Like, I don't know, re-covering from an almost catastrophic fall from height. You sure you're okay?'

'Okay.' I let out a laugh that tasted bitter to me. 'Awesome. Everyone I've ever met has lied to me and I have no clue who I am and I'm developing an unhealthy case of paranoia and I have NO idea who I can trust. Other than that, I'm great.'

'Me,' said Eve, quietly. 'You can trust me.'

I stopped, let the papers fall back into the tray, and fought back the threatening tears. 'I know I can.' I shook my head, another jab of pain. 'Hey, I meant to ask, did you send me flowers?'

Eve blanched. 'No, I mean, I was going to, only I didn't know if ...'

I grinned, waved her fumbling defences away. 'I didn't mean it like that. Someone sent me lilies. No name. I'm just trying to figure out who.' My stomach twisted. My amygdala supercharging my danger detection again. 'They forgot to put their name on them,' I finished, quietly, testing it as a theory, to see if I believed it. That,

96

of course, is the trouble with fear, it creates nightmares from every curtain crease.

My computer pinged, and I glanced at the screen, an email, an address I didn't recognise. I frowned, studying it.

'What?'

'Some guy from Sacramento, Ben something or other, says he's a screenwriter working with Fox and is looking for some advice on creating characters. Wants to know what makes fraudsters into killers, if, and I quote, that means they are "crazy".'

Eve snorted. 'That's a big fat yes.' She leaned over me, looking at my computer screen, at the papers spread out before me. She looked at me. 'What the hell is this?'

I shifted, sheepish. 'The psychology of abandoning parents. There's some really interesting stuff there ...'

'Holy shit.' Eve spun me about, aiming me towards the door. 'Up. I'm taking you for lunch, before you do any more damage to that broke-ass brain of yours.'

The Tipsy Cow was quiet, lunch rush already gone, and I picked at my grilled cheese one-handed, stretching it out into a long line of yellow.

'So,' said Eve through a mouthful of burger, 'how you doin'?'

I shrugged, taking a bite of crust. 'I'm fine.'

'Liar.'

'Eve ...'

'How are you doing?'

I sighed, settled my sandwich back down onto its plate. 'I don't know. I mean, the research, it says that for foundlings finding out about their adoption as an adult, there's a higher risk of anxiety and depression, so I have that to look forward to. Only, the studies show that generally there is a delay in reaction, so I guess you could say I'm in some kind of shock period right now.'

Eve shook her head, a line of ketchup rimming her upper lip. 'Jesus, you're a nerd.'

I laughed, the sound of it startling me. 'Seriously, that feels like the only damn thing I know about myself right now. Nerd and proud of it, baby.'

'Are you going to look for them?' Eve dabbed at her mouth with a napkin. 'Your family, I mean.'

I picked up a fry, studied it with more focus than it required. 'They say that the common thread in abandonment is the sense that the pregnancy is not socially acceptable. Poverty plays a role too. The mothers who do this, leave their babies, often they're poor ...' I looked up at Eve to find her staring at me, an eyebrow raised. 'I don't know what I'm going to do,' I murmured, setting the fry back down again. 'Everyone's telling me not to go digging. That I could be opening a can of worms.'

'And you?' said Eve, quietly. 'What do you think?'

I sat there for a moment, those three letters circling around my head again, then shoved my plate away. 'You done?'

'Sure.'

'Wanna walk?'

We stepped out onto King Street, into the cool of a twisting breeze. The Indian summer had begun to retreat now, leaves flecking the sidewalk, reds and browns pocking the grey.

Eve tucked her hands into her pockets, shivered ostentatiously. 'I understand what your family is saying. I really do. I mean, they love you. They're trying to protect you.'

'But?'

'But it's your life. I think you need to follow your instincts.'

The Capitol building loomed ahead, the white dome of it vivid in the sunlight.

'I'm not sure I have any instincts any more,' I muttered, waiting for a break in traffic.

'Okay, fine.' Eve's voice shuddered as we jogged across the road, connecting onto Main Street. 'You may not have instincts, but you have research. You know, on account of you being ...'

'A nerd. I know,' I finished. I looped my arm through hers, fell into thought. Then, 'The ones who do it, the ones who search, they show better recovery. In terms of acceptance, a sense of closure, I mean. Even if they aren't successful, even if they don't find anything. I don't know, maybe it gives them some sense of control.'

Eve squeezed my arm. 'And what do you feel about that? You don't have to remain an academic robot, you know.'

'Babe, I kind of think I do.'

'Why?'

'Because if I feel, then I'm pretty sure I'm going to fall apart.'

Eve slipped her hand into mine, and we walked on in a heavy silence. As we turned off South Carroll Street, along one of the spokes that led to the Capitol building, I could feel my heart rate begin to climb. It was not now, but twenty years ago. Was not me, but a young Laurie.

'You okay?' murmured Eve.

I nodded, not meaning a word of it.

'Where?'

'Up ahead. Right beside the front steps.'

It was a patch of grass, a speck of green to break up the ascending white of the wide stairs.

'I was tucked in here. Right behind this post.'

'Maybe they figured it wouldn't take long for someone to find you there. Figured you'd be safe.'

Ah, birth family romance.

I crouched down, let the palm of my hand rest against the cool of the white stone. The place where the life of Rosa Fisher had begun.

And in that moment, I knew what I had to do next.

Chapter 8

Six weeks later

The rain battered against the windows, a steady, relentless stream of it, bringing the day to an early close, premature night coming in hard. I sat, lit by the glow of the open laptop, and watched the raindrops spatter against the glass. The orange glow of lamplight behind me, white-lit laptop before me. Curtains open wide. Nothing between me and that wild night.

They say time heals. I flexed the fingers of my left hand, narrow flashes of the memory of pain arcing up towards my elbow. Six weeks had healed my broken elbow, had allowed the eyeshadow bruising of my black eye to fade out to nothing.

Six weeks.

For six weeks I had waited, the echoing memory of the sound of footsteps punctuating my every move. I had waited. I had watched. And yet, nothing. No sense of being stared at. No hang-up calls. No mystery figures on the security camera.

And around five weeks and two days, I had somehow, miraculously, healed, I had settled into that welcome feeling of having been utterly wrong. There had been another break-in, a mile or two away. This time they had come while the family were at work, had stripped the house bare. No forensics. I'm betting it was the same guy, said Gray. We'll get him.

And so I had lulled myself into it, a run-of-the mill break-in. All connections to my long-lost past illusory. Co-occurence masquerading as causation.

And I had done my best to forget about the flowers, about 'Sorry'. A misworded note of sympathy from a well-meaning friend. That was all.

'I thought you were going to come down to the family room?' Mom said plaintively. '*CSI* is coming on soon.' She stood in the doorway of the dining room, cosy in sweats, a family-sized bag of popcorn tucked beneath her arm.

'I will,' I murmured, attention on the screen before me. 'I just need to check in for my flight, is all.'

We had reached a detente, an unsteady truce. I asked no more questions for which my mom had no answers, and Mom, she got to pretend that nothing had changed. Addie and Drew had unknotted, relaxing finally as it became apparent that I had taken their advice, had stopped digging.

Of course, they didn't know about the DNA. One little swab, a whole lot of patience, and an entire world of possibility at your fingertips. I had tucked the swab into the envelope, the name Family Finders emblazoned large across the front of it; had felt the faintest flush of guilt. The research. The research had said that searching was an effective way to reach acceptance. And acceptance, that was important for all of it, wasn't it? If I was going to move on, if I was going to reach a point of closure. So really, when you thought about it, I was doing it for all of us.

In the past six weeks, my rationalisation skills had become super honed.

Mom sighed, the movement causing the bag to crackle. 'Look at this weather. They're saying we'll be looking at snow soon too, as if all this rain isn't bad enough.' She sighed again. 'You sure you have to go? I don't like the idea of you travelling when it's like this.'

'It's rain, Mom. I'm sure the plane can handle a bit of rain.' I clicked onto the Delta website. 'Besides, it's an important conference.'

'Well, I just don't like you going all that way on your own. Especially after what happened. You know you're not good at being on your own.'

'I'm not going to be on my own. Will is meeting me there.'

She fell silent for a moment, then said, 'I'm getting awful palpitations again.'

I worked really hard not to look at her. 'I'll be gone four days. I'm sure you'll survive four days.' My cellphone rang on the tabletop, a welcome escape, and I grabbed for it, the movement sending sparks up my arm. 'Hello?' If it was a cold-caller, I was going to keep them talking until midnight.

Mom sighed heavily, turning on her heels with a tut.

'Rosa. It's Will.' My PhD supervisor's voice sounded

tinny across the line, his mosaic accent distinct.

'Hey. How's Beijing?'

'Oh great. You know how it is. One university is pretty much like another. Food's better though.'

It was the curse of a hotshot supervisor, that he was gone far more than he was here. It was fine. Supervision from a distance worked pretty well for me.

'I just wanted to check you're all set for your presentation?'

I closed the browser, pulled up the PowerPoint I had spent the last three weeks working on, the words 'What turns white-collar criminals red?' large across the screen. 'Yup,' I said, glancing over it. 'I'm good to go.'

It seemed like I could hear him nod. 'And you? You okay? After ...' His voice faded away.

I looked to the window, puckering raindrops, dark night beyond. 'Everything's fine.'

'That's good. We were worried about you for a while there.'

I moved the cursor, the sound of my supervisor's voice winding its way through the thundering rain, and clicked on the icon for the security system Gray had installed. It had been three days since I had checked it last, my fear slipping away, my vigilance going with it.

'And there were some fascinating data points from the Hong Kong study ...'

I clicked on the camera feed of the previous day, sliding through it frame by frame, twenty-four hours slipping by in minutes.

'So, we need to see if maybe we can apply some of

your techniques to this group. I think it could be really valuable for you ...'

I nodded, watching the screen. There was me leaving for work. There was Mom letting Fleck out into the garden. There was Drew pulling up in his jeep, loading Fleck inside. I'm borrowing him. Just for the day. He'd looked sheepish, Need some, uh, protection. A kernel of anxiety twisted in my stomach. What the hell had my brother gotten himself involved in now? Me arriving home. Dusk settling.

And then ...

I must have gasped, because Will said, 'What? What's wrong?'

I stared at the laptop. A figure stood right at the edge of the screen.

I put my hand to my mouth, felt my throat tighten.

'Rosa?'

'Nothing,' I lied.

Man or woman, impossible to tell. Just some ill-defined shape standing in the shadow of the trees, watching the house.

And then it all came back, that storm surge of fear that the past six weeks had laid low, and I jumped up from my seat, pulling the curtains tight, heart beating in my head.

'Rosa?'

'Sorry,' I muttered. 'Will, I'm getting another call. Can I just see you in New York?'

His goodbyes vanished as I hung up the phone. I stood, hidden by the dense fabric of the curtains, adrenaline coursing. I had been right. All this time and it was like I had worked to convince myself how wrong I was. Only I wasn't wrong. There had been someone in the house that night. Someone had climbed the stairs, had taken the photo, had left the flowers, the 'Sorry' note.

I tried to control my breathing, wild panic rising.

Had someone been in here today? I stuffed my phone into the pocket of my sweater, hurried from room to room, searching for what, I wasn't sure. Something missing, something added.

I grabbed my raincoat from a hook in the hall, slipped out into the rain, using my cellphone as a flashlight. A little voice in my head. Someone could be out there. Someone could be watching you now.

I ran the patch of light over the lawn, squinting towards the treeline. Nothing there now but shadow. Then I pulled the light back towards the walls of the house.

I found it by the kitchen window.

A patch of grass protected from the rain by the overhang of the roof. And in that patch of grass, a shoeprint.

I stood, frozen, deafening rain battering against my hood. My entire body sparking with fear. Standing here, you could see into the kitchen, to the family room beyond. I could see my mother in her La-Z-Boy recliner, bag of popcorn open on her lap. Could see the sofa, where I had sat only an hour or so ago, my book still waiting on the arm, Fleck stretched across the length of it.

I was going to be sick.

You're guided by those around you. Social influence. Look it up, it's a thing. So when the world tells you you're wrong, you believe it.

Only I hadn't been fucking wrong, had I?

I turned, sneakers squelching through sodden grass, moving as fast as I could. Gray. Gray, would want to see this.

I hurried inside, throwing my coat onto the coat rack, my mother's voice rolling from the family room. 'What in God's name are you doing out there in all that rain?'

I ignored her, pulled my phone from my pocket, dialling Gray, working hard to keep the panic from my voice, failing spectacularly. He answered with a mouthful of food, voice thick. The camera. Someone's been here. Shoeprint. A stretched-out silence, then a brisk, I'm on my way. And then pacing and pacing because sitting, that was impossible, and knowing that I was only biding time, until the inevitable would come and my mother would ask, and then the entirety of this would reach a whole new level of crazy. And the minutes crawling and flashing by both, so that suddenly my brother-in-law is there, raincoat pulled on over joggers and worn-out sneakers, his face hard in that cop expression of his.

'Show me the footage,' he muttered, tersely.

Then my mother, 'Gray? Is that Gray? What in the Lord's name are you doing here, on a night like this?' And her appearing in the hallway, looking from me to him and back, her face draining of colour, mouth going slack. 'What? What is it, Gray?'

My brother-in-law patting her quickly on the arm, a train in motion, 'Nothing for you to worry about, Nora, I just need to do a quick check of the cameras.' Him blowing on past her in the hope that that will be an end to it, but, of course, it never was going to be. My mother trailed along behind him like an avalanche after a snowball.

Then the screen, and the figure shrouded in shadow, and my mother shrieking, because of course, and Gray's voice stern, clipped. 'Nora, stop it. Probably same guy, checking to see if you've upped security, looking to make another pass at it. The cameras, the alarm system, it's all marked up. That'll have put him off. But I'm going to call down to the station now, get someone to come on out here, do a check of the place.' He glanced at me. 'You wanna call Drew? Get him to come on over, maybe spend the night? Yeah, Bob? Hey, it's Gray.' This last into his cell, his back turning to us now.

I tucked my arm through my mother's trembling one, guided her back into the living room, settling her into the chair. I then moved from window to window pulling the curtains tight shut, trying to still my breathing, trying to ignore the sound of her high-pitched chatter. Telling myself that Gray was right, that I had overreacted, no reason to think this was anything other than what he had said. Burglars doing what burglars do. That my mother was hysterical enough for both of us, no need to pile any more crazy onto the fire. Waiting for patrol and for my brother and for my heart to stop beating through my eyeballs and for my mother to stop crying, and then …

I wouldn't have heard the pinging of my phone had I not been perched beside it, balancing on the arm of the sofa, chewing on my thumbnail. Wouldn't have looked at it, only I thought it would be Drew, an ETA on his arrival, or, at worst, an excuse why his white knight suit was in the shop.

But I did hear it, and I did look at it, and that, well, that changed everything.

Family Finders – DNA match found.

Chapter 9

It smelled of coffee, the earthiness of it overlaying the faintest tang beneath, of urine and sweat. The girl at the desk fussed over the computer, did not bother to look up when I walked in. Her black kohl eyes studied the screen, purple-tipped fingernails tap, tap, tapping across the keyboard. And I briefly considered running.

It was a feeling like no other. We have a DNA match for you. It was the sense of drifting on the open sea and suddenly being pulled up short by an anchor you hadn't suspected was there. It was moving through a crowded room, strangers all of them, your senses being assaulted by alien voices, unknown smells, and suddenly walking into your identical twin. My hands had shaken, breath coming in short sharp stops, and I had thumbed open the email, a feeling like plunging from a cliff. My DNA, it had connected me to a woman, my maternal grandmother. And it had included a number, an area code I didn't recognise. I had quietly excused myself, had told my mother that I needed to use the bathroom, had locked myself in and dialled.

'Hello?' A woman's voice. She sounded cheerful, bright, and absurdly I took comfort from that.

'Hi …' My voice cracked. I sounded neither cheerful, nor bright, rather like I was in the process of being strangled. 'I got a match. On Family Finders. DNA.' Holy shit, Rosa, pull it together. 'Sorry. It's just, they gave me your number …'

A long silence. I couldn't blame her. Then, 'I don't think that can have been me. I've never given my DNA.'

'Are you …' I stumbled over the name, 'Lilian Gauthier?'

'Oh,' said the voice on the phone. 'You're looking for the woman who lived here before us. No. She left, a year or two ago.'

My stomach plunged. 'Do you have a forwarding address?'

'No … I think she went into a care home. I don't know where though.'

I stopped, shifting pieces in my mind, looking for a solution. 'Where are you?'

'York County. Ontario.'

I had heard the front door slamming, the rolling thunder of Drew's voice, a little looser now, the Michelob already beginning to work its magic. I'd hung up, telling myself to keep it together, to compartmentalise. One crisis at a time. Easing my way back downstairs, working hard to remember the appropriate expression for my face, finding my mother weeping, settling for an eye roll. Sitting on the sofa while she set out the whole sorry saga to my brother, who sat, his gaze locked on his rough-toed boots, giving little more than a grunt in return, and trying not to let my hands shake.

Then Gray and the patrol officers, and catching fleeting words of it: checked grounds, no sign, get someone to take a cast of the print, keep the house locked up tight. And thinking only of escape, of answers laying north, in Canada.

My mother looking at me, expression plaintive, 'Do you think you should cancel your conference? I'm not sure you should be away from home right now.'

And she was right, wasn't she? There was danger here, wherever it came from, and it was watching my family. And if I was responsible and caring, I would stay.

Only that DNA, it pulled at me, like a wire cord pulled tight about my waist, and the thought of staying, of not chasing the answer dangling right up ahead of me, it stopped up the breath in my chest.

My voice seemed to come from a long way away from me, saying, no, I have to go. It's critical to my PhD. Critical. I remember actually using that word. Funny how the mind works, isn't it. Then excusing myself and grabbing my laptop and slipping upstairs and calling Will and telling him that there had been a family emergency, that the burglars had returned, that I just didn't feel right leaving my mother home alone, that I would not be in New York. And the sympathy and the of course I understands and me hanging up, feeling like an asshole. Only that feeling, it didn't last long enough to do any real damage. And so I began calling. Any care home within York County, the Google list waiting patiently on the screen before me. Please can you help me. I'm looking for my grandmother.

I found her in the sixth.

'I'm coming to see her. I'll be there tomorrow.'

The woman on the phone had made a noise that sounded a lot like a tut. 'You're not an authorised visitor.'

'What?'

'Only authorised visitors.' She sounded bored. I wanted to slap her.

'Okay,' I said, my grip on my patience loosening. 'How do I become an authorised visitor?'

'Sorry. You'll have to speak to the manager. She's in Monday to Friday, nine until five. Call back then.' A click, and the phone disconnected and I considered throwing it against a wall.

I had sat on my bed and had listened to the waning activity downstairs and I had considered, how did you get somewhere you weren't supposed to be? And I realised that my entire life had prepared me for this. That my basket of deplorables, as Eve liked to call them, had taught me all that I needed to know. So I had planned my strategy, only dimly bothered by conscience.

I had left the following morning. Because, after all, the New York conference was critical to my PhD. Had waved away offers to drive me to the airport. I comfort myself that before I left, I did make sure that the alarm was set, that the cameras were working, and Drew was staying. But I still left. Apparently deplorableness is contagious.

It was an eleven-hour drive from Madison to Caledon, the little town just outside Toronto. Eleven hours that seemed to pass by in minutes. I had checked myself into a Best Western a couple of miles away, clinging to consciousness long enough to pick up a pizza from a nearby takeout. And to collect my parcel from reception. Thank you, eBay. And then I had fallen into a restless sleep, punctuated with confused wakings and a creeping feeling of being watched.

Now I strode closer to the purple-nailed girl, tapping my own unpainted fingernails on the desk, clearing my throat with just a touch of attitude. The keyboard clacking stopped and the woman – or girl rather, from this distance could be little more than eighteen – raised a densely pencilled eyebrow.

'Help you?' Her lipstick was cerise, the lack of interest the same as it had been on the phone.

I gave her a steady look, didn't smile, and waved the badge at her. 'Sergeant Rebecca Leland from the RCMP. Need to talk to one of your residents.'

Her purple lips rounded into a perfect O, smoked-up eyes widened. I got the badge off eBay. The name of the sergeant off the RCMP's website. She does exist, is based up in New Brunswick. And if you looked her up online, you would find a woman, maybe a decade older than me but looks younger, who could be mistaken for me in a pinch. I haven't spent years studying white-collar crime without learning a few things.

'Um, sure, I ... Sure. Who? The resident, I mean.'

'Lilian Gauthier.'

Lilian Gauthier. Aged seventy-six. Born in Nova Scotia. Moved to Ontario in her early twenties. Joined Family Finders a decade ago. My maternal grandmother.

I waited while she tap, tapped into the computer, running my fingers along the alien heft of the RCMP badge, aware that I should be feeling something now, guilt probably, and yet instead feeling an electric thrill that made the hairs across my arms stand on end. Duping delight. The thrill of the lie. Jesus Christ, who the hell was I?

I tapped the RCMP badge on the faux-wood desk in a show of impatience. When you thought about it, it wasn't like I was doing any harm. It was a lie for a good cause. And the care home, they'd kind of boxed me into a corner.

The girl glanced up, nervous. 'Sorry, I have to … What did you say you needed Lilian for?'

I gave her a flat look, raised an eyebrow right back at her. 'I'm afraid I'm not at liberty to discuss that. All I can tell you is that it's in regards to an investigation.'

I was rationalising, justifying my lies. Could you call them frauds? Oh no, Rosa, stealing someone else's identity and using it to achieve your own ends … why would anyone ever think of that as a fraud? Perhaps it was like a virus. Perhaps I had spent too long, amongst liars and cheats, had learned too much.

The girl bit her lip and jiggled the mouse and I quested about for that sense of guilt; for the little voice that should right now be banshee-screeching at me, telling me that I was doing the wrong thing, that I would get caught, that punishment would follow. Once again coming up short. Where was it, my fraud-avoiding inner voice? Seemed like where my conscience should have been instead sat a devil, hopped up on tequila and egging me on.

'Yeah, okay, sure. So, she's in room sixteen. Only…'

'What?'

The girl pursed her cerise lips. 'She's not … I don't know how much help she'll be.'

I smiled coldly. 'I'm sure she'll do fine. Room sixteen, yes?'

The girl nodded, indicated a corridor leading off to my left. 'Fourth door along.'

It felt like my legs were being operated by someone else, like I was watching myself, from a great distance, my heart thumping in my chest. Fourth door along. My grandmother, the first person I had ever met who was related to me, was mere feet away. I arranged my face, experimenting with a slightly bored, all in a day's work expression. Sergeant Rebecca Leland, remember?

I pulled up outside room number sixteen, allowed myself a moment to breathe. My gaze resting on a pink-framed print on the wall adjacent, motel art, an unreasonably slim woman wafting through a staggeringly flowered garden, and then I rapped quickly on the door, letting myself in before I had the chance to change my mind and run like hell.

Dull early-morning light spilled in through French doors, and it took a moment for my vision to shift, acclimatising to my new surroundings. Then I saw her.

She sat in a high-backed chair before the window, dressed in spite of the early hour, in a long skirt, a high-necked jumper. White hair was pulled up, coiled on top of her head. Her nails were painted, a dark red, and I found myself moving closer, trying to make out the features of her. The nose, with its upturned tip, was just like mine; her eyes, the same verdant green as my own. My grandmother studied me, frowning, a spoon held in her hand, forgotten now. A bowl of porridge sat before her, filling the room with the scent of it. Beside that, a china teapot, a bone-china cup, set into a thin saucer.

'I'm sorry to disturb you so early.' My voice didn't sound like mine, suddenly seemed younger, on the verge of tears. But then, I was, wasn't I?

She set the spoon down carefully and squinted at me, green eyes flitting across my face. 'I know you, don't I?'

'Well, I ...'

'Oh, Camille. Where have you been?' She clasped her hands together, the clap of them echoing through the small room. 'I told them to call you, but you know how they are here, just won't listen. Well now, and you look so well. And the boys? How are the boys? Well, I'm so glad you came, sweetheart.'

I floundered. 'No, I'm ... sorry ... I ...' I glanced back towards the door, closed, and yet lowered my voice anyway. 'The thing is, I'm ... well, I'm your granddaughter.'

She stared at me, her lips moving in a silent litany, and then she shook her head, once, twice, as if trying to dislodge a persistent thought. 'You're not Camille?'

'No,' I said, the sense invading me that I was Alice tumbling down a rabbit hole. 'Sorry. I ... I found you, that is, my details were matched with yours on Family Finders. I'm you granddaughter.'

She sat back, a crestfallen look, 'Oh. I ... It's happened again, hasn't it?'

'What?'

'I ... My mind ... it feels like it just won't stay still. I thought ... You look like her. My daughter.' A beat. 'Are you?'

I felt a sinking feeling. 'No.' Moved closer, into the light, so she could see me, so that if I reached out, I could touch the papery stretch of her skin. 'I'm your granddaughter.'

She frowned then, sitting up straighter. 'No, you're not.'

'I ...'

'My granddaughter is dead.'

A sharp rap on the door, my head spinning towards it, heart beating fast, and it opened inwards with one deft movement, admitting a woman in her late middle age, broad shoulders, a wide forehead, her hair scraped back into a bun. She studied me, her face showing every sign of preparation to be irritated.

'You're with the RCMP?'

'I ... Yes ...'

'ID?'

I silently handed her my fake warrant card, offered up a silent prayer as she examined it, frowning, then handed it back, showing little sign that it had improved her mood.

'Esther Moody. Manager. My receptionist said you needed to talk to Lilian as part of your investigation?'

'That's right.'

The woman looked over at my grandmother, painted a false smile across her face. 'And how are we today, Lilian?'

My grandmother stared at her, seemed to be considering her responses. 'Oh, do fuck off.'

It was certainly concise.

Esther Moody pursed her lips. 'She has good days and bad days. Looks like this is a bad one. You won't get much help here, I'm afraid.'

I nodded. 'It's ...'

'Dementia. She's been going downhill for a while, but now it's more bad than good.'

Shit. I should have done clinical psychology. I glanced back at her, my grandmother. She had gone back to studying her spoon now, frowning at it, as if she was trying to decide, should she eat from it or throw it at Esther Moody. I could certainly see the appeal. Perhaps it was a genetic thing. And I felt a sense of sinking, of hope lost.

No. There was always a way.

'I guess,' I said, 'she's not going to be able to tell me much.' I frowned, faux thinking. 'Look, I probably shouldn't be telling you this, but ...' I hesitated, sighed dramatically, thinking that my mother would have been proud. 'We have identified Lilian on a DNA database known as Family Finders.'

The manager nodded, 'I know the one. A number of

our residents have gotten into that, looking for long-lost relatives, family trees, that kind of thing. I know Lilian used to take part in our genealogy group, back before … well,' she gestured towards my grandmother, 'you know.'

I nodded, slowly, delivering my words with a studied indifference. 'What about family? Does she have anyone visiting? Perhaps they might be able to help.'

The manager folded thick arms beneath her chest. 'Lilian doesn't really get visitors. Don't think she's got any family. Not after … Well, I'm sure I don't need to tell you.'

She did in fact need to tell me, because I had no clue.

I studied the manager, could see it, in the twitch of her eyes about the room, the way her fingers danced across her arms. She wanted to know why I was here, wanted to know what tragedy Lilian Gauthier could help with. She assumed knowledge in me, that she wanted. And so I waited, kept my mouth shut, my gaze trained on her until the silence stretched out, becoming gluey and uncomfortable.

Finally, 'She still talks about it, you know. Not when she's … calm. She'll not be drawn on it then. But if she's having one of her episodes. Sometimes she'll have screaming fits, loud enough to shake the walls, and there's just nothing you can do with her, no calming her. Staff here say she's reliving it, that day, the finding out.'

A snaking hand of fear gripped my insides. 'Understandable.'

'Terrible thing,' muttered Esther. 'Just terrible.' She considered. 'We don't have much on record for Lilian. Like I said, don't think she's got much in the way of family left, and if she does, well, we don't know about them. But I know she keeps a box of papers, documents and such.' She gestured towards the chest of drawers, pulling open the topmost drawer. 'Maybe there'll be something in there that would be of use to you? Names of old friends and the like?' She pulled a box file out, presented it to me, a cat delivering a field mouse. 'I mean, this investigation, is it related to ... well, you know, what happened?'

I took the box off her, gave her my very best smile. 'I'm afraid I can't say.'

Her lips puckered, the taste of something sour, and her gaze flitted back to Lilian, a small sigh escaping from her. 'No, of course.' The old woman had turned her head sideways now, her gaze fixed on the window, the garden beyond. A single branch of a tree tapped against the glass. Her lids drooped.

'I must say how much I appreciate your help,' I said, quietly. 'So many people in your position wouldn't understand just how critical they can be to our work. It's such a relief to meet someone who is aware of the needs of an investigation.'

The manager stood up taller, her ample chest puffing out further still. 'Well, I do like to consider myself an informed individual. Can I ... Coffee? Can I get you one?' She indicated a desk, a chair tucked beneath it. She glanced at Lilian, her head dropping to her chest, mouth slack with sleep. 'Looks like Lilian is out for the count, why don't you take a seat? I think I can rustle up a cookie or two, as well.'

I smiled widely and placed a hand upon her arm. 'Esther, you truly are a godsend. Yes. That would be wonderful.'

I sat, placing the box on the desk in front of me, and waited while she bustled her way from the room, humming. As the door closed behind her, I shifted my gaze to the box before me, was suddenly aware that my hands were shaking.

I eased open the lid.

The newspaper sat on the top, so that every time Lilian opened it, she would see the headline. The page old, faded, the colours of it leaching to sepia. A photograph of a building, standing alone in a field, engulfed in flames.

Above the picture, in bold letters, the headline.

FAMILY DEAD IN BARN FIRE

The bodies of four members of the same family were found at the scene of a barn fire in York County.

Firefighters were called to the scene of a blazing barn on farmland near Brampton by a neighbor who spotted the flames at about 5 p.m. last night. Extensive efforts were made to quench the flames of what was initially believed to be an industrial accident. It was some hours later that firefighters were finally able to enter the structure, believed to be empty. Inside, they found the bodies of 37-year-old

Camille Lynch, her husband, 39-year-old Hadley, and two children, 17-year-old Kyle and 5-month-old Mia.

Lilian Gauthier, mother to Camille, described herself as devastated. 'They were such a wonderful family and my grandchildren were the light of my life. I've lost my only child. I don't understand how something like this could have happened.'

Neighbors described themselves as devastated by the loss of the family. Investigations into the cause of death are still ongoing. Anyone with information is asked to contact Ontario Provincial Police.

Chapter 10

Lilian Gauthier snored softly in the chair, her chin dropped down to her chest. A strand of hair had worked its way free from her bun, blowing in the breeze of her out breath. I held the paper tight between my fingers, aware suddenly that I was shaking, that the room had taken on a sheen of unreality. Because, in spite of all expectation, she had been right. Lilian had said that her granddaughter was dead, and there it was, in black and white before me.

I laid the newspaper down on the desk, worked hard to breathe. It had been a mistake. There was no other explanation. DNA companies, they weren't infallible. They had gotten it wrong, led me down a rabbit hole, assigning me to a history that was not my own.

I looked to Lilian, the rhythm of her breaths lyrical. I had imagined our likeness. It would be understandable, that in my own need to find a place that I belonged I had projected a similarity that wasn't there. And it crashed over me. What was I doing here? In Canada, pretending to be an officer of the RCMP? What the hell had I been thinking? This wasn't me. And with the thought of that came the sudden urge to flee, to drop the box that sat on my lap still, to run home, to not look back.

I had made a mistake, had imagined I was someone I wasn't.

Mia was dead. I was not. Ergo, whoever I was, it could not be Mia Lynch.

It was a form of insanity this, brought about by the footsteps on the stairs, by the fall, the sense of being hunted. I had needed so much to find certainty in my world, a definitive answer of who I was, where I came from, that I had clung to the DNA results, never stopping to question their veracity.

I felt like crying then.

It should have ended there. I should have stood up, walked out, given it all up as a bad job and retreated back into the life that I had always known. But something kept me glued to that seat. Curiosity, perhaps. And so I lifted the weight of papers from within the box file, set them onto the desk before me, driven by nothing more sophisticated than the urge to read of the great tragedy of Lilian Gauthier's life.

I glanced across at her. A bubble of saliva had worked its way between her lips, growing and shrinking with each breath that she took. Poor love. Was this why? Had the trauma of her past wormed its way into her brain, causing it to fold into confusion? I had a dim memory of reading of it, the link between post-traumatic stress and dementia. Atrophy of the hippocampus perhaps. Injury heaped upon insult. I let my mind linger here, meandering through the mechanics of it all, finding relief in the science. In science there was evidence, and questions could find their answers.

I sighed, looked back down at the near-empty box, to see that, even with all the papers removed, something still remained, a small yellow packet. I picked it up, feeling its lightness, flipped open the folded lip of it to find within a wad of photographs, the contrast of them dulled with age.

My fingers selected one, unmistakably Lilian, only far, far younger than the Lilian who sat before me, her white hair blonde, hanging loose about her shoulders, her arm slung across a girl right on the cusp of being a woman. And there time hung. Because I had seen this photograph before, even though I hadn't. Of a teenaged girl, long dark hair with the slightest hint of a wave, the green eyes, the upturn of the nose. It was me. Only, of course, it wasn't. I turned the photograph over. In neat script, the words *Nova Scotia, August, 1975, Lilian & Camille*. The room swam about me, and I turned the photograph back over, studying this girl/woman hybrid. It was like looking in a mirror. I found myself casting about, searching for a memory of standing on a cliff in Nova Scotia, of a woman's arm slung about my shoulder. But, of course, no such memories existed. I'd never even been to Canada before. The girl in the photograph, she wasn't me, was someone else.

She must be Lilian's daughter, the daughter she had mistaken me for. And the likeness between us, it was staggering.

My mind spun. Think. Camille and her daughter

had died in a barn fire. And yet I looked so much like Camille, it was breathtaking. Was it possible that she had had another daughter? One that she had chosen not to keep?

But ... More pictures lay beneath. Of Camille, her face still unlined and innocent, holding a baby in her arms, a toddler at her side. *Camille with Kyle and Elliott, 1978.* Of two boys, with the stretched-outedness of a child who is leaving childhood behind, heading straight for puberty. *Kyle and Elliott, 1990.* Then one of Camille, again holding another baby, smaller this time, only now Camille's face had taken on a worn look, lines tracing her nose and mouth, the boys teenagers standing beside her, expressions uncomfortable. *Camille, boys, baby Mia, 1995.*

I was born in 1995.

I stared at the photograph. Was that me? But ... it couldn't be. Because the baby had died. But then, the dates matched, there or thereabouts. When the barn fire happened, I would have been five months old, the same age Mia was when she died. And by the time I was left in Madison, both Camille and Hadley were already dead. And Mia's mother, she was the image of me. And then there was the DNA ...

Only for all of the points in the conclusion's favour, the problem that remained was a substantial one.

That Mia was already dead.

I leaned forward, ran my fingers through my hair. None of this made sense. Was it possible the DNA had mistakenly matched me to a family in which my looks

127

matched like a finger in a glove? Could that possibly be a coincidence?

Keep it together. Keep it together. Time was running short and soon the manager would return and I would have to be on, be what she expected me to be.

My fingers shaking, I moved on to the next page. Lilian gave out a low snore.

BARN DEATHS ARE MURDER-SUICIDE

I stared at the headline, breath caught in my throat. Beneath the awful words, a large picture, a portrait of a man, late thirties probably, with a rounded face, receding hair, his mouth set into a grim line.

In a shocking twist, authorities have revealed that the family found deceased in the barn fire near Brampton were the victims of a murder-suicide plot. Police say that Mrs Camille Lynch and her two children were killed with gunshot wounds to the back of the head. Mr Hadley Lynch, a postal worker from Markham, was found to have a gunshot wound to his right temple. The gun, a .22, was found at his side.

Mrs Elizabeth Barrow, a neighbor, said that Mr Lynch was well known to be a heavy drinker and was reportedly abusive to his children. The Lynch family are survived by Mrs Lynch's eldest son, Elliott, who was out of town at the time of the tragedy.

My stomach lurched. Tempting now to throw the papers back into the box, to call it a mistake, to walk away, never look back. You could be opening up a can of worms. Everyone had been right, I had been wrong.

Only I never could bear an unanswered question.

The next page was a typewritten sheet, a police report. I scanned through it, trying not to absorb words like muzzle burn, catastrophic damage. Told myself it was just like doing research, reading a story, the tragic tale of people wholly unconnected with me.

And then, everything changed. It was a small note at the bottom of the description of the murder scene, almost missed as I tried to parse through it. That the body of the baby was never conclusively identified, that the newspaper had been wrong, in one point at least, that there was not enough left to make a positive identification. But they had found Mia's clothing, pacifier, and family and friends had reported that she was there with her mother on that day. They had assumed that she had been thrown first onto the point of origin of the fire, that the heat of it had consumed her little body quickly.

Only that wasn't true, was it?

Because somehow I had escaped the gunshots and the fire. And somehow I had made my way to the Capitol building in Madison.

Somehow, I had lived.

I was Mia Lynch.

I had to be.

I held the paper tight in my hand. I had found my

parents, but it was already too late. They were dead, and their deaths had not been an accident. Rather, they had been murdered by my father, a man who had contributed half of my DNA.

Be sure if you ask a question that you want to know the answer.

Why? Why did I not die along with my mother, my brother? Did my father spare me? If so, how? Because the barn fire, the murders, they had taken place in the September. Yet I was not found in Madison until the November. Where was I for those six intervening weeks and how did I make it from here to Wisconsin?

And where was my eldest brother?

'You're not her, are you?' I hadn't heard Lilian wake, had been too lost within my own thoughts, trying to make sense of it all. But when I turned towards her, she was watching me with rheumy eyes. 'You're not Camille?'

'No.'

She squinted at me. 'And I'm willing to bet you're not RCMP either.' It was a statement, not a question.

I stared at her, then, putting the papers back into the box, slowly rose, crouched down at the side of her chair, could smell lilacs.

'My name,' I said, 'is Rosa. But ... I think it used to be something else. I think it used to be Mia. I think I'm your granddaughter.'

She studied me, and gingerly raised a hand towards my face, one finger grazing the side of my cheek. What was she seeing when she looked at me?

Then, from beyond the door, I heard the distant sound of footsteps. I sprang up, putting a respectable distance between us, arranged my face into an expression more befitting Rebecca Leland of the RCMP. The manager let herself in, a mug of coffee held carefully in her hand, looked from me to my grandmother and back.

'Everything okay?'

'Fine,' I said, coolly.

'You know,' offered Lilian conversationally, 'her name is Rosa. But she used to be my granddaughter, Mia.'

My heart stopped in my chest, and I worked to keep my face level, voice even. I gave the manager a smile, the faintest of winks. 'That's right, Lilian. Well, it's been so lovely to meet you today.'

I took the coffee, hefted the box file into my arms. 'You don't mind if I borrow these, do you?' A glance at the old woman sitting alone in the chair. 'Poor love. It's terrible to see it when their minds go like that, isn't it?'

Chapter 11

The sugar grains tumbled into the black beneath, and I watched them fall, mesmerised, mind a million miles away, so that in the end the mug was more sugar than coffee. The diner was busy, a lunchtime rush that I had inadvertently become a part of, but the voices, the clink of cutlery against china, the smell of fries, of burgers cooking, it all felt such a long way from me. Had I meant to stop here? I had meant to get in my car, to drive out of the parking lot of the care home, to put some miles between myself and the hopeful-eyed manager, between myself and Rebecca Leland. And even the woman I now knew to be my grandmother. It was all too much, all too suffocating. I had needed to run, to find space in which to breathe, to be for a moment simply Rosa. I don't know how long I had driven before the Denny's sign had punched its way through the grey of the day, the yellow of it glowing with familiarity, and the car had pulled in, of its own volition, so it seemed to me then.

A family sat in the next booth, mother, father, toddler twins, one of the girls singing 'Come Alive' at the top of her lungs, voice unsteady. What must that be like? To grow up alongside someone whose face mirrored yours, to never have that sense of being somehow irretrievably different? I had always pushed myself, in all the ways that one can push oneself, so determined to be the perfect daughter, the perfect sister, the perfect student, as if deep down I had always known that my place in this family was not assured, that I would have to earn my belonging.

I took a sip of my coffee, too sweet, the heat of it burning my lips, and let my fingers run across the top of the box file that sat atop the table beside me. It was remarkable what you could achieve when the world perceived you as having some kind of power. I had simply informed the manager that I was taking the file with me and she had acquiesced without a murmur, had walked me to my car, the journey stuffed with a litany of chatter. Please, she had said, if you need anything else, make sure you call me. I had glanced up at her, had opened my mouth, hesitated. Her eyes had widened. And then I had smiled widely. You've been a great help. Take care now.

I carefully flipped open the lid of the box file and from within pulled free the police report, the official story of my family's destruction. The twins were playing I spy now. I spy a polar bear. I'm not sure they entirely understood the point of the game. I took a long pull of coffee, set the mug down and, with a sense of bracing oneself for a crash landing, picked up the paperwork.

It had apparently been a normal day, little indication of the disaster to come. The family had lived in a farmhouse on the outskirts of Brampton, a modest affair that had come with minimal land. But what it had offered was a barn. According to the victim's mother, Lilian Gauthier, they had lived at the farmhouse for around ten years, had bought it with the hope that one day life would shift, would become kinder to them. That land would open up, that Hadley would be able to give up his job in the postal service, become a farmer like his papa. Life, however, had other ideas. Camille had lost her job and their finances had taken a downswing, and when it did happen that a neighbouring parcel of land came onto the market, there was barely enough food to feed their growing family, never mind to invest in a land purchase. According to Mrs Gauthier, they managed, muddling through even when times were tight.

According to their nearest neighbour, Elizabeth Barrow, the family's struggles were more acute than anyone suspected. She claimed that the boys had expressed their discomfort with their father, that she'd had the sense for some time that all was far from well.

At approximately 4.30 p.m., Mrs Barrow was in her kitchen, and heard a car approaching. Upon glancing out of the window, Mrs Barrow recognized it as being Hadley Lynch's. The car took its usual path toward the house.

Camille Lynch returned home approximately thirty minutes later. Mrs Barrow reports having been in the yard at the time, and having seen her in the car with baby Mia. She reports that Mrs Lynch slowed the car, rolled the window down to pass the time of day, promising that Kyle would come down later that evening to help her take her trash to the kerb. The car then continued up the narrow road that led to the farmhouse.

Around an hour after that, at approximately 6 p.m., the first smoke was seen coming from the barn.

First responders attempted to raise the family from the farmhouse. When this failed, it was assumed that they had left the premises. It was only later, in speaking to Mrs Barrow, that it was confirmed that no cars had passed by her premises and that both vehicles had in fact been left to the rear of the farmhouse. Upon elimination of the fire, emergency personnel were able to confirm the presence of bodies within the burnt-out barn.

It is believed that Mr Lynch summoned his family to the barn, perhaps on some pretext, and that he there killed them using his .22. It is believed that sometime after the murder of his family, Mr Lynch piled their bodies up, with that of baby Mia at the bottom, and, using gasoline as an accelerant, set fire to them. He is then believed to have shot himself.

Family and friends confirmed that Mr Lynch had become more withdrawn in recent months and that he had expressed his frustration with his family situation. It is believed that the family were suffering from some financial strains, and that these were a source of intense pressure for him.

'Honey? You got a patty melt?'

It took me a moment to pull back, to remember where I was. I looked up at the waitress, shockingly young, face thick with make-up that failed to cover the acne.

'I ... yes ... sorry.' I shifted the papers, allowing her to slide the plate in front of me, suddenly aware that my cheeks were damp.

'Here you go.' She hovered. 'You okay?'

I looked from her to the sandwich, back again. 'I'm fine. Thank you.'

Because, honestly, what else do you say? Well, I just found out that I'm actually a foundling whose birth father tried to murder her and succeeded in murdering the rest of her family. How are you?

I folded the police report closed and slowly picked up a fork, doubtfully moving a fry about. They had assumed I was dead. Because a baby cannot transport herself from the heart of a crime scene to the depths of the Midwest. Only somehow I did.

What had happened on that day to push my father over the edge? What was wrong with him that could make such a thing even possible? And then a creeping thought, that the same blood ran in my veins, and so what if whatever was wrong with him was wrong with me too?

No.

I couldn't go there, couldn't allow that thought oxygen. Because if I did, it would become an all-consuming fire.

Focus, Rosa.

I came here looking for two things – family and answers. What I had found had been incomplete at best. And yet somewhere out there was my brother. Family. And, odds were, he could also provide answers.

I sighed, took a reluctant bite of my sandwich and pulled my phone closer to me, typing the name Elliott Lynch into the search engine. It wasn't an uncommon name, common enough in fact to send my adrenaline spiking, again and again. But by the time I had finished my food, it had become obvious that he was nowhere to be seen. He was not on Facebook or Twitter or Instagram. There was no record of him in the White Pages. I had managed to locate a birth record, but nothing since. It seemed that my brother had simply dropped off the face of the earth.

I shuffled through the papers and pulled free the photograph of us – my mother and brothers and I – and studied Elliott. He wore his fair hair short, was lean, the faintest hint of muscle beneath his T-shirt. He had not smiled for the camera, but rather was looking through it, so that the overall effect was that he looked past the lens and straight at you. He had my eyes.

'Where are you?' I muttered.

I leaned back, staring into space. Two survivors, him and I. Had he somehow rescued me? And yet, if he was going to rescue me, surely he would at least have attempted to save our brother as well?

It seemed to me then that I could smell smoke, an acrid trace that lingered at the back of my throat, beneath it, bitter gasoline. I could feel heat, that raced across my body, flushing my cheeks. Was it a memory or a fantasy?

They said that they had found signs of me, the clothing I had worn, my pacifier. It was almost ... It was almost as if someone had wanted them to think that way, that someone had wanted the world to believe me dead.

But why?

The investigation had been flawed, had been based on a faulty assumption of four deaths rather than three. I needed to go back, to begin again. I flipped through the police report, locating the name of the neighbour, Elizabeth Barrow, her contact details, and I plugged them into my cell, muttering a silent prayer. After three rings, a woman answered and I could dimly make out the sound of dogs barking in the background.

'Hey, Mrs Barrow? Hi, I'm Rebecca Leland, Sergeant for the RCMP. I've been tasked with looking into the Lynch murders and your name is on the original case file. I wonder if I could come out and talk with you?'

To the woman's credit, she managed her surprise well. 'Oh, sure. I'm surprised to hear from you after all these years. But sure, I'm here. You want to come on out now?'

'I do, Mrs Barrow. You want to give me your current address?'

She recited an address and I scribbled the details onto a napkin. 'Okay, I'm maybe thirty minutes out. I'll see you soon, okay?'

I was dimly aware of a server approaching my table, of someone crouching down beside me. I glanced side-ways as I hung up the phone, to see the same waitress who had brought me my food. From this distance, her make-up looked patchy and worn, her eyes tired. I gave her a half-smile.

'Hey,' she said, voice quiet enough that I had to lean in close to pick out her words from the thrum of sound that filled the diner. 'Look, I don't want to worry you, only there's a guy over there that's been staring at you this whole time.'

Chapter 12

My stomach lurched and I twisted in my seat, scanning the faces surrounding me. 'Where?'

'Over there by the ...' The waitress leaned away from me, gaze focused on a booth near the door, 'Oh. I guess he left.' Colour flooded to her cheeks, and she shook her head quickly, 'I'm sorry. I shouldn't have scared you like that. Only, you know how it is, how guys are. Us girls, we got to stick together, right?'

The twins at the next table were arguing now over whether My Little Pony could beat Minnie Mouse in a fight. And I focused on the table, trying to bring myself back to some kind of reality, trying to ground myself.

Breathe. Just breathe.

'You sure he was watching me?' I asked, gaze still running over the diner, the people within it.

The waitress pulled a face. 'Pretty sure. It kind of creeped me out. But look, I'm sorry. He was probably just one of those guys, thinks it's their right to look.' She glanced about her. 'Anyways, he's gone now.' She smiled brightly. 'Can I get you some more coffee?'

I shook my head, sharp. 'What did he look like, this guy?'

She hesitated, something in my tone catching her attention. 'I don't know. I guess middle-aged, glasses. Your average guy. You know, not the type you pay much attention to.' She leaned on the table, standing up tall. 'I really wish I hadn't said anything now.' She glanced about. 'You want me to get someone to walk you out? Y'know, if it'll make you feel better and all?'

It was nothing. It was a coincidence. I shook my head again, 'I'm okay. And ... thank you. I appreciate you telling me.'

She grinned. 'Be part of the solution, right?'

I stood up, my legs unsteady, gripped the table for balance and scanned the diner. My breath was out of control, the sense of having a target on the back of one's neck. I should go home. I should run. I blew out a slow breath, trying to get my panic to ebb, my vision to coalesce, my heartbeat to stabilise. But then, wasn't home where this had all begun? I stuffed the papers back into the box file, then darted between the seats and the booths, feeling fear, a big hard block of it settling on top of my chest, waiting for the sound of a shot to puncture the air.

Then I was out and free, only freedom is not safety, and the wind had whipped itself up into a bitter-cold frenzy that tugged at my hair, whipping at my face. And with it came the first drifting flakes of snow, the vanguard of an impending army. So I ducked my head down low and hurried towards my car, keys pushed through my fist of fingers, the tension pulsing in my arm, waiting for the sound of breath behind me, for running footsteps. Survival is a matter of breaking the world down into tiny goals. Now it was the car. Get to the car and you will be okay. Get to the car and you'll be safe. I cradled the box file to my chest, could feel my heart beating against it, and tugged the door open, all but throwing myself inside and slamming the door behind me. The click of the lock.

I couldn't breathe. Couldn't think.

I leaned forward, peering into the grey at the cars surrounding me. Was he in one of them, watching? Whoever he was, had I seen him? But no. If I had seen him, if my eyes had actually landed on his features, I would have known. Surely? There would have been something about him, some warning.

I dumped the box file onto the seat beside me, my hands shaking, trying to force my brain to calm, to think. That likely this was nothing, some creepy guy staring at a woman in a diner. Happened every hour of every day. A world away from home, where no one knows who I am, to assume that this was in any way connected to the burglary, to the fall, that was my fear talking.

Snow had begun to tumble now, flakes of it coming on fast. If I was going to make it out to Brampton, I should go now. I reached for my phone, quickly thumbing out a text to Gray.

Everything okay at the house?

A moment, two, then three dancing bubbles, followed by the words, Everything fine. Okay in NY?

A billow of guilt and I replied, the thumbs-up emoji. It wasn't lying if it was in emoji form. Right?

I shook my head, sliding the phone into the centre console, and jammed the key into the ignition, pulling out of the parking lot fast, a quick right turn into traffic. My fingers dug into the steering wheel, my attention on the rear-view mirror, on the cars behind. That grey sedan. Had I seen that back at the diner? I sped up, moved out a lane, watched as it hung back.

An off-ramp appeared up ahead and, at the last possible moment, I cut across two lanes of traffic towards it, plunging off the highway into the streets below. Slowed. Whoever it was, they weren't behind me now.

It took close to an hour to reach the house of Elizabeth Barrow. The sky lay heavy above, thick with a dense layer of cloud, snow falling in a steady barrage. I slowed as I approached, a straight road through patchwork fields, the pattern broken only by the occasional farmhouse. Or barn. And I tried to forget that I had been here before, in a time beyond memory. That my mother would have driven this road, me wrapped up at her side. And that my father would have driven this road on the day that he murdered her.

I tried not to think of that, tried to turn myself into Sergeant Rebecca Leland. I had no idea who she was, but could not shake the vague impression that she would have her shit together more than I did.

I pulled up outside the cottage of Elizabeth Barrow. In spite of the weather, she was waiting for me on the wraparound porch. She had a thick padded coat pulled on over a roll-neck jumper, and she blinked into the drifting snow and gave a quick wave. Yes, it's me. You're in the right place.

I took a deep breath, arranged my features and climbed sedately from the car, a quick glance to the road behind. Was anyone watching?

'Mrs Barrow?' I asked.

'It is.' The woman was perhaps in her seventies and yet held herself as if she was far younger, her white-blonde hair pulled back into a loose ponytail. 'You best come inside. Snow's coming down hard.'

I nodded, steadily climbing the steps, following her into the small house. Although perhaps, on reflection, it wasn't that small, rather stuffed with every conceivable manner of item, such that it seemed there was no room left for air.

Soft toys lined the walls of the living room, sitting three-deep in some places, giving the effect of entering an arena, a fight to the death with a lovey audience baying for your blood. A mantel overfilled with framed photographs, of a wedding, of a baby, of an elderly couple, so many damn faces. She waved me towards the sofa, brown leather, covered with cushions, perhaps an inch square remaining for sitting. There was a musky smell, like the place had been dotted with mothballs.

Or perhaps that was the smell of decomposing soft toys. A teddy bear death scene.

It's possible I was becoming delirious.

A pot of coffee was waiting, positioned carefully in

amongst a kaleidoscope of old magazines, a plate of home-made cookies beside them.

'Oatmeal raisin,' Mrs Barrow said, pointing to them. 'Fresh from the oven. Tuck in.' She had pulled her coat off, slinging it over the back of the recliner, and shoved a sleeping Pomeranian to one side, carefully perching beside it. 'So.' She studied me, and I sat up straighter under her gaze. 'Why is RCMP interested in this again? Been a long time.'

'Some new evidence has come in,' I said, voice deliberately calm. 'Sure it's nothing, but you understand that we have to follow up.'

She nodded, approvingly. 'Well, you've got me. What is it you want to know?'

'You knew the Lynches well?'

She considered. 'Well enough. She – Camille that is – she was a delightful girl. Pretty too.' She stopped, studied me, and my stomach flipped. 'Had a bit of a look of you about her. Strange that, isn't it?'

I felt unsteady, as if I had risen above my body, looking down on the scene.

'And the boys. They were just lovely. They'd come down here and they'd say to me, "We've come to help you with the chickens, Aunt Liz."'

'What were they like?' I was aware of a note of longing creeping into my voice, a quick cough, a useless cover.

She sighed, brushing a twist of hair from her forehead. 'Elliott, he was a quiet soul. Reserved, you know. A thinker. Handsome boy, too. But Kyle, he was more

145

of the social butterfly. He would come on down here, would sit with me out on that porch and we would drink lemonade and chat and just watch the world go by. And kind. Nothing was too much trouble for that boy. Said he liked coming down here, that it was peaceful here.'

'Peaceful,' I said, carefully. 'Does that mean that home wasn't peaceful for him?'

She pursed her lips, shifted like she was settling in for a long tale, her hand resting on the dormant Pomeranian. 'Well now, that Camille, she loved those boys, no doubt about it, they were the two eyes of her. But Hadley ... I guess it's normal, for fathers and sons to have trouble. Only Hadley, he was mean. Not that you'd know it to talk to him. That man, he could charm the birds from the trees. That nasty streak of his, that only came out behind closed doors. Kyle had it the worst of all, bruises, big black welts all up and down his stomach.'

'Did you tell anyone? Social services? Cops?'

She gave me a long look. 'Don't you think I wish I had. I couldn't have known that he would go off, would do what he did. And Kyle, he begged me, begged. "Liz," he said, "you can't tell anybody what I told you. He'll kill me if you do." Course,' she said, 'I didn't think he actually would kill him, thought it was just a turn of phrase.'

'What about Camille? Did she know?'

Elizabeth snorted, and the dog started, its chin lifting from the chair, giving her a look of disgust. 'It's okay, Odie. Mommy's sorry.' She stroked the wild white fur on his head and shook her head regretfully. 'Hard to imagine she didn't. What with them all living in that house together. How could you not?' She sighed. 'Why she didn't do something, make some move to protect those boys, it's more than I can say. I guess, maybe she just gave up.' She looked down. 'You know, I never told anyone this, but I'm angry with her. They were good kids. They deserved better than they got. And Camille, sure, she had troubles, but you protect your babies. As a mother ...' Her voice trailed off, then she looked at me again, eyes shining. 'I'm sorry. I just ... it's still hard, you know?'

I nodded. She couldn't even begin to imagine.

'You remember that day?' I asked, carefully.

She wasn't looking at me, her gaze instead resting on the mantel, on the army of photographs, and it took a moment for my words to reach through to wherever it was she had gone. When they did, Elizabeth gave the ghost of a laugh. 'Remember it? I still have nightmares about it, all these years later. I wake up, and I'll think I can smell burning, and it'll feel like it's happening all over again. It was a clear day, still warm after the summer. I wasn't working by then. That was back in the day, before my husband died, and he was pretty sick – Parkinson's, you know – so I'd quit work to take care of him, didn't tend to go too far from the house. I guess Camille and Hadley would have headed out to work. Can't say I saw them, but even if I did, I'm not so sure I'd have remembered. I mean, nothing special about that.'

'So, that road outside, is that the only way in and out of the Lynches' farm?'

She nodded. 'It is. Nowadays, I tend to see most of what passes by my door. But then, I'm old now, haven't got anything else to distract me. My husband, he died a couple of months after the fire,' she said, matter-of-factly. Her gaze drifted again to the mantel, the wedding photo, the bride in a high-necked, puff-sleeved dress, the groom standing to attention. She shook her head, patted the dog absently. 'That day, the day of the fire, I had gone outside, guess it must have been a little after six. I told Harry I was too warm, that I needed some air. Truth is, I was smoking. He never did like it, so I just figured what he didn't know wouldn't kill him, certainly not before the Parkinson's did. And, as soon as I opened that door there, I just knew something was wrong. I could smell it, the fire, I mean. Only it didn't smell like your usual fire that you get on a farm. So, I walked down the road a little ways, trying to see if I could figure out where it was coming from, and then I saw it, that whole barn alight.'

'You called 911?'

She nodded. 'Figured it had been some kind of accident. I called the fire department, told Harry I was going on up there, that I'd bring the kids back with me—' her voice cracked. 'I said, "Camille will be desperate. I'll bring the children on down here, don't want them hanging about with all that smoke, especially little Mia."' She plucked at a loose thread on the cushion beside her.

'I had no idea. Had no idea at all. Who could ever have imagined it would end up as badly as it did.'

I watched her in silence as tears drifted down her cheeks. Mrs Barrow pulled a handkerchief from her sleeve and dabbed at her eyes, once, twice, then shot me a grateful look, and I realised that she thought my silence was for her.

'Sorry,' she muttered, voice thick. 'I don't talk about it often.'

'Of course,' I said, sympathy laid on thick, catching hold of her impression of me and clinging tight. 'I have of course gone through the original report closely, and I know you were of great help to the original investigating officers ...'

She nodded proudly.

'But, obviously, a lot of time has passed since then and memory, it can be a funny thing, can keep things squirrelled away until years later. So, I just wanted to ask if there was anything else you can remember from that day, anything that might have surfaced after all of this was closed up. Anything might help,' I added, 'no matter how small.'

She frowned, considering, then, 'There was something. I didn't think of it at the time, because it was all just so ... awful ... and the timing, well, it didn't seem to make any sense, and by the time I remembered, they had already closed the case, so I didn't think it would be important ...'

'That's fine. That's absolutely fine. What is it?'

'Well, I remembered afterwards that there had been

a car here that day. Well, not here, I mean that a car had gone up the road, oh, I suppose it would have been about lunchtime. I was washing the dishes, there in the kitchen, and I saw it pass me.'

'You see who was driving?'

She shook her head. 'Just saw it once it had passed.'

'What car was it, do you recall?'

'A sedan. Silver. Pretty dirty, as I remember.'

'And what time did it leave?'

She shook her head. 'I don't know. I didn't see it pass again.'

I paused. 'Could you ... I mean, is it feasible it could have passed and you missed it?'

'Sure. I mean, Harry, he kept me pretty busy, so I wouldn't like to say for certain I'd have noticed.'

I thought back to the police report. No mention of a silver sedan being found on the scene, so, one way or another, whoever it was had left before the fire.

The dog had stirred now, had rolled in the narrow gap, his belly pointing skywards. Elizabeth ran her fingers across the smooth skin of his stomach. 'Who's a good boy?' she murmured. She glanced at me. 'Odie here, he's the only family I've got left now,' she said, a simple statement of affairs. 'Time marches on. And before you know it, you're the only one left.'

The only one left.

Only I wasn't, was I? 'What about the older boy?' I asked, working hard to keep the note of desperation from my voice. 'Elliott? You said you were pretty close to the boys. Did you see him after?'

She shook her head. 'Not since the day of the funeral. Poor boy was just devastated. I did hear that he went to live with his grandmother, but that didn't last long. No idea where he is now.' She sighed. 'Just imagine. Being the only one left behind after a tragedy like that. You have to ask yourself, what would that do to a person's life?'

Chapter 13

I pulled my coat tighter around me, walking slowly up the narrow road that led back to the beginning. Elizabeth Barrow's house was behind me, the orange light from its kitchen window throwing shadows onto the snow. It had begun to fall properly now, large flakes swirling through the air in front of me in an elaborate dance that warned of worse to come. My fingers burned with cold, and I considered returning to my car for my gloves, my hat. But there was something appealing about the pain, the sparks keeping me present on this silent road, reminding me to stay in the moment, not to slip back into an unwieldy past. You are an RCMP officer. I am the child of a murdered family. You are Rosa Fisher. I am the daughter of a madman. It felt like a dark room briefly illuminated with strobe lights, the image shifting and changing, so that in the end I was not sure where I was or when I was or who I was.

Familicide. The killing of multiple members of your own family.

It was like the flicking of a switch for me, the mounting panic dwindling in the face of cold hard facts. I am Rosa the nerd.

The perpetrator – your father, Rosa, one half of your DNA. No. The perpetrator. The perpetrator generally falls into one of two camps. The angry killer, the one with a bone to pick with his wife, who gives off to the world this sense of a pan on the cusp of bubbling over, a history of lashing out, of anger and violence.

What had Elizabeth said? That he had hurt my brother, that she had seen the marks.

Or the sad killer, one for whom life seems to have nothing but anguish, weighed down by a sense of impending doom. A feeling that they are offering a mercy to their wife, their children, rescuing them from this cruel, cruel world.

I turned my face up to the falling snow and tried to kid myself that it mattered, the why of it. That separating my father into one of the two camps would somehow make a difference. Only it wouldn't, would it? They were still dead. I tried to breathe, tried to push down the rising sense of horror. The research says that the common thread, the tie that binds these two different types of killer, is a sense of ownership. The view that their family are somehow possessions of theirs, to do with as they will. Images flashed in my head, of my long-forgotten mother, of my helpless brother, not people, but my father's toys. And I felt sick.

Then, the thought of being watched. I stopped, turned to look back towards the main road. Had anyone followed me here? The weather and the diminishing day had plunged the world into deepening shadow. I studied the lines of the road, the stretch of the trees, looking for signs of a figure hidden amongst them.

But there was only me.

Whoever that was.

I turned away from the road again and began to walk on, snowflakes hitting my cheeks, laying thick upon my hair. How many times had I passed along this road before? I should feel something, surely? Not memory perhaps, but there should be something in me that sensed a familiarity with the shape of the trees, the curve of the road, the emerging shape of the distant farmhouse. But all I could find in there was fear, a sense of walking a tightrope, a plunging drop beneath.

It wasn't too late, I could still turn back.

But it was, and I couldn't.

I rounded a chink in the road, trees giving way to a wide-open space, a farmyard quiet in the snow. A house, narrow red brick topped with grey wood slats, orange lights glowing from its downstairs windows. And from somewhere within, the distant sound of a dog barking.

The farmhouse door swung inwards, spilling warm light out onto the grey of the yard, and a liver-and-white spaniel came rocketing towards me, its ears flapping wildly with the movement. Its tail began to wag, and it circled me, letting loose yips of pleasure.

'Tory! Tory, goddammit.' A figure moved into the doorway, backlit by the glow beyond. A woman, but more than that I couldn't tell.

I paused, hunkered down to fuss over the dog that danced at my feet.

'Can we help you?' The tone suggested that she sincerely hoped she could not.

I stood up, squared off my shoulders. Now I remembered who I was, for today at least. 'Rebecca Leland, RCMP. Need to ask you a few questions.'

'What about?' She stepped closer, her features emerging; she was about forty-five, give or take a decade, wore a face free of make-up and dark hair cropped short. She also looked supremely pissed off to see me. Which was nice.

'You the homeowner?'

'Yeah. Why?'

'You heard about the murder that happened here?'

'That was a long time ago. You folks be better off letting sleeping dogs lie.'

I stopped in front of her, gave her a steady look. One that said that you were entitled to your opinion no matter how wrong it may be. Until finally she sighed. 'You better come in, I suppose. Name's Anne Martin.'

I don't know what I had been expecting. Perhaps that walking into the home of my infancy would bring long-forgotten memories screaming back to me, that unknown smells would trigger my limbic system, give rise to emotions that would make little sense to me.

Instead, it was just a house. The door gave way to a wood-floored hallway, spreadeagle kitchen beyond. It smelled of spaniel and dust and my limbic system remained entirely unmoved. It felt to me that my gaze was everywhere, trying to connect this barren kitchen, with its scuffed breakfast bar, dishes still piled upon it, to some long-lost part of me. Was it truly possible that I had called this place home once?

'Don't know what you think I can tell you. We didn't buy the place until maybe five years after the fire. Stood empty for a long time. Too many people knew what happened here.'

I turned to look at her. 'But it didn't bother you?'

She shrugged. 'We were looking for a farm. Everything else was too expensive. Besides, it's not like we had to look at the barn every day. There wasn't much left of it, anyhow, not after the fire. We bulldozed the remains, built a new one.'

I nodded, trying to get my mind to work. Because the truth of it was, there was little this woman could tell me. She had not been a part of the original picture of my life. And I had come here, less because of some wildly optimistic belief that it would lead to answers, more because I could not bear to be where I was, less than half a mile from my childhood home, the place where everything began and ended, and not see.

That, however, would be unlikely to be convincing as an investigation strategy.

'Your neighbour has brought some new information to our attention. I was wondering if you might be able to shed any light on it.' Sure. That would work. 'She's told us that she remembers seeing a silver sedan entering the premises on the day of the murder. Probably nothing, but there's no mention of it in the original police report. I don't suppose it means anything to you?'

She frowned at me. 'No ...'

'What?'

She folded her arms, leaned against the kitchen counter. 'No, I mean, it may have nothing to do with it … Look, when we first bought the place, I mean, it was a mess. Utter nightmare. It took us months to get everything straightened out, get the fields ready for planting again. We were working through the top field and we came across the bumper of a car, looked like it had been torn off and just left there.'

I frowned, tried to work it through. 'So … what, someone went for a drive across the fields and came back without their bumper?'

She shrugged. 'Guess so. Couldn't tell you what colour it was, but I know we thought it was kind of weird at the time.'

'And the top field, that's …'

'If you go out through the back of the yard, it's maybe a mile to the north.'

I tried to remember the map screen on my GPS, the lay of the land surrounding us. 'Can you get to any roads that way?'

'Ah, yeah, I guess … if you cut across the fields you'd eventually make it onto Collywood Lane, which loops back onto the One Twenty Five.'

I nodded, going for just the right level of interested, my mind spinning. A car seen entering the property, but never leaving. A baby – me – seen entering the property and presumed dead, and yet somehow ending up across the border. Surely the two together were more than a coincidence? What if that was how I left? And yet who had been driving the car, who had taken me out? And why?

Then my cellphone began to ring, its tones echoing in the cavernous kitchen. 'Hello?'

I felt the woman look at me. Should I have said 'Sergeant Leland'? Surely detectives identified themselves in more official terms. Then, from the voice on the other end, I picked up the words 'Care Home' and every other thought vanished.

'I'm sorry,' I said, 'who is this?'

'It's Esther. The manager at Littlebrook. You said I should call if anything unusual happened ...'

'Okay,' I said. 'What's going on?'

'Well, remember I said that Lilian doesn't get visitors?'

'Yes.'

'Well, someone has just come to see her, he's in with her now, and given your visit, I thought it would be a good idea to call and let you know ...'

'Who? Who's there?'

'He says his name is Jackson Wolf.'

Chapter 14

The snow came heavy, billowing flakes of it spiralling along the tunnel of light from the car's headlights, so that my vision became unsteady. My hands clenched tight on the wheel. Hurry. Hurry. Hurry. My entire body fighting between good sense and an irrepressible need to just get there, this need to know. Who the hell was with my grandmother?

Could it be a member of my family, someone unknown to Esther Moody? Could it be someone else who was a part of me, someone with a firmer grip on the here and the now? Someone who would have answers to the questions I was asking?

A knot of fear twisted in my stomach.

Or was it something else?

I thought of the man from the diner, of the footsteps in my house.

But that, that was only fear talking.

Wasn't it?

The name Wolf had hung in the air, stopping the breath in my throat, and I had clutched tight to the cell, aware of Anne's gaze on me. 'Is he ... I mean, is she okay?'

'She's fine,' said Esther Moody, 'I've left someone in there with them, just in case, one of the orderlies. But I thought you'd want to ...'

'Yes. I do.' I'd glanced at Anne. 'Look, keep him there. As long as you can. I'm on my way.'

I'd hung up the phone, my feet twitching to run, and forced my face into an awkward smile. 'I'm so sorry, I have to go.'

Anne had nodded, to her credit keeping her lips sealed tight, any questions she might have kept to herself.

'Hey,' I'd said, 'the name Jackson Wolf mean anything to you?'

The woman had frowned. 'Don't think so.'

'No connection to the Lynches that you can think of?'

'Nuh-uh.'

There must have been more words exchanged, a polite goodbye, an exchange of details, but in all honesty I could remember none of them.

I pulled the car out around a sedan doing thirty, could feel the tyres loose against the slick road surface.

I pushed my foot closer to the floor, squinting into the spiralling snow. Who are you? They had said that Lilian never had visitors. What were the odds of her having two on the same day, completely unconnected to one another.

My brother-in-law always said that there was no such thing as a coincidence in a police investigation. But I am a scientist, and I can tell you that the law of averages means that there are coincidences everywhere, that within complex mathematics coincidences fall like snow.

And yet here I was, travelling through my past on a slick highway, topping the speed limit by far more than I was comfortable with, chasing ghosts. Could I even call myself a scientist any more? Where was the logic in this? Where was the reason?

I felt the car begin to slide beneath me, reluctantly raised my foot from the gas. My death would not be useful at this point. It was the trauma, I told myself. The fall, the discovery of my adoption. All of those things were designed to shake one's world and the perception of a place within it. It would make sense, therefore, for my behaviour to lack reason, to be guided by impulse and the need for truth.

Nerd-girl, fighting back academic-style.

I steered the car onto the off-ramp, the uncomfortable recollection of something I had recently written in a paper on the psychology of the financial fraudster settling over me. Everyone has the ability to rationalise bad behaviour. Even me.

The streets were quiet now, the world driven inside by the first real snow of the season, and I drove with my attention split between steering and watching the world outside. It had taken me a long time, far longer than I had expected. Seemed too much to hope that he would have remained there, just waiting for me. My attention focused on a car driving in the opposite direction, its headlights dazzling. Is it you? I slowed, turned my head to watch it pass. An elderly woman, pulled up close to her steering wheel, face taut with anxiety.

No, then.

The care home sat ahead, lights punching through the gloom, and I pulled into the parking lot. A layer of snow had already begun to settle across the expanse of it. I didn't bother with a space, figured I didn't need to. RCMP, remember? I switched the engine off and plunged out into the winter weather, striding with long steps towards the entrance, wishing suddenly that I really was a detective, that I had a gun, or some mace, hell, even a big stick.

'Sergeant.' The manager and the wall of heat from the lobby reached me at about the same time. 'I'm so sorry. He left. I tried to delay him, but I think he realised ...'

My stomach flipped. 'How long?'

'Maybe fifteen minutes? I tried to call you, but it went straight to answerphone.'

Shit. I glanced down at my phone, signal bars empty. Damn. It must have lost signal somewhere along the drive and then failed to pick it up again.

Think. Think.

'You have cameras here, yes?'

The manager nodded, wringing her hands. 'Yes. Of course. In my office. You want to ...'

I nodded grimly, not even having to feign my irritation, slipped into step beside her. 'Lilian ... she's okay?'

'Oh yes. She said it's the best day she's had in years, so many visitors. Of course, I think she's forgotten

162

about you both by now, but still ... nice for her while it lasted.'

'And she didn't say anything about who he was?'

The manager stopped in front of a door, pulling a key from her pocket and stuffing it into the lock. 'Nothing. I did ask her. She just said, "He's a wolf." Poor dear.' She pushed the door open, stepped aside to let me enter.

The room was small and institutional, its walls apparently held up by inspirational cat posters. What doesn't kill you makes you stronger. Hang in there. Life is a gift, that's why it's called the present. I fought off an eye roll, not entirely successfully.

'Here you go.' She had pulled up a screen on her desktop, footage of the front lobby, timestamped twenty minutes ago. The screen frozen on a man on his way out, his head ducked low, face buried beneath a mass of curls, a large belly protruding over the top of loose-fit jeans, thick-rimmed glasses. I gestured for her to hit play, willing him to look up, but it seemed almost that he had planned this, that he knew where the camera was, was showing me only what he was willing for me to see.

Now just who in the hell are you?

'You got any footage from the parking lot?'

She shook her head. 'Sorry. Our camera is out. We're waiting for the company to repair it, but you know how it is.'

I grimaced. 'What about his car? Anyone see it? You get a plate?'

She looked slightly like she wanted to cry. 'Sorry,' she repeated.

Shit.

I pushed my snow-damp hair from my eyes. Was thinking of finding a bar and drinking myself into oblivion on tequila, when a thought crept its way to the fore. 'Wait … you …' but she hadn't told me, had she? She had told Rosa. 'Um, it was my understanding that visitors were limited to those on the authorised list. Why did you let him in?'

She blinked at me. 'Well, he was on the list.'

I stared at her. 'What?'

'Yes, we checked, but he had been placed on the list by one of the authorising agents, so we had to let him in.'

'So, by authorising agents you mean next of kin?' My heart had begun to beat faster.

'No, sadly Lilian doesn't have a next of kin. Her lawyers are in charge of her estate and care. It was her lawyer who called and got Mr Wolf placed on the visitors' list.'

I nodded, could feel a laugh bubbling up, because you really had to admire the nerve of it. I washed it away, sliding my expression into neutral. 'And when did you speak to the lawyer?'

'Perhaps a week ago?'

'Uh-huh. And how did you know it was the lawyer you were speaking to?'

'He told me. Oh.' She looked stricken.

I gestured to the phone on the desk. 'Call them, please. Let's see if he is who he says he is.'

I lingered, biting my lip while she dialled, her voice

low, suitably chastened. Telling myself that it would be above board, that the lawyers would know who Jackson Wolf was, that Jackson Wolf could have answers for me. But that fear, it just wouldn't settle. I watched Esther Moody, listening to the voice on the other end of the phone, watched her face sink.

It wasn't above board, was it?

'Thank you. Yes, thank you.' Esther Moody hung up, looking at me, her gaze lingering somewhere about the level of my chin. 'You were right. They never rang. They never added anyone to the visitors' list.' Her voice clambered, increasingly hysterical. 'Someone else did it, someone pretending to be the lawyers. You think that was that man? That Jackson Wolf?'

I hesitated, trying to remember who the hell I was meant to be. Was it wrong that in amongst the irritation at missing him was something else, annoyance at myself that I hadn't thought of the same move, that if I had I would now be standing here as Rosa Fisher rather than Rebecca Leland of the RCMP. 'It looks like it.'

The fear should have been unleashed now, terror justified. Instead, I felt a numbness sliding over me, felt my breathing slowing, my thoughts slipping as if greased. Someone had lied to get close to my grand-mother. Someone other than me, that is.

So. Jackson Wolf. Who the hell are you? And what the hell do you want with Lilian Gauthier?

'And he didn't speak to anyone?' I asked 'Didn't make any mention of why he was here ...'

She shook her head. 'He came in, gave his name,

and because he was on the list, he was shown right in. Luckily I was coming out of my office as he was being led into Lilian's room or I'm not sure I'd have known.'

Was it a coincidence? A man whose visit was prefaced with a lie coming to see Lilian on the same day that her long-lost granddaughter arrived? The abundance of coincidences in nature notwithstanding, that one felt like a bit of a stretch.

My mind flitted back again, to the footsteps on the stairs, to hands rummaging through my mother's dresser. To the flowers, the Sorry, the missing graduation photograph, the disturbed folder of my origin story. To the figure standing in the shadows of my home, watching.

All of those things, sliding into order, one behind the other, until it felt like a story I had already read.

There was a connection here.

'Okay,' I sighed, theatrically. 'Could you print me out a copy of this picture.' I gestured to the screen, the fat man in front of me. 'I'm just going to go and look in on Lilian.'

I let myself back out into the corridor again, knocked loudly on the door of room sixteen. A querulous 'Come' from inside.

She sat in the same chair. The light beyond the window had faded now, the darkness punctured by the mesmerising drift of the falling snow. Someone had put a CD on, Vivaldi's *Winter* playing low, and Lilian hummed softly, her gaze hooked on the window.

'Hey, Lilian,' I said, softly, closing the door behind me.

She shifted her gaze to me then, studying me with a ferocity, as if she was struggling to remember something she had once heard about me. In truth, she probably was. I opened my mouth to explain, then closed it again. I would tell her. She would forget. And on we would go in a never-ending cycle. And in the warmth of the room, with the lullaby music and the spiralling snow, I felt like crying.

I stepped closer, my gaze falling on the bedside table, the glow from the lamp creating a puddle of light beneath. It was my name within it that drew my attention. I picked up the sheet of paper, my heart thudding in my chest. The word Rosa scrawled across the folded-down front of it. I unfolded the sheet, leaning closer to the light.

Some things are best left in the past. For your grandmother's sake, leave it alone.

'You know,' my grandmother said, conversationally, 'they all loved her. Very very much.'

I struggled to focus, the entirety of my attention clinging to the words, to the threat of them. 'Who?'

'Mia, of course. Oh, they loved that child.'

A burning at the back of my eyes, and I swallowed hard, stepping closer to my grandmother. 'Lilian? Do you know who I am?'

Then, like a cloud sweeping across a clear blue sky, her expression changed. 'Who are you? Are you the cleaner? Because I've been telling them, my sheets need changing, and do you think they'll listen to me …'

It was more than I could bear. Forgive me, but I turned from her then, stepping out into the blessed relief of the empty corridor, nothing left to me of Lilian but the distant tones of Vivaldi that seeped beneath the door. I blew out a slow breath, tucking the note into my pocket, could feel it all, hovering over me, a storm cloud of all that I had learned and all that I had seen.

'Sergeant?'

I looked up, schooling my face once more. The manager waving the printed photograph at me. All that I had to show for a wild dash through the snow. That and a name.

Jackson Wolf.

Chapter 15

I sat in the darkness, hard-backed chair pulled up close enough to the chipped table that my knees bumped against the wood. The sleeves of my oversized sweatshirt were pulled down across my hands. I took a sip of the vodka I had taken from the minibar, could feel the heat of it extending down through my torso, into my belly. I stared out at the night, the parking lot dimly visible beyond my window, one solitary street light fighting through the near blizzard, illuminating my car in a sickly yellow glow, and tried to pretend that my hand wasn't shaking, that the chills that ran up and down my spine were trickles escaping from my shower-wet hair. Unfortunately, I am a scientist, I cling to facts. And the fact was, I was scared shitless.

The hotel room was dark, the only light in it spilling from the laptop that stood open upon the table before me. I had searched for Jackson Wolf online, looking for anyone that matched the image laid out beside the computer, had sat in that same seat, picking at a curled-edged room-service sandwich, for hours, crawling through the Google pages. But, page after page, no Jackson Wolf that would work, mostly a bunch of listings for a college-level athlete, too young to be my guy.

I leaned my head against the cold of the window. Watched as a snow sweeper made its way steadily down the street, cutting a clear path, flinging a sheet of white out in its wake. And I thought of Wolf.

The note lay on the table before me, illuminated by the glow of the computer. Who the hell are you? And why are you trying to drive me away from here?

My cellphone rang, and I set the vodka down on the table, Eve's name flashing up on the screen. I answered on the second ring.

'Hey.' The words came out clumsy, my tongue made unwieldy by the liquor. 'Sorry. I've had a drink.'

'Hey yourself,' said Eve. 'So, weird thing. I saw your sister, down at Monona Terrace earlier, and she tells me that you're in New York. That you're working very hard. Conference, apparently. And yet, not only did Will tell me that you couldn't make it to the great NYC, but I'm pretty sure you told me you were going to Chicago ...'

A figure walked along the outer rim of the parking lot, indistinct in the gloom. A reluctant dog towed along behind it. I watched as they trudged towards the road, turning right up towards the gas station.

'I'm in Canada.'

'Of course you are.'

'I'm looking for my family,' I heard myself say. 'Mom, Addie ... I told those guys I'm away with work. I ... I'd rather keep this to myself. For now.'

A hefty silence, then, 'Okay, so ... are you ... I mean, have you ...'

'It's complicated.' I couldn't say it, had not understood that as an unavoidable truth until this moment, just knew suddenly that if I broke it down, if I put it all into words, then it would overwhelm me, and I couldn't afford to be overwhelmed, not now. 'I promise I'll explain. When I can.'

My laptop beeped, an incoming email alert, and I moved my fingers across the mousepad, unthinking, pulling up an email from the Sacramento screenwriter. Apparently his enthusiasm for my work was unquenchable. I had replied to his last email, as kindly and as briefly as I could, sufficient information, I had hoped, to satisfy him, not enough to encourage him.

'Shit,' I muttered.

'What?'

'Oh, nothing, just that Sacramento guy again. I'd hoped I'd shaken him off.'

'You and your creepy dudes,' muttered Eve.

Honey, you have no idea.

I scanned the email quickly. Profuse thanks for my reply, appreciation for my time, yada yada, and, inevitably, more questions. My finger moved the cursor over the trash can, then stopped, a single line catching my attention.

I'm particularly interested in your mention of
behavioral thresholds for the use of violence amongst
white-collar criminals, specifically the sense that

once one has shaken off the natural restraints against using violence for the first time, the threshold for subsequent acts of violence is likely to then become lower.

I read the line, once, twice, dimly aware of Eve on the other end of the phone, her voice distant, a long and meandering story about a recent date, her subsequent ghosting. Something nudged at me, a little voice at the back of my mind harrumphing softly, and I opened my Sent folder, pulling up the reply I had sent him, looking for that line, for any mention of behavioural thresholds.

Only I hadn't said it, had I?

Not there. I hadn't said that anywhere publicly. Where I had said it was in my journal article, the one that was out on submission now, waiting for its chance to be published. The one that had vanished from my house on the night of the burglary.

My insides clenched.

'Eve,' I said, cutting her off mid-flow, 'you know that paper I asked you to proofread? The red-collar crime one?'

A long silence as my best friend processed the conversational U-turn. 'Uh ... yeah?'

'You give a copy to anyone? Let anyone read it?'

Eve snorted. 'What, because violent crime is such delightful bedtime reading?' She hesitated. 'No offence, obvs. No. My copy ...' I heard rummaging over the line, 'it's right here. Why?'

'And ... seriously, is there any way someone else could

have read that? Someone from outside the department?'

'Well, I mean, I guess you gave it to Will, right? So maybe he ... Rosa, what's going on?'

I stared at the email, at the name, Ben Folger. 'You know a Ben Folger?'

'No. Dude, you're starting to freak me out.'

'Sorry. It's fine. It's fine. I must have made a mistake. Look, honey, I gotta go. I'll give you a call tomorrow, okay?'

'Okay, just ... be careful, yeah?'

'Yeah.' I hung up, moved the cursor back to the email, to that line of Ben Folger's. My mind instantly moving to quiet my gut, a coincidence again, that he had picked out a line from a paper I had written, that it was mere happenstance, a co-occurrence of wording. Only my gut was getting pretty sick of being shouted down.

I pulled the cursor over to the Safari window, googling Ben. The screenwriter out of Sacramento. The one that worked with Fox. I searched. And I searched. And I searched. Each time coming up empty. I couldn't find him, the screenwriter Ben Folger. The person who seemed to know what I had written in a paper that had thus far been read by two people.

And then I remembered a scam, one I'd gotten from a con artist out of Chicago. He hadn't begun life as a con artist, had started out as a regular Joe, just trying to make ends meet. Yet opportunity and fear, and the lack of a company paying close attention, had ended up with him embezzling three million dollars. What was weird, said his boss, was that he was so good at covering his tracks. He would never do anything if there was anyone around who could catch him. It was like he always knew where we were.

So, I opened up Facebook, found a photograph of myself from the Christmas before last, smile bright, entirely unknowing of what was to come, copied the URL, opened up a website, one I had never heard of before my Chicago friend, and pasted the URL into its field. You see, you generate an email, you include a photograph. And when they click on the photograph, it sends you the IP address of the computer they are using.

See? It's amazing what you can achieve if you don't care how you do it.

I typed quickly. This might be useful for you. Hit send, waited.

It took only seconds to bounce back, but each one of them felt like an hour, before the screen changed, flashing up with an IP address. I grabbed it quickly, searching for its location. That rational brain of mine still mocking the crazy of this, the voice in my head saying that it would return as Sacramento, and then I would look like a crazy person, sending a picture of myself to some random stranger.

The result flashed up on the screen and my heart stopped beating. IP address – Orangeville, Ontario.

My hotel.

Chapter 16

I couldn't breathe. Or rather, I could breathe, but the breaths were coming shallow and fast, a runaway train of oxygen converting to carbon dioxide. I pushed myself back from the table, could feel a rush of blood to the head that made the world swim.

Gut and brain were in sync now, both singing the same song. That whoever came into my house that night wasn't there to steal. He was connected, to me, to my family. And he had followed me here.

I turned around in a useless circle in the middle of the hotel room, like if I just rotated, I would figure it out, would know what to do.

Shit.

Shit. Shit. Shit.

I grabbed the still captured from the care home's surveillance footage from the table. It was him. It had to be him. Right?

Right??

Who the fuck was he? What the fuck did he want with me?

I had to calm down. I had to think.

First things first. He knew where I was. I grabbed the

chair, towing it across the room towards the door, and, tilting it back, slid it beneath the handle, wedging it good and tight. Then, I turned about on myself, scanning the room again, this time looking for a weapon, something I could use in place of my little-league baseball bat. My gaze fell on the lamps, one standing guard on each side of the king-size bed. I ducked down, unplugging the one closest to the window, and wrapped the wire about its body. Hefted it in my hands. Light enough that I could lift it. Weighty enough that it could do some damage if swung with enough enthusiasm.

I carried the lamp over to the bed, laid it beside me like a weapon of war, and sat down next to it. I could cry. Crying seemed like a pretty rational response right now. Unfortunately, crying also seemed like it would be spectacularly unhelpful.

I had stumbled into something that I didn't understand. And, if I knew nothing else, I knew of myself that when I didn't understand, I had to find information.

Lilian, bless her heart, was unlikely to provide much in the way of insight, unless I was spectacularly lucky in my timings. And other than Lilian, who was there left?

There was Elliott. There was my brother.

I pulled my laptop onto the bed and opened up Safari. What was most important was finding my brother. If I could do that, then all would fall into place. I expanded the window to fill the screen, again feeling that wash of disappointment. I had searched everywhere: marriage records, White Pages, social media. Had even, with a sense of dread, looked for him amongst the deaths. And yet there was nothing.

I sat, stared at the white of the screen, willing my mind to conjure up a new angle.

He was the only other survivor. He had to be out there somewhere.

I sighed heavily, scrubbed my sweaty hands across my face and left them there for long moments, cocooning myself in a bubble of terry cloth. He and I. Him and me. Of the Lynch family, we were all that was left. So was it him? Did he somehow find a way to rescue me from the cataclysm that was descending upon our family? The police report, it said he was out of the country. But they didn't know there was anything left unexplained, so would they even have checked?

Someone got me out. And if it wasn't my brother, then who the hell was it?

I thought for long moments, then reached into my bag, pulling the police report free and searching through its pages. There. Elliott had been enrolled at Schirmer High School. I moved to Google Maps, located the school, a dozen miles away.

And now I had a plan.

I had begun to settle into complacency, warmed by the heat of the vodka and the room, and the soft glow from the laptop. My adrenal response had begun to settle, my mind, for the briefest of moments, forgetting to feel afraid. Then came movement beyond the window, through the snow and the deep darkness. A figure walking slowly through the parking lot, thickly bundled inside a winter coat, a woollen hat pulled down low. I watched the shape, could feel a chill running through me again, slid the lid of my laptop closed to shut off the lights of it, and ducked off the bed, closer to the window.

It was the speed of it, the figure's pace meandering almost on this bitter-cold night. It was the way their head swivelled, casual, from left to right. They were making sure they were not being observed. It was the bulk of them, distantly familiar even beneath the winter clothing.

I shifted, pulling back so that the shape of me would be hidden by the curtain. And I watched. Waiting.

The figure came to a stop, movement easy, nothing to see here. Just someone getting to their car on a snowy winter night. Only it wasn't their car. It was mine.

It ducked down beside my Mini, peering into the back seat, the trunk.

My fingers moved without thought, reaching for my phone, pulling it up, aiming. A snap of the camera. Which would have been fine. Had I thought to turn the flash off first.

A burst of light, the darkness more complete in its wake. My heart pounding and I dived backwards, throwing myself behind the curtain.

Shit.

Shit. Shit. shit.

I waited there, trying to get my breath to slow, my heart to stop beating out of my chest. Wanting to kick myself for being so stupid. It felt like hours and yet, in truth, was probably seconds, little more, before I risked a look, a cautious movement of the curtain, peering out into the darkness. Telling myself that perhaps they hadn't seen, that perhaps I was overreacting.

It took a moment for my eyes to acclimatise, to make out what stood beyond the second-floor window. My car. And the figure beside it. Standing now, hands loose at its sides, staring up at my window.

I let the curtain drop, falling back against the wall, head racing. Because there was something in the shape of him, in the easy confidence of him, that confirmed what I had feared to be true. It was Wolf. The same man who had gone into the care home, who had lied his way into my grandmother's presence and left me a clear message, stood now before my hotel window. He knew my car. He knew my room.

Who are you? What the hell do you want? Why are you watching me?

Nausea raced through me, the urge to run turning my feet towards the door. But where was there to run to, when he stood beside my car?

I gripped the fabric of the curtain and fought to regain control. I had to think. The people who play you, they work on your emotions, they get you so that you are all reaction, not enough thought.

So you do things like taking a covert photo without turning the fucking flash off!

I edged closer to the window, peering out.

The figure had moved now, was standing closer to the road, the detail of him hidden by the falling snow.

I was going to have to leave, find a different hotel, somewhere where he couldn't find me. A quiet whisper of a thought at the back of my mind – how did he find me? How did he know where I was?

But that was tomorrow's problem, because today's was what came next. Because I had to leave. And in order to leave, at some point I was going to have to get out of this room.

I tugged open the wardrobe door, flipping open the lid of my suitcase, clothes a crumpled pile within. There had to be something. I found a scarf, a deep teal, the faintest tracings of vines clambering across it, and I wrapped it around my head, turning it into a hijab. I sat there, on the floor, for long moments, thinking, then moved to my handbag, digging through scraps of paper and scraggly handkerchiefs, before finding my sunglasses. Target bargains, crumbs accumulated in the hinges of them. I grimaced and, with my thumbs, pushed the lenses onto the carpet, leaving behind empty frames. It wasn't perfect, but it would be better than nothing.

I tugged the scarf from my head and, keeping close to the wall, moved back towards the window.

He was gone. Nothing left now but an empty parking lot.

I stared out into the falling snow and, for the briefest of moments, wondered if I had imagined it all.

Chapter 17

'Hey. My name is Sergeant Rebecca Leland, and I'm with the RCMP. I was wondering if you could help me ...' I smiled brightly.

It took the school administrator a few moments for my words to work their way into her consciousness, pulling her from whatever pressing matter absorbed her on her computer screen. And then she looked up, blonde ponytail swinging, and leaned back in her chair, the round bump of a pregnant belly emerging from beneath the desk.

'Sorry,' she said carefully. 'Who did you say you are?'

I waved my eBay badge in front of her, one quick swipe and then away. 'Sergeant Leland. Need to look at your records.'

The sky had just begun to lighten when I left the hotel, dark night bleaching its way towards the dawn. The snow had stopped, leaving behind white foot-print-lined sidewalks, a bitter-cold breeze. I had stood at the window of my room for a long time, watching the waking world, looking for that figure, but seeing only an empty parking lot, my Mini half buried beneath a mountain of snow, a purple sunrise.

I had opened the door cautiously, peering out into

the empty corridor, painfully aware of the carefully arranged scarf that covered my hair, of my ludicrous glasses with their heavy frames and empty eyes, had eased the door shut behind me, walked with quiet steps towards the stairwell. In my head, reminding myself to be someone new, someone whose strides are narrower, whose shoulders do not rise up, arms do not swing. But it seemed that this character work was for me and the pigeons. I eased open the rear door, scanning the parking lot, empty, my poor Mini sitting there, waiting and alone. I didn't head for it, but rather hugged the side of the building, hurrying out onto the road that ran behind the motel to where an Uber sat waiting, the driver some pock-faced kid, who barely glanced at me, before pulling out into the early-morning streets.

I had breakfasted in a coffee shop, a block or two from Schirmer High, waiting as the sky lightened as much as it likely would, as the day got moving, people heading to work, children to school. I drank cup after cup of coffee and toyed with chewy scrambled eggs, my attention flitting from the door, to the tables surrounding me, to the flurry of pedestrians that passed by the windows. And I looked for a figure that seemed familiar, for the sense of being stared at.

For Wolf.

And yet, as the hours slipped away, the watery winter sun coming up full, I could feel my shoulders begin to unravel, the tension behind my eyes begin to ease. It had worked. He had kept watch on my car, had assumed that because it remained, I did too.

I slid a twenty-dollar bill onto the table and slipped into the ladies' room, pulling the scarf from about my head, slipping the glasses off. A muted copper lipstick, hair twisted up into a chignon. A different character now. Sergeant Leland, reporting for duty.

The school administrator's expression had cleared, light entering her eyes. 'Of course,' she said. 'Anything we can do to help.'

We often say that there is little to tie together con artists. They each approach their crimes from a different direction. But their victims, it is they who share a profile. They have a need for something, a desire for more than life is currently offering them, and the fraudsters, they reach out, apparently presenting them with an opportunity for precisely what has been lacking.

I sighed heavily, running my fingers through my hair. 'Honestly, this case has been a pain in the ass. Even just trying to locate witnesses twenty years later … it's impossible.'

She pushed herself up to standing, one hand resting on the mound of her belly. 'Well, let me see if I can help. We keep pretty good records of our alumni. Reunions, that kind of thing …' She leaned forward, a staged whisper. 'Sometimes fundraising. Principal feels it's important to "keep connected". You said twenty years, right? You have a name of the student you're looking for?'

I stood up a little straighter, allowed a look of relief to cross my face. 'If you had anything that would help, that would be awesome. It's Elliott Lynch.'

183

And there it was. The reaction. Her gaze lingering on me for just a fraction too long.

'You know the name.' It was a statement, rather than a question.

The administrator flushed. 'Sure. I mean, I grew up around here. What happened with the Lynches ... I would have been, I don't know, I guess, twelve. It was all anyone talked about. For months.' She ducked her head down, teeth bothering her bottom lip, a question she was working very hard not to ask. She shook her head. 'Horrible thing,' she said, carefully.

'Yes,' I agreed.

'So ...' Her fingers danced quickly across the keyboard. 'Okay, we have an address for Elliott, but, look ...' She twisted the screen towards me, ran her finger across a line of text. 'I'm pretty sure that's his grandmother's address. Last I heard, she'd gone into residential care. Dementia,' she said, confidentially. 'There's no listed number for Elliott. No other address.'

I groaned softly, didn't have to stage it. 'Dammit. Okay. I'm trying to just confirm the location of everyone involved in the case. Now, according to the original investigation reports, I have Elliott as being in the US, New Orleans, on a school trip at the time what happened ... happened. You wouldn't have any records of that? Any way I can definitely say, yes, this kid was in this location, so I can move on to the next?'

She shook her head slowly. 'I'm so sorry. We just don't keep records for that long. Not on things like school trips.'

I sighed. 'I'm not surprised. I told my supervisor you'd say that, but you know how it is.'

The administrator drummed her fingernails against the desktop in a rapid staccato beat. 'What if we try ... Wait a second. I'll be right back.'

She pushed her chair to one side, moving towards the rear office in a waddling motion.

I turned on the spot, studying the glass partition separating me from the rest of the school, could feel a prickle across my spine. But there was no one there, just an empty hallway, first period well under way now. Somewhere, someone played the violin. Badly. I scanned the hall beyond. Seemed it was becoming ever-present, that feeling of pursuit, that even in utter loneliness there was always a sense of feeling hunted.

The woman came back, carrying a leather-bound book. 'Here you go. Yearbook from Elliott's senior year. Might have something.' She flipped up the partition and beckoned me around to the rear of the desk, placing the book down onto its surface. She opened the pages, fingers sliding across their slick surface. 'Here's Elliott Lynch.' She pointed to a picture about a third of the way down the page, a half-man, half-boy, looking at the camera as if embarrassed by its presence, his lips curled into a doubtful smile. 'I don't know that will help you any, but still ...'

I tried for a smile of my own, my gaze tracing the arc of his eyes, the line of his nose, and seeing a glimpse of it in the face that looked back at me from the mirror each morning. 'No. I suppose not.'

She turned the page, pulling my brother away from me before I was ready. 'See, there are a lot of candid shots in here. Groups the kids were in – band, football. I don't know if there are any of Elliott, but ...' She steadily turned the pages, running her finger across them, totally committed now to this detective work that had become her own. After a couple of turns, a face shone out at me.

'There,' I said, quietly.

Elliott was laughing, a split-apart smile, one arm looped around the shoulder of a shorter boy, as dark as Elliott was fair.

'Who is that?' I asked.

'Um ... Sadiq Baram,' read the woman. 'Same year as Elliott.'

I jotted a note in my notepad, watching as she turned the next page. 'Wait.'

My brother again, smile pensive this time, standing amidst a group of boys. Sadiq once again beside him. I studied the picture, tapping the image of the other boy. 'Can you check and see if you have a recent address for this guy?'

'Sure.' She moved away from me, fingers dancing quickly across the keyboard. 'So, he's local. I have a Toronto address for him. There's a phone number here too, if you want it?'

'Please.' I passed her my notepad, watched as she scribbled it down.

She handed the pad back to me and returned to my side, resuming her slow turning of the pages. But that was it for the presence of my brother. Three small pictures, that was all that remained to testify to his life here.

As she reached the rear of the book, a sigh escaped me. 'Okay. And there's no one here who I could talk to about that New Orleans trip? No teacher who might have escorted it?'

The woman tapped her fingers against the book cover. 'No. Marie was the longest-serving teacher and we lost her last year.' Cancer, she mouthed. 'Wait ...' The woman clapped her hands together. 'You know, I've just had a thought. Wait here.'

She vanished again, back into the rear office, before reappearing, holding a large box file. 'Okay, so we don't keep records dating back that far, but what we do keep is copies of the school newspaper. It's been going since the school began pretty much and they release an edition every month.' She flipped open the file, the smell of must sweeping across us. 'Now, I can't say for sure, but they often feature the bigger school trips, so there might be ...' She lifted a stack of newspapers out, handing me half of the pile.

We sifted through the decades-old papers, print staining my fingers black.

'Here,' I murmured. 'This is the year. And the month.'

I turned through the pages, and there, on page three, was a photograph of perhaps twenty students, a frazzled-looking teacher standing in the midst of them, holding a sign: New Orleans, September 17, 1995. And for a moment I could not find him, and I believed that

I had found my answer, that my brother had somehow been at the farm that day, that it was him that had gotten me out.

'There,' said the administrator.

She rested a long starry fingernail on a figure in the middle row, a man-boy with my eyes and my nose and a diffident smile.

Elliott Lynch. My brother.

He was there. He couldn't have saved me.

Chapter 18

The bell had rung, the signal for second period, a harsh industrial buzzer echoing through the taupe corridors. The briefest of moments in which it seems that the world holds its breath and then five hundred chair legs all scraping across linoleum in an off-key symphony, the rustle of five hundred bags being slung onto five hundred shoulders, and then a thousand feet, all marching to a beat of their own. I weaved through them, a feeling of being flung back in time; a different city, different country, all else just the same. I could feel the barely contained impatience, the low-key anxiety, to grow, to change, to be gone from this place and out into the world.

And for a moment I allowed myself to mourn it, to wish myself back there, when life was simple and all was possibility, when I was Rosa Fisher, just another part of the homogenous mass.

I slid in between them, with their bulbous backpacks, their watchful eyes, a space opening up around me as eyes turned to me, figuring I didn't belong there, kept my gaze towards the door, the wide world beyond.

Then out through the doors and the wind scoured at

my cheeks, burning with the cold of it. Down the steps and along the footpath, mounded on either side with waist-high heaps of snow. Feeling the first flakes, tiny and delicate, begin to land on my nose, my lips.

A tear broke free, winding its way down my cheek, and I dashed it roughly aside.

It was not Elliott who had saved me. He was not there on that day. It was the feeling of reaching a finish line and seeing it dash off into the distance, a cruel practical joke. My brother could not possibly have been the one who rescued me, who brought me to Madison.

A Volvo slid by, sending a spray of slush sideways out from its wheels, and I picked up my pace, needing to be away now, to put the school and the past behind me.

'Okay,' I muttered to myself. 'Think. What do you know?'

I knew where I had come from, knew that I had been born Mia Lynch, had started life in the farmland of Ontario. Daughter to Camille and Hadley Lynch. Sister to Elliott and Kyle. I knew why I had ended up alone. Because, on one autumn day, Hadley Lynch had taken a .22 to the heads of his wife and his youngest son before setting fire to their bodies and turning the gun on himself. I knew I was supposed to be dead. And yet I wasn't, and I didn't know why. And I didn't know who was driving that silver sedan or if it had any connection to my survival.

I had reached the main road, cars flying by now, one following the other, and a spark of electricity shot through me. I had forgotten about being followed. I was no longer paying attention. I turned on the spot, let my gaze track across the snow-banked roadway behind me, empty but for the trail of my footprints in the slush.

I could not stay here. And, in the absence of any better ideas, my thoughts returned to where they had begun. That I had to find my brother. That even if he had not been there, if he could provide me no answers, he was my brother and I needed him.

I reached into my pocket, pulled out the notepad, the administrator's writing shaping out the name Sadiq Baram, the number beneath. Nothing ventured.

I selected the numbers on my cell, fingers clumsy with the cold, listened as it began to ring. Thinking that it was a long shot, that he would be there, that he would know how to find Elliott.

But still I waited.

It was on the fifth ring that the answer came. Long enough that I had begun to give up hope.

'Hello?' A woman's voice, breathless.

I floundered for a moment, thrown by the female voice, 'Hi. Hello. This is ...' Who? Rosa? And who the hell is Rosa? 'This is Sergeant Rebecca Leland of the RCMP. I'm looking for a Sadiq Baram?'

There was a lengthy silence as the woman on the other end weighed my words, balancing their implications, and my stomach flipped with guilt. Was she wondering now what her husband had done? Was she wondering if her whole world was about to unravel?

'It's nothing to be concerned with,' I said, belatedly. 'Just a couple of questions about a case I'm dealing with.'

'Oh, sure. Well ... I mean, he should be at the station. He texted me, maybe an hour ago, and I know he was there then.'

I stopped. 'The station?'

'Yes, he's based out of headquarters.'

The pieces slowly slid into place and I could feel what little colour remained draining from my cheeks. 'You mean he's police?'

'Yes ...' she said, hesitantly. 'He's a detective. You didn't know that?'

I chose my words carefully. Shit. 'No. I didn't realise. Okay, so ...'

'Here, let me give you his cell. I mean, I'll pass the message on, but I don't know what time he'll be home. Best you call him direct.'

Shit. Shit. Shit.

'Uh-huh.' I scrawled his number on my notebook, fingers shaking. 'Okay, Mrs Baram, well, thank you.'

'Oh, you're welcome.'

I hung up, scrubbed my fingers across my face. What the hell had I just done? I'd pretended to be RCMP to the wife of a police officer. And now, if I didn't contact him, she was going to tell him about my call, and maybe he'd try and find me to find out what I wanted, and then he'd figure out that Rebecca Leland, the real Rebecca Leland, had no damn clue what he was talking about. I kicked at the mound of snow at my feet, causing a miniature avalanche. Dammit. I'd have to leave it. I'd have to run home and hope for the best and stop goddam pretending to be someone I wasn't. But then ... but then I wouldn't find my brother and then I wouldn't find my answers and then I would have to live the rest of my life forever looking over my shoulder, always wondering what happened and just who in the hell was Jackson Wolf.

It was not a decision I made, not in my head at least. My body, it seemed, was willing to decide for me as my fingers pushed the numbers for Sadiq Baram into my phone, heart thumping. My hand raised the phone to my ear, and from a great distance, I heard the words, 'Detective Baram, this is Sergeant Leland, RCMP.'

He stood in the lobby of police headquarters, a tall, slender man with swept-back hair that had begun to recede, a dark suit, tie pulled open at the throat. I walked slowly down the wide steps, careful to not be myself but to be someone far more impressive instead, and, catching his eye, nodded solemnly, my stomach bucking and twisting.

'Detective Baram? Rebecca Leland.' I stuck my hand out, a firm shake.

A brief smile flitted across his face. 'Hey. Sadiq, please. You want to come inside?'

'Well, I was just thinking, I haven't eaten yet today. How about we grab some breakfast?' I said it with a smile, keeping my gaze on him, not on the booth behind him, the entry into the building, where they would inevitably ask to see my RCMP ID. My eBay-bought RCMP ID.

'Sure. We can go to Fran's.' He shrugged. 'Let me just grab my coat.'

I lingered in the foyer, casual, as if I had seen all this a thousand times before, and then, when he returned, smaller now, buried inside a fur-hooded puffer jacket, fell into step with him. I walked as I imagined Rebecca Leland would walk, with long, confident strides, down the front steps of the building and back out onto College Street, where the snow had begun to fall again in earnest, dense flakes of it that blurred the world before me. Half a block and then beneath the highlighted canopy, beneath the fluorescent lights, into the restaurant.

Sadiq slid into a booth, tugging his coat off as he went. 'What'll you get? Benedict is good here.'

I thought of the eggs I had eaten a couple of hours ago and felt a wave of nausea pass over me. 'Maybe I'll get a sandwich.'

We made small talk while the waitress brought us coffee, took our orders. The weather, the fate of the Toronto Maple Leafs. I nodded a lot, tried to keep up.

Then, 'So what's this case you want my help with?' Sadiq poured sugar into his coffee, his gaze flicking up to me.

Keep it together.

'I'm trying to find someone. Thought you might be able to help. Elliott Lynch.'

He set down his spoon with a chink, sat back in his seat. 'Now that's a name I haven't heard in a long time. Why you looking for him?'

'I believe he may have some information on a case

I've been working on. Only trouble is, no one seems to know where he is.'

Sadiq didn't respond, was watching me, waiting for more.

I selected my way carefully, aware now that I was striding out across a thinly frozen pond. 'Look, I can't give you too much. It's ... delicate.' I lowered my voice. 'High-profile, you know? But it's important we find Lynch.'

He nodded slowly. 'And you're asking me, why?'

I leaned back as the waitress arrived, slid a chicken and avocado club in front of me, steak Benedict in front of him. 'Thanks. I went out to the high school,' I said, as she disappeared, 'hoped they might have some records. Found you and him were pretty tight back then.'

He sat, unmoving, dark eyes watching me intently, and I could feel pins and needles in my fingers, the sudden thought that I'd said too much, gone out too far on this thin ice. A sudden rogue thought – what was the sentence for impersonating a police officer? To a police officer.

Then he shrugged, picked up his fork. 'Sorry to say,' he said, breaking into his egg, 'but that was a long time ago. After what happened, with his family, I mean, Elliott pretty much dropped off the face of the earth. Just about finished up high school, but he was out more than he was in. He'd had big plans, was going to go to college, study law. But after his folks died ...' He sighed, took a bite of meat. 'Poor guy. I tried reaching out to him, a bunch of us did, but he just ... It was kind of like he died too. I know he lived with his grandmother for a while. Then, the last I heard, he'd joined the military.'

A thrill moved through me. 'The military?' I didn't look at him, carefully picked up my sandwich, kept my voice steady. 'Which branch?'

A glob of hollandaise lingered at the corner of his mouth and he dabbed at it with a napkin. 'Ah, air force? Don't hold me to that.' He shook his head 'Think he'd have joined ISIS if it'd have gotten him away from here.' He sighed, leaned back. 'You know, twenty years later and I still can't imagine what it must have been like for him. I mean, one day you're a normal kid, you got your whole life in front of you, next you find out that your entire family has been massacred by your stepfather.'

I froze, the sandwich an inch from my mouth. 'I … I thought it was the father.'

Sadiq shook his head. 'No, Hadley, he came on the scene … I guess Elliott must have been five? Six maybe? He adopted them, right when he and Camille married. Baby Mia was his … Elliott's half-sister.'

I felt a wave of dizziness, disappointment crashing hard on the heels of fleeting hope. That there had been a momentary chance that I was not the child of a man who murdered his family quickly vanished.

I forced myself to take a bite, to chew. 'Step-kids, they're always at a higher risk in cases of familicide,' I muttered through a mouthful of bread.

Sadiq glanced at me quizzically for a moment, then set down his fork. 'You know, if you find him … I don't know … it's been a long time. I just, I always hoped he was doing okay, you know? That he'd figured out a way to make life work for him. Because a thing like that, it changes who you are as a person.' He shook his head. 'You know that's why I do this job, right? I mean, as a kid, you just think that that kind of shit, that it only happens in movies and on TV. And then one day you wake up and it's on your doorstep and it's one of your best friends. It was like our childhoods, they just stopped on that day. What with the Lynch murders, and, I mean, that's bad enough, right? Then there was that whole thing with Clay. Just seemed like our entire worlds got flipped upside down. Guess I figured that if the bad stuff in life was going to land on my doorstep anyway, then I'd rather get a jump on it, be in a position to do something about it.'

'Clay?' I asked.

Sadiq took a sip of coffee. 'Clay Rutherford. Local stoner kid. Vanished, I guess maybe a month or so after the Lynch thing.'

I laid my sandwich down slowly, something pulling at my gut. 'This Rutherford kid … he have a car?'

He frowned. 'A car? Yeah. I guess, although from what I remember, they never found it.' He paused. 'A silver sedan.'

Chapter 19

I lingered beneath the canopy of Fran's, watched as Sadiq walked away, long loping strides back towards the police station, my mind racing. As he neared the courtyard, he glanced back across his shoulder towards me, and I lifted my hand in a wave. He waved back, gaze considering, and my heart beat faster, the sudden thought flitting that I had made it to within inches of the finish line, that I was about to stumble. I pulled my cell from my pocket and began talking into it, expression serious, turning my gaze off towards the steady stream of traffic, for five seconds, ten. When I looked back, he had gone.

I lowered the phone, blew out a breath. A silver sedan. That was it. The missing link in the story.

'Why are you asking about Rutherford's car?' Sadiq had studied me, curious, eggs forgotten now in the unfolding mystery before him. 'You got something on it?'

I stared back at him, holding a pair, playing it as a flush. 'It's not something I can get into right now.' I picked up the sandwich again, reminding myself to breathe. 'So ... this kid. Who is he?'

'Clay? He was trouble. High-school dropout. Tough

home life, from what I remember. He was the kid everyone went to if they wanted to get high.'

I nodded, the bread dry against the roof of my mouth, and tried to slot his words into the incomplete jigsaw, equate this kid with someone who would rescue a baby, keep it for six weeks, care for it, then leave it outside a fire station a whole country away, watching over it to ensure it was safe. I swallowed, hard.

'Was he ...' grasping at straws, 'this kid, was he a friend of Elliott's?'

Sadiq pulled a face. 'Elliott was a nerd. A good kid. He didn't hang around with assholes like that. Clay, he did a couple of odd jobs for Hadley. Hadley had a business, a car shop, and Clay, he worked for him, for, I don't know, maybe like six weeks, back in the day. Let's just say it wasn't a good fit for either one of them.'

'And he was how old? This Rutherford kid, I mean.'

'Seventeen? Maybe a little younger.'

That placed him closer in age to Kyle. 'What about Elliott's brother? Kyle. He hang around with him?'

Sadiq drained his coffee, a quick shake of the head. 'That's why Hadley let Clay go. Must have been a year before the murders, Kyle comes to school one day with this massive black eye, I mean, a real shiner. Said he'd gotten into a fight with this Clay kid. He liked to pick on the local kids, especially the smart ones, the ones who were doing well in school. I'm pretty sure they didn't become BFFs after that.' He studied me. 'Look, I don't know what you think you've got here, but Rutherford, he's in the wind. Far as I know, he hasn't been seen in twenty years. His mom, she's still kicking around here somewhere, surviving on sheer stubbornness alone, from what I hear.'

'You got a name?'

'Ilianna Ruez. She's married a couple of times since, lives out in North York.' He watched as I wrote it down. 'So, where is it you said you're based?'

I didn't look up. 'Nova Scotia.'

'You're a long way from home.'

I smiled brightly, waved at the falling snow. 'Weather's better.'

I turned, the police station at my rear, and began to walk slowly into the falling snow, leaving Sadiq behind me with a feeling of relief. The wind scrubbed at my cheeks, snow soaking into my hair, and I pulled a woollen hat from my pocket, pulling it down low. I could have taken the subway, but I was flushed and flustered and I needed to feel the cold against my skin, to breathe in the frozen air. Along Bay Street, the double-wide road busy now with slow-moving traffic, putting Sadiq and my lies behind me. It was an answer of sorts, although perhaps not an obvious one. For although Clay Rutherford did not sound like anyone's idea of a hero, the evidence suggested that somehow he had been there that night, and that he had gotten out. It was a small leap of logic then to assume that I, as the only other survivor, had gotten out with him.

I moved my thumb across the screen of my cell, looking for Ilianna Ruez, but the falling snow landed heavy and the screen was slick, and so I sighed, tucking it back into my pocket as I wove through the bundled-up crowds. I would need shelter to find her.

Then a vibration, my cell ringing in my pocket, and I sidestepped, tucking myself into the overhang outside a nail shop.

My mother. I suppressed a sigh.

'Hi.'

'Rosa? It's Mom.'

I winced, the sound of her voice bringing with it the smell of home, reigniting a memory of who I was before. 'Hi, Mom. How are you?'

She sighed heavily, sounding somehow more like wind than the wind itself. 'Well, oh, you know ... You didn't call last night. I said to your sister, she hasn't called. It isn't like her. I was worried.'

Sorry. I was imitating an officer of the law and hiding from a creepy dude and figuring out a disguise to go with my new identity. 'I was busy, Mom. You know how these conferences are.'

The line fell silent, and for one brief, terrifying moment, I thought that she was gone, hung up on me. Then she sniffed, and I realised she had only been waiting, allowing my words to hang there, her disapproval to seep across the line to me. Irritation washed over me.

'Are you eating?'

'What?'

'Food. Are you eating? And not any of that millennial nonsense, hummus and the rest. Are you eating actual food?'

'Mom. Of course I'm eating.' A truck rumbled past me, spraying slush in its wake.

'Is that traffic? Do I hear traffic? Where are you right now?'

'I ...' I fumbled. 'I don't ... Fifty-second and Fifth. I just got lunch, and now I'm going back in for my next seminar.'

'You're not alone, are you? I don't like the thought of you out alone in New York.'

'If Macaulay Culkin can handle it ...' I muttered.

'What?'

'Mom, it's Midtown Manhattan, not central Baghdad. I got this.'

I turned my face away from the traffic, letting my gaze fall into the nail bar, its clientele with their calm and collected lives, and I wanted to bang the window, to scream at them. See the crazy lady arguing with her mother in the snow?

The line fell silent again, and this time I prayed she'd hung up on me. But when her voice returned, it was patchy and broken. 'Rosa, do you think they'll come back?'

I stood there for a moment, my mind so far away from my Madison home that her words made no sense. Then I remembered. About the burglary and the figure watching the house. And I remembered that, for her, that was the story of it. Whereas for me, that story had bucked and shifted and followed me across an international border. 'No, Mom. I'm sure they won't,' I said, more gently this time.

'Drew,' she said. 'He said he'd stay here with me, but most nights he's off with his friends, and it's just me and Fleck, and you know how useless that dog is.'

I suppressed a smile.

'I'm not sleeping, Rosa. I keep thinking that every sound is someone coming into the house. I was thinking, maybe I could get Gray to teach me how to shoot a gun.'

Sweet Lord in heaven.

'Mom, yeah, I don't think that's the best of plans. Look,' I said, soothing, trying to ignore the billowing guilt, 'you have the cameras, you have the security system. And Fleck, keep him inside with you. I'm sure if someone got in he'd go for them.'

Unless they had steak.

My mother snorted. 'Unless they had steak,' she muttered.

I grinned, felt tears spring to my eyes. It would be so easy now to say it, what she wanted to hear. That I was returning home, was on my way. I could almost taste it, that sensation of laying something before your parent, your eyes watching theirs in the search for approval, a cat who has caught a sparrow. It would be such an easy thing to do.

I wiped my hand across my face and turned back towards the Toronto traffic. It would also be the wrong thing to do. Because my answers were here.

'Mom,' I said, quietly, 'it's going to be just fine. I'll call Drew and chew him out, make sure he stays over from now on, okay? And besides, I'll be back in a day or two. Just try and think of what Gray said, that they'll have seen the security system, they won't try again.'

And 'they' is following me around Canada. I kept that last bit to myself.

It seemed like I could hear my mother nod. 'Okay. Well, you'll ring me tomorrow, right?'

'Yes, Mom.'

'And you'll stay safe?'

'Yes, Mom.'

Quiet, then, 'I love you, Rosa-bel.'

'I love you too.'

I slid the phone from my ear and turned back towards the window of the nail salon, the glass of it reflecting myself back on me. I didn't recognise her.

I should go home. But instead I slipped my phone back into my pocket, fingers stiff with the cold. I needed to get somewhere warm, out of the snow. Then the sign caught my attention, the PATH right ahead. I moved off, limbs awkward now, hurrying through the crowds, ducking down into the underground pedestrian walkway, the heat clambering up the staircase to greet me.

I paused at the bottom, taking stock, a moment to breathe. Thinking that this would be perfect, were it not for all the people in it, an underground hollow, a hobbit hole burrowed beneath the earth, beyond the snow and the wind. A place to hide. Only it wasn't, was it?

Sounds pinioned off the walls, footfalls and voices echoing back on each other. Bodies pressed together, smelling of damp wool and BO. A group of schoolkids flooded by me, a flock of birds with their high-pitched calls, gaudy backpacks taking the place of wings. I watched as they tumbled by, a little girl in a thick duffel coat bringing up the rear, skipping as she walked, her pigtail snaking its way from beneath a luxuriously bobbled hat.

And then I looked up, back towards the stairway through which I had entered the PATH. A wall of people, patches of grey light just visible between them. And through a gap in the crowd, I caught a flash of a figure, bulky and broad, a woollen hat pulled low. The same figure that had stood beside my car on the previous night, the same one who had stared up at my window.

Wolf.

My breath caught in my throat and I stepped back, ducking inside a candy store.

Why was he here? The mathematical opportunity for coincidence aside, it seemed unlikely that he would happen upon me, in amongst the Toronto crowds, that, by chance, he would find himself in the same PATH entrance.

I slid behind a counter of fudge, keeping low, and watched the movement of the crowd through the window, looking for the shape of him, for the dark knit hat. There. He had reached the base of the staircase and had stopped in almost the same spot where I had stood, was looking about himself, left to right, head swinging, searching for something.

For me?

He knows I'm here.

I moved closer to the door, keeping hidden behind a rack of M&Ms. Turn. I reached into my pocket for my phone, flipping the camera open, and angled it towards him, finger and thumb flicking the screen to zoom in on him. Looking for more than I currently had. A shape, face turned, a quarter profile. I checked the flash was off – no one ever said I was a slow learner – and quickly snapped a photo of him. He turned, moving away from me, the movement of his head suggesting a search still under way.

And then my body moved, driven by an instinct that had nothing to do with the smart part of my brain, forcing my feet out of the store, pedestrians buffeting me as I cut through them. My frontal cortex screaming to regain control, but pure instinct had gotten hold of the wheel now, steering me through the people, right towards him.

And I am there, am almost on him, my hand reaching out to snake through the crowd, to grab hold of his elbow, and my phone vibrated. I stopped, pulled up sharp, the crashing realisation of having entirely lost my mind, and stepped backwards, further away from the turned shoulders of him, my heart beating inside my head. Fear tuning out the sounds and the smells until it was only me and him.

Did he hear my phone? Have I blown it?

Only he was distracted, was looking down at a phone of his own.

And instinct stepped up again, nudging at me, warning me to pay attention, that something was happening here I was not going to want to miss. I looked down at the screen of my cell. A text message, Addie's name.

He looked down still, his focus absorbed in the phone in his hand, and I moved into the wide slipstream of an elderly woman, her fluffed-up purple coat making it appear that an ostrich was cutting its way through the crowd. She ambled past him, humming a tune I didn't recognise, and I followed along behind her, close enough that I could see his face.

If only I had looked.

But I didn't. My attention captured instead by the phone in his hand, the screen of it. A text message, Addie's name.

And then I knew why he was there, and I knew how he had found me.

And I turned tail and I ran.

Chapter 20

I dodged through a gaggle of tourists trailing behind a flag-holding guide, ducklings behind their mother, with their bobble hats and brand-new Canada Goose jackets, and I turned wildly, looking for somewhere to hide. He was blocking the steps. And, even if he wasn't, he would know where I had gone if I didn't act quickly. I pushed my way back into the candy store, awkward ingers moving across my phone, sliding it to off, fumbling with the battery until it separated out from the body of the phone.

I watch *CSI*.

I slipped the phone and the battery into my pocket, tried to breathe without crying.

'Ma'am? Can I help you?' The shop assistant had come from the back room, was watching me, concern etched heavy on her face.

I'm fine. It's nothing.

I'm a police officer on a stakeout.

I glanced back towards the window, the crowd of tourists tailing off now, searched for the shape of him, yet could see nothing, no one that stood out as familiar. I turned back to her, hurrying closer. 'I'm sorry. I think

I'm being followed. There's this guy ... he's watching me and I think he's followed me in here.' I squeezed out a tear. It wasn't hard. 'I'm really scared.'

The woman, maybe ten years my senior, with enough make-up to make her look twenty, nodded swiftly and stepped back, opening the door to the rear office. 'In here.'

I glanced back over my shoulder one more time, then followed her in, pulling the door closed behind me. A small storeroom, lined with shelves, heavy with the aroma of chocolate, led to a narrow office. A single desk, a single chair, a leaning pile of paperwork.

'There's a back exit,' she said, quietly. 'If you follow the corridor, right to the end, then through the doors. He won't see you then. Here.' She rummaged about in an oversized patent handbag, handed me a dark wool beanie. 'Switch out your hat. He won't be looking for this.'

I took the fabric, stared at her and searched for the right words, and she laid a hand on my forearm. 'I'm a survivor. Rape. Keep the hat.'

Another tear fell then, unbidden this time, and I gripped hold of her hand, the sudden urge filling me to spill it all. To tell this woman whom I had never met before the whole of my story, to cling to her, beg her for guidance.

'I ...'

'It's okay. But you should go. Just stay safe, yes? There are a lot of dangerous people out there.'

I nodded swiftly, pulled my hat off and handed it to

her. 'You keep this one. Please.' A lump in my throat, that it was so little to offer in return. Pulled her beanie onto my head. And then I hugged her. 'Thank you. So much.'

She pulled away and unlocked the door to the rear of the office. 'No problem. Go now.'

I slipped along the passageway, narrow and breeze-blocked, hard-edged light thrown out from fluorescent tubes, and wiped at my face. I had to get it together. I had to focus. This was ... If it wasn't serious before, it was now. Somehow this man, this Wolf, had gotten hold of my phone, had had hands on it long enough to install spyware on it. Which meant ... which meant he had gotten extremely close to me and I had never known.

I walked with quick steps, trying to think. When? I was a millennial. My phone rarely leaving my sight. It had remained in my pocket almost my entire time in Canada. Apart from at night. When it had been plugged into the charger, laid on the motel room's bedside table.

My steps slowed, a prickling sense of horror. Was that it? Had he gotten into the room, while I slept? While I showered?

I stopped, a wave of panic threatening to crash over me. Who the hell was this guy? What did he want with me? I reached into my pocket, fingers grasping the defunct phone. I should call Gray. I should call Sadiq. I should tell someone that I had bitten off more than I could chew.

And then I thought of my brother's picture, of the

memory of a burnt-out barn, and my feet moved on regardless.

I wasn't ready to give up yet.

I reached the end of the corridor and carefully eased open the door. It let out further down the concourse, close to the entrance to the subway, and I peered about me, looking for the shape of him in amongst the crowds. Nothing. I slipped out, closing the door behind me.

I paused on the concourse, dug out the address of Ilianna Ruez, a quick study of a map, and with my finger traced the route out to her home in North York. My heart thumping. I should go home. I should do as my candy-store friend had suggested, should keep myself safe.

Only some things mattered more to me than safety.

I pushed my way through the crowd, finding the train to York Mills.

I had asked myself who I was now. Turns out I was someone who could not take a hint.

I arrived in York Mills and ventured above ground into the thickly falling snow and caught a bus, through suburbs that would once have been green, now shrouded in dense white.

The house, when I finally found it, was a small duplex. It would have been pretty once, but its heyday had long since passed, the porch railings all but rusted through, a broken-down chair dumped on the front lawn, the seat of it filling up with snow. I trudged up the short drive, and breathed in, giving myself a moment to remember who I was this time, why I was there.

Sergeant Rebecca Leland.

I knocked, the way I imagined she would knock, and waited, the cold seeping through the thickness of my coat. I waited long enough that I had begun to conclude that no one was home, and then I heard the shuffle of slow footsteps within, the sliding back of a chain.

Ilianna Ruez came up to perhaps my shoulder. She must have been fifty and yet had an air about her of being little more than a child, with her stick-slender arms, the collarbones that protruded sharply upwards. She wore a wide-knit sweater that hung loose about her, its sleeves pushed up beyond her elbows, her grey-rooted blonde hair scraped back into a bun. On her arms, she had track marks.

She studied me with an intensity, like she was struggling to focus on me, her pupils large and dark. 'What?'

I held my card up in front of her wavering gaze. 'RCMP. Need to talk to you about your son.'

She stared at the card, then at me, and then, finally, my words seeped through the drug fog and she started, her face twisting into a sudden look of terror.

'No. It's not ...' My heart beat faster. 'We haven't found anything. It's not that. I just, I need to ask you some questions, that's all. For the file.'

She stared at me, one hand reaching out to grip the frame of the door, and I saw it sink in, saw the mist begin to descend again. 'Better come in.'

The house was spartan, dense with a pervasive smell

of cigarettes and rotting food. She waved me into the lounge, although it had little to distinguish it as such, just a sagging sofa, a small television. A narrow cat sat on the arm of it, watching me with suspicion. I sat as far away from it as I could get.

'Been a long time since we've had police here. Thought you weren't interested.' She didn't stand but rather hovered before me, a ghost haunting her own home.

The cat glared at me.

'It has been dormant for too long,' I said, injecting a tone of apology, comforting myself with the fact that, strictly speaking, that was true. 'I was wondering if I could hear about your son's disappearance from you? You know, so I can get a real understanding of what happened.'

She stared at me, through me, then shrugged. 'He just ... vanished. Just stopped calling. Stopped showing up. I don't know ...'

'Just so I've got everything exactly right, he disappeared in the October?'

Two weeks after the murders.

She nodded, pulling a packet of cigarettes from her pocket and lighting one in a burst of flame. ''S'right.'

'And, what did he say to you before he left that day? Can you tell me about that?'

She took a long drag of the cigarette. 'No. Didn't see him that day.'

I frowned. 'I'm sorry?'

'He'd called me, couple of times in work. I used to

work in a packing plant down by the city. But he must have gotten my shifts mixed up, never managed to get hold of me. Just left messages to say he was staying with a friend, out in Aurora.'

'Okay, he give you a name for this friend?'

She shook her head, blowing out a long train of smoke. 'Never heard of anyone out that way. Not surprising though. Kept his life pretty private.'

I bit my lip, the pieces shifting. 'So, when was the last time you actually saw Clay? With your own eyes?'

'September 17. I remember 'cos it was my birthday.'

The day of the murders.

I pulled in a breath. Holy shit. 'And what did you guys do that day? You go out to celebrate?'

She shrugged. 'Nah. I went out with some girlfriends. Got pretty wasted. Clay, I saw him, it was early. I know, 'cos I was mad at him waking me up, it being my birthday and all. Said he had things to do, he'd had a call to go meet someone. Said he'd be back later. Never did show up.' She slid the cigarette between her lips. 'That was Clay though. Never did know where that boy got to.'

'And he didn't say who he was meeting?'

She shook her head. 'Not that I recall.'

I was willing to bet her recollection was about as accurate as my dementia-ridden grandmother's. 'Did the original investigating officers check his phone? You said he'd had a call?'

'Never found his phone. Car neither. Like the whole lot of him just upped and vanished into thin air.'

I nodded, choosing my words carefully. 'What about Clay's childhood? How was that?'

She blew out smoke, scowled at me, awareness suddenly punching through the fog. 'He had a good childhood. Gave that boy all I had. People been saying I didn't? That I was a bad mother?'

I smiled soothingly. 'Of course not. No one has said anything of the sort. It's just a standard question that we have to ask everyone in this kind of situation.'

She moved to the windowsill, sifted through a stack of papers and returned with a business card. 'You should talk to her. This woman runs a missing-person website. Got one of them podcast things too. She's been trying to help. Not that she's gotten anywhere, but still. Least she was interested. More than can be said for you guys.' She handed me the card and stood, studying me, more alert now than I thought was possible. 'Why now? Huh? Why are you here talking to me now?'

I looked up at her, searching for an answer. Failing.

Because I'm afraid. Because I need answers. And because somewhere in amongst all this mess, lies the truth, and maybe, somehow, Clay is connected to that truth.

Chapter 21

The glass sparkled on the densely packed snow, the shards catching the light from the overhead street light, splitting it into a rainbow of colours. I stood beside the sorry remains of my Mini and gazed at the smashed-out windows, a perfect arc of them. It was as if someone had circled the car, smashing one, then another, then another, until there was little left solid about it. The harsh wind had swept snow in, through the broken windows, so that it filled up the bucket seats, giving the car the appearance of one that had been dug from an avalanche. So caught up was I by the dancing lights of the shattered glass that it took me long moments to realise the damage did not end there. Each of the four tyres had been slashed through, were now little more than rubber puddles against the snow-bound tarmac.

I stood there, the wind tugging at my clothes, in the rapidly descending darkness, frozen by more than the cold. Because I had had a plan, that I would change hotels, would sneak out in the early-morning hours. I would find somewhere where I could stash the car away from the road, where I could make sure he couldn't find me. But now ... now I was trapped here.

I stood, locked into this moment, the horror of what it meant, unable to align my thoughts. And then a creeping fear, instinct tapping on the locked door of my brain. You are standing alone in a dark parking lot. I looked up at the hotel windows, a patchwork quilt of lights punching their way into the gloom, looking for a shape at a window, for someone watching. If he was watching, he was better at it than I was.

I spun on the spot, searching the mounded snow banks, the sleeping bodies of the other cars, expecting to see the silhouette of him. The wind snaked through the alley between the buildings, driving a surge of snow before it. I was alone.

I took one last look at the car and hurried inside, trudging with wide, effortful steps, my skin sparking, brain conjuring up the sound of footsteps echoing behind me, the feel of breath on the back of my neck. Up the stairs and along the landing, head swivelling, gaze falling left and right, to my room, key into the lock, and now my heart beating faster still because it seemed to me that nowhere was safe, not now. Flipping on the light and closing the door behind me, movements reluctant, because what was I doing? Locking danger out? Or locking danger in? And searching, the bathroom and the wardrobe and beside the cabinet and beneath the bed, and then tugging the curtains tight across the window, and checking to make sure there are no gaps, and all the while, my chest tight enough that it feels it will explode at any moment.

I grabbed the table from before the window and,

using my whole body as leverage, shoved it across the room, past the bathroom, until the edge of it was pushed up against the door.

I stopped. Leaned against the table. Breathe.

Tears twisted down my cheeks, and I stood, slumped, made little effort to stop them. What the hell was I doing? What the hell had I gotten myself involved in?

My brain twisted and writhed, panic fighting to take hold, and I turned, leaned my forearms against the table. No. You can't panic. If you panic, you're finished. Breathe. Just breathe.

I blew out a breath, pulled open the minibar and fished out a miniature bottle of rum, taking a long swallow of it. Fighting back the urge to gag as it hit my stomach.

Okay. First … I needed a car. I couldn't stay here. He had smashed up my car for a reason, perhaps more than one. To frighten me? Probably. To keep me cut off, trap me where he could find me? Yes. Which meant that whatever happened, I needed to circumvent that. I took another swallow of rum and, rummaging through my purse, found the emergency breakdown number, dialling it from the corded phone in the hotel room. Who knew they still made corded phones. Yes, my car has been damaged. No, I haven't called the police. Yes, I need you to come and get it. How fast can you do it? Two days? Not fast enough. I need it by tomorrow. I'll pay extra. Am I going to be there when you arrive? I thought of the plunging light of the parking lot and the shadows that rimmed the edges of it. I thought of a pickup truck pulling in and a man getting out and how was I to know that that man was not him? He would know I would need a rescue service. No. I won't be there. I have a thing.

I hung up the call, sank down onto the floor, head fuzzy from the fear and the booze. My stomach had knotted itself up. The earlier sandwich sat there now like a cannonball.

I pulled my laptop from the dresser drawer and looked it over for any sign of tampering. If it had been touched, I couldn't see any sign of it. I paused for a moment, considered my options, painfully limited at this point, then I sighed, flipped the lid open, entered my password, waited. The screen surged to life and I searched for local car-hire places, found one, maybe a couple of miles away. Reserved a Toyota Yaris for collection within the hour. And now I had a plan. I would call an Uber, get a new car.

I pushed myself up to standing, moved about the room, throwing things into the suitcase. I couldn't stay here. Whatever happened, to remain here felt like a deer settling down beside the hunter's car, just waiting. So once I had a new car, I could find a new hotel.

I moved the cursor to my inbox, looking for anything further from Ben Folger. Only there was no reply to my photograph. He knew what I had done. He knew that he had been made. And while that should have made me feel triumphant, instead the thought brought with it fear. Because if he knew there was no need to hide now, what else was he capable of?

Like smashing up a car, perhaps?

I rubbed my hands over my face. I had forced him out of the shadows. What the hell came next?

My inbox pinged, and I looked down at an email from Eve.

RING ME RIGHT NOW BECAUSE I AM WORRIED SICK!

I sank onto the bed, pulling the phone down onto the comforter beside me and dialled Eve's number.

One ring. 'Hello?'

'It's me.'

'Rosa? God, I've been trying to call you all day. I was starting to freak. I mean, what the hell!'

I rested my head in my hands. 'Yeah. Sorry. Problem with my phone.'

'What kind of problem?' she asked, suspicious.

And I wanted to tell her the truth. I so wanted to tell her the truth, only the truth came with sharp edges and dark corners, and somehow it seemed to me that I could not get my mouth to form the words of it. 'Signal's rubbish,' I said, instead.

'Rosa, look, you think you should come home? I mean, you're up there, all on your own, and ... I mean, have you found anyone? Have you found your family?'

I fought back the urge to laugh. Now there was a question without an easy answer. 'My grandmother,' I said. 'Only she's in a home. Gets confused. Can't tell me much.'

Eve fell silent for long moments, then said again, 'Rosa, come home. I got a bad feeling about this.'

I mumbled, 'I'll be back soon. I promise. Another day or two. I just have a couple more leads I need to follow up.'

Eve let out a sharp laugh. 'You sound like a detective.'

I didn't tell her I'd been practising.

A beam of light shone through the thin curtains, lighting up the room. I looked up, pushed myself carefully to standing and moved towards the window's edge, keeping my body well back from the seam at which the curtain met the wall. Could see a light in the darkness of the parking lot. A tow truck, the driver pulling up beside the glass, clambering awkwardly from the cab. Was it him? Thick jacket, baseball cap. I waited for him to look for me, for his gaze to fall on my window, but there was nothing. No curiosity, just purposeful movement, hooking up the car. A man with a job to complete.

'Gotta go, girl. I'll call you tomorrow.' I hung up on her protests, and shifted closer to the window, watching the figure as he raised my car up onto the truck, tucking his hands into his pockets and, head down, trudged back to the cab of it, not once looking in my direction.

I let the curtain fall back down.

I stood, contemplated. I wanted little more than sleep, but the exhaustion of my body was far from the buzzing of my brain. I considered the bottle of rum. But my head already felt thick, my thoughts already swimming. Unlikely then that more alcohol would help.

I thought of Ilianna, of her long-lost son. Ilianna knew all there was to know about drowning your sorrows, by the look of her. Was that why Clay had done it, vanished the way he had? Seemed a good chance that there had been little life there to return to. But, say that was it, say he had been there, had seen what was happening, had saved me ... why take me all the way to Madison? If he didn't trust the police, if he didn't want to get caught up in it all, why not just dump me outside an Ontario hospital? And the six weeks? Why keep a baby that long. Must have been an almost impossible burden for any teenage boy, not least one with pretty shitty impulse-control skills.

I moved back towards my laptop, thinking that somewhere within the cavernous internet there must be some clues as to what happened to this missing boy. Only I didn't get that far. Because I had left my inbox open, and I suddenly realised that in amongst what I had taken to be junk mail, from Geiko and Sephora and Pottery Barn, was one more email.

> Dear Sergeant Leland,
> I tried calling you on the number you left for me, but I couldn't get an answer, so thought perhaps emailing would be best. I'd like to speak to you at your earliest convenience. It's important.
> Best wishes,
> Elizabeth

I read it, read it again. Felt a blossoming of hope in

my chest that Elizabeth Barrow, my family's former neighbour, had something for me.

I pulled the phone towards me, punched in the number she listed beneath the signature line of the email and waited. Connecting. One ring, two, three, four. Then a click, a pause, a man's voice.

'Hello?'

I opened my mouth, all sound lost. Was it him? Was he there?

'I ... Elizabeth?' My voice sounded unlike my own.

'Can I ask who's calling?'

'A friend. Rebecca.'

Another pause, then a soft sigh. 'Okay, I'm here with the Ontario Police Department. I'm very sorry to have to tell you this, Ma'am, but Mrs Barrow is dead.'

Chapter 22

It would have been an accident. A fall, perhaps. Or else something else. A heart attack. A stroke. It would be a natural death, an uneasy coincidence, and after all, wasn't nature dense with coincidence? I had said it, again and again, the mantra becoming a chant, on the Uber ride to the car-rental place, on the long drive through the heavy falling snow, back out to where it had all begun. Along still highways bounded with snow-heavy fields, the past drawing nearer with each mile that fell behind. A feeling, of going home almost, even though it was a home my memory had entirely forgotten. And so, by the time I made the final turn, towards the farm and the sad, sad story of Elizabeth Barrow, I had all but convinced myself that I was heading out there to observe the close of a life that had simply sputtered out of time. That the hourglass had just run out of sand.

I pulled up, parking the Yaris on a snowy verge, maybe a quarter-mile away. Yet still, in spite of the distance, a row of parked cars stretched out before me, abutting the highway. I sat for a moment in the driver's seat, trying to take it in, to steady my breathing. There were so many cars here, all parked at odd angles on a wide country road. A dozen perhaps. None of them marked up as police. Reporters. My stomach lurched, another understanding sliding into place. Reporters did not come out, not in such numbers at least, for a nice old lady who sat before her fire one night and simply drifted off into an eternal sleep.

Then I saw the blue swirl of police lights and I understood instantly the hourglass had been smashed instead.

I pulled the dark wool hat low on my head, zipped up my padded coat and slipped the notepad into my pocket. Because it wasn't just detectives who carried notepads, but reporters too. I climbed out into the dark night, made my way gingerly along the snowy verge.

As the house emerged from the darkness, any remaining hope that Elizabeth's death had been a peaceful one evaporated in a puff of smoke. Beyond the gaggle of well-wrapped reporters that ringed the lot like spectators on fight night, narrow strips of police tape twisted in the wind. They had brought lights in, large, standing halogen affairs, that threw a blue glow against the snow. White-suited technicians moved in and out of the hanging open front door. A uniformed officer stood beside the cordon, steadfastly ignoring the questions thrown to him by the waiting crowd.

'Officer, who was the victim?'

'Do we have any leads on a perpetrator?'

'Do we know what kind of gun was used yet?'

I thought of Elizabeth, of her piled-up grey hair, her faintly bemused smile. In my mind, I saw her as she had been, and then, like a split screen, with her torso punctured with a litany of holes, of dark blood seeping through her gypsy blouse, a spray of it flying up and out and spattering drops against the stacked-up piles of newspapers, the confused-looking row of stuffed toys. I placed my hand over my mouth, swallowed hard.

'First one?'

It took me long moments to realise that the words were directed at me, that I had drifted into the crowd of reporters, was thoroughly enmeshed now. I glanced up at the speaker, a middle-aged man, middle-level attractive, and watched him assess me, his gaze running from my face, down across my body, before flicking back up. He had a smile that he thought was charming, but read instead as predatory.

'Not easy when you first start out.' He leaned close to me, words confidential and designed to be ensnaring. 'Don't worry. You'll get used to it.'

My body wanted to lean away. Although, to be entirely accurate, my fist was tempted to smack him. I could feel the put-down, fully formed at the back of my tongue. But instead I smiled, working hard to look grateful, allowed a catch to sound in my voice. 'Oh, I hope so. It's awful. Isn't it?' In spite of the protest of my limbs, I stepped closer. 'So, the poor lady. What happened to her?'

'Dead,' he said shortly, then grinned, leaned in. 'GSW. Sorry.' He patted my arm. Like I was a dog he'd met on the sidewalk. 'That's gunshot wounds.'

I wasn't entirely sure his information was worth the sacrifice of not punching him.

'We know who?' I cocked my head, going for inno-cent.

'Nah. If they do, they're not saying.'

'What about witnesses?'

He turned full towards me then, the smell of his breath hitting me full in the face, peppermint and enough cologne to suffocate an ox. 'See now, that's all I'm pre-pared to give you for free.' His gaze roamed over me again. 'Any more and you're going to have to buy me dinner.' He leaned in, voice dropping to a low growl. 'I could provide dessert.'

I smiled, suppressed a shudder, and waved my gloved hand at him. 'Sorry. Married. I appreciate the help though.'

I stepped back, slipping away from the crowd, further along the road that ran perpendicular to the highway, along the side of the house. Past the fir trees that ringed the property, towards its rear. Could see lights on in the downstairs window, the one closest to the front door, the movement of bodies within. Search team, perhaps? Was that where she had been killed?

'Detective?'

I heard the word, didn't react, because it meant nothing to me. Then, in some dark place in my hippo-campus, a memory shook free, of a voice I had heard before, of that word addressed to me. I spun on the spot.

Anne Martin, also known as the current occupant of my former house, stood some distance away, wrapped in a thick jacket, feet encased in knee-high boots, arms wrapped tight about her waist.

227

I shook my head, struggling to change tack. Not a reporter now. A detective. 'Anne. Hi. I was just going to come up and see you,' I lied, wildly.

She nodded towards the house, face pale. 'I heard what happened. Friends of hers. They came up to the farm, wanted to know if I'd seen her. Said she hadn't shown up to choir. I was ...' Her voice cracked. 'I was kind of rude to them.' She looked at me, pleadingly. 'I didn't realise. Thought they were just silly old women making a fuss.'

I cast about for a response, landed on a platitude. 'You couldn't have known.'

She shook her head, light catching on tears that shone in the corners of her eyes. 'I didn't know you were here. I was just ...' She waved towards the house, where a woman in a brown North Face coat had come out the back door, was talking into her cell. 'I saw the police. Wanted to come and tell them what I saw.'

My heart began to beat faster. 'What did you see?'

'It would have been ... I guess about 3 p.m. I was coming home from the store. Saw this guy going into the house. Had this ...' she gestured towards her torso, 'um ... you know, like what utility workers wear, like one of those yellow jackets. I figured, I don't know, maybe she had a problem with one of her services.'

I pulled my notepad from my pocket, more for show than for anything else. After all, I was unlikely to forget this. Even after extensive therapy. 'What did he look like?'

'I didn't see his face. I was coming along, just as he

was heading inside. Seemed pretty tall. Maybe, I don't know, six foot, maybe more. Seemed like he was quite a big guy. Stocky, I mean. He was wearing a baseball cap.'

Any doubts that had lingered now vanished into the night. It was him. It was Wolf.

I could feel my knees loosen, a nausea rising up through me. The sudden sense that all before had been little more than a game, that now we had finally gotten serious. He had nipped and worried, working to drive me in one direction, to steer me away from places he hadn't wanted me to go. Only that hadn't worked and I had ignored him and carried on regardless. And so now he had come to killing.

I looked away from Anne, towards the house, trying to ignore the heat, the urge to lean over into the snowy verge and vomit. He had killed Elizabeth. He had killed her because he knew she could tell me something. He had killed her to make sure she didn't.

What? What was it that she knew? And why was it so important to him that she told no one else?

Then another thought struck me. 'You said it was about three? That you saw the man going in?'

Anne nodded. 'I know it was, because I had to get home for a phone call at 3.15 and I was worried I was running late. I remember checking the clock, just as I turned in past Mrs Barrow's.'

I had seen him at 11 a.m. The email from Elizabeth, that was sent at 1 p.m.

Two hours later, she was dead.

My brother-in-law was right. When it came to murder, there was no such thing as coincidence. She had emailed me, saying she had figured something out and, within hours, Wolf came for her.

He had access to my emails.

I turned to look towards the house, fighting a rising panic, could feel Anne step up beside me, looking towards the once-was home, now crime scene.

'You think,' she said, hesitantly, '... you think we're safe? Me and my kids, I mean.'

I glanced across at her, this woman who had made a home in the place where it all began. I didn't know what he wanted, could not begin to guess what it was that he was fighting so hard to keep secret. But if he had decided that Elizabeth was a threat to him ...

'No one came up to the house?' I asked. 'After you got home? No one knocked on your door? You didn't see anyone hanging around?'

She shook her head. 'Not that I know of. But then I was on the phone, up in the office. That's ... It's in the back of the house, so sometimes, I mean, I don't always hear the doorbell.'

I bit my lip. 'Maybe ... maybe it would be a good idea to go to a hotel. You and the kids. Just for a couple of days. Just until the police catch him.' Then she looked at me strangely, and I heard it, what I had just said. 'Until we catch him. And we will, Anne.'

She considered me for a moment, then nodded slowly. And I felt a crashing sense of horror at what I was doing now, what I had done. That I had come to Elizabeth, impersonating a police officer. That I had been inside her house, could have left behind fingerprints and DNA, and if I had left niether of those things, I had certainly left behind my contact details, my number, my email address. And the police, they would be following back the thread of Elizabeth's life, would be looking for anyone she had spoken to in recent days, and so wouldn't they be highly interested in this RCMP detective, this Rebecca Leland, who had visited her, such a short time before her death? Wouldn't they reach out to her, try to find out what she had wanted, look to see if there was any connection between that investigation and Elizabeth's own death?

And once they did that, then I was screwed.

Then, another realisation. That Anne now thought she had passed on her information to a detective. Only she hadn't, had she?

She had told me.

Which meant the police still did not know about the man in the utility jacket who had come to Elizabeth's house and murdered her.

I felt an overwhelming urge to vomit.

'Poor woman,' said Anne, quiet beside me. 'Maybe it's true.'

'What?' I asked.

'Maybe this place is cursed.'

Chapter 23

It was a perfect family scene. The long, clothed table surrounded by Mom and Drew and Addie and Gray and the girls. Their voices were high-pitched and excitable, the chatter from one designed to outdo that of the other. The remnants of a pot roast sitting in a red ceramic dish, meat ringed with the relics of root vegetables, like the drifting survivors in a shipwreck. Fleck sat beneath my chair, occasionally letting loose a heavy sigh, his wagging tail hitting periodically against my leg. I moved the food about my plate, my fork leaving streaks through the heap of pallid mash, and felt the chair shimmy beneath me, my vision swimming with exhaustion. I glanced up, could feel my mother's gaze on me, took an overlarge bite of meat, ignoring the lump that sat inside my throat.

'You look tired,' my mother said, flatly.

I nodded, forced a smile. 'I am tired. It's been a long week.'

I half listened as Addie chirruped, some story about a school bake sale and GMO produce, and half watched as Drew shovelled potatoes into his mouth, his head down, the movement of his fork like it was driven by a piston. But my mind, that was a whole country away.

I had backed away from Anne, made some empty excuse, had filled the distance between us with cold night air and prayers that it would not occur to her to ask why I remained so steadfastly on the wrong side of the police cordon. Had moved beyond the fir trees, towards the swell of reporters, gaze moving across them. And there he was, Mr Middle-Age, Middle-Attractiveness. I'd slipped into the pool, appearing at his elbow, a bright smile, and, leaning in towards him, whispered, 'I'm returning the favour. Lady over there,' I'd nodded towards Anne, 'she says she saw him. Three p.m. Big guy in a utility vest.' I'd smiled, patted him on the arm. 'Let's call it in lieu of dinner.'

And so I ran. From the police tape and the woman lying dead. From the gathered reporters and from the remnants of me that tied me to a murder scene. Admitting defeat, the certain knowledge that I had gone too far, had bitten off more than I could chew. I'd crossed the line from courage into recklessness, and because of that, a woman was dead.

The potato felt gluey in my mouth, sticking to my soft palate, and a wave of nausea swamped me. I swirled a carrot about my plate, watching the shapes left behind in the dark of the gravy, feeling suddenly like I couldn't breathe. The words chased around and around in my head, had chased me all the way back from Canada. It's your fault. It's your fault. He told you to stop. Everyone told you to stop. Only you wouldn't and you didn't and now a woman is dead.

I'd lingered in Canada long enough for my car to

be repaired, an endless, sleepless, watchful night. Then a never-ending drive across stretched-out highways, from country to country, state to state. One eye always behind me, watching for the following wolf. Finally bowing down, admitting defeat. You could call it logic, but, in truth, all that had powered me was the instinct to run, as far and as fast as I could, hoping that by doing so, by leaving, by stopping, he would be satisfied, would leave me alone.

'So, how was your flight?' Addie asked, carefully removing a steak knife from her four-year-old with one hand, wiping her mouth with the other. Was there a tone to it? The laying down of a gauntlet? Or was that just my guilt?

'Full. I got to sit next to a guy with BO, so that was nice.'

'Rosie, what's BO?' asked Gabriella.

I glanced at my niece. 'It's when people are stinky, honey.'

'You and your brother,' Mom ladled another slice of brisket onto her plate. 'You make a proper pair. Drew's been working non-stop, haven't you? We haven't seen him.'

My brother grunted around a mouthful of vegetables.

The conversation washed over me, words of it rising to the surface, sinking away again. Me looking down at the remnants of my plate, seeing instead the dead body of Elizabeth Barrow.

Then another thought, that somehow Wolf had gotten close enough to me to access my phone, my emails. I looked around at my family, the sudden thought that I was now a piece that stood up at the wrong angle, that I no longer fit here, now no longer seeing my family but ... what? Suspects? Was it one of you? Did someone here get to my phone? To my emails?

I pushed back my chair, and Fleck leapt up, all fur and enthusiasm. The scrape of legs against wood cutting across the conversation, pulling everyone's gaze up to me. 'Sorry. I'm exhausted. I need to go to bed.'

Murmurs of concern, sounds of sympathy, my niece's 'Can I have her biscuit then?', all fell away. I could feel Fleck's weight behind me, his heavy breath against the back of my leg. I slid inside my room, waited for the dog, closed the door behind us, and stood in the darkness, gaze fixed on the window, the yard beyond.

Are you out there?

Are you waiting for me?

Fleck sat down beside me, looking up at me in the darkness. A low whine.

'It's okay,' I said, rubbing his head. 'We're okay.'

My cell rang in my pocket. Not my cellphone, but a throwaway, grabbed from a Walmart on the route home. A number I didn't recognise.

'Hello?'

'Oh, hi. You left a message for me earlier? It's Leah. From the missing-person website.'

I had called the number on the business card Ilianna Ruez had given me. This was from the hotel room, before the death of Elizabeth Barrow, before I knew just how much my digging would cost. I had listened as the

235

phone rang out. I'm calling about the Clay Rutherford case. Call me as soon as you can.

I'm sorry, you've got the wrong number. I'm sorry, I don't know what you're talking about. I should stop this, should shut it down, should do what I had been told to do.

My mouth opened, the words fell out. 'Yes. Hi.'

The dog sighed heavily, lay down on the floor beside me, his head on his paws. He was judging me. I didn't blame him.

'You're police, yes?' Leah asked.

I hesitated. Because, really, hadn't playing with identities cost me enough already? But you had to meet people where they needed to be. And Leah, she was waiting for me to say yes.

'Yes.' I sank down onto the bed, snapping on my bedside lamp.

'And you're calling about the Rutherford kid?'

'His mom gave me your details.'

She made a noise in the back of her throat. 'You must have caught her on a good day.'

I allowed a smile into my voice. 'Yes, she seemed like someone hit hard by life.'

'Sure. Let's say that.' She sighed heavily. 'Look, I've pulled out my notes. This case, it's been pretty dormant for years now. What do you need from me?'

'Well,' I said, pulling my legs up towards my chest, 'Mom filled me in from her end. What she was less keen to talk about was his childhood, her role in this whole thing.'

The voice on the other end of the phone sighed heavily. 'Yeah, that certainly sounds like her. See, these cases, once we take them on, we stay in touch, y'know. Often, the families, they'll do their own events, bring public focus back to the case, maybe once a year, something like that, so we think it's important that we stay in contact with them. Ilianna, she stopped having much to do with things a long time ago.'

'So ...' I considered, 'you think she could have had something to do with his disappearance?'

A pause. 'No. Not really. Look, from what I've heard, Ilianna's been a mess for pretty much as long as she's been standing. Started drinking as a teen, got pregnant at, what, fifteen maybe. The father, he was nowhere to be seen. Sounds like Clay, he pretty much had to raise himself. By the time he was in high school, she was a full-blown alcoholic. Had bouts of sobriety, you know the drill, I'll do better this time, I'm putting my kid first, that kind of thing. Never lasted. And Clay, well, I guess he figured out how to make his own way in the world.'

'He was dealing?' I asked.

'Ilianna would say no. I talked to friends of his, back in the day, and they said a big fat, hell yes. Started off small – weed, prescription pills from wherever he could steal them. But, from the look of him, he was just heading up into the big league – heroin, coke. That was when he vanished.'

I pursed my lips. 'Could that be why he vanished?'

'Could be. Could very well be. I mean, in that world, you do not want to piss off the wrong person. You do, well, you could easily find yourself gone, whether you want to or not.'

'And what about after? Ilianna, she was a bit unclear.'

'Let's just say that Clay disappearing was all the excuse that woman needed to up her medication. I'm pretty sure she's boarded the heroin train herself now. And look, I'll be honest with you, Ilianna was a shitshow of a mother. Wouldn't surprise me if her son decided to clear out and leave Momma to her own devices.'

'Is there anything on him? Police stops or bank withdrawals? I mean, staying hidden for twenty years, that's no mean feat.'

'Okay, so according to our files, we have evidence of him reaching out to Ilianna, right up to October 8. Then all contact, it just stops. But what we do have is a single transaction on his debit card, about five weeks after his disappearance.'

I sat up straighter. 'Where?'

'According to the bank, it was a Texaco just outside of South Bend, Indiana.'

I considered my drive of mere hours ago, flashing back to a signpost – South Bend, 2 miles. It was on the way. If you were driving here, to Madison, and you were coming from Toronto, that's the way you would go.

'And they're sure it's him?'

'Pretty sure. CCTV was out, but the clerk gave a pretty good description and it matched Clay.'

'Okay,' I said. 'This is going to sound weird ... were there any reports of him having a baby with him?'

A long pause. 'A baby? No.' Another pause. 'I got to say, I'm pretty sure Clay, he wasn't the paternal type.'

'What about after that?' I said, hurriedly 'Any idea where he went from there?'

'Nuh-uh, and see, that's the thing. That is the last sighting we have of him. There at that gas station. I mean, the absolute last. After that, there's no bank activity, no contact, he never got a ticket or a citation for dealing. Nothing.' She sighed heavily. 'Look, I've been doing this for a long time. I've dealt with cases, hell, through pretty much all of North America, and I got to tell you, when someone goes this cold ... I mean, it's been twenty years. With nothing. Nothing at all. I'm sorry, but I got to say, I think it's likely this boy is dead,' she said, voice low. Then she snorted. 'I mean, either it's that or he's become someone else entirely.'

Chapter 24

I pulled my legs up towards my chest, wrapped my arms around them, was dimly aware of Fleck watching me, a low whine curling from the back of his throat. It still wasn't too late. I could still walk away, could still do what Wolf had told me to.

Only it was hovering there, this answer, just beyond my reach. And I've never been great at being told what to do.

Fleck looked up at me, big-eyed.

'What do you think?'

He sighed again.

'Yeah. I know. I'm incorrigible.'

A murder scene. A surviving baby, one that no one knows about. A missing boy driving a car last seen approaching the murder. An untraceable half-brother. They had to be connected, had to somehow link up in some way that I was missing.

I pulled my laptop towards me. Pulled up the missing-person website, the photograph of Clay Rutherford, made uneven with age, posed and unwilling. It had the feel of a yearbook photo. Yet even in this, he looked at the camera as if daring it to capture him, his gaze head-on and piercing, the left of his lip curled into, not a smile, but a snarl almost: Come on. You think you can get me? Bring it on.

He looked like someone destined for a life of crime. Like someone who didn't give a shit about the world or anyone in it.

He did not look like the kind of person who would rescue a baby, care for a baby, take that baby to safety.

I sighed. Leaned back against the cushions that arched across my bed. Didn't I know better than most that what one saw was rarely the sum of the story. That all of us have hidden depths to us, secrets that the world at large would never guess from merely a photograph. After all, wasn't that how the fraudster did his job? Or her job. They paint a picture of themselves, as the person their victim wishes to see. They play the part of the perfect employee or boyfriend or colleague, and they play it so well that when it all falls apart, when the world finally realises that beneath the surface is layer upon layer of lies, those that they have fooled will then take up the baton, often fooling themselves, because it couldn't be true. He was a good man. And so the victim takes up where the fraudster left off, sometimes spinning their own lies to make their beliefs in his goodness to be well founded.

We lie to ourselves. All the time. We believe that we know far more about people than we ever truly can.

So what if that was true of Clay? What if there was something to him that the world at large had not seen yet? He was eighteen, plenty of time then to change, to adapt to a challenging world. That still did not answer the question of why he was there that day, and if he was, why he survived. And why bring me here, to Madison? Wouldn't you just hand me over to the police, then and there? Why the secrecy?

I tapped my nails against the hard edge of the laptop. There was nothing in the police files, no connection between the disappearance of Clay Rutherford and the Lynch murders. But then, why would there be? According to Ilianna, his presence was accounted for until two weeks after. Only she hadn't seen him, had she? So, really speaking, he could have been anywhere by that point. And the police, they didn't know about me, didn't know there was a survivor. Maybe they'd never connected him to the case because they didn't know there was any need to.

And now the question – was I cocky enough to believe I could do better than the police who had investigated it?

Probably.

Fleck looked up at me, another whine, and I shook my head. 'Fleck, I have to find my brother.' It was the only place I could think to go for answers. That was what I told myself. But the truth of it? It was like a tug, deep down in the belly of me, that I had discovered this invisible thread connecting me to someone who maybe looked like me. Maybe thought like me. And the thought of not following where that thread might lead, it was simply unbearable.

Fleck jumped up to his feet, tongue out, tail wagging,

and slid his nose beneath my knee. I would take that as agreement.

I pulled my laptop closer. Sadiq had said that Elliott had joined the military. He'd also said that Elliott and Kyle, that they were the product of my mother's first marriage. Reasonable then to think that Elliott would not be keen to keep the name of the stepfather who went on to murder the entirety of his family.

I did a records search, looking for the name of my mother's first husband, for marriage certificates that would match the place and time frame, finally coming up with a name – Dylan Ebert. They had married young, my mother eighteen, her husband just a year older. They had divorced three years later. Just long enough to produce two little boys. A death certificate followed. Dylan, it appeared, had died ten years ago, a heart attack.

I switched over to the military website, searching the database for an Elliott Ebert, offered up a swift prayer.

And there he was. No longer a boy, but now a man, stocky-framed, resplendent in air force uniform. My brother.

'Holy shit,' I muttered. 'Fleck, I got him.'

Fleck nudged me, gave a low woof of agreement.

Then my gaze tracked down, to the words 'discharged'. 2014.

I blew out a breath, could feel my stomach waiting to drop. 'Okay, but we got a name. We got a name.' I navigated quickly to a second window. Looking for an address. The Canada 411 search brought up hundreds of potentials. Then another thought, one that sent sparks across my skin. How did I know that he had remained in Canada? Couldn't he be here? A White Pages search then. Another couple of dozen to add to the list.

I bit my lip. Would have to ring each of them individually, a list that amounted to nearly two hundred people.

I did a social media search across the usual culprits – Facebook and Twitter and Instagram – and came up with another couple of hundred potentials to add to my list. There had to be some way to narrow this down, based on what I already had.

I considered, then typed into the search engine – finding discharged military personnel in Canada. Then sat up straighter as the results flooded in. A service, one that allows people to reach out to those who have served, that offers to track them down for you. Under the right circumstances.

I looked down at Fleck. 'What do you think? Who do I need to be?'

I could be Rebecca Leland. Although the thought of her clenched my stomach up into a tight knot, the thought again of the body of Elizabeth Barrow, of the left-behind remnants of the fictional Leland all over a murder scene.

Maybe not.

Maybe a journalist?

Or the care home, wanting to talk to him about our grandmother?

Or …

I picked my cellphone up, dialled the number on the screen. Waited through an automatic message, through Mozart's Symphony No. 40, then, 'Hello? Military Reunions.'

I took a breath, stepped out onto the ice, and let the words spill from me. That my name was Rosa Fisher. That I had recently learned that I was adopted. That my search for my family had taken me to Canada, to the site of a murder, to a dementia-ridden grandmother and a family of ghosts. That all that was left was my brother, that he had served, that I couldn't find him alone. And as the words tumbled from me, so did tears, a solid, steady stream, brought about by exhaustion and by the overwhelming story, by the fact that there was so much to say, so much more to leave out. Fleck rested his head in my lap, sighed.

When I finished, the woman remained silent for long enough that I began to wonder if she had given up, had hung up somewhere in the midst of my saga.

Then, 'Well. That's quite … You've had it pretty tough, I'm guessing.'

More tears then. I dashed them away with the palm of my hand. 'Yes.'

'Okay,' she said softly. 'Give me everything you have on your brother. I'll do what I can.'

I reeled it off, giving her my cell number, my email address, then hung up. A distant feeling of defeat almost. That I had come so far alone, and that finally that hadn't been enough, that I had had to place something of such importance into the hands of another.

245

Then a sound from beyond my door, of footsteps on the stairs, and the hairs stood up on my arms, flashing back to that night, two short months and an entire life-time ago. Fleck let loose a growl.

'It's okay,' I muttered.

Three sharp knocks on the door, and Drew's voice. 'You awake?'

I snapped the laptop shut, slid it beneath my pillow. 'I'm awake,' I called.

He eased the door open, slipped inside, looked like he had slept little more than me of late, the bags beneath his eyes dark and bulbous, hair standing up on end. 'Mom said to tell you we got pecan pie if you want some?'

I rubbed my face. 'I'm fine, thanks.'

He studied me. 'You look wiped out.'

'Right back at you.'

He snorted. 'Work. My boss is a prick.' He stopped, considered, 'Look, I just wanted to say, I know things have been tough for you lately. You know, your fall, the adoption thing ... I just want you to know, if you need anything, I mean, I know I'm not the best talker in the world, but, you know, I can listen.'

I nodded, could feel the words sitting on the tip of my tongue, the urge suddenly to be what I once was again, the little sister, the one who could hand over responsibility, could rely on the family around her to make everything all right.

Only I wasn't her, was I? Not now.

'I'm fine, Drew. I'm just tired, is all.'

He studied me, overlong hair flopping before his eyes. 'New York it was, yes?'

A whisper started at the rear of my brain. 'Yes.'

He nodded, gaze locked on mine. 'How was the weather?'

I met his gaze. 'Pretty mild actually. Bit of rain, but nothing too bad.'

Because the very best of con men, they pay attention to the details. Like what the weather is like in the place that you are supposed to be.

A buzzer rang downstairs, the doorbell, and Drew turned, frowning. 'Who's that now?'

Then my mother's voice, 'Rosa? It's Eve.'

I frowned, stood up, careful not to lean on my hidden laptop, could hear my best friend's voice, her footsteps on the stairs.

Drew opened the door up, waved a greeting. 'Hey. I'll leave you guys to it.'

Eve smiled broadly, hiking the backpack further up her shoulder. 'Hey, Drew, good to see you.' She shut the door behind him, turning to me. 'Girl!'

'What?'

'You have stressed me out. Off on your little adventures. You know I haven't slept a night since you went, right?'

I sighed, sank back onto the bed. 'I'm okay, Eve.'

'Well, I'm gonna put that down to luck instead of judgement.' She plumped herself down on the bed, tugging the backpack from her shoulders, and studied me. 'Seriously, can you honestly tell me this is worth it?'

'If I find my brother ... yes, it'll be worth it.'

She stared at me, 'Honey, you already got two siblings. How many does a person need? Let me tell you, I got a brother, and that guy, he's an ass. If you're so desperate to get another one, have him. Please.'

I gave a laugh. 'Eve, I don't know how to explain it. It's like, for all these years, I believed that I was this one person, that I was surrounded by my family, but I always felt that I was different. Just not quite like anyone else. And I thought everyone felt like that. That that was just how life was. Then all of a sudden I realise that there's a reason why I feel the way I do, that I am different, that I don't fit. And then, I can't explain it, but ... you feel like this need, you know? To stand beside someone who looks like you, who comes from the same place you do, who makes you feel that you aren't entirely different after all.'

She pursed her lips, nodded. 'I guess I get that. Just, you gotta promise me, you're going to be careful, yes?'

I nodded. 'I'll be careful.'

She pulled the backpack around, tugging a box file free. 'You're covering that statistics lecture for Will tomorrow morning, don't forget? I brought the stuff from the office for you, figured it would save you going up to get it.' She dumped the box into my hands. 'Better you than me.'

I grinned, 'Thanks.'

She studied me, again. 'I better go. I got a bunch of papers to mark. You'll call, if you need anything?'

'I'll call.'

She gave me a quick hug, pulling the backpack round onto her shoulders, and slipped out, footsteps quick and light on the stairs.

I sighed, had entirely forgotten about the following morning's lecture, had done nothing to prepare. I rubbed my eyes and dreamed of sleep, flipping open the lid of the box file. Downstairs, the front door slammed shut. I lifted the sheets of paper out, the undergraduate programme of qualitative analysis.

And there, beneath it, the missing journal article, my edit notes still scribbled in its margins.

Chapter 25

My hands trembled. I sat there, staring at the paper, thoughts ricocheting. I had been wrong, it hadn't been taken on the night of the break-in. That somehow, for reasons that I couldn't quite grasp hold of, I had instead put it into this box file, in between the sheets on content and thematic analysis. Only that couldn't be true, could it? Because I remembered sitting at the dining-room table, papers spread about me, pen in my hand, What turns white-collar criminals red?

A heat moved through me. My breath came in short and uneven bursts and I pushed myself up to standing. Fleck, ears pricked, his pace matching mine as we marched, back and fore, across the bedroom floor. Because there would be a rational explanation for this. I was panicking, was losing my grip. I had to calm down, to think.

I stopped, blew out a breath.

'Okay,' I said, softly. Fleck sat back on his haunches, looked up at me attentively, 'I didn't put this paper in that box. It was there, before the break-in. I remember that it was there.'

Fleck did not protest.

'And so ...' I turned, walking back towards the window, the pulled-tight curtains, 'that means that sometime after the break-in, someone else did it.' I looked at Fleck.

He whined, clambered to his feet, and followed me about the room.

'The box file, it was in my office, right? Because where else would it be. It's just teaching stuff. So, okay, it's in my office. So, someone comes in, maybe Eve has left the door open, has gone to grab something from the lab, they let themselves in, they slip the paper inside. A little psychological game, a way to say fuck you.' Then another memory, and I stopped walking, sudden enough that the dog collided with the back of my leg. 'Only ... the file ... it was in the filing cabinet. I remember because it almost didn't fit, and I nearly gave up and just left it on my desk, because the filing cabinet, that's usually just for the confidential stuff, only, only then it went in, so I just left it in there. And Eve wouldn't leave the filing cabinet open.' We called it our Fort Knox, the home to our confidential files, our participant data, joked that we needed an eyeball scanner fitted to it, save having to carry the keys about with us.

Which meant that someone had gotten into the filing cabinet.

I sat down hard on the bed. It was hardly a stretch. If you could track my phone, if you could read my emails, stood to reason you could probably figure out how to open an Office Depot filing cabinet. But a buzzing had filled my ears as another thought snuck in, worming its way into my consciousness.

That there was another option.

That Eve had a key. That it would be nothing to her to open up the drawer, to find the right file, one she knows I'm going to need for class. To slip this paper inside. That she had access to my phone, while it sat charging at my desk, when I went to the bathroom or to make coffee. That no one else could quite so easily see my email password, just look up at the right time, just pay attention.

No. That was crazy.

But how else to explain a break-in with no forced entry. A tracker on my phone, access to my emails? One way or another, someone I trusted had betrayed me.

My face flushed, hands tingling, and I stood quickly, tugging my boots on, pushing past Fleck, heavy footfall on the stairs, a quick 'I'm going out, be back in a bit' thrown over my shoulder as I grabbed my duffel coat, car keys, into the frigid night. Frost had already begun to form across the lawn, crunching underfoot as I ran towards the car. All tiredness was gone now, swept away in a wave of adrenaline. The sky was clear, carpeted with stars. I climbed into the car, fingers trembling, stuck the key into the ignition.

Because if I was right, if Eve was somehow involved in this, then she was linked to the man who called himself Wolf. She would know who he was and, more importantly, she would know why.

I pulled out of the drive, steering loose on the gravel,

252

tyres whirring, and shot down the hill, taking a hard right at the bottom of it. Leaning close to the steering wheel, squinting into the darkness, my thoughts a kaleidoscope.

That it couldn't be true. That Eve was my friend.

That it had to be true. That Eve had lied to me.

It all coming back to that one inescapable truth, that none of us can truly know the mind of another. That the world we inhabit, the people we call our friends, we see of them only what they allow us to see, and that buried within them sit myriad other people, strangers in a friend's clothing.

I pushed the gas closer to the floor, driving far too fast on pitch-black country roads, over rolling hills, around tree-lined bends.

I no longer even knew myself. How then could I ever expect to know someone else?

I watched the speed creep upwards, adrenaline spiking, my brain split now between devil and angel. Speed up. Slow down. You'll be killed. Who cares?

I was Rosa Fisher. I was Rebecca Leland. I was the good girl. I was a woman who told whatever lie would gain her what she needed.

How the hell could I expect any more from my best friend?

Then, up ahead, looming through the darkness, the red glow of brake lights. I came up on them fast, hand on the horn, lights flashing. A pause, then the car in front pulling away from me, speeding up.

Shit.

I hesitated, angel winning long enough for me to glance up at the straight stretch of road ahead, then slammed the gas to the floor, pulling around Eve's car until my passenger-side window was level with her window. I pushed the button, window sliding down, a gale of bitter-cold wind slapping against my cheeks, my throat.

'Eve. Pull over.'

She was leaning close to the steering wheel, was keeping her gaze locked on the road ahead. Then a single fearful glance to her left. A moment. Then another, longer look. Then an explosion, her window slipping down, letting loose a string of expletives.

'Holy shit, Rosa. You scared the shit out of me, what the hell are you thinking, girl. You're gonna get us both killed ...'

'Pull over.' I eased my foot off the gas, sliding my car back into lane behind hers, followed her until we hit a clearing, her blinker flashing. She rolled to a stop, was out of the car into the dark night almost before the engine had died.

'Rosa, I swear to God, if you ever pull that crap again ... You, you've lost your goddam mind ...'

I pushed open the car door, grabbed the paper from the passenger seat, marched towards her and shoved it into her face. 'What's this?'

She stared at it, stared at me. 'What?'

'You heard me.'

A moment then, where she scanned my face, processing, as if trying to find within it the Rosa she knew. Good luck with that.

'Rosa,' she forced her voice to calm, 'I don't know what is goin' on here, but ...'

I held the paper up. 'This. This was in the box file you brought to my house.'

'Okay?'

'This paper? This was the one that was stolen. During the break-in. Someone put a tracker on my phone. That could only have been someone close to me. Someone got into my emails. Someone,' my voice cracked, a blend of frustration and fury, 'someone came into my house, took this paper, left me for dead. Who is he?'

'Who?'

'The man, Wolf, the one in Canada. The one who followed me.'

'I ...'

I stepped towards her, almost screaming now. 'Eve, he killed someone. He killed a woman. Because she said she had something to tell me, and he goddam killed her. So, whoever it is you've been helping, however you got yourself involved in this, Eve, he's dangerous. You have no idea what it is you're tied up in.'

She stared at the paper. 'I ... Honey, I don't ... Rosa, please, you need to take a breath.'

It seemed that I had left my body, was watching the scene play out from far away. The one woman, staring, hands out, placating. The other, screaming and wild. A distant feeling that I was playing the wrong part in this particular play.

'Please,' I said, pleading now. 'Just ... I won't tell the police anything about your involvement. I promise. I

255

just have to know, tell me who he is. Tell me why he's after me.'

Eve stared at me for moments that stretched out endlessly. Then she stepped close to me and slowly, like she was dealing with a rabid animal, plucked the paper from between my fingers, squinting at it in the darkness. 'Rosa,' she said, softly. 'Honey, this is the copy you gave me. You photocopied the paper you were working on. Remember?'

My heart thudded in my ears. 'What?' I said, voice hoarse.

She moved closer, gingerly, holding the paper up to me. 'There ...' she said, gently, 'see that? That's the coffee stain, where I spilled my latte. Remember? You were there. It was right after you gave it to me. In that coffee shop down on State Street.' She studied my face. 'Remember? I must have put it in the box file, I guess. After I'd read it.'

I stared at the paper and I stared at her, and I felt hot tears bubble over and spill down my cheeks, my lips moving in a useless apology that never made it past a low moan. 'I ...'

'Rosa,' Eve took hold of my hands, gripping them tight within her own. 'I think this has gone too far. I think you need help.'

Chapter 26

My chest was tight, skin stretched across a drum. My heartbeat came in quick, unsteady pulses, felt that it would shoot soon from my chest, like I was some kind of lovelorn cartoon. My palms slippery with sweat where they rested against my forehead. My view was only of the cracked linoleum beneath me, of the darkness of my thighs, the dense material of my pants splayed wide, the toes of my boots, scuffed on the edges. I needed to polish them, I thought. Would they last another winter, or was their time nearly up? My thoughts scattered and collided and scattered again. I was losing my mind.

'You okay?' Gray's voice came from oceans away.

'Fine,' I muttered, studying the linoleum, the edging of a stain that crept from beneath my brother-in-law's desk, spreading towards the tips of my toes. Was it dried urine? It looked like dried urine.

'You want some water?'

Maybe it was water. No. Best face facts. It was probably urine.

'Please.'

The scraping of chair legs on urine-stained linoleum, heavy footsteps, the opening of Gray's office door, a flood of over-baked air, heating turned up high to counteract the impending snow. This movie of my life made no sense to me. Someone should sack the director. And the main character, what a wimp, sitting in her brother-in-law's office in a downtown Madison police station, her head in her hands, doing her best not to cry. What kind of protagonist was that?

I don't know how long I had stood on that dark country road, my head resting on Eve's shoulder. I know I had sobbed and sobbed, her hand patting me limp on the back, 'there, there's' lost to the wind. A sense of my own mind turning against me, sending my thoughts spinning and spiralling until everything I knew seemed to be wrong and no one was who I thought they were. A distant thought that this must be what it was like to be my grandmother, must be Lilian Gauthier's every waking moment, suspicion and confusion and doubt battering her every thought.

'I'm sorry,' I mumbled, into Eve's mass of dark hair.

A snort in return. 'Whatever. I'm kinda flattered you think I have it in me. I'm like one of those Bond girls.' Then, her tone sliding to serious. 'This guy, he killed someone?'

I nodded, a hiccough, 'Yes.'

'I'm taking you home, Rosa,' said Eve, firm. 'You're going to tell Gray what you know.'

My nieces were asleep by the time we returned to the house, two heads, one blonde, one dark, hair twisting together on the sofa's edge, a patchwork blanket pulled up around their chins. And the rest of the family, they sat, the television bright with *Seinfeld*. A rerun, but that hardly seemed to matter. My mother's eyes were heavy, head thrown back in the recliner. Addie and Gray, bookending their girls, Gray looking like he would give anything now to take flight, to escape the family bonding over decades-old TV. Drew playing on his phone.

My mother looked up as the door closed behind us, her eyes snapping open. 'Where'd you go?' Then looking, from my reddened eyes, to Eve, alarmed. 'What? What's wrong?'

I had opened my mouth, only words, they failed me.

'I have a little bit of a problem, Mrs Fisher,' said Eve, quietly. 'I know it's late, but I was wondering if maybe I could have a quick word with Gray?'

Gray's eyes grazed me, and he pushed himself up to standing, careful to disentangle himself from his eldest daughter's limbs. 'Let's head on into the kitchen. Don't wanna wake the girls.'

He had led the way, my mother and sister's gazes boring into my back. I'm pretty sure Drew hadn't noticed we were there. We followed Gray into the kitchen, waiting while he closed the door tight behind us.

'So,' he said. 'What's up?'

And so I told him, of my hidden history, of my search for a beginning, of my grandmother and Laurie and Canada and of Jackson Wolf. Gray sat, leaned back in his chair, arms taut across his chest, like he was bracing. As well he might. I told him of the tracker on my phone, the figure in the parking lot, the glass of my car shining like scattered crystals in the snow. And I told him of the murder of Elizabeth Barrow.

'Holy shit, Rosa,' muttered Eve.

'Yes.'

Gray stared at me, face grim. 'You talked to the Ontario PD?'

I looked down at my lap. 'No.'

'Why?'

I felt the colour begin to creep across my cheeks. 'Because, while in Canada, I repeatedly impersonated a Canadian detective. I got a badge and everything. eBay,' I added, redundantly.

Eve put her hands over her face, and Gray let out a low snort, that I took to be derision, but, looking up, I realised was a laugh. 'You know how Addie always says about you being the good girl? Seems my wife doesn't have a goddam clue what her sister is about.'

I grinned in spite of myself.

Gray shook his head. 'Okay, look, let me see what I can do. Eve, in the meantime, watch her and make sure she doesn't try to steal any identities or cross any international borders. Rosa, tomorrow morning, come down to the office. I'm going to go call our friends in Ontario PD and see if I can't smooth this over.' He turned, head still shaking. 'Detective. Son of a bitch.'

'Yes,' I said. 'Sorry,' I added. 'Gray?'

'What?'

'You think I'm going to prison?'

He grinned, shrugged. 'Probably.'

Another thought, streaking in from left field. 'Hey, Gray?'

'What?'

'Could you check something out for me?'

'Length of prison sentence for impersonating a police officer?' muttered Eve.

'Good one. No. It's about when I was born ... or, not born, left. Was there ever any mention of a silver sedan associated with that case?'

Gray studied me, was silent for long moments. 'Why?'

My lips sealed shut of their own accord. But then, what was the point of that? Hadn't I already told my brother-in-law everything else? I unsealed my reluctant lips and told him about Clay, about his disappearance, about the great theory of my arrival in Madison.

Gray nodded slowly, not saying a word, the heavy crease of a frown lining his face. 'Let me see what I can find.'

And so I was here, in his office, waiting. I closed my eyes briefly, lack of sleep making the office swim about me. Forced myself to breathe, until Gray's footsteps returned, an icy-cold plastic bottle shoved into my hand.

'You should drink some.'

I nodded, twisted the cap, took a large mouthful. 'Sorry,' I muttered. 'Had to get myself together.'

Gray didn't look at me, shifted through papers. 'You sure you're ready to do this?'

'Uh-huh.'

He sat down across from me, studying my face. 'Okay, so, first thing – Clay Rutherford. Found a report in the system. Kid was pulled about an hour after you were found, next county over. Was stopped for speeding.

261

Silver Sedan. Gave his name as Rutherford. Officer let him off with a warning.' He looked at me hard, lips pursed. 'Looks like your theory has legs. This Clay, he was in Madison the day you were left here.'

I closed my eyes briefly, in amongst the tumult of the day, the relief of being briefly right, of having an answer of sorts.

'Okay,' said Gray, 'so, let's assume you're right. Let's assume that the burglary, that it was somehow connected to your search for your family, my question then is why? Why that night? If it was this Wolf guy who came into your house, why then? You hadn't started digging then. At that point, you didn't even know there was anything to be digging for. So what brought him there?'

I shrugged expansively. 'I don't know. I've been driving myself crazy trying to figure that out.'

'I mean, your logic for the connection is the paper, the one that you think was taken during the break-in. That Wolf must have had a copy of that paper when he emailed you under the guise of the screenwriter from the hotel.' He pulled a face. 'That's pretty thin.'

I groaned. 'I know. Seriously, I get how this sounds. Only it just feels too much. Too coincidental to be unconnected.'

Gray leaned back in his chair, studied me. 'Okay, so go on then.'

'What?'

'Well, I know you. You always have a theory. About everything. What's your theory? If you think it was Wolf in your house that night, why?'

I plucked at a loose thread on my trouser leg. 'The best I can come up with is that there was something in our house that he wanted. I don't know what it was, and I don't know how the hell he would have known it was there. But all I know is that he came in on a night when he thought the house was empty, that somehow he knew we were planning on being away, and that the only place he targeted just happened to be my mom's dresser. The place where she kept all the stuff about my past.'

'And he also took the time to lift an academic paper and your graduation photo,' offered Gray.

'That too.'

'Why?'

'No clue.'

'There's something else,' said Gray

'About Clay?'

'No. About Jackson Wolf.'

'Okay?'

'Turns out, there's an alert on the system. We are not the first people to be asking questions about Jackson Wolf. The alert comes with a warning to not approach, as he is considered armed and very dangerous. I called it in, spoke to some detective based out of London. Let's just say she was mighty interested.' Gray gave me a long look. 'Rosa, I don't know what this is about. I don't know why this guy is interested in you and I don't know if he is in any way connected to the break-in. But what I do know is that this guy, he's dangerous.'

Chapter 27

I drove beneath the overarching trees, along the narrow driveway leading up to the house. I kept one eye ahead of me at the twisting flakes of snow, one on the rear-view mirror, watching for shadows in amongst the trees. I told myself that I would be safe now. That I had done the right thing, handed it over to the people who knew what to do. Only the thought rang hollow, my stomach tight with the sense that I wasn't in control here, that Wolf would choose how much of a role I had to play, whatever my thoughts on the matter. Patrols will come by the house more regularly, Gray had said. I've spoken to Drew, emphasised to him the need to be there, to be watchful. My brother-in-law had arched his eyebrow, given me a wistful smile, Let's hope that gets through. You need me, I can be there in a hot minute, yes?

I wondered how many minutes Elizabeth Barrow had had between the realisation that she was in danger and the moment that she died.

I eased the car to a stop, pulling up beside Addie's SUV, turning the engine off. It felt like an ending, like my part was done. I wonder if Wolf felt the same?

Then the front door opened, spilling light across the deck, and Fleck came bounding down the front steps, a ripped-up stuffed duck clutched tight in his mouth. I looked up at the door, at the figure of Addie silhouetted against the light, and raised my hand in a wave. How much had Gray told her? Just how much trouble was I in?

I pushed open the driver's-side door, Fleck's nose burying itself in my side with a low whine of excitement. Not looking at him though, but looking beyond, to the treeline. Are you out there? Are you watching?

'Hey?' called Addie. 'You coming in?'

I breathed in a last drag of the bitter-cold air and climbed from the car, fingers entwined in Fleck's fur. I pushed the door closed, hurrying up the steps, trying to arrange my face, so that it did not scream out all of my secrets.

'Come on,' said Addie. 'It's freezing out there.'

I paused a moment to look over my shoulder, looking for shapes in the darkness. But it was only me and the dog and the twisting snow. And so I sighed, and shook my head and stepped into the light and the steady warmth of a log fire and the sugar-sweet smell of cookies baking. Addie hovered, reaching out a hand to take my wet coat, watching as I pulled off my slush-covered boots.

'You're here late,' I said, tugging at my recalcitrant right foot. 'Where are the girls?'

'Hmm?' She hung my coat on a peg, her voice a study of nonchalance. 'Oh, they're down in the family room watching *Trolls*. Mason is trying to figure out how to fart glitter. Come on into the living room, honey.'

It was in her tone, in the carefulness of her movements. All the warnings were laid out before me. Unfortunately, I was too stupid to see them.

My sister tucked her arm through mine, half leading, half dragging me towards the living room, my steps slowing as I neared, as the sound of the fire got louder, the smell of cookies stronger. My mother was sitting in the La-Z-Boy. The back of it was poker-straight, her hands flat on the arms of it, mouth a straight line. I glanced from her, to my brother, seated on the sofa, folded forward, elbows planted on his knees, fingers locked together. Very definitely not looking at me. And I looked at the coffee table, the pot of coffee, the four cups, fresh-baked cookies ringed on the good china plate.

Oh shit.

'What?' I asked, looking from sibling to sibling to parent. 'What's going on?'

'You wanna sit down, sweetie? Look,' my sister said, steering me towards the sofa, 'I made cookies. Oatmeal raisin. You want one?' Sometimes my sister has trouble remembering who is her child and who is not and so simply sets 'mother' as her default setting. 'We just thought we'd all have a little chat, is all.'

Fuck.

'Is this ...' I let out a strangled laugh. 'Is this an intervention?' I looked at my family, sinking to the sofa, mainly because I thought Addie might push me into it if I didn't. 'Seriously, guys, I know it's been rocky, but my Dr Pepper addiction is under control these days.'

No one laughed.

'Rosa,' said my mom, carefully, 'we know what you've been doing.'

I was dead. I didn't have to wait for Wolf to kill me. I was already dead.

'What ...' My stomach sat in my throat. 'What do you mean?'

'Canada,' muttered my brother, still not looking at me. 'We know about the DNA.'

Gray. I was going to kill him.

I stared at Addie, wondering just how much he had told her.

'You mustn't be angry with him,' said Addie, quickly. 'I bullied him into telling me. Sweetie, we know you've tracked down your ...' she hesitated, picking her way over thin ice, 'birth family. We thought ... We figured it would be a good idea to talk about it.'

'You figured,' muttered Drew.

'We're worried about you,' said my mother, quietly, her voice rough-edged, and I looked at her more closely, eyes red-rimmed with already shed tears. She picked at a handkerchief clasped tight in her fingers, and guilt billowed inside me.

'I'm fine, Mom,' I said, not even sure I was convincing myself.

'I feel like I don't know you any more.' Gone was the anger in her voice, the ever-present righteous indignation. She sounded quiet and small and so unlike my mother. 'And, Rosa, I'm frightened. You went off to Canada. You didn't tell anyone where you were going. If anything had happened to you there, Rosa, we would never have found you. We wouldn't have even known where to begin.' She looked at me then, a tear rolling down her cheek.

Nausea built up in me.

'We're just worried about you, is all,' said Addie, quietly.

And what could I say? That there was nothing to worry about? Well, that would be a big fat lie now, wouldn't it?

'The hell you thinking?' muttered Drew. 'These people, they left you on the street. You honest to God think you're going to have some kind of happy family reunion?'

I opened my mouth to say that given the decades-old deaths of most of my immediate family, a reunion get-together seemed unlikely. Then I shut it again, the realisation sinking in that Gray had not told them everything. A wash of relief. Then, choosing my path. Truth or lie?

'No, I just …'

My mother held up her hand. 'Rosa …' She took a deep breath, 'I understand that you feel you need to do this.' She dropped her gaze down to her lap. 'If I'm honest, I wish you wouldn't. I wish we could just go back, have things be just like they always were.'

I opened my mouth and my mother clucked at me, waving her hand to quiet me. 'Listen, child. I wish you didn't need to do this. But I understand that you do.'

I couldn't breathe.

'All that we ask of you, Rosa, is that you remember that family is more than blood. That for the whole of your life I have raised you and loved you, and I may not have been perfect, I know I made plenty of mistakes along the way, but I did the very best that I could for you. Look for these people if you must. But please don't forget that you already have a family, right here, where they have always been.'

I nodded slowly, not trusting myself to speak.

'Mom,' said Addie, softly.

My mother glanced at her, wiped a hand across her cheek and nodded briefly. 'I know, Addison. I haven't forgotten.'

I looked from one to the other. 'What?'

'There's something else, Rosa,' said Addie, carefully. 'Mom, she's been talking to people ...'

'James Beck,' said my mother, proudly, a flicker of the usual her forcing its way through. 'Was police chief. Retired now. But, back in the day, back when you were found, he was a lieutenant, down in Madison. Good man. He's kept in touch, over the years. Christmas cards and stuff.' My mother took a deep breath. 'He called me today, wanted to give me a heads-up. Seems he'd heard about your little Canada jaunt.' An acerbic edge crept its way into her words.

I frowned. 'How?'

Addie shrugged. 'Gray, I guess. Beck was his captain, back when he first started.'

'Okay?'

'He wanted to let me know,' said Mom, 'about your brother.'

Drew grunted beside me, shifted in his seat and I turned to look at him.

'No,' said Addie. 'Your other brother. Elliott.'

I sat up straighter then. 'What about him?'

Drew, the brother beside me, snorted. 'He's a thug.'

'Drew,' murmured Addie. 'Rosa, Chief Beck, he's gotten hold of Elliott's service record. He knows people. You know how it is. And it turns out, Elliott, he ...'

'He's an asshole,' supplied Drew. 'Dishonourable discharge. Guy beat the shit out of his commanding officer. Wound up with a term in military prison, then got booted out.'

'Andrew,' snapped my mother. 'That's enough.' She glared at him, then shifted her gaze to me. 'Chief Beck, he thought you ought to know. The thing is, Rosa, you're out there looking for this brother, and the truth is, you just don't know what you're getting into. Your brother, he is not a good man.'

Book Two

Book Two

Chapter 1

It had been seven days. One hundred and sixty-eight hours since I had run home from the Canadian snows. It felt closer to a year. Each hour stretching itself out endlessly, minute by minute punctuated with flashes of the empty body of Elizabeth Barrow, the sound of footsteps on stairs, the image of a figure in the shadows. I would have assumed that I would stop sleeping, that each night would see me propped upright, a book on my knees, something fantastic and comforting, my bedroom billowing with lights. Instead I had gone in the opposite direction, each day punctuated with a swamping exhaustion that dragged me into bed at a little past eight each evening, plunging me into a sleep that felt closer to a coma. I had thought that I would dream of Wolf. But instead I slept and slept and slept, with little memory of any of those limitless hours but the steady ever-present sense of running. Always running.

I stood on the front deck, looking out over the rolling hills, white stacked under heavy grey skies. The snow had been coming down hard the last couple of days, a low-pressure system that had swept down from the north, dumping a teenager-sized mound of snow in one twenty-four-hour period. They said it would get worse, that there was talk of an ice storm in the offing. I pulled my chin deeper into my padded jacket, the whistling wind scouring my cheeks.

'Why are they coming out here?' I asked. 'Why do they want to meet me?'

'They said they wanted to talk to you,' said Gray softly. He glanced across at me, snowflakes settling on his long eyelashes. 'It's nothing for you to worry about. I think they just want to get some information about your experiences. You know, with him.'

With Wolf.

In the distance, beyond the trees, where the road curled around the hill, headlights punched through the grey day. I lifted my chin, gesturing towards the car as it turned towards the house, vanishing from sight beneath the tunnel of the trees. 'Here they come.'

I watched the trees, waiting for the car to break through, my stomach wound up into a tight knot. I thought of Mom. She had been quieter since the 'intervention', softer, had made little mention of my family or my search. And yet I would catch her watching me, at times when she thought my attention was absorbed, her gaze full of worry. She would be done with her appointment now, would she have picked her way safely across slick sidewalks to my sister's waiting car, would they have made it home safe to Addison's? Perhaps I should have called, checked in, made sure everyone made it through safe with this weather and all. But I simply stood there, watching the Audi slow, gliding to a stop at the base of the front steps.

I watched as the car doors opened, first one, then the other. A man climbing out of the passenger side, good-looking, broad shoulders made broader by his thick winter coat. He looked up towards us, raising a hand in a wave. From the driver's side, a woman, smaller, slighter, buried beneath a thick woollen hat.

We waited there, in the blowing snow, as they trudged up the front steps, bodies slanted forward into the wind.

'Hey,' called Gray. 'Come on inside.'

My hands had begun to shake, shuddering against the insides of my pockets, and I kept my head low, gaze on the snow-slick deck, into the hall, the wall of heat jarring against my cheeks, tugging off my coat, shaking the snow from my hair, sucking in a deep breath. Reminding myself that I could do this. That although I was suddenly swamped by it, the feeling of being a kindergartener, watching the adults around me work, that I had survived thus far. My face flushed, irritation with myself sweeping the cold away.

'So ...' Gray pulled the door closed tight behind us, voice unnaturally jovial, 'Rosa, this is Captain Gabriel Otero from the NYPD.'

The dark-eyed man engulfed my small hand in his larger one, gave me a wide smile that made me blush.

'And this is Detective Sergeant Alice Parr from the Metropolitan police, London. England,' he added, re-dundantly.

The woman tugged the wool hat from her head, and, tucking it beneath her arm, reached out, taking my hand in hers. 'Rosa,' she said, rolling the r and turning my name into something I didn't recognise. 'Thank you so much for agreeing to talk with us.'

I stared at her. I attempted to pull my eyes down and away, but each saccade returned my gaze again and again to her face. She was scarred, a twisting map of fire that traced its way from the left side of her forehead, down across her cheekbone, pushing back her hairline, the mahogany choppiness giving way to an edging that was thin and wispy, proto-hair. But it wasn't that that made me stare. There was something about her, an edge impossible to define. In the way she spoke and the way her gaze tracked across you. It felt like she was unshakeable. Like she had walked through fire and come out the other side.

And, in comparison, I felt smaller. The little girl.

I forced my gaze away, leading the three of them through the hall, into the wide expanse of the living room, home and yet not home. The fire clambered across thick logs, popping and crackling, the heat from it stretching out across the room towards me. Fleck lay before it, head on his paws, feigning sleep, eyes half open, watching the visitors with barely disguised interest. I felt outside of myself, a drowning sense of unreality.

'You guys have a seat.' Gray gestured to the sofa, picking up the host ball that I was busy fumbling. 'You want a coffee or ...'

DS Parr shook her head. She perched on the edge of

the sofa, reaching a closed hand to Fleck to sniff, then ruffling beneath his chin. 'Hey, guy.' She looked back at me, smiled. 'Nice dog.'

I nodded stiffly, still feeling ever so young in her presence. Words bubbling up, and I clamped my teeth shut to stop them from spilling out. What happened to your face? Watching the way she held herself, with her chin raised up, shoulders straight, like this woman, she knew exactly who she was, like she didn't give a shit for the opinion of anyone else.

I sank into the La-Z-Boy, hands folded into my lap, and felt a sudden urge to curl up into the smallest of balls.

'So,' said the woman, 'Gray tells me you're doing a PhD in psychology?'

'Yes,' I said. 'The psychology of fraud.'

She looked at me then, long moments, considering. 'Interesting.' She glanced at Captain Otero, a moment of silent communication I could not decipher. 'So how did you get into that?'

At the moment she might as well have asked me why I had two arms instead of six. I shrugged, 'Just ... I find them interesting ...'

'Them?'

'People who play others. Who deceive them. Who become who other people want so that they can get their own way.' I thought of Canada and Rebecca Leland and a flush clambered up my cheeks. 'It's just interesting, is all,' I finished, lamely.

Interesting. Interesting. I was like a record player,

needle stuck in a groove. I coughed, could feel my cheeks flushing. 'So, um ...' How to say why the hell are you here without it sounding like an accusation? 'Gray said you needed to speak to me? I mean, I don't know how much I can tell you.'

The woman watched me, something behind her eyes, some calculation or other.

'Are you here because of Wolf?' I asked, giving up all efforts at diplomacy.

The man smiled, one side of his mouth hooking higher than the other, a calculated attempt to charm. 'We've been looking for him for some time.'

'Why?' I asked, bluntly.

Shocking I'd never been approached to work at the UN really.

It was like the sliding on of a mask, his smile becoming fixed, gaze wary. 'He is wanted in connected with another case.'

I opened my mouth, caught the woman's look, lips pursed, eyebrow raised, and closed it again. They were here to take information. Not to give it. Apparently.

Then she leaned forward, clasping her hands together, looking at me intensely. 'So, if I can ask, your experience with Jackson Wolf ... where did that begin?'

And so I told her, all that I knew and all that I didn't know. I give myself credit for telling her the hard bits too, of my RCMP badge, of Rebecca Leland. Although, given that Gray knew, that was probably credit I didn't deserve. And something flickered behind her eyes then, something changing in the way she looked at me.

Judgement, maybe? You couldn't blame her. I told her of the break-in and the fall and the figure that watched the house. Of the DNA and Canada and the visitor to the care home and the death of Elizabeth Barrow. I told her of my birth family's untimely demise and the disappearance of Clay Rutherford, and of a baby girl found at the base of the Capitol building. And as I spoke, she and the men, they sat in silence, three faces turned towards mine, the only other sound the crackling of the fire in the hearth, the wind buffeting against the windows.

Eventually, my voice petered out, worn and scraggly from the outpouring, and I fell silent, my gaze dropping to the hands still clasped tight in my lap. 'I left Canada. Like he told me to. I'm hoping that that will be enough.' I did not mention the phone call from the Military Locator Service. I'm going to claim poor memory. I'm lying.

DS Parr glanced at Captain Otero, one of those looks again, then back at me. 'So, just so I'm clear, the night of the break-in, do we know exactly what was taken?'

Gray cleared his throat. 'Some cash from the mother's room, drawers were turned out, but there were plenty of valuables left laying about, so we've been operating on the theory that it was a burglary that was interrupted once he realised someone was in the house.'

'There are other things too,' I said, quietly.

They looked at me, the three of them.

'A photo of me taken on my graduation day. A research paper I was editing, about what makes white-collar criminals kill. And some stuff from a folder, it had the information in it about my discovery, newspaper articles, things like that. My mom, she said there should have been a bunch of photographs in there, only most of them were missing. I can't be sure they were taken that night,' I allowed. 'They may just have gotten lost over the years, only …' He followed me to Canada, he went to the care home, he smashed up my car, he killed Elizabeth Barrow. I sat up a little straighter, forced myself to look at the faces looking at me, 'I think he took them.'

'The problem we have, obviously,' interjected Gray, 'is that this is all stuff that may have simply been misplaced, and we just have no way of knowing …'

'The research article,' said DS Parr, quietly, 'it was about why con artists kill?'

I nodded. 'There's something else, too.' I told her of the screenwriter, of his questions, of the IP address that told me that he was in fact Wolf.

The woman's face split into a wry smile, and she looked at Captain Otero, her voice low. 'He's trying to understand,' she murmured.

'Understand what?' asked Gray.

'Himself,' offered Captain Otero, quietly.

I looked from one to the other, wanting to ask, but knowing if I did that their expressions would slide shut again, that their mouths would seal.

'Okay,' said DS Parr, turning to face me again, 'so, the night of the break-in, you said it was likely he thought the house was empty. Did you have plans that night?'

'We were meant to be in Chicago.'

'And who knew about that?'

I shrugged. 'I don't know. I mean, it wasn't a secret. Anyone could have known.'

She drummed her fingernails together, then looked at Gray, at Captain Otero, back to me. 'Okay. I think he knew you were going. I don't know what specifically he was looking for when he came into the house. But, given what I know about Jackson Wolf... Rosa, I think it is highly likely that this man, that he is someone you already know.'

Chapter 2

I stood at the window, was dimly aware of them, my brother-in-law, the two detectives, hovering around the dining table, sifting through all that I had collected, about my family, about the tragedy, about Wolf. Was I supposed to involve myself? Or was my role exactly what it currently was, hovering in the space between the dining nook and living room, drowning in unreality?

I heard them muttering, about MO, victims, jarring terms when they are being applied to you. 'Am I in danger?' I blurted out, looking back at them. 'Is my family?'

The three of them exchanged glances, like a five-year-old had just asked for the truth about Santa. You tell her. No, you tell her. It was DS Parr who finally broke the silence.

'I think it's fair to say he can be a very dangerous man. So yes. Yes, I think you might be.'

I nodded, the information somehow not penetrating fully, and looked back out to the snow. 'I guess it would depend on whether harming me would serve any instrumental purpose for him. Whether it would do him any good. Psychopaths, they tend to be less reactive in terms of their aggression. It's not about anger for them. It's about what purpose violence will serve.' I gave out something that was supposed to be a laugh. 'So I suppose it depends on whether killing me is the instrumental choice.'

'Rosa ...' Gray began, his voice trailing away when it became clear to him that there really was nothing he could say.

DS Parr moved closer to me. 'So you're confident that's what he is? A psychopath?'

I shrugged, all nerd-based confidence vanished anew beneath the threat of imminent death.

'But you know about psychopaths, right, Rosa?' asked Gray, tone pleading almost. 'That's, like, what you do.'

'It's ... it's part of what I do. It can be a feature of fraud. It isn't always.' I was being disingenuous, overly modest.

Because, if you had asked me ten days ago if I could have spotted a psychopath, I would have told you yes.

But if DS Parr was right, if Wolf was someone I knew, then shouldn't I have been able to tell?

'His behaviours could fit the profile,' I allowed, grudgingly, my mind spilling inexorably on to the next question. I looked back at her, 'But if he is ... I don't know who he could be. If I've met him, if he's someone I know ... how have I not noticed?'

The woman gave a wry smile, lost in thought. 'Because, Rosa, he is just that good. There's something you need to understand – this is a game to him. And it's a game he has been playing for a very long time. You could stand next to him and never know that you are standing beside a monster.'

I nodded, giving myself the out. 'It can go that way, especially with psychopaths. Sometimes, an extended relationship with them, it can make it harder to spot the cues. They are good at playing a part. The more time you spend with them, the more chance they have to con you.'

She looked at me, sympathetic. 'You shouldn't feel bad. For not knowing. He's … he's conned an awful lot of people.'

'Alice.'

DS Parr turned towards Otero. He stood at the table still, in his hand the folder that I had 'borrowed' from Lilian.

'What?' she asked.

Wordless, he pulled the newspaper article from its cardboard sheath, the image of the barn, of my family burning inside it, the reds and oranges of the flame still vivid after all these years. 'It's here.'

'What?' I asked.

No one answered.

The New York cop moved to stand at her shoulder, handing her the sheet of paper, the room thick with silence as they read the words accompanying the photograph.

Finally, DS Parr looked up. 'Rosa, this is you? The baby they talk about, the one who died? That was you? This is what happened to your family?'

It felt strangely like pride. 'Yes.' Then, 'Why? What's

so important about that piece of paper?'

There was a hefty silence and for a moment it appeared that no one was going to answer, and then she looked up, her words reluctant. 'We've seen this image before. But we had no idea what it related to.' She stared at the article, deep in thought. Then she glanced at Otero, and set the newspaper cutting down on the tabletop. 'Okay, I need to show you something.'

Relief washed over me, accompanied by a spark of thrill. They were going to pull the curtain back, reveal the wolf behind. And I moved closer to the table, movements perhaps more eager than they should have been.

She reached into her messenger bag, pulling out a single sheet of paper.

'What is this?'

'I need you to take a look at this.' She handed it to me. 'It's a list of Wolf's known aliases. It's not exhaustive, but it is all we've been able to gather so far. See if you recognise any of them.'

I stared at her, disappointed, then down at the list, my gaze grazing the letters, nothing yet punching through the fog.

Then a flutter, the faintest stirring of recognition.

'I . . .'

'What?'

I handed her the list, stepped back from the table. 'Give me a minute.'

I hurried up the stairs, Fleck following close behind me, breath hot against my leg as I pushed open the door of my bedroom. I kept my paperwork, the kind of stuff critical to lead a grown-up life, in a shoebox in my closet. Because, obviously. I pulled the box out, sank down onto my bed, Fleck parking himself to the floor beside me, tongue lolling. I sifted through it until I found my PhD paperwork. A scholarship application, the letter of notification of a grant being awarded, and then, at the bottom of it all, a letter from the university, confirming payment. And in the midst of that, a name.

Edward Griffin.

I sat on the bed, stared at the letter, a tremble beginning in my fingers. Had I looked at this before? Had I ever paid attention? After all, all that had mattered to me was the simple fact of its being, that my studies were paid for, that I would have an if not generous, then comfortable stipend. Had I ever looked before at where that came from?

No. This, it had to be a coincidence. Because I had applied for the scholarship, had gone through all the proper channels. Had received an email, confirming my acceptance. And ... A new memory brought a rush of heat to my cheeks. Because there had been another email, hadn't there. One that made no sense. 'We're sorry to inform you that you have been unsuccessful in your application to our scholarship program.' Only, I had been successful. And I had called the number on my acceptance letter and a man had answered and ... and he had been soothing and kind and said they'd had a glitch in the computer system that had sent the emails out, and that I shouldn't worry, that I had been accepted and everything had been taken care of.

I had called the number on the acceptance letter.

Not the number on the application.

It was him.

It was Wolf.

They were waiting for me, still gathered around the kitchen table, looked like they had not moved since I left.

I handed the scholarship paperwork to DS Parr, pointing to the name.

'Edward Griffin,' I said, quietly.

She studied it. 'He's been paying for your scholarship?' She looked back at me. 'How long?'

'Eighteen months.' My words felt flat. Not my own.

A long silence, then Gray putting our thoughts into words. 'Why?' he asked. 'Why would he do that?'

I waited for someone to answer, willing them to. But no one looked at me in return.

Then Parr said, 'The newspaper, it says that you had an older brother, that he was away at the time of the fire.'

'Yes,' I said, 'Elliott.'

'You have any idea where he is now?'

I shook my head. 'I haven't been able to find him. I know he was in the military.'

'You know that because ...'

'His best friend from high school, Sadiq. He told me.'

'Sadiq, he happen to mention what he was like? I mean, was he a smart kid?'

I nodded. 'I think so. There was talk of him going

on to be a lawyer. Then, you know, what happened … happened.' I hesitated, the words that had formed stumbling on my tongue. 'I … He has a record. Elliott. Assault on a senior officer.' Then, inevitably, the justification, 'I mean, after what he went through, it's not really surprising …' My voice frittered out, suddenly aware that no one was listening to me.

A yearbook lay on the table, already open, and DS Parr pulled it closer. She studied it, face heavy in a frown, then passed it to Otero. 'It could be.'

'What?'

He studied the photograph, nodded. 'You're right. It could.'

Then a sinking realisation. 'You think … you think Wolf is my brother? You think he's Elliott?'

No one answered.

Then DS Parr smiled, a kind, staged smile. 'You know, I hope you don't think I'm cheeky, but I'd kill for a cup of tea.'

I nodded, turning towards the kitchen, a childish sense that if I was fast enough, if I made the tea well enough, then they would trust me, would let me in. And so I filled the kettle from the tap, careful, set it on the stove, careful, and all the time the wild snow swirling beyond the window and the sense of eyes searching through the blizzard, watching.

I lit the stove. Could it be Elliott? I thought of what Sadiq had said, of my careful, quiet, clever brother. And felt a strange warmth. That he somehow cared for me. That the fall, that had been an accident. The flowers, the Sorry, making that clear. I batted away an image of Elizabeth Barrow in her overstuffed home. He didn't want to hurt me, just to guide me, to steer me along the correct course of action.

And it settled over me, a quiet confidence, that, one way or another, Wolf and I were inextricably connected.

The kettle began to sing, and I picked it up, careful, poured the steaming water into the pot, careful. Arranged cookies on a plate, just so. I set out mugs, wishing I had cups, saucers of delicate bone china, placing it all on a tray, hefting it carefully, and stepping around the inert form of Fleck, who had followed me to the kitchen.

'Sorry,' I said, 'I'm rubbish at tea.' I nodded towards the sofas, my best hostess voice. 'Please, do sit down.' I carefully set the tray down onto the wooden coffee table, aware now of the woman's gaze on me. I sank onto the chair across from her, my fingers inadvertently moving to the hem of my sweater.

'Rosa,' said DS Parr, 'I need to ask you, just what are you hoping to get from this?'

That was the question, wasn't it. What did I want? And I'm not sure that I had the answer. But then again, it wasn't about the truth. Because if I said too much now, let slip the wrong thing, then they would smile politely at me and drink my oh-so careful tea and then they would shut me out, and I would never understand just what it was that had happened to my life.

'I want ... I want to know what happened to me.' I chose my words with care. 'I need to understand, I don't know, why it all changed, I guess.' Because sometimes it pays to be the little girl, I allowed tears to spring to my eyes. 'How could we go from where we were to ... that.' I picked up the newspaper, a lost child looking for answers, both a lie and the truth. 'I want to know why.' And then more truths, inadvertent almost. 'And, I guess, in spite of everything, I just want to find him.' I looked at the list, the names familiar enough that it felt that I had always known them. Then I looked up at DS Parr. 'Whoever he is, I just want to find my brother.'

She nodded slowly, looked down at her hands. 'Rosa ... I understand this is personal for you. I do have sympathy for your situation. But ... I just want you to be careful. I ... I have some experience with him, with what he's capable of.' Was there the slightest break in her voice, or was that my imagination, looking for weakness in steel? She looked up at me, her gaze pinning me in place. 'It's important that you get it, I mean really get it. Wolf, he is a con man. He is clever, he is cunning and he is very, very dangerous.'

Chapter 3

I could hear the television, the canned laughter snaking its way up the stairs from the living room, bleeding beneath my door. Every now and again, I'd hear my mother's voice, words lost, only the tone remaining. She spoke as if to herself. My brother was down there, in body if not in spirit, settled in the La-Z-Boy, gaze locked on whatever cacophonous show they were watching. Drew, my knight in shining flannel.

I leaned back in my desk chair, my literature review untouched before me. I tried to breathe. If I concentrated hard enough, I would be able to quiet the bustle of my brain, the tightness in my chest. I threw my pen onto the desk in front of me, suppressed the urge to scream.

'We don't know where he is,' DS Parr had said. 'We don't know what he's planning. But we know he represents a danger to you.'

I'd opened my mouth, a protest on the tip of my tongue. That he was my brother, after all. And that changed things, surely?

But then I saw the woman's face, expression brooking no argument.

'We're looking for him. But for now, best be safe.' She had been gathering up documents, sliding them into her messenger bag, no longer looking at me. 'Best you work from home for the time being.' She looked at me then, a parent scowling at a child. 'I don't want you going anywhere alone, okay?'

No. Not okay. Of course it's not okay.

I'd smiled, working hard to make it reach my eyes. 'No problem.'

And so they had gone. Off hunting the Wolf. And here I sat. The little girl once more.

I pushed back my chair, moved towards the window, the night dark outside, flecked with light flickers of falling snow. Quested for that feeling of being watched, but came up empty. Was it wrong that I somehow missed it?

I told myself that it was over. That I had learned all that I could. And isn't that what I had wanted, all along? I knew who I was, where I came from. Why I was set adrift. I knew that it was Clay who had brought me here, even if the why of that remained out of reach. That what we had suffered had been sufficient to turn Elliott into a wolf.

It was over. I was done.

My phone pinged and I grabbed for it.

A text from Gray, in answer to my own.

No news. Think they've gone to Canada now to follow up on the Barrow case. Try not to worry. The professionals have got it now.

Irritation sparked and I threw my phone back onto the desk, my gaze returning to the snow.

As she was leaving, DS Parr had stopped at the doorway, had paused in the zipping of her coat and studied me. 'You do understand,' she'd said, 'this guy, he's a monster.'

And I had nodded, tight-lipped.

I leaned closer to the window, the outside cold seeping through the edges of the frame. The thing was, it was they who did not understand. Monster, after all, is simply a shorthand for that which we cannot explain. The detectives, they were looking at him only through the lens of his crimes. But me, I was different, my lens shining a refracted light. And what I saw was not a monster, rather a young man, his life torn apart by the catastrophic actions of his stepfather.

They didn't understand that violence begets violence, that youngsters who experience violence are more likely to grow up to use violence. That losing the entirety of your family to familicide can warp everything within you.

I tapped my fingernails against the window frame, cold pressing against the pads of my fingers. The detectives believed that what Wolf needed was a trap. But they said themselves that even he didn't understand why he did what he did. So perhaps, rather, what he needed was someone who did.

I sat back down at my desk, pulling the cardboard storage box, heavy with notebooks, towards me. Reorienting. Go back to your life, they had said. Go back to being who you are. I pulled my notebooks, hundreds and hundreds of pages of my handwriting, curled and slanted. Gathered notes from a lifetime of psychology articles.

'You do it your way,' I muttered. 'I'll do it mine.'

I opened the yearbook, propped it in front of me, Elliott's face looking back at me, light and hopeful, back before it all changed.

'Think,' I murmured to myself. 'This is what you do.' I studied my brother's photograph. 'What have you become?'

She called him a con man. A white-collar criminal at heart then, crimes turning red when the proper pressure was applied. But then, wasn't such crime always about the pressure, when you really thought about it? Some great weight that settles down on top of you. A job lost, a medical bill that you just can't pay, your checking account showing zero and the mortgage due.

And for Elliott, alone in the world suddenly, an orphan and adrift, how much pressure must there have been then? How much of a weight, simply to survive?

And then, add to that, opportunity. Because no weight is sufficient without there being, somewhere, an open window. A wallet left in plain view. A business account offering easy access. A fifty-dollar bill falling from the pocket of the man in front. Elliott, he was smart, personable. And to have had the success that he has had dipping and diving in and out of identities and lives, he had the capacity to adapt, to seek out opportunities, weaknesses in the system, where fraud became a possibility.

So the final piece of the puzzle. Rationalisation.

Well, it's not much money. The business can afford this. The thing is everyone does this. The twisting of facts to make actions acceptable.

What did Elliott say to himself? What story did he use to make it all okay?

'He's not a monster,' I muttered. 'He's my brother.'

Trying not to think of Elizabeth, of her overstuffed house, her crooked smile, her faint smell of cinnamon.

I blew out a breath. Turn the lens, look at it from a different angle.

Elizabeth had threatened him, knew something he didn't want her to know. For someone like Elliott, for someone whose life was so finely balanced, the threat of exposure, well, that was like a threat to life, a challenge that cut right to the core of existence. So when you thought of it that way, he had lashed out, a desperate bid to protect the life that he had built.

I drummed my fingernails on the desk. The professionals have got it now. Which was my brother-in-law's code for: be a good girl, stay in your lane, don't do anything too ... Rosa.

Okay.

Sure.

I shuffled through my collected papers, the folder labelled simply 'family'. And I pulled out a number, took a deep breath and dialled.

Sadiq answered on the second ring. 'Hello?'

I froze for a moment, caught in a place I had not thought through. Because he knew me. But he didn't know this version of me. Wolf's sister indeed.

I took a deep breath, opted for the truth.

'Sadiq, you know me as Rebecca Leland. We met in Toronto last week.' My voice shook. 'I'm afraid I lied to you. My real name is Rosa Fisher. I'm Elliott Lynch's sister.'

Nothing. Just a staticky emptiness across the line. He had hung up on me.

Then, 'Yes. I just spent an interesting couple of hours with some people who know you. The Rosa Fisher version of you at least. Parr and Otero. They filled me in.' His words were clipped, all hard edges.

My stomach clenched itself up tight. 'I'm sorry,' I offered, limply.

'You understand you could be arrested? Impersonating a police officer. You get that, right?'

'I get that.' I paused, this time didn't have to try for the contrition that flowed out. 'I'm really sorry. I ... I just wanted to understand, what happened to me, to my family. It ... I know this isn't an excuse ... it just felt like the only way at the time.'

Then a different silence, softer. A sigh. 'Yeah. I get it. I don't like it,' he said, voice stern, 'but I do get it.' Another sigh, sadder. 'So, Rosa Fisher, what can I do for you this time?'

'Same thing, I suppose,' I said, carefully. 'I want to ask you about Elliott.'

'Didn't we already do that?' he asked. 'Also, the detectives, they just spent the last two hours asking me about Elliott.' He hesitated. 'Do they know you're calling me?'

296

I opened my mouth, closed it again. A sinking sense of the futility of lies, the salvation of the truth. 'No,' I admitted. 'They … they're looking for him. Elliott. They say he's done some things, bad things.'

'So I hear. You think they're wrong?'

'No. I just think that maybe that's not all there is to know. And that maybe … I mean, you knew him before … before it all went wrong. Maybe you can help me understand how he became who he is now.'

Silence. Then, 'Yes, I guess I'd want to know the same if I was in your shoes. Okay. Go ahead.'

'When he found out, Elliott I mean – when he learned about the family, about what happened to them, how did he react?'

Sadiq blew out a long breath. 'You know, I still dream about it? All these years later, still hasn't left me. It was the morning after. We'd just finished breakfast and were heading out for the day, and one of the teachers – Mr Barbery – he comes over to us, says that he needs to speak to Elliott. Tells me I should probably come too. And I'm thinking that we're in trouble, that he knows about the beers we snuck into our room last night, that we're about to end up in the shit. And he takes us into this conference room, place is all empty but for us, and he makes us sit down, and then he tells us.'

'What did he tell you?'

'No one knew then, you know, how bad it was. No one had figured out that it was the dad.' He paused. 'Your dad. He just said there'd been a fire. A bad one. That Elliott's family had been caught up in it. That they had all gone to be with Jesus. Those were the words he used, because I know for a moment I didn't get it, just didn't understand what he meant. And then I figured it out and I thought, Mr Barbery, he must have gone crazy. No way Elliott's whole family just died, just like that. And Elliott, he just sat there and sat there. I mean, even after I'd figured out that it was the truth, he's still just sitting there, and Mr Barbery, he's looking freaked, like he just doesn't know what to do now, because Elliott, he's just not reacting. Then the kid, he just folded, I mean, like his head just dropped to his knees and he started screaming. It was crazy after that. I guess I don't remember much from there, just bits and pieces. But Elliott, I mean, I'm a cop, I've seen lots of people get bad news, lots of people in pain. I don't know that I've ever seen anyone as cut up as Elliott was. He just lost it. I tell you, it was like everything, all of who he was, just left his body with that scream. After that, all that was left behind was an empty shell.' He fell silent for long moments. 'Bad. It was really bad.'

Tears had begun to pool. I closed my eyes, one hand gripping on to the cool of the windowsill. Sadiq was right, wasn't he? Elliott had lost everything. And when he began again, it was as someone new. No wonder then that identity was so malleable to him. He had learned early that who you are can vanish in the blink of an eye.

'Did he mention me? The baby, I mean.'

'I remember him saying that you hadn't gotten to live at all. How unfair it was. Seemed like he couldn't bring himself to talk about you much, like it was just too painful.'

'Did he ever mention Clay to you?'

He paused, taking stock. 'Clay? Clay Rutherford?'

'Yes.'

'No. Should he have?'

I didn't answer.

Sadiq sighed again, 'Look, Rosa ... That Parr woman, she told me about him. Elliott, I mean. About what they think he's been doing. Whoever he is now, that's not your brother. That's not the Elliott I knew. This thing your dad did, it broke him, turned him into someone he would have hated once. I know why you're asking these things. I get it. But don't fall into the trap of thinking that just because he's your brother, just because he's been hurt, that you can help him. If he is who they say he is, if he's done what they say he's done, he's dangerous. And there's nothing you can do to help him.'

I nodded, gaze once again on the falling snow. 'I know,' I said. 'I just need to understand.'

'I get that,' he said, gently. 'Look, I'm here. And now that I know who you actually are, I want to help. So, if there's anything else I can do, any questions you need answered, just reach out. Yeah?'

'Yeah,' I said. A tear spilled. 'Thank you.'

I hung up. Minutes ticking by. The clank of pipes. The sound of running water from somewhere within the house. Frozen in this moment. At the bifurcation of a path into two.

Left or right, Rosa?

I turned from the window, kicking off my slippers as I went, bare feet all but silent on the floor. The floorboards threatened but did not groan. I knew them well enough to know where the pressure should be applied. I eased my bedroom door, looked out into the dimly lit hall. The lights downstairs had been switched off. A solitary line of light seeping beneath the bathroom door, the sound of the shower running. I walked along the hallway, keeping tight to the wall where the floorboards were quietest, and eased my way into my brother's bedroom. The spare room in truth, but he was here often enough that it had always remained Drew's bedroom. Felt my way to his chest of drawers, third drawer down, and felt inside it.

The laptop was old and slow. Had been Addison's once, before she had upgraded, gifting it to Drew in the wild hope that she could draw him forth into the twenty-first century. It had been a spectacular failure. The laptop was ringed with circles, the marks from coffee mugs, dust in its clasps, so rarely was it opened. I slipped the laptop under my arm and eased my way back to my room.

It took far longer than I had expected. A dead battery, a hundred or so updates. Just waiting, waiting, for technology to catch up with my need for it. And then, finally, the screen oozing to life.

I blew out a long breath. There was still time to turn back. To turn a different path.

But there wasn't really. I'm not sure that there ever had been.

Because I was me, and because I needed to find my brother before anyone else did.

I opened Drew's email, a troubling collection of loan opportunities, of Russian brides and erectile dysfunction drugs. And I typed out an email, addressing it to my own email account. And I prayed he was still watching.

Wolf,
I need to see you. Just you and me. No police. Meet me at Monona Terrace, 10 p.m. tomorrow.
    I know who you are.
    Rosa.

Chapter 4

The cold was breathtaking, a wicked wind kicking up across the almost frozen Lake Monona. It was hard to think in it, hard to allow your brain to work its way up from the baseline recognition of just how damn cold it was. I pulled my chin further into my tightly wound scarf, trying to suppress the shivers that shook me, and shifted around in a 360-degree arc, my gaze roaming across the empty parking lot.

10.03 p.m.

There was still time. No reason to think at this point that he would not show. I felt for my cellphone, a force of habit, that sudden sinking feeling at the emptiness of my pocket. But of course it was empty. My cell still sat on my desk at home.

It had been so reasonable, the need for an early night. After all, I had been through a lot. Mom had brushed my hair back from my forehead, letting her hand rest upon my cheek. She had taken my hand, guided me to the foot of the stairs, like I was a kindergartener, like I required shooing towards bedtime. You go on up now. Everything is fine now. Drew and I, we're right down here. You get some good sleep. A thought, then – You want some cocoa? I could bring you some up?

It had felt to me that I was playing a part in a play.

No, I said. No cocoa. I had tried to look grateful, had tried to feel grateful. I forced a weary smile. Thanks, Mom.

She had stroked my cheek.

And I had trudged slowly up the stairs to bed, the feeling of my mother's gaze heavy on my back. Had closed my bedroom door tight behind me, sighed heavily.

And then a pivot, from little girl to ... what? Lunatic, probably. Had pulled a pair of sneakers on, had stuffed my bed with pillows, like this was Alcatraz and I was Clint Eastwood. Had eased the window open, a blast of icy-cold air buffeting me. The distant sound of the television, of my mother's voice, a steady stream of one-sided conversation. Out onto the ladder I had left propped beneath my window. Picked my way around the house in a wide, looping arc, along the tree-tunnelled drive towards the road. A car idled there, lights off.

'You know I don't like this, right?'

Eve's voice floated out to meet me as I tugged open the passenger door, shivering in my inappropriate sweater. I slid inside, easing the door shut, and gratefully took the thick parka she handed me.

'Here. As requested. This is crazy. You know that, right?'

I tugged the borrowed jacket on, the blast of hot air from the heater suddenly suffocating. 'Probably,' I

303

agreed. I shivered, glanced across at her. 'Appreciate you helping though.'

She snorted, pulling away onto the snow-bound road. 'Someone's got to make sure you don't wind up dead.'

I nodded, looking out into the darkness ahead. 'You know you can't come with me, right. You've got to stay out of sight. Else he'll rabbit.'

Eve pursed her lips. 'You going to get in trouble for this?'

'Not if no one finds out,' I said, grim.

I stamped my feet, shaking the snow from my sneakers. I should be afraid. Any rational person standing about in an empty parking lot on the shores of Lake Monona in the freezing darkness, they would be afraid. I listened, straining to hear the crunch of footsteps in snow. Turned on the spot. The distant lights of cars on John Nolen Drive, slow-moving and few and far between. Was he in one of those? I looked across the parking lot, orange street lamps puncturing the dark. Up at the looming shadow of the parking ramp, its concrete layers all but empty at this hour on this day.

I should be afraid. He was, after all, a killer. And yet all I could feel was a chirruping sense of anticipation. That I was about to meet my brother.

10.10 p.m.

He would come. He would check the area first, would make sure that I was alone. That this was not some kind of elaborate police sting, a SWAT team waiting in the wings. He would circle about, would check from all angles, making sure that he was safe, that he had an escape route, that I was where I said I was. It was, after all, what I would do.

He would come.

I paced, trudging slowly, backwards and forwards, the cruel wind from across the lake yanking at me. It was okay. This. It was a rational choice, when you considered all the facts, was in fact the only thing I could have done.

I almost believed myself.

10.15 p.m.

He wasn't coming.

Then a feeling, my hand shaking within my pocket. The odd sensation of disconnection, a fleeting thought, perhaps I was having a stroke. Then I remembered. The burner phone. I had grabbed it from my desk drawer, had shoved it into my jeans pocket, an insurance policy against my own madness. I slid my hand beneath my borrowed jacket, pulling it free.

Who the hell would be calling me on this?

Who the hell had this number?

'Hello?'

A silence, then a voice, heavily corrupted, 'Hello, Rosa.'

I stopped, facing out towards the frozen lake, face hot in spite of the searingly cold wind. A spurt of adrenaline twisting my stomach up into a painful knot.

I fought to keep my voice level. 'Can I assume that this is Jackson Wolf?'

A pause, then, 'You can.'

'I thought we were going to meet,' I said, calmly.

'Best not.' The mechanical voice cut through me, sparking gooseflesh to spring up across my arms, my neck.

'Please,' I said, cajoling. 'I came alone. Just like I said I would.'

'I can see that.'

Then the first real wave of fear washed over me. I turned on the spot, looking for him, seeing only emptiness and shadows. And for the first time, the sense of what I had done hit me. The realisation settling, that I could die here today.

'Where are you?' I asked, fighting to keep my voice even.

'Don't worry about that,' said the voice. 'You're not being a great friend to Eve. Leaving her alone up there on Wilson.'

Another wave of fear, panic tinging its edges. Had he done something to her? Had he hurt her?

I pushed it down, gathered myself together. Because panic, that was what he wanted, wasn't it? To push me into emotion, to bring my ability to think and to reason to a crashing halt. I breathed, in and out. Felt my feet against the snow. The wind against my face.

'You've been following me,' I said.

Silence.

'Can you tell me why?' I asked, quietly.

A soft, mechanical laugh. 'Maybe it's because you're interesting, Rosa.'

'Can I see you?' I asked. 'I know you're here. Will you come and meet me?'

'I can't do that.'

'Why not? I thought you could do anything you wanted. That's what they say, anyway. That you can be anyone, do anything.'

'Touché. Fine. Let's say instead I'm not going to do that.'

My gaze swept the lakefront, the parking lot. Then landed back on the parking ramp, its curved layers of concrete.

There.

I turned towards the parking structure, addressing my words towards it. Towards him.

'I think I understand,' I said, slowly.

A pause. 'Understand what?'

'What happened to you. How you came to do ... what you did?'

He fell silent for long moments. Then, 'What is it you think you understand?'

I took a deep breath. 'I think that you're my brother.'

It seemed to me then that the shadows within the ramp pulled deeper.

'I don't think you're what they say you are. You have to believe that. I know that you've done things. Things that I'm sure you didn't want to do. And I understand. I know you felt like you had to. In order to survive. Just ... please, let me help you.'

My heart thrummed in my throat.

A heavy sigh. 'Rosa. I need you to stop this. I need you to leave it alone.' The voice fell silent again, then, 'Please don't make me hurt you.'

A click and then he was gone.

I took off running, pulling my feet through the snow. Towards the ramp. No thought now, just pure flight. Slip-sliding on the concrete spiral. Floor one, a concrete cavern, dim-lit orange. Empty but for me. Breath raged in my chest, my thighs burned with the exertion.

He was here. He was here.

I felt like panic. All thought gone now, just pure fear remaining.

But there was no shadowed figure, no wolf waiting in the wings.

I stopped on the top deck, face burning, hands on knees. And, slowly, as my heartbeat eased its thunder, the edges of a thought began to push its way into my consciousness.

The mechanical words, his voice distorted by some device you could buy at Radio Shack.

But the thing was, there was only one reason why he would need to do that.

DS Parr was right.

He was someone I knew.

Chapter 5

Blue lights punched through the darkness, blinking swirls against the black. They cut through the shadowed arms of the trees, there and then gone again. A portent of danger ahead.

'Oh, shit,' muttered Eve. She slowed the car, her instinct to keep her distance as pronounced as mine to rush forward.

'Hurry,' I murmured.

The car rounded the corner, the treeline giving way to empty space. My house aglow with lights in room after room. A figure pacing across the front porch, back and forth. Gray, a phone to his ear, face precipitously aged. Police cars, two, three.

My stomach twisted.

I jumped from the car as Eve steered it to a rolling halt, and ran towards my brother-in-law, taking the porch steps two at a time.

'What is it?' I shouted. 'What happened? Is it Mom?'

'Holy shit.' Gray let the phone slide from his ear. 'Rosa. Jesus. Are you okay? Did he take you? How did you ... Are you hurt? Nora! Nora! She's okay. Nora. She's here.'

Mom came hurtling through the already open front door and threw herself on me, wrapping me up in a bear hug. 'Baby girl, baby girl. Are you okay? How did he get you? Did he hurt you? Is it ...'

'I'm fine, Mom.' I sucked in a breath, drowning in the heavy scent of roses and Momness, her wide chest pressed into my face. 'I ...'

'But what happened, I mean ...'

I should lie. I should say he took me, that I managed to escape.

I should tell the truth.

I looked up at my mother's face, red-blotched from tears, eyes swollen and heavy, looking searchingly into mine. The sudden realisation that she would want me to lie, would rather a kind untruth than the burden of her daughter not being who she wanted her to be.

'I ...' I pulled backwards, creating a distance from the woman who had raised me. 'I just ... I needed to get out. It all got too much for me, what with being watched all the time and feeling like a prisoner in my own home. So I ... I just asked Eve to come get me. That's all. I wanted to go for a drink. Catch up. You know, just be normal for a while.'

My mother had stepped back, her hands gripping my arm, the pressure of her thumbs painful. Was studying me, as if she had never seen me before. 'You ... you left?'

I did not have to work hard for contrition. 'I'm sorry. I didn't mean to worry anyone.'

'I ...' Her gaze left me, landing somewhere over my

shoulder, and I turned to see Eve, looking terrified. 'You came to get her? So she could go drinking?'

Eve looked at me, face tight, then nodded, once. 'I thought she could use a break.' She bowed her head. 'We didn't mean to cause ...' She waved vaguely at the police cars, the flashing blue lights. 'All this.'

My mother drew back, let go of my arms, her nostrils flaring, lips pressed vanishingly tight together. 'You have both behaved extremely irresponsibly. I am disappointed in you both.'

Eve dropped her head, fingers picking at the toggle on her coat.

'Mom.'

'No. This was a very selfish thing to do. I thought you were more mature than this, Rosa. I really did.' She turned her back on me, throwing back over her shoulder, 'It's time you grew up. Stopped acting like a child.'

I could feel it, sticking in my throat, everything I wanted to say, from sorry to screaming. But I kept my lips sealed shut, ducked my head down, watching as my mother swept back inside the house.

'Sorry, Gray,' I muttered.

He shook his head. 'Gotta say, I'm surprised. Didn't think you were the type. Eve, best you get yourself on home. Rosa, I think we'll call it a night here. I gotta call off the troops, let them know it was a false alarm.'

Heat stained my cheeks.

I nodded, watched him turn away. Shared a quick look with Eve, the you-owe-me clear from her expression. I watched as she walked back to her car, doing her best to be inconspicuous. Watched as the first of the police cars pulled away. Could hear Gray's voice, loud in the darkness. 'Yeah, seems they thought a night out would be a good idea. I don't know. I know. What can I say? Kids, huh?' Felt an overwhelming urge to throw something.

As Eve started the engine, she threw me a quick, sympathetic look, and then she too was gone.

I turned, walked quietly up the stairs, my mother's voice, loud from the kitchen, the words 'foolish', 'spoiled' floating up behind me. I let myself into my bedroom, closed the door quietly behind me and kicked my trash can across the floor.

I sank onto the bed, let my head rest in my hands. It had all been for nothing. They were right. It had been wildly irresponsible, a foolish gambit. I had boxed myself in now, had guaranteed myself a seat on the sidelines.

My cellphone, a chastising banner – twenty-six missed calls.

I ran my hands through my hair, fighting back the urge to scream. But that was just the panic talking, and now was not the time for that.

Now was the time to problem-solve, and for that I would have to be calm.

I stood before my desk, focusing on the palms of my hands, their pressure against the cool of the wood, of the sound of car doors slamming and engines dwindling into the distance, of my mother's heavy footsteps, the slamming of her bedroom door. Then the silence.

I breathed out, slowly.

I had to find him. I had to understand, to understand him, what had happened to me. I had to find the answers to my questions. And I had to explain him to the world.

He was, after all, my brother.

I pulled out my desk chair, sat down slowly, the back of it groaning with the weight of me, and looked at the yearbook, the photograph of my brother with his tentative smile.

Who are you? I thought of the distorted voice across the phone line. The voice beyond it, the real one, stripped of its mechanical edges, what would that sound like? My stomach gave a little flip, as my mind parsed through faces, names, any man I had ever met, at least the ones impressive enough to have etched themselves on my memory. Are you in amongst them? Have I spoken to you in a coffee shop? Exchanged work discoveries with you?

It was a crawling feeling of unease, a further flipping on end of my world. I'm not who I thought I was. Old news now. And now an extra layer, that someone around me is a liar, a con man. A murderer.

The London detective. She'd said that he had done this before, that he was good at playing this game. So then, don't focus on him. If he's that good, he will have covered his bases, established a solid façade.

What if, instead, you looked at the victim?

When forensic accountants are investigating red-collar crimes, murders that are committed because the perpetrator has a need to keep a fraud hidden, they are advised to look at the victim and to ask themselves the question – what did they know that could have posed a threat?

I pulled a notepad towards me, flipping open onto a clear white page, and scribbled the name Elizabeth Barrow at the head of it. He had killed her for a reason. But what?

I thought of her email. It's about Jackson Wolf. But … how did she even know the name Jackson Wolf. I had never heard of it before that night, before the call from the care home, the flight back to my grandmother.

And then it hit me. Anne. I had asked Anne if she knew the name.

I searched through my papers, looking for the number. Dialled, and only after the ringing began considered the time. A little after 2 a.m.

Shit.

'Hello?' Her voice sounded sleep-heavy. And perhaps a little fearful.

But then no one ever called at 2 a.m. with good news, did they?

'Anne, I'm sorry for the late hour. It's Rebecca Leland,' I said, without thought. 'RCMP.'

A long pause, presumably while she pulled herself awake. The sound of shuffling, of a light snapping on. 'Is there a problem?'

'No problem. Just a quick follow-up question.'

'Okay …'

'In reference to Mrs Barrow. I was just wondering … you remember I asked you if you knew the name Jackson Wolf?'

A silence, then, 'Sure.'

'Did you mention that name to Elizabeth?'

I could hear a shuffling on the other end, a yawn. 'I saw her, I guess, the following morning. Told her what you'd said. About Jackson Wolf.'

My stomach tightened. 'And what did she say?'

'She didn't really say anything. Just ... she just kind of went quiet, and said she had to go. And she scuttled off. I guess my impression was that she knew him.'

Chapter 6

I slept for an hour. Two at the most. An uneasy sleep, punctured by unsettling dreams that would vanish as soon as I attempted to reach for them. Gave up at 6 a.m and allowed myself a long hot shower, an attempt to wash it all away, doomed to fail. I dressed slowly, jeans, a thick shawl-necked sweater, and pulled my hair into a loose plait. My mind hummed.

I could keep it to myself, hold the information close like a prize. I had a sudden image of Golum curled about the ring. Precious.

I wiped condensation from the steamed-up bedroom window. It had stopped snowing overnight, but it lay heavy still, mounded piles of it, and an icy wind crept its way around the wooden frame.

Elliott. My brother. He had killed Elizabeth because she had figured it out, had connected him to Jackson Wolf.

And yet I was his sister. Whatever else he was, he was family. And he had no one, no one looking to help him.

I pulled on my winter boots. I had to find him. One way or another.

The kitchen smelled of cinnamon, Drew chewing

on a bagel, standing, leaned up against the counter. He looked at me over the top of it, an eyebrow raised. 'Didn't expect to see you up so early.'

I forced a smile. 'Couldn't sleep.' The kitchen mess from the night before had been all tucked away, the counters shining brightly. 'Where's Mom?'

Drew drained his coffee. 'Basement. She couldn't sleep either. She's already rage-cleaned the kitchen. She's going after the family room now.' He set his cup down, giving me a long look. 'Do yourself a favour, kid, and stay out of her way today. She's pretty damn pissed.'

I nodded, my stomach clenching. 'Hey, can you do me a favour? Take me over to Addie's?'

'You're only going to Addie's though, right? Not going to hop on a Greyhound to Chicago, have the place swarming with cops again?'

'Just Addie's,' I said. 'Come on. No doubt she wants to yell at me too. Best get it over and done with.'

A crash worked its way up from downstairs, then the sound of Mom swearing ferociously.

Drew pulled a face. 'Probably a good idea. I'll go brief the dragon. You ... you just stand right there, okay?'

I was only going to my sister's. What harm was there in that?

Drew's jeep smelled of cigarettes and gasoline. I pushed a pile of newspapers and candy wrappers from the passenger side, slid in, tried my best not to breathe. The radio burbled, Dolly Parton pleading with Jolene to leave her husband the hell alone. Drew hummed along, tunelessly, saying little as snow-lined country roads turned to highway, to city streets. He slowed, stopped at a red, the grey day punctured with the brake lights before us, the entire world on the road now and heading into work. I glanced at my watch, muttering a silent prayer that I would be in time.

'You got someplace to be?' asked Drew.

'I'm thinking of you,' I lied. 'Don't you have work?'

'Not on shift till ten. But appreciate the consideration.'

He eased his foot down on the gas as the cars before us began a slow crawl forward.

'So . . .' he said, 'last night, huh?'

'Yup. Last night.'

'Gotta admit. Surprised me. Stunt like that. Something I'd pull. Not you.'

I didn't answer, stared out the passenger window at an SUV, at the driver, male, dark hair, glasses. Felt a prickle across my skin. That could be Wolf. Or the guy behind us in the red sedan. Or the guy coming out of the Panera carrying a bag, a takeaway cup. He could be all of them or none of them.

'You know,' said Drew, breaking the silence, 'Mom, she'll get over it. Once that temper of hers has cooled down a bit.' He glanced across at me. 'Figure she's just surprised too, what with you being her baby and all. Shock takes longer to pass then.'

I nodded, bit my lip.

Drew slowed, took a right turn into Addie's street. 'Just . . . take care of yourself, okay, kiddo?' He eased the jeep to the kerb, glanced up at Addie's neat little house, then back at me. 'I can trust you, right? I got some stuff to do over in Middleton. You'll stay with Addie and Gray until I come back. Right?'

I gave a small smile. 'I promise. Thanks Drew. You're a good brother.'

Drew snorted. 'Been telling you that for years.'

I grinned, pushed the passenger door open and picked my way along the snow-shovelled path towards the house, rapped quickly on the door, then twisted the handle. A quick wave back to Drew. 'Guys? It's me.'

'Auntie Rosa, Auntie Rosa.' The girls tumbled down the hallway, a whirlwind of blonde hair and lily-white skin in various stages of undress.

'Put your sweater on! Gabriella Swiggert, your pants are on inside out!' My sister spared me an exasperated look. 'Hey. Gray's in the kitchen taking his own sweet time over his morning coffee.' She blew out a breath. 'You go on through while I get these two ... No ... Mason! No! Why are you taking your socks off? Oh for the ...' Addie shooed me along the hall towards the kitchen, then caught my arm. 'Hey, don't let him give you a hard time, okay?' I smiled at my sister, but already her attention had whiplashed away. 'Teeth. Come on. Brush your teeth.'

I followed the smell of coffee, pushed open the kitchen door.

Gray stood, leaning against the island, staring wearily into a cup. He looked ashen, and I felt colour flush to my cheeks.

'Hi.'

He set down the cup. Gave me a level look. 'Hi. You look like shit.'

I grinned. 'Right back at you.'

He sighed. 'Yeah, well. Part of the job.' He leaned across the island, pulling car keys from a turquoise bowl. 'Better head in.'

I selected my words carefully. 'Gray, I found something. And I think you need to know about it.'

Gray turned towards me, face sliding to flat. Studied me. 'Okay,' he said, slowly. 'So tell me.'

My stomach clenched. 'I know why he killed Elizabeth.'

My brother-in-law folded his arms. 'Okay. Why?'

I took a deep breath. 'I'll tell you ... but I want in.'

'You want in,' repeated Gray, quietly.

'Yes.'

'You ...'

'I want to help you. To be involved in the investigation.'

'Jesus Christ, Rosa,' muttered Gray. He threw his car keys back into the bowl, the clatter of them jarring me. 'Kid ... look, this is ... I mean, he's your brother. He's also a complete psycho. You already have a goddam target on your back. And now you want to make that worse?' He was looking at me with an expression I didn't recognise, hard as rock. 'And, to be frank, after last night, I don't want you in. You're reckless. I don't know what the hell you were thinking last night, I don't know where you went ...'

'I ...'

'Yes, you "felt like a drink". I remember. I also think you're full of horseshit. And, after that, you want me to bring you onto a police investigation, give you another opportunity to play chicken with oncoming traffic?'

I didn't move. Didn't react.

'Jesus Christ,' muttered Gray again. 'You do understand, you could be charged with hindering an investigation?'

'I'm sorry, Gray,' I said, quietly. 'I just think that it's important that I'm involved.'

'Why?' he asked, a plea almost. 'Why is it this important to you? Why can't you just be ... I don't know, normal? Why can't you just get on, do what you do, let me do what I do?'

I stared back at him, searching for an answer that would work. Turned out that the answer I found was the truth. 'Because it feels like I don't have a life any more. Or ... I do, only it just doesn't fit me now. I don't expect you to understand, but it's ... it's like, after all that's happened, I'm just not the same person. I can't go back to being who I was. That person is gone. And if I want to figure out who I am now, I have to find my brother, figure out how I came to be here and why.' I threw my hands up. 'There is no one else. No one who can possibly answer my questions. There's only him.' I was aware that I was pleading now, was losing my poker face. 'Look, I'm not just his sister. I have spent years studying fraud, the kind of people who commit it, what they do, why they do it. Those detectives, they've spent all this time trying to catch him using policing techniques. And they haven't caught him. Maybe it's time to try something different.'

Gray frowned. 'So what are you saying?'

'I'm saying ... I don't know ... we need to understand him, I guess. Figure out not just what he's done, but why he's done it.'

'Rosa ...' Gray leaned forward, palms flat on the island countertop, face serious, 'you get that my goal, our goal, is to arrest Wolf. My personal hope is that we can put him in prison for a long time.'

And me? For me it was all about the answers. And if I stayed where I was, on the outside, the answers would remain lost to me. Only by helping Gray, by standing alongside him, could I get close. And if those answers brought him to Elliott's door? What would I do then? Who would I be? Which way would I jump?

I strode forward, with no clear idea of which way I would turn, safe in the knowledge that the crossroads was still some way ahead, that I had time.

I nodded, slowly. 'I understand that.'

'So why ...'

'Because I think he needs help. And I need to find him to help him. And ... whatever else is true, Elizabeth Barrow did not deserve to die.' My voice shook, the truth of it making my breath catch.

It was only silence then, my brother-in-law staring at me, assessing. 'Rosa,' he muttered again, shaking his head. He ran his fingers through his hair and blew out a breath. 'Fine. Fine. Look, holy shit, look, I don't like this. I don't like this even one tiny bit. But at least if you're with me, you're not out there, rampaging around and getting yourself into trouble.' He stood up straighter, a single shoulder shrug. 'And, I guess, maybe you do know a couple of things that may be useful.' He turned, retrieved his backpack and pulled a dense file from within it, and held it tight, studying me. 'But if you're going to do this, you need to know just what it is you're dealing with.' He slid the file across the island towards me. 'I'm warning you though, kid, this ain't good. This brother of yours, he is a very bad man.'

I nodded, my fingers reaching out of their own accord, grasping the file within them.

'Nuh-uh,' said Gray, not relinquishing his hold. 'Before I show you mine, you gotta show me yours. What've you got?'

I took a deep breath, nodded and sank onto a stool, deliberately not looking at Gray. 'Elizabeth Barrow. She knew Jackson Wolf. That was why she wanted to speak to me. That was why he killed her.' I glanced up then. 'Elliott was close with Elizabeth. She could easily have heard that name back then, and would have realised the connection when she heard it again. I'm betting that this was his first alternative identity. The beginning of his life as it is now. My guess is, the risk of exposure, of the Wolf identity being connected to Elliott, that represented a massive existential threat to him, to his very idea of himself. Elizabeth, in his view, she simply had to die.' I let the silence settle for a moment. Then, 'Your turn. What do you have?'

Gray coughed. 'Look, Rosa …'

'No,' I said, quietly. 'A deal's a deal.'

I looked from Gray to the file, his fingers still pressed down tight upon it. He sighed heavily, then nodded, finally relinquishing his hold.

'Read the file. Then you'll understand just how bad this is.'

I nodded, slowly, struggling to make sense of the words. Dimly aware of a phone ringing, of Gray answering it. Then a ping from my cell, and I looked at it, automatic. An email notification.

My thumb pressed on it, unthinking.

Rosa,
I think we should meet. I'll be at the food court of the
West Towne Mall in two hours.
    Elliott.

Chapter 7

It was madness, utter madness. I walked through the West Towne Mall, steps slowed by the weight of my own sheer recklessness. This was stupidity of the highest order. And yet I persisted.

I had parked at the farthest end of the mall, close to Sears. I don't know what my logic was, perhaps some kind of cognitive-distancing mechanism, some way of rationalising to myself that the choices I was making had some tactical merit. Past Gap, past the sparkly chaos of Justice, my amygdala on high alert, the tinny sounds of music, of chatter, of footfall, all vanishing away, as my brain poured every ounce of attention I had towards the faces that surrounded me. Looking for ... what? An impression rather than a face, a sense of familiarity. Is it you? Or you? Or you?

I had read the email, my hands shaking, could feel my heartbeat thundering in my ears, loud enough that I was certain Gray had to be able to hear it too. Then had replied, thumb moving quickly across the keys, I'll be there. Had slipped the cell into my pocket, willed the colour to return to my face, worked on slowing my breathing. The file, my brother's file, still sat before me, and I smoothed across the cover of it, wondering if Gray would notice the tremble in my fingers.

My brother-in-law hung up the phone, turned back towards me, must have seen something in my face. 'You okay?' Softness breaking through his irritation, sunshine through clouds.

I cleared my throat. 'I wonder if ... maybe there's somewhere I could go, somewhere private, where I can ...' I tapped the cover of the file. 'I feel like this is going to be a lot to take in.'

'You can use my study. Addie's already gotten the kids out the door and she won't be back for a while. I gotta make some calls, so have at it,' said Gray. He moved towards the kitchen door, gesturing for me to follow, and I ducked my head, slid into step behind him, file clutched to my chest.

I would call Eve. Once I got to his study, I would call Eve. She would drive me.

Only, after last night ... would she?

Could I call Drew? Tell him I needed something at the mall? Only he would insist on coming in with me, and then ...

Gray pushed open his study door, showing me to the desk. A splayed ray of watery sunlight had broken through the clouds, puncturing the gloom. 'You can read it in here. I'll be in the kitchen. Give me a call when you're done.'

I nodded, holding the file like a shield. 'Thank you.'

He stood for a moment, lips pursed, nodding to himself, his gaze at his feet. 'Rosa, I don't know who you are any more.' Then he turned, closing the door tight behind him.

I stood, staring after him, at the closed door, his Canada Goose jacket hanging from the back of it. 'Neither do I,' I murmured.

And then …

Then I set the cardboard file containing the story of Elliott Lynch, of Jackson Wolf, down onto the desk, and I walked towards that door and that coat and I searched through the pockets until I found the keys for my brother-in-law's Chevy Suburban, and then I pulled the coat on, drowning inside it, and I slipped out of the study, along the hallway and out through the front door.

A group of teenagers flocked by me, buffeting me closer to the Pottery Barn window, voices loud enough to shake me to attention. A smell of cheap perfume and weed.

What the hell are you doing, Rosa? Who the hell have you become?

It was crazy, this choice. No matter what sympathy I had for my brother, he was dangerous, and I knew he was dangerous. Only my feet continued to walk and my heart continued to race, and it seemed to me like the entirety of my body had turned against me. Because he had killed already. Elizabeth was dead because she could link him to Jackson Wolf. And I had told him, had said the words, I think you are my brother. Familial affection likely would only take me so far. So the question was, had I already pushed it further than it would stretch?

Too late to go back now. The only way was forward.

Because he was my brother. Because he was my flesh and blood. And the need to sit across from him, to study his features, his mannerisms, was utterly overwhelming. And, if I was honest with myself, wasn't there something else alongside that fear, a spark of something, thrill perhaps? That ever since the fall, I had gotten into the habit of rolling the dice, of walking on paper-thin ice, the whole of it one big game, playing chicken with an oncoming train.

Because he was my brother. And I was his sister. And some of that wildness lay within me too.

He sat on the edge of the food court, a table close to the door, the tactical choice, all ready for an easy escape. There was no question in me. No doubt about who it was I was seeing. He sat hunched over, his hands knotted together on the table before him, his head down. Just waiting. And I slowed, awash with this sudden feeling of déjà vu, familiarity with the unfamiliar. It felt to me like a Snapchat trick. My face turned to male. Me but not me. The same nose and the same jaw and just this unerring sense of looking in a mirror, only from an unfamiliar angle.

He looked up, drawn by the power of my gaze.

'Rosa.'

I moved closer. 'Elliott.' It came out strangled and small.

I had expected something different. I had expected that, in looking at him, I would see it. The wildness of him, the danger. And yet he looked utterly average, a certain carefulness to his expression, a wariness that I echoed. And for a moment I allowed myself to believe it, to feel that wash of relief, that they had been mistaken all along.

And I searched for the thing that I knew would be there, the memory of him, circling my life somehow. Only there was nothing, no recollection, no familiarity in his face beyond what I could see in a mirror. I felt a sinking sense of dislocation, that I had been wrong after all, that I had never met him before.

I stepped closer to the table, sank to the seat opposite him. He had been here for a few minutes at least, a cardboard cup sitting almost empty before him, a thin layer of black coffee staining the bottom of it. Sugar granules had spilled from packets, sparkling crystals scattered across the table. A plastic spoon.

He gazed at me, his attention roaming across my features, taking me in. Then, 'I didn't think you'd come.' He sounded nervous, a shake to his voice.

I smiled slightly. 'Neither did I.'

But the thing was, this was not a normal conversation, not a level playing field. His psychopathy would allow for his ability to read others, to assess their feelings. And his success, the way in which he had for decades moved through society, convincing the world to accept him, to like him even, suggested that he was very good at reading the emotional landscape of those around him. He watched me, a laser-beam gaze, and I felt myself begin to squirm under the heat of it. Are you reading me, studying the flicker of my eyes, the pallor of my skin, the bitten edges of my fingernails, so that you can see through to the heart of me? So that you can figure out just who you need to be for me. Are you looking for weaknesses here?

I watched as his fingers plucked at a napkin, shredding the edge of it into a frayed curtain.

Thought of a paper I had read, sitting in the family room, watching the snow fall beyond my window. Of psychopaths and their ability to mimic emotions, of their capacity to fool those around them into thinking that they can feel.

Fear shot through me.

Do I know you? Is the sense of familiarity I'm feeling some deep-seated pull towards a long-lost sibling? Or is it something else? Have you moved through my life somehow, hiding in plain sight, somewhere I would have seen you, once, twice, a thousand times, but never thought to look at you? Or are you, rather, a voice on the phone, words on an email, a social media 'friend'?

I smiled again, letting a wobble into the edge of it. I could feel him watching me, reading me. Best to let him believe that I was little more than a girl, wildly outmatched here.

'I'm glad you reached out,' I said, quietly.

He nodded slowly. 'You look just like Mom.'

My heart beat faster. 'I do?' Was aware that there was a pleading edge to my voice, one that had not been deliberate, and I cursed myself silently for my weakness.

'You could be twins,' he offered.

Only I had shown him, hadn't I, how much that

statement meant to me. I had given him a way in, an opportunity to give me what I needed, and for him to gain my gratitude in return.

I suddenly felt swamped, frightened. What the hell was I doing? I should call Gray. I slipped my fingers into my pocket, fingered the cell. How long would it take them to get here? If they sent the closest unit, five minutes maybe. Ten. And then it would all be over and my brother would vanish into the system and with him would go any chance of answers, any hope of under-standing how I came to be where I was.

No. Focus.

I ducked my head, allowed the tears that stood there, right on the periphery, to flood my eyes and dabbed at them with my sleeve. Then a hard clang echoed through the food court, and both of us jumped,

I laughed nervously. 'Sorry. I'm … This is a lot.'

He studied me, expression one of sympathy. 'I know. For me too. I …' He wrapped his fingers tighter to-gether. 'I can't believe you're here.'

He had to believe I needed him. That he was im-portant to me. And, really, wasn't there enough truth in that?

I nodded, dabbing at my eyes again. 'I … There are things I need answers to. To move forward. You know?'

He nodded, slowly.

'I want to understand,' I said, quietly.

'Understand?'

He thought I was asking about his crimes, about what he had done, who he had become. Only it turned out I was more selfish than that. That what I needed from my brother was all about me.

'Our parents. Kyle. What happened when they died. What happened after. I didn't mean ...' Your crimes. But why didn't I mean that? Surely, of all the questions I should need answering, those should head the list? 'I just want to know why our father did what he did. And I want to know why I ended up here, in Madison.'

He lowered his head. 'I've asked myself that. More times than you can imagine. Hadley ... he always ... I know this doesn't make sense, but he was a good father. Before ... that. I mean, he kept a gun. For protection. It was always in the top drawer of his desk, but, I mean, you never think ... What happened, what he did, I still don't understand what made him do that.'

Elizabeth Barrow had told me he was abusive, that he hit Kyle. I nodded slowly, schooling my face so that he would not know I had caught his lie. 'So there was nothing? No warning signs?'

'He'd been ... quieter, I guess. Seemed preoccupied. Mom, she said the business was stressing him out. He was a mechanic, ran his own shop. Afterward, the police said the business was on the brink of bankruptcy, figured that was why ...'

I bit my lip, stared at him. His eyes were the same as mine. Same moss green, same long lashes. Tears pricked the back of my eyes.

No. Focus.

Financial despair. Fear of economic ruin. A commonly cited motive for family annihilators, who cannot see a way out of their free fall, who justify their family's destruction to themselves by saying that they will be better off, that they are in fact sparing them the pain of poverty and shame.

'Do you think he planned it?' I asked. 'For that day. Knowing that you wouldn't be there. Despondent husbands, the type that commit familicides like this, they tend to premeditate, get all their ducks in a row before they act.'

He studied me.

'Psychologist,' I muttered. But then, of course, he knew that.

He looked at me for a moment longer, then shook his head. 'I don't know. I don't get why it was me that was spared.' He nodded towards me. 'And, of course, you.'

'Did you ...' I chose my words carefully. 'Did you arrange for me to be brought here?'

He looked up at me, frowned. 'Did I? No, I thought you were dead. That's what the police told me. For years I believed I was the only one left.'

My brain ground to a halt. 'But then ... I mean, why did Clay ...'

'Clay?'

A hard vibration against my hip, the phone ringing, loud through the fabric of my jacket. I pulled it out, Gray. My finger moved to disconnect the call. Then I stared at the screen, a sudden sinking feeling. That I had forgotten. That Elliott had caught me, swept me up into believing his carefully constructed presentation. The research, it says that it's easier for people to detect signs of psychopathy when they only see the psychopath fleetingly, a minute, less. Because any longer and the arsenal gets deployed against you, the charm, the penetrating search for vulnerabilities, the conversational loops, until in the end you get swallowed up, convincing yourself that where you first saw danger there is in fact only vulnerability and warmth.

Shit.

'So ...' I said.

My cell began ringing again, harsh in the echoing space of the food court. Gray.

What was I doing here? What did I think this would achieve?

And I thought of the file, left lying on Gray's desk, unread. Of his words – This brother of yours, he is a very bad man. Of my own rationalisations, of trauma turning him callous, psychopathy in all but name. And I thought of Elizabeth Barrow.

I pushed my chair back.

'I have to go.'

'What?' He was startled. Or, at the very least, was doing a good impression of it.

'I shouldn't have come.'

'Rosa...'

'I'm sorry,' I said. 'I understand how tough it must have been for you. I get what something like that, losing everyone you love, I get what it can do to you as a person, how it can change you. But Elizabeth, she didn't deserve it.'

He pushed his chair back, coming up to standing, a

sudden sense of a predator looming over its prey. 'Listen to me ...'

'No!' It came out as a shout. Heads turned towards us, conversations surrounding us petering out. 'This ... I've been stupid. I've only been thinking of myself. And, I can't ...' I looked at him, fighting to keep my voice steady. 'I'm leaving now. And when I get to the parking lot, I'm going to answer this phone.' It had begun ringing again, as if cued by my words. 'And I'm going to tell them where you are. I'm sorry things couldn't have been different. Goodbye, Elliott.'

I turned, walked quickly through the food court, the phone ringing loud in my hand, could feel heads turning to follow me as I went, the searing burn of Elliott's gaze on my back. I waited for it, for the sound of the gun, for the rush of feet, the burning thump of a knife in my back. But there was nothing, only the cresting wave of sound that followed behind me.

I rounded the corner onto the main concourse, walking faster, almost running. Fifteen minutes. I had been with my brother for fifteen minutes, after twenty years without him. It was not enough. It would never be enough. Because he was not who I wanted my brother to be. He was the wolf.

The phone rang off and then, within seconds, began ringing again.

I kept walking. I had given my word. And it was all I was able to give. I padded the outside of my brother-in-law's jacket pocket, could feel the shape of Elliott's plastic spoon within, and the thrill of fear. Would there be DNA on it? Should be fingerprints at the very least. In my head, I muttered an apology to my brother.

I took a hard left by Sears, the door to the world beyond sliding open in anticipation, a swill of cold air washing over me, the heady smell of snow.

I stepped outside into the cold.

I answered the phone.

'Gray, look, I'm sorry, I ...'

'Rosa. Jesus fucking Christ, Rosa, where the fuck are you?'

'I ... I'm at the West Towne Mall. Look, I can explain ...'

I heard him turn from the phone, voice muffled, the words: 'She's at the West Towne Mall. Get a unit there, now.' I felt sick.

'Gray ...'

'Rosa, I need you to stay inside.'

'I'm out ...'

'Jesus!' he shouted. 'Go back in. Go to the nearest store. Get them to call security for you. Do not leave. Stay at the register. Stay where people can see you. We have units on the way to you now.'

'Seriously, Gray, I'm okay, I ...'

'No. You listen,' he barked. And in the background of the call, something else. The sound of crying. I heard my brother-in-law draw in a deep breath. 'Something has happened, Rosa. It's bad.'

Chapter 8

And then...

Then it was only fear. The omnipresent sense of having pushed too hard and gone too far, of chickens coming home to roost. What is it, Gray? What's happened? Just wait. We're coming to you. A feeling of being far above my body, of floating over myself standing alone in the ice-slicked parking lot, the floating me waiting for the standing me to crumble, to simply give up, fold up right there into the snow. Because whatever was coming, both 'me's, the floating and the standing, we knew enough to know it would change everything.

'Are you inside? Get inside, Rosa.'

My feet moving then as if they are directly linked to Gray's command, watching with fascination as my boots kick up little showers of snow as they walked. A dim and distant sense of having forgotten something important, that there was something I was going to do here, something I was going to say, all of that lost now to the rushing sense of foreboding. Back into the mall, artificial heat burning my face.

'Where are you? Which store?'

'Barnes and Noble,' I muttered. Because when seeking safety, I run to books.

The sound of Gray's voice, muttering to someone else, then louder to me, 'They're coming, Rosa. Just stay where you can be seen.'

I didn't ask again. Didn't ask what had happened. Just allowed him to guide my feet towards the bookstore. Somewhere inside, aware that I wasn't asking because I did not want to know, wanted to have these last few moments of ignorance.

And then the inside, engulfed with the paper-fresh smell of new books, and wanting to feel comforted, yet missing the mark, and, under orders from Gray, my feet propelling me direct to the front desk, and the middle-aged man with the dreadlocks and the moth-holed shirt looking askance at me, and rather than trying to explain, simply handing him the phone, watching as he listened, his expression moving from bewilderment to self-importance. Then the call going up for security. Urgent. Two men, who should have been sitting on a beach somewhere sipping Margaritas and listening to Jimmy Buffett, rounded the corner at an awkward half walk, half run, looking between me and the store clerk, their faces changing when they heard their charge, then ushering me to the side of the desk, taking up position beside me, two guard dogs.

Holding my cell in my hands, suddenly aware that I had disconnected the call, had cut Gray off, and a feeling of wild relief, like if he couldn't talk to me, then he couldn't tell me, and everything would remain as it was.

And throughout, that feeling, of having forgotten to do something, to say something, and what was it? Yet each time I reached for it, I was aware of nothing but a deep, cavernous fear in the pit of my stomach.

Then the sound of running, the heads of my two guard dogs snapping towards the door, and two patrol cops rounding the corner, their gazes sweeping left to right, expressions hard and soft both.

I would ask now.

The woman smiled at me, tight and reassuring. 'Rosa? Gray sent us. You want to come with us?' She handed me her ID, waited while my sightless gaze scanned it, while her partner handed me his.

I handed the IDs back, opened my mouth, and her face took on a careful look, a guardedness warning me not to question, so I closed it again. Grateful for the brief reprieve.

They walked me out, one either side of me, heads of passers-by turning to watch us, a ripple of murmurs that followed their frank stares. I heard the word shoplifter from a young mother with a double buggy. Was faintly surprised how little I cared.

Outside, face burning in spite of the cold. Into the squad car. Watching as the grey world slid by, piled-up snow flecked with dirt.

I should ask now.

Opening my mouth and closing it again. Because these were it, the final moments. And so, instead, listening to the burr of the snow chains on the road, to the low thrum of conversation over the police radio, to my breath, in, out, in, out.

The woman pulled the car to a stop in front of the police station, and I looked up to the doorway, half looking for answers, half afraid to find them. Gray stood waiting in the cold, parka zipped up to his chin, face white pale, and tight.

I sat. I did not move. Did not unbuckle.

Just one more moment.

Just one.

The door opened.

Moment's over.

'Rosa.' Gray reached out, curling his arm about my back, voice soft. 'Let's go inside.'

I stopped, legs becoming granite. 'Tell me.'

'Inside,' said Gray, gently.

'No,' I said. 'Now. Who is it?'

'It's your mom.'

Then being guided through the beige hallways to an office, a hunched-over figure sitting in a chair at the corner of the desk, that I looked at, once, twice, before recognising as Drew, crying. The oblique thought that I had never seen my brother cry before, that even with my father's death, my brother had always appeared red-eyed yet in control. Then a figure sweeping towards me, arms engulfing me. Addie, the wracking sobs of her shaking me.

'Mom,' I said, a question and a statement both.

Addie's grip only tightened, her sobs growing deeper, more guttural.

'She's gone, Rosa,' said Gray, quietly.

Everything coming to me then as if from a long tunnel, sounds whittling themselves down to whispers. A feeling as if my soul was trying to escape from my body, as if being here, amongst all this, was just too much for any decent soul to bear.

I wriggled free from Addie's grasp. 'Was it ... It was her heart?'

Please. Please say it was her heart.

'It wasn't her heart,' said Gray.

The rest, that was merely a kaleidoscope of sounds, technicolour-bright images. It had been Drew who had found her, had found the front door ajar, the toe of her once white pump holding it open so that the snow swept in with the wind, turning the dark-stained wood white. Then the blood. To be fair, no one told me about the blood, rather an image painted itself in my imagination of a spreading pool of it, of brain matter sprinkling the chintz wallpaper.

She had been shot in the head.

Just one bullet wound, they said. But then, one had been enough.

My mother had been dead before she hit the floor.

I remember asking why.

And then, impossibly, it getting worse. That he had murdered my mother, that he had stepped over her where she lay, that he had trailed blood through the hall and up the stairs and into my bedroom.

'Rosa,' Gray had said, his voice searingly gentle, 'I think he was there for you.'

His words oozed their way through my brain. He had killed her. He had killed her because he was trying to kill me, because I had told him that his secret was out, his identity known. And so he had murdered my mother and had searched for me, only I wasn't there, was I? Because I was busy finagling my way into the investigation, trying to find him, to get close to him, this beloved brother of mine. And so he had stepped once more over the dead body of my mother and had emailed me, knowing how stupid I was and how gullible and how desperate for this mythical family of mine, and had summoned me to the West Towne Mall, and I had gone. And how frustrated he must have been, how wild with it, that before he could get me alone, before he had a chance to kill me, I had fled.

'He was at the West Towne Mall,' I said, quietly. I plunged my hand into my pocket, pulling out the plastic spoon, set it carefully onto the desk. 'I met him. It must have been,' my voice cracked, 'right after he did it.' The thought then, of the brutality of it, of murdering my mother, of coming and sitting across from me, never a sign of what he had done. 'This spoon, this may have his DNA on it. Should have his prints at least. So you can be sure.' I looked up at Gray.

Because that man wasn't my brother. My brother was Drew, who sat slumped in the corner, a marionette, his strings cut, silent tears rolling down his cheeks. My brother was Gray, who stood, his hand rhythmically stroking his wife's back, his face twisted with the pressure of holding back tears. Elliott/Wolf, he was a monster, a ghost who could sit across from me, could play soft and kind, mere fractions of an hour after he had shot my mother dead.

I could feel Gray's gaze on me.

'He's a monster,' I said.

'Yes,' he said. 'He is.'

I nodded slowly.

'Catch him.'

Chapter 9

I did not cry. I sat there, on the floor of Gray's office, my knees drawn close to my chest, head resting back against the hard lines of the bookcase. I should be crying. Yet it felt that I was too empty for that, that I had been hollowed out by my own culpability, the weight of what I had done.

The words circled, around and around my head. This is your fault. This is your fault.

'It's not over,' Gray said. 'If he went to the house, looking for Rosa, he didn't find her.' He looked to my sister, her eyes red-rimmed and heavy. 'It's not safe. For any of us.'

'The girls.' Addie looked up at him, voice spiked with horror. She flung herself across the room, towards the phone, punching in a number with trembling fingers, then her voice coming, a heavy layer of faux calm draped across the top of it. 'If you could pull them from class. Yes, a ... a death in the family.' Her face was pale, but hard now. 'I'm on my way. Don't ... don't release them to anyone else. Anyone.' She hung up, turned to her husband. 'Can you ...'

'I got two patrol cops waiting to take you.' Gray laid his hand on his wife's cheek. 'I could ...'

'No.' An Addie I didn't recognise. Harder. Tougher. 'Stay with Rosa. I'll be right back.' Then she turned on her heel and was gone.

'We need to get out of town,' muttered Gray, to himself or to Drew and me, I wasn't sure. 'All of us. Bob's got a cabin. Ski place. Out in Portage. I'll talk to him. See if we can use it. Drew?'

My brother sat in a chair, his head in his hands, fingers raking through his hair, his shoulders shaking steadily. It took him a moment for his name to punch through. He wrenched his gaze upwards. 'What?'

'Are you coming with us?'

He stared at him, blank. Then he shook his head. 'I'll go to Steve's.'

'Rosa,' Gray said, 'can you think of anyone else that Wolf might target? Anyone you're close to?'

I bounced my head off the shelves behind me, Gray's voice coming from a great distance, and, with difficulty, pulled my gaze towards him. 'I ...' What had I done? Who else had I endangered? What other damage had I done? 'Eve,' I said, slowly. 'He saw her, out at Monona Terrace. He mentioned her by name.'

Gray nodded once, reaching for the phone. 'I'm on it.'

I leaned my head back, closed my eyes. A mistake, as it turned out. Because there waited for me that image, of my mother laying prone on the ground, blood spattered up the walls. Because of me. Because of what I had done, who I had become.

I snapped my eyes open again, heat and nausea rising through me.

Gray hung up the phone, the click of it making me start. He moved around the desk, crouched before me. The expression on his face a preternaturally forced calm. His police face. 'They're going to find him. We got people all over the mall. We got him on camera, we got the car. It's just a matter of time.'

My head nodded, mind far away.

A scrape of chair legs, Drew pushing himself up to a lurching stand. 'Restroom,' he muttered. He shoved his way out the door, letting it swing shut behind him.

I felt my brother-in-law's gaze on me. 'You okay?' he asked, then grimaced. 'Stupid bloody question. Of course you're not okay.'

I stared at him, foggy-eyed, and he ducked down before me in an awkward squat.

He sighed heavily. 'Okay, look, I don't like this, but I need your help, kid.'

'What?'

'I think you might be right.'

I stared at him. I had never felt less right in my entire life. 'About what?'

'I think you might be able to help me catch him. I know this is a shitty time, Rosa. Look, if you don't wanna ... fine. I totally get that. But ... the thing is, you've gotten closer to Wolf than anyone else has.' He gave me a long look. 'Seems like you're inside his head.' He leaned in. 'You told me that you could do something I couldn't. That you could help me figure out not just who he is, but why he's doing this. If you're right, if you can do that, maybe you can figure out what he's going to do next.'

I opened my mouth, closed it again. Then, 'I ... This is my fault. I should have told you the truth. I shouldn't have gone. Only I did, and Mom ...'

Gray reached out, awkwardly gripping my hand inside his bear paws. 'No. This isn't you. This is him.'

A tear rolled down my cheek. 'What if ...' The words came, unbidden. 'What if I am like him? I've done things in this, things I would never have imagined I'd have done.' I looked to him, voice almost a plea. 'Gray, I'm afraid that I'm not who I thought I was.'

I was crying now, a silent stream of tears. Felt Gray's large hand squeeze mine tight.

He was silent for long moments. Then, 'I get it, kid. I do. Things like this happen, you find out who you are. Trouble is, that's not always who you thought it would be.' He considered, then said, 'Look, I been doing this a long time. And you know what I figure? Who we are, it's not set in stone. Not ever. You got guys out there, bad guys, who don't think twice about walking up, shooting someone in the head for looking at them the wrong way. Those same guys, they go home and they play with their babies, kiss their wives. Some of them, you look at how they were raised, and you think, well yeah, I mean, what other outcome was there ever going to be? And then you see these other guys, raised in exactly the same environment, and they turn it around, join the military, or the church, they make a choice.

They do something different.' He sighed. 'We think who we are, for good or bad, that it's set in stone. Only look at this Wolf guy. He's a smart guy. He could have been anyone, done anything. He chose this.' He leaned down, pulling my gaze onto his. 'Rosa, who we are, it's mostly about the choice we make.' He gave a quick flash of a grin. 'I don't know, maybe you do have a bit of the wolf in you. But what that means for you, who that makes you, for my money, I'd say that's up to you.'

'What do I do now?' I asked, quietly.

He pursed his lips. 'That has to be your decision.'

'Whatever he's been through, no matter how bad ... it doesn't excuse this.'

'No.'

'I want to catch him,' I said.

'Good.' Gray slapped his palms against his thighs and pushed himself up to standing, 'Then let's do that.' He turned back towards the desk and picked up a file, the one I had left unread. 'But first, you need to read this.'

I do not know how long I sat there, trapped within the world of Wolf. I have a dim recollection of a knock on the door, of Gray excusing himself, of my sister's voice, a low-level argument, the words, 'She doesn't need to be involved in this. She isn't safe.' My brother-in-law's voice, firm but kind. 'I'll take care of her. Bob said the cabin is ours for as long as we need it. I'm going to get the guys from patrol bring you and the kids up to Portage. Get Drew dropped off wherever he wants to go. Once we've done what we need to do here, we'll follow you.'

I put my hands over my ears. And I read and read and read, and even when the moment came when I wanted to stop, needed it like oxygen following a deep dive, I carried on.

I had allowed myself to believe all was as I wished it to be. Now it was time to know the truth.

I finished. I closed the cardboard cover of the file. I leaned back in my chair. I felt tears bubble over, streaking down my cheeks.

'Hey,' said Gray, awkward. 'It's ... I know ... You okay?'

I dashed my hands across my cheeks, gave a short bark of a laugh. 'Awesome.'

He grunted, handed me a cup of coffee and slid into the chair beside me. 'So?' he said. 'What do you think?'

'What do I think?'

'Not you, the sister. You, the psychologist.' He reached over, tapped the top of the file. 'What does *she* make of this guy?'

I shifted my gaze to the dark coffee, breathed out slowly. Me, the psychologist. 'I think,' I heard my psychologist self say, 'that based on what I've read here, Wolf ... Elliott ... I think it's likely he'd score pretty highly on the PCL-R. Sorry. Psychopathy Checklist. Given the ease with which he lies, his ability to manipulate, his lack of empathy ... seems a pretty logical conclusion.'

'You've sat across the table from him,' offered Gray. 'You'd know.'

Only I hadn't, had I? Not Rosa the psychologist at

349

least. Rather Rosa the sister. And she, she had not been looking for what was there, but rather what she had wanted to see. The damaged brother. The brother who loved her, who needed only to be saved.

'You know,' I said, conversationally, 'talking to a psychopath, it can feel ... I don't know, like being a deer caught in headlights. It's almost like you lose all sense of yourself, that you become simply a passive audience for their monologue. It's weird. Being around them. It's almost like ... I don't know, possession.' I flushed slightly. 'Afterward, you kind of find yourself thinking about them a lot. Almost obsessing, so that in the end it feels, this is going to sound so weird, but it kind of feels like a crush.' I did myself the favour of looking away. 'It's the charisma,' I finished, quietly.

'Oh.' An uneasy silence settled. Then, 'So, is this how you felt? With Elliott?'

I thought of my brother. Of the table between us, of the hollow echoing sounds of the food hall, of the smell of meat and of fat, and of the shape of his hands resting on the tabletop. Tried to live again the conversation, dissecting the wild flow of emotions that had made my heart thump, my hands shake. Because Gray was right. I had sat across the table from him. And I understood, where he'd come from, how his brain worked. So I should see it, there in him. Right?

Gray was waiting for an answer.

'I just ... I can't see it. The psychopath in him, I mean.'

'I know it's rough,' said Gray, voice soft. 'He's your brother.'

'No, it's not just that. I feel … I feel like there's something I'm missing. Something about what he said, what he did.'

And then, from somewhere beyond the closed office, came a bang, a careless door slamming, and I felt my adrenaline spike. An exaggerated startle reflex. A fitting tribute to a murdered mother. And then it came to me, the memory pulled forward by my body's response. The bang in the food court. Both Elliott and I starting in unison. And I put my hand to my mouth.

'Shit.'

'What?'

'Gray … I don't think it's him.'

'What?'

I breathed slowly, trying to steady myself, to get my thoughts in order. 'Okay,' I said, placing my hand, palm down, on top of the file, 'this guy, Wolf. Everything he's done, his behaviour, his responses, all of those are indicative of someone with significant psychopathic personality traits. Right?'

'Okay?'

'Okay, so what research tells us is that psychopaths show much lower startle response for things they're not paying attention to than do the rest of us.'

'Okay …'

'Okay, so, in the food court, someone dropped a tray. He jumped.'

Gray studied me, a sense of him carefully choosing his words. 'Rosa …'

'No, I know. And it's not evidence, I get that. Maybe

351

he just … jumped. Maybe it doesn't mean anything. Only, it's not just that, Gray. It's the way he talks, the way he uses his hands, even his expressions … none of them feel like psychopathy to me. I just don't see it. And if I'm right and that's true, then that means … Elliott isn't Wolf.'

We sat in silence, staring at each other.

'But,' Gray fumbled, 'if that's true, then who …'

I bit my lip, neurons firing wildly. 'Clay,' I said, quietly. 'If Wolf isn't Elliott …'

Then Gray's cell rang. That damn startle reflex again. 'Hey.' He glanced at me. 'Oh, okay. That's great. Yeah, see you soon.' He hung up, looked to me. 'Guess we're about to find out. They picked Elliott up on his way out of town. He's on his way here now.'

I leaned forward, resting my elbows on my knees, head in my hands.

'Rosa, look, we're close. Okay?'

Another ringtone, another startle response.

Gray hung up, looked at me. 'Your friend Eve is safe. She's left town. Gone to her parents.'

I nodded. 'That's good.'

'Yeah. Based on what we've seen, anyone with the kind of information she had, about you, about your life … seems like he's going to see them as a pretty big threat.'

I glanced across at him. 'What about my grandmother? I mean, I know she doesn't remember much…'

'Already taken care of.'

I thought of Lilian, alone in her room, thought of

Eve, running because of me. And then I thought of the man who had rescued a baby left alone in the cold, of the place where this all began.

'Oh God, Gray. Laurie. He's going to go after Laurie.'

Chapter 10

'I don't like this,' I muttered.

Gray grunted, pushing the gas pedal down towards the floor. 'Try him again.'

I hit redial on my cell, listened as Laurie's phone just rang and rang. Maybe he's out. Maybe he's gone to the store. Maybe he's gone on vacation.

'Maybe it's nothing,' said Gray, echoing my thoughts. He took a corner hard. 'Maybe we're overreacting.'

I nodded, not trusting myself to speak. Then a thought. 'You have a gun, right?'

Gray glanced across at me. 'I'm a cop and a Republican. Of course I have a gun.'

'I'm a psychologist and a Democrat. Can I get one too?'

'Nope.'

'Awesome,' I muttered.

He had told me to stay, in much the same tone one would use with a golden retriever. You stay here. It's not safe. And I had stood up anyway and walked by him and told him that I was going regardless. Rosa, he's after you. Yes, I had said. But he's also after Laurie and

Laurie saved my life and there is no fucking way I am just sitting here while he dies.

Gray took a turn into Laurie's street, braking hard outside his cheery ranch. He turned the engine off, twisting in his seat to scan the street, the surrounding lot. I looked to the house. The garage door was shut tight. Snow had accumulated before the door, drifts building beyond the unshovelled path, unmarked by footprints.

'There's no one here,' I said. 'Gray, I have a really bad feeling.'

'Right there with you,' he muttered. He looked at me. 'Is there any point in me telling you to stay in the car?'

'Nope.'

Gray sighed. 'Let's go then.'

I pushed open the door, stepping out onto the cleared sidewalk, and then, beyond that, onto Laurie's path, the snow on it calf-deep, our footsteps pocking the pristine white of it. Gray, his head turning this way and that, the prickling realisation that he was searching for danger, his hand moving to the holster at his hip. And me, my gaze locked on the front door before me, my vision of it shifting, so that suddenly the pale blue door stood ajar and the snow had begun to sweep its way into the foyer and, through the thin line of it, there was the image of puddling blood. I stopped, footsteps frozen, and Gray turned to look at me.

'You okay?'

I swallowed, shook my head slightly, focusing my gaze on that door. Closed now. Locked up tight, the snow banked against it like a scene from a Christmas card. Could feel the heat of relief rushing through me. Telling myself that it was normal, not a sign of impending madness, that in any situation our brain shows us what we expect to see, rather than the truth of what is there. But that the brain is a muscle, the brain can be controlled, if you breathe, and you calm down, and you think, paying attention to the details, the truth that lies before you.

'I'm fine.'

I trudged closer, my gaze locked on the door, on the seam of it, where the opening had been in my imaginings. Unthinking, I reached a mittened hand towards it.

'Careful,' murmured Gray.

I let my hand drop. The sudden realisation that for him, this was a crime scene. I looked back at him, his expression closed, the lines of his jaw hard. He thought that Laurie's dead body was in there.

The thought held me in place, and I merely stood there, hand still frozen, inches from the door, and watched as Gray picked his way across the front of the house towards the picture window. He leaned forward, cupping his hands around his eyes, breath fogging the glass.

Did I want to see this?

I pulled my boots through the snow, moving towards the window. Because it felt like a betrayal to not see, to not bear witness. If it had happened, if he too had died for me, then surely the least I could do was look upon it.

I leaned close to the burning-cold glass, gave my vision a moment to clear, my brain a second to calm, so that it could process what lay before it.

Nothing.

No carnage. No corpse. Just a living room, neat as a pin.

'Where is he?' I muttered.

Gray didn't answer, his focus still on the inside.

'Could Wolf have taken him?' I asked.

It seemed that I was talking to myself. But then finally Gray turned to look at me, an expression I couldn't identify. And then the ringing of his phone, and he shook his head as if he too needed to shed visions that would not serve him, and pulled the phone from his pocket. 'Yeah.'

I turned away, shifting my body towards the wind. Where was he?

Then, over the brow of the hill, I spotted a fleck of colour, vivid against the snow. A figure, the dark shape of a dog loping at its side.

My heart skipped. 'Gray.' I didn't wait for a response but picked my way through the snow towards the sidewalk, breath coming fast, vision blurry with adrenaline. Pulled in a slow breath and my vision cleared and my heart sank. Because the figure I had taken to be Laurie was in fact a woman, swaddled deep inside a thick down jacket, a wool hat pulled down low to her eyes. I shifted my gaze towards the dog. A golden retriever, the colour of burnt butter. And then I smiled, the pieces shifting, coalescing into a picture that made sense.

I started walking towards her, my hand raised in a half wave, and the woman slowed, expression one of wariness. Archer wagged his tail, the entire rear end of him shimmying with excitement.

'Hey,' I said, reaching down to ruffle his ears. 'I was looking for you, boy.' I glanced up at the woman, frowning down at me. 'I'm sorry. I just ... You're Laurie's wife, right?'

She stared at me. 'No.'

I looked to Archer, back to where Gray stood before the house, phone to her ear, watching me.

'Oh, okay, only ... I mean, that's Laurie's dog, right? Archer?'

The retriever sat back on his haunches, gazed at me with liquid eyes.

The woman took a small step back, tightened her hold on the leash. 'I think you've gotten us confused with someone else.'

I looked from her, to the dog. 'So, this isn't Archer?'

'This is Henry,' she said, reluctantly.

I stared at the dog for a moment, then back to the woman. 'Okay ... I ... Look, we're looking for Laurie. Have you seen him? Or his wife?'

She hesitated, looking from me to the distant figure of Gray.

'We ...' I hesitated, starting over. 'That guy there, he's a detective. He needs to talk to him.'

That did it. Her face cleared, and she looked at me properly for the first time. 'Oh right. You mean the guy in number 186? Older? Glasses?'

'Yes. You seen him? It's pretty important.'

She shrugged. 'Sorry. Not for, I guess, a week, maybe more.' She looked past me to the house. 'I just assumed his lease was up.'

I opened my mouth, closed it again. Had they moved? If they had moved, if they were already gone before Wolf got here, then likely they were safe. I looked back towards Gray, stopped. The colour had drained from his face, phone still held to his ear. And my stomach knotted up tight. What now?

I turned, forgetting about the woman, the dog, and hurried back towards him.

'What? What's happened.'

Gray looked at me. 'Yeah, give me a sec,' he said into the phone. 'Rosa, they have Elliott back at the police station.'

'Okay.'

'The timings don't work out. They got him on camera at the mall at the same time your mom was ... y'know. You were right. Elliott isn't Wolf.'

My knees felt weak, head cotton-candy dense. Relief or horror, hard to tell.

Then a voice behind me. 'Hey, you said you were looking for the ones who lived here?'

Gray looked beyond me to the dog walker. 'Trish,' he said into the phone, 'I'll call you back.' He hung up, smiled. 'Yes, Detective Gray Swiggert. You seen them around?'

She shook her head. 'No. But ... I never saw a woman here.'

I thought of the house, of the photograph, the smiling woman. 'He's definitely married,' I said, defensive almost.

The woman gave me a sharp look, shrugged and turned, the dog pirouetting at her heel.

Gray called after her. 'Hey, how long would you say he'd lived here?'

The woman glanced back over her shoulder. 'I don't know. Not long. A month, maybe?'

She turned, carried on her way towards the neighbouring house, slid up the latch on the garden gate, pulled it open, shooing the dog inside.

And I saw it all.

How easy it would be to make a house into a home, a couple of photographs angled here and there, a smattering of magazines, two coffee cups left to drain beside the sink. And, of course, the dog.

'Hey,' I called, my voice shaking, 'you work?'

The woman looked back at me. 'Mondays through Thursdays. Why?'

'And the dog?'

'He has a doggy house in the backyard,' she said, defensive. 'He's fine.'

I felt light-headed, nauseous, and bizarrely like laughing. Because few things make a house a home like a dog. And all it takes is the lifting of a latch, maybe a few doggy treats to tempt him out, to follow this man he doesn't know. And suddenly he's Archer, not Henry, and the world looks entirely different from how it really is.

And when I came for him, it would appear that he had always been right here, waiting.

Because, with a crashing sense of inevitability, I realised that I had been right. That Wolf had disguised his voice because I already knew it, would have recognised it had I heard it. That I had been wrong. That Wolf was not Elliott.

He was Laurie.

Chapter 11

It had been a lie. All of it. Everything of me. I sat in the passenger seat of Gray's car, hunched forward, my head in my hands, as close as I could come to the foetal position. I could not think, could not breathe. Everything about me, the totality of my life, one lie stacked upon another. Tears spilled down my cheeks, a steady stream of them, the dam that had held firm since my mother's death busting open.

Tears rolling, I fixed my gaze on the world beyond the car. My mind blank. The police tape was up now. The search teams and Gray inside the playhouse of the wolf. I cradled my phone in my hand. Why, I didn't know. Who could I call with this? There was no one left. I looked beyond the window to the sky, grey clouds breaking apart, an insulting blue beyond.

I had thought that Wolf was interested in my origin story. But the truth of it was, he had written my origin story. Likely now that there was no swaddled baby left against the walls of the Capitol building, no life-or-death moment wherein exposure could have claimed her. That that narrative had been a lie, designed to disguise ... what? That he had brought her from Canada himself?

We had stood in the snow, the sound of sirens rapidly approaching. Gray and I, two stooges, fooled once more.

'Gray, he has to be Clay.' It had crashed over me, a sense that I had thought this once, had allowed myself to be distracted by the thought of my brother. I had heard the panic in my own voice, 'Wolf. He has to be. There are no other possibilities. We know that Clay went missing at around the same time as the murders, and we know that he was in Wisconsin hours after I was found. The missing-person woman, the one from the website, she said he's either dead or someone else. What if this is who he is? Wolf.'

Gray hadn't answered, had just looked at me, a slow shake of his head, like he too had suddenly found himself in far deeper water than he had anticipated, and the panic grew in me. If he couldn't handle this, what the hell hope did I have?

I leaned my head back against the headrest, watched as a crow landed on the power lines above, its gaze locked on the house below, on the thrum of activity. I wiped my hand across my face.

It was a lie. Every last piece of my story.

I was a construction, a creation of Wolf's imagination.

And then a new feeling rose up in me, of white-hot fury.

No. I was not.

However I had begun this life, I was someone else entirely now.

What had Gray said? Who we are, it's mainly about the choices we make.

So who did I choose to be? I could be curious and clever and, yes, I could be cunning and I could lie. But I cared deeply about the people around me, the world at large.

'Fuck you,' I muttered.

I wiped at my cheeks with the sleeve of my coat and reached into the back seat for my messenger bag.

He had created me, but in so doing, he had created someone uniquely qualified to stop him.

I pulled out my notepad and pen. I wrote the name *Laurie* across the top of a blank page. The word *hero*. The word *firefighter*. *Rescuer*. My pen hovered over the page. And that was why it had worked. Wolf had pulled off an affinity fraud, on a massive scale. You become a member of a group so that you can con the group. He had presented himself as a rescuer, a member of the kind of group one looks to for salvation. And he had presented himself in this way to not just anyone, but to police officers. Had taken me directly to the police station, the firefighter and the lost baby. And they had bought his story. Because why wouldn't they? What threat could he pose? He had saved a child from certain death. They had looked at him, judged him as one of their own. And so they had stopped paying attention, had stopped looking for discrepancies that could have revealed a lie. Because that's what we do as humans, we use shortcuts to help us navigate our way through the world. And one of them is: you are like me, ergo, you are worthy of my trust.

I scrawled the words *affinity fraud* across the page and

studied the shape of them. These kind of cons, they are potent and long-lasting, often stretching on for years and years. Because the victims have established emotional bonds with the fraudster, and therefore the mere consideration of a lie becomes too painful to consider. The police had trusted him. And so my mother had trusted him. And so I had trusted him. So, for years and years and years, he had kept this up, had succeeded in the con.

Not one of us had ever stopped to consider – what if this entire structure is built on a lie?

I thought of Elliott, of my mother's words. He has a criminal record. She said the information had come from the former police chief. Only Laurie, Wolf, whatever we were calling him now, he told me that they remained good friends. What if Wolf himself had fed the information to the chief, encouraged him to warn the family. Because, after all, hadn't he wanted me to stop digging, to leave it all the hell alone. And what better way to achieve that than to make the brother I sought seem dangerous, like someone best avoided.

I studied the paper. What are you going to do next, Wolf? You like us to believe that you're one of us. You make a habit of hiding within the ranks of those we trust.

I grabbed my cell, dialled Gray's number. 'Yeah.'

'It's me. You need to check all of the on-scene personnel.'

Silence. To his credit, he didn't ask me why. 'Already done,' he said. 'He's not here, Rosa.'

365

I bit my lip. Then thought of the police station, of my brother inside it. 'The police station. Elliott is there. He's going to present himself as someone they trust.'

He hesitated. Then, 'I'm on it.'

I hung up. A sudden sense of sickening heat, and I leaned over, dumping my notepad onto the driver's seat, shoved open the car door. Out into the blue sky, bitter against the white snow. I leaned against the car, ice-cold against my back. I stood there, watching the twisting tape. Could feel the tears building again. Muttered, 'No.' Because this is what he wanted, what the murder of Mom was meant to do to me, to devastate me, force me to grind to a halt. I watched the crow shift its way carefully along the wire, setting free a sprinkling of snow. Then I looked back to the house. Something was niggling at me. What was it?

The front door opened, Gray slipping out into the snow, gaze tracking towards the car, locking on me, a quick wave of acknowledgement.

'Well?' I asked, bracing.

'House is clean,' he said. 'Like, crazy clean. We found a burn pit out back, but nothing salvageable. Just the remnants of some old Polaroids, but whatever they showed, it's long gone now.'

I stared at him. 'Polaroids.'

'They're old photographs,' he offered.

I gave him a long look. 'I know that. Just … wait a second.' I took my phone out, dialled Addie, waited as it connected.

'Rosa?' She sounded flustered and fearful.

'I'm fine. I just … I need to ask you something. That stuff Mom had. About my adoption?'

'Yes? I remember it.'

'You'd seen it right? You'd looked through that folder? I mean, before I found out.'

Silence then, like she was afraid to give the answer.

'Adds, I'm not mad, I just need to know about what was in there. You remember?'

'Oh, it was like, a bunch of newspaper articles, court documents on your adoption, photographs …'

'Okay, wait, photographs of who?'

I could hear high-pitched whining in the background. 'Girls, would you quiet down! Um, I don't really remember. You, obviously. From like right after you were found. From your foster home. And I think some with the rescuers.'

The rescuers. Laurie.

'You know,' continued Addie, 'Mom said to me, maybe a month before it all happened, before your fall and all that, that she thought it was time, that you needed to know the truth about where you came from. She said she was going to give you everything, once she could figure it out, how to say it to you, I mean. She said she'd been talking it over with Laurie, that she'd told him she was going to hand everything over, only he thought maybe you weren't ready.' Her voice cracked. 'I know you were mad, Rosa, at her, at all of us, but you need to know she was planning on telling you the truth. She really was.'

I couldn't breathe. 'Thank you, Adds. I love you.'

'Love you too, sweetie.'

I hung up the phone, looked at Gray. 'It was the Polaroids. That was why he came into the house that night. My mother had spoken to him, had told him she was going to tell me. And I'm going to bet that she also told him she had photographs, of him. And he knew that if anyone went digging, those photographs would have connected him with a boy that vanished from Toronto. They would prove that he was Clay, and he didn't want anyone knowing that. That was why he came.'

Gray stuffed his hands into his pockets. 'Shit. Rosa, I think you're right.' He looked back towards the house. 'Jesus. He's probably already someone else by now.'

I looked back towards the house. 'You're saying that because that's what you'd do.'

He looked at me. 'Fair point. So,' he folded his arms, 'what would Wolf do?'

I thought of the nerve it took to place himself right beside me. Of how much risk that had entailed. 'He doesn't understand risk. Not the way you and I do. I think that he has some goal, something that matters to him. And until he achieves that goal, I don't think he's going to let any sense of danger stop him.'

Gray's cell began to ring. 'Hey.' A lengthy pause, 'Okay … hey, Trish, let me just put you on speaker, okay?' He glanced at me. 'It's the station. You need to hear this.'

'You are not going to believe this.' A woman's voice came tinny across the line. 'We ordered a check of the station. This clerk out at the front desk, she notices that

368

one guy, he slips out once he sees her going from person to person checking their IDs. And get this, when he first got there, he introduced himself to her as Elliott's lawyer.'

Gray and I looked at one another.

'You were right,' said Gray. 'He isn't done.'

I looked back to the house, seeing Laurie, that sense of safety he had brought to me. And then the thought that had been hiding within my subconscious. The photograph that had been inside the house. The woman with the flame-red hair, looking at Laurie like he had hung the moon. The wedding dress.

'Gray,' I said, 'somewhere out there, he has a wife.'

Chapter 12

Gray hung up the phone with a sigh. 'Okay, so we haven't been able to find any evidence of a woman in the house. Rosa, I think we need to consider that the woman you saw in the picture with Wolf may be already dead.'

Elliott groaned loudly, leaned forward in the chair, his arms wrapped about his stomach as if somehow that would ease the pain.

I found myself staring at him, studying the shape of his eyes, the slope of his nose. He looked up at me, attention drawn by my gaze, gave me a weak smile.

We had been sequestered, Elliott and Gray and Addie and the girls and I, sent off into the Wisconsin wilds, on the world's most uncomfortable family reunion. To be fair, Addie had attempted it, had made a pass at making small talk with my long-lost brother and, until hours earlier, the suspected murderer of our mother, before finally giving it up as a lost cause and retreating to bed with the children. I'm going to sleep with the girls tonight, she had murmured. Make sure they feel safe. A glance at my brand-new brother, the weight of it enough to sink a ship.

Make sure they feel safe. Make sure they are safe. And, in truth, who could blame her? Who the hell knew who to trust any more?

And so my sister had vanished up the stairs to her children, armed with a cellphone, a copy of *The Time Traveller's Wife* and a rolling pin taken from the kitchen.

The fire had been built up in the hearth, Gray apparently thrilling in the manliness of the task, thick velour curtains pulled tight against the night. The blue sky had morphed to grey and then to howling winds and twisting snow. Could have been cosy, were it not for the ever-present threat of death.

I looked back at my laptop. The lengthy oak tabletop was littered with paperwork, the police files on Wolf, on the deaths of Elizabeth and my mother, my own research into my family of birth, my notepad, dense now with scribbles.

'I can't find anything on NamUs,' said Gray. 'No bodies matching the description of the woman you saw in the wedding picture.' He tapped his pen against the tabletop. 'File says there are kids. But no one knows what happened to them. No bodies matching their description either.'

'You really think this guy would kill his own kids?' asked Elliott.

'Do we think that, Rosa?' asked Gray.

I leaned back in the dining chair, the spine of it digging into my back. What did I think? The trick, of course, is in seeing the world as it is, not as you want it to be. 'If he has children, his relationship with them …

it won't be like other people's relationship with their kids.'

'Would he love them?' asked Elliott.

I considered, gaze moving to the endless parade of open tabs on my laptop. Because it had been my question too, not an easy one to answer. 'I think … it's fair to say that psychopaths, they have a theoretical understanding of what love is. Whether they are capable of feeling it …' I shrugged. 'What we do know is that for a psychopath, relationships are about what others can do for them.' I chewed on my fingernails. 'For him, his children … they are likely to feel like a possession to him. They are important, because he owns them.' Elliott winced. 'The other thing to be aware of is that for psychopaths, their own sense of social standing is really important. Not in terms of how others view them, but in terms of how they view themselves. And there is a certain cache to being a single father, valiantly raising his children alone. These children, they have value to him.'

'And the wife?' asked Gray.

I grimaced. 'Okay, based on what's in that file, he moves from woman to woman pretty easily. Children would be useful to use as a currency in this.' I thought of the woman in the photograph. 'Beth, whoever she is, I'm going to guess she's someone who enhances his sense of his own social status.' I looked at Gray. 'The other thing we know … psychopaths are really good at spotting vulnerabilities in other people. They can read people, can sense their weaknesses. It makes them really good at selecting victims. Beth … perhaps he chose her

372

as a partner because he sensed a vulnerability in her, something he could use to control her.'

'Holy shit,' muttered Elliott.

I rubbed my face. 'Look, the wife, the children. They are tools for him. He will keep them with him for as long as they are useful.'

'And when they aren't?'

I grimaced. 'According to the file, he's learned hard lessons about what happens when you leave someone behind to tell the tale. I think he's going to kill them.'

'I can't believe this,' muttered Elliott. 'I mean, I remember Clay. He was an asshole. But this? This is so far beyond that. This is … evil.'

I turned to look at him. 'You know, victims will often say about the people who con them, "It's so out of character for them." Truth of the matter is, what they did, it was always a part of them, always something they were capable of. It's just that the victims were never allowed to see that portion of their personality. They just didn't know them as well as they thought they did.'

Elliott studied me and I felt myself colouring. My brother. I had thought him to be a monster. And now? The truth was, in spite of the familiarity of his face, the uncanny déjà vu of the way that he moved, he was my brother in name alone. In truth, he remained a stranger.

'Why did he save you then?' asked Elliott, quietly. 'And if he was going to save you, why leave Kyle to die?'

I shook my head, 'I don't know.'

'How do we find him, Rosa?' asked Gray, quietly.

I shook my head, fingers sending the pages of my notebook fluttering. 'Everything he has done, his crimes, his vanishings, it seems that there is always a trigger point for him. A point at which he decides that someone is getting too close, and so his time in that identity is done. And then he flees.'

'Or kills,' murmured Gray.

I nodded. 'The question then becomes, too close to what?'

'What do you mean?'

'Psychopaths, they often have a problem with the way in which they deploy their attention. They become fixated on a goal, and that makes them kind of impervious to environmental cues, signs that the rest of us would take as warnings, that we should back up. It's almost like they can't control their level of fixation on what's important to them.'

'So ... what are you saying?'

'Throughout, he's been fixated on making sure no one gets too close. We thought it was so they didn't figure out the con. But what if it's more than that? All this, all that he's done here. None of it makes sense. Not when you compare it to his past behaviours. Why stick around here? Why keep exposing himself again and again, why not just move on like he has before, become someone new?' I fell silent, thoughts swirling. 'What if this is something else? Something that goes right to the heart of who he considers himself to be.'

They both stared at me, and I drummed my pen against the table.

'Okay,' I said, 'we know that psychopaths place a high value on social status, where they perceive themselves to be in the hierarchy. The file, it's pretty clear that he has said he only kills where he has to.'

'Okay,' agreed Gray.

'He's justifying, rationalising it to himself in a way that allows him to keep thinking of himself as a person of high social standing, not some grubby murderer. That idea, it doesn't fit with his own sense of who he is at all.' I stood up, moved around the table, movements hurried, and reached across for the file containing my research, flipped it open. 'What if, in digging into my own origins, I have inadvertently also been digging into his? And what if there's something there that even he cannot justify to himself?'

I laid the newspaper clipping in the centre of the table, the red of the burning barn looking a lot like blood.

Chapter 13

We stood now, the three of us gathered around the rough oak table, our heads bowed, so that if anyone had looked in, had the heavy curtains not been drawn tight on the dark night outside, it would have looked to them almost like we were praying.

'There were victims,' muttered Gray. 'And so Wolf gave them a culprit. He made sure it was tied up with a pretty little bow. No one is going to investigate a crime that has already been solved.'

'You're suggesting . . .' Elliott's voice wavered. 'You're saying that Hadley . . . that Dad . . . he was murdered?'

I reached out a hand to him, placed it on his arm, and he looked at me like he was pleading, begging me to tell him that he had not spent the past two decades castigating his stepfather in vain, that everything he knew was the truth and not a lie. I tested the idea, nibbling at the edge of it. My father, the monster, the murderer. The victim. The skeleton in our closet, the monster under our bed.

Only what if it was all a con?

I looked to Gray. 'The police report. All they had on Hadley was the positioning of the gunshot, the use of his gun. They looked at the scene and they assumed they knew what had happened.'

'He set it up to look like a familicide,' said Gray. 'Because then …'

'Because,' I said, 'if it's a familicide, then it's not a red-collar crime. It is a crime scene contained within itself. And the money that was missing from the business? That becomes a symptom, rather than a motive.'

'They said the business was on the verge of bankruptcy,' said Elliott, his voice hollow. 'They thought … I thought … that was why.'

I looked at him. 'I think it was why. Clay would have known the business. He could have gained access to its finances.'

'And then?' asked Elliott. 'You think that Hadley … Dad, that he found out, confronted Clay, that Clay got angry?'

'Not angry. When psychopaths commit crimes, it's not about emotion. Or, not usually. They … I guess a better way to look at it would be that they see the crimes as a solution to a problem. You gotta ask, what did the victim know that could have posed a threat to the con?' I reached across the table, pulling out a photo of Hadley. 'If we consider Hadley as the victim …'

'He'd found out about the missing money.'

Gray made a noise in the back of his throat. 'So a teenage boy decides to take out an entire family?'

I tapped my fingers against the table, my gaze on the crackling fire in the hearth, thinking of another fire. 'What if … what if it wasn't like that?' I said, quietly. I

377

watched the flames, thinking of a teenage boy, standing in a barn that was not his, a gun in his hand, taken from the desk of his former boss. Perhaps he is waiting, perhaps he has asked his former boss to meet him there, an empty promise of an explanation for all that has passed. The gun heavy in his hand. Knowing that the man has to die, that it is the only way to disguise what it is he has done. It is clearly the only logical solution.

But a murder. When there is a murder, then there are questions.

And when there is a murder, there has to be a murderer.

But a suicide ...

And so he waits, and he is hidden, because, of course, the man is so much bigger than he. But he has the gun, and a gun is such an equaliser. And he waits and he waits and then finally there is the sound, loud against the anticipation, of a car engine, the slamming of a door, footsteps.

And as the man walks through the doorway of the barn, the boy steps forward and places the gun against the man's temple and he pulls the trigger. Because it is the only logical solution. And perhaps he looks down at the crumpled body and feels – what? – relief. Or does he feel anything at all?

Only then, perhaps, he hears another sound.

'What if they weren't meant to be there?' I murmured. 'We. What if we weren't meant to be there? Maybe he'd assumed that Hadley would come alone. But what if he didn't?'

'So,' said Gray, forehead heavy in a frown, 'he never intended to kill Camille and Kyle. He just ... reacted to changing circumstances. And now what? He feels guilty?'

I shook my head. 'I don't think so. Not guilt. I think that Wolf sees himself as a chameleon. I think he takes pride in his ability to take what he wants and vanish. As far as he's concerned, these things aren't crimes. They're simply him gaming the system. Only the murder of a family, even he struggles to defend that. If it stays a secret to the world, then at least he can pretend to himself that this is not who he is.'

A movement then, Elliott slumping down heavily in the chair. 'Holy shit,' he muttered, head in his hands. 'Holy shit.'

'This is great,' said Gray. 'But it gets us no closer to catching him. And he's still out there somewhere.' He rapped his knuckles against the tabletop. 'You said social status matters to him. The way he sees himself.'

I nodded.

'What if we release it to the media? The reopening of the Lynch case. The exhumation of the bodies ...'

'I think ... I think it might provoke him. Might make him act rashly.' I looked about me. 'And I think I know how to draw him out.'

Chapter 14

Headlights punched through the darkness. Slowing, slowing, stopping, the brakes of the car squealing in protest, pools of light dazzling. I could not breathe. My fingers clutched tight to the wheel. Chest tight, the bulletproof vest feeling more like a straitjacket.

It had gone out on the morning news. The reopening of a solved case.

'Investigators announced today the reopening of a twenty-year-old closed case after a baby girl, long believed dead, was found alive in Madison. Rosa Fisher had no idea when she sent her DNA off for analysis just how big a can of worms she would be opening. Because it turned out that Rosa Fisher was not in fact Rosa Fisher at all, but rather Mia Lynch, the baby daughter of an Ontario family, long believed murdered along with her mother and brother in a tragic murder-suicide. The perpetrator, her own father. The survival of baby Mia has thrown new light onto this decades-old tragedy and has prompted investigators to begin the process of exhuming the rest of the Lynch family victims in search of answers.'

I had sat beside Elliott, the crackling of the fire all but drowning out the reporter's words, had clenched my hands together to stop their shaking. 'Here we go,' I'd muttered.

'You don't have to do this.' My brother's voice had cracked. 'Let me go instead.'

I'd tucked my hands into my armpits. 'It has to be me.'

'He's going to kill you,' said Elliott, bluntly.

I'd glanced at him, the ghost of a smile. 'Hopefully not.'

The car ahead came to a rolling stop, the bumper of it just feet from my own car. The empty turn-in on the dark country road now suddenly feeling breathtakingly full. The driver's door opened, a shadow against the light, a figure emerging.

They had fought me, as I had known they would, had said it was crazy, that they would not allow it, but I understand people and I understand how to apply pressure on precisely the point that matters to them the most. We aren't going to be safe, Gray, not until he's caught. You, me. Then the clincher – Addie and the girls. We have to get him, before … And then I had left it unsaid, because the imagination has so much more power than mere words, and I had watched as my brother-in-law's face had played out the movie to its final scene.

And in the end, it came down to simple math. My

life balanced against the lives of limitless others. The solution to the problem was obvious.

They had sat around me, Gray and Elliott, the three of us gathered about the kitchen table, still strewn with paperwork. I had weighed the cellphone in my hands, trying to remind myself to breathe. And then I had dialled, the faint sound of my fingertips against the flat of the screen deafening in the pregnant silence. Had held my breath as they stared at me, a communal vacuum of waiting.

Then, 'Hello?'

His voice had sounded cautious, edged in doubt. I closed my eyes, letting go of me, letting loose the wolf within.

'Laurie?' I said. My voice quavered. To my surprise, a tear slid down my cheek. 'It's Rosa.'

He needs to feel like he's in control, I had said, studying the picture of the barn fire. See, I've been getting it wrong, this whole time. I've been trying to force him out, to confront him. But what if, instead, I let him win? Let him be who he wants to be. My protector, my hero. The one I can turn to to make everything okay again.

I could hear it, his mind working.

'Did you see it on the news? Did you see what they said?'

Silence, then a careful, 'Yes.'

'They think someone is still out there, Laurie. They say they're no longer sure my father did it. They think he's going to come after me.' My voice had scrambled up an octave or two, panic coursing through me. The dim realisation that I was sufficiently adept at lying that I was conning myself. 'I don't know who I can trust.'

A pause. 'What about the police? Are you with them?'

His voice was rich with concern, and I allowed myself a moment to admire it.

'I think ...' I could feel Gray's gaze on me. 'I feel like they're using me. All they care about is catching this guy.' I took a deep breath. 'Laurie, I just don't know what to do. I didn't know who to turn to.'

'You did right,' he said, softly. 'Tell me where you are. I'll come meet you.'

I watched as the figure stepped into the headlights of my car, squinting into the glare of it and shadow, and I fought my body's urge to fling open the door, to run to him, to throw myself at him and to gouge his fucking eyes out. I saw the outline, long arms, hands that had held a gun to my mother's head. And I felt my foot flex above the gas pedal, my hands tighten on the wheel, hard enough that they blanched white. Logic battling sheer wild emotion.

And then my vision cleared, the figure coalescing into familiarity. Laurie. And someone else. A sense like déjà vu, but not. My heart began to beat faster, time grinding to a halt. Stripping away the grey hair, the glasses, looking beyond it all to the eyes, the shape of the jaw. He had stopped just inside the puddle of the headlights, and feeling flooded me again, of standing somewhere I had stood before.

And then it happened, the whole world erupting into light and sound, cars and people and guns pointing at the figure in the light. Voices shouting, words lost in the tumbledown chaos of it.

I shoved open the car door, knowing I shouldn't, but doing it anyway. And stepping towards the mass of bodies, the hard lines of the pointed weapons. Searching throughout it all for him, not standing now, but rather pushed face down onto the hood of his car. I pushed my way forward, until I could see him, until he could see me. His head had twisted to one side, cheek pressed up against the cold metal of the hood. His gaze scanned the line of SWAT, finding me in amongst them and locking on to me. On his face, the slightest of smiles.

'Rosa.' A new voice now, breath warm against my cheek.

I pulled my gaze towards Gray, a sudden awareness that I was crying.

'It's okay,' he said. 'It's okay, Rosa. You did it. You got him.'

And then my brother was beside me, Elliott, with his arm wrapped around me, and me looking up at him, only his attention, that was trapped somewhere else, glued on the wall of police, the figure of Laurie within.

'Oh my God,' he breathed.

I followed his gaze, 'What?'

Laurie was moving now, SWAT either side of him, guiding him towards a waiting van.

'Elliott, what?'

'Oh my God,' he muttered again. 'We got it wrong.'

'Got ... what?' Gray's head snapped towards him. 'Elliott? What did we get wrong?'

The doors of the SWAT van hanging open, the figure stepping up and in, and turning and looking back at me, and that same smile on his face.

'That's not Clay,' said Elliott. 'That's Kyle.'

I looked to Elliott and I looked back towards the SWAT van and Laurie, and it seemed that my brain had slowed, that I could not make sense of what was before me. And then it happened, the pieces falling into place. That the best way to commit a crime is to make sure there is no culprit left to look for. And that to do that, you need a body.

Clay.

Not a hero. Not a villain.

A victim. A cover.

Dead, so that the police would find the burned corpse of a teenage boy, and so that Kyle could take his family's money, could vanish. Could become Jackson Wolf.

Chapter 15

Eighteen months later

He looked thinner – Kyle, Laurie, Wolf. The lines on his face had deepened and the shadows beneath his eyes had darkened. But his hair, naturally salt-and-pepper now, was neatly cut, and he was clean-shaven, and on his face, an expression of softness. Of grief almost. His hands were clenched together on the table before him, his long fingers twitching, one against the other.

It had been a year and a half, there or thereabouts. A year and a half in which it had seemed that the whole world was one large exhalation. Of starting anew, of patching together the pieces of an old life, turning them into something new.

My PhD was behind me, Dr Rosa Fisher. Or Doc, as Elliott did insist on calling me. And I had found a new identity, no longer the student, but now a researcher out in the University of Chicago. Still researching con men. I think we could all agree I was singularly qualified. I visited with my family, both old and new, as often as I could. Elliott's sons called me Aunt Doc.

I glanced to the right of me, to my girlfriend, Gina.

Another new thing, risen from the ashes of my old life. She gave me a nervous smile, her thumb stroking across the back of my hand. Nearly there, she mouthed.

Was that what this was? An ending? It seemed to me now that this me, she had been shaped in the fire of the hunt for Wolf. Were it all to end, what then?

But then, of course, there remained the wife, the children.

An interview room in Madison PD, the sterility of it made harsher by the flatness of the camera, the small screen. I had sat in a viewing room packed tight with cops and Elliott and half of Madison, so it had seemed. Perhaps it was the press of bodies that had made it so damned hard to breathe. Elliott beside me, and he was just crying, a steady stream of silent tears, his gaze locked on the screen before us and on the serene face of our long-dead brother.

'How could he?' he'd murmured, to himself or to me, I never was sure. No one answered. Because, of course, there were no answers. Nothing that would make this thing any better. For your brother to cheat and lie and steal. And then, rather than risk the exposure of all he has done, to make a plan. To choose a boy, right age, right build, the right amount of stupid. And to murder him, all so that no one will come looking for you. Why would they? You're already dead.

And our father, left to carry the burden of guilt.

No one left who knew the truth.

Then Camille. My mother.

Gray sat across from him, solid as a rock. He had already won.

Wolf had watched him, his gaze absorbing every feature.

'Why hasn't he gotten a lawyer?' muttered Elliott.

'Because it's a game,' I replied, quietly.

Wolf sat, his head tilted in faux sympathy, and listened as Gray laid it out. Our theory of the Lynch murders. How Kyle Lynch became Jackson Wolf. And Wolf had simply sat there, mouth tugged into an almost smile.

'You didn't expect your mom to come home when she did, did you?' asked Gray, voice deliberate. 'She wasn't part of the plan, was she?'

A reaction then, brief enough that for a moment I thought that it might have been a flicker of the screen.

'He's got him,' I murmured.

Wolf leaned further back in his chair, his face sliding to flat.

'Did she see them? Clay and your dad? Did she see what you'd done to them?'

No answer. No reaction, but the briefest tightening of his forehead.

'I bet that must have broken her heart.' Gray tapped his pen against the table. 'You know we're going to get the bodies, right? You know that it's over?'

And then my brother had leaned forward, had set his hands upon the table as if he was reaching for him, and had set his face into a plea. 'Detective Swiggert, I'm just so relieved that it's all finally done with. That I can stop hiding.'

388

A low cheer went up from somewhere behind me, and I held up my hand. Wait.

'Now that I know that my father is actually dead, perhaps I can begin to feel safe again. I can't tell you how hard it's been all these years, always waiting for him to hunt me down, to kill me like he killed the others. If I had known, if I had any idea he had died that same night ... how different my life would have been.'

'Shit,' muttered a detective from Ontario, flown in for the occasion.

'Can he do that?' Elliott looked to me, to the cops, back again. 'Blame our father? After all everyone has already said about him ...'

'He can do what he likes,' said the Ontario detective. 'It's called building a defence.'

Gray had fallen silent, the way he held his fingers taut against the arms of the chair telling me he was rattled. For long moments, no one spoke. Then he said, 'Tell me ... Kyle. Where's your wife? Beth, isn't it?'

It seemed that his face had frozen, that his breath had stopped. Then he shifted, that same tranquillity moving across him. 'I'm sorry,' he said. 'I don't believe I know anyone by that name.'

Gray nodded, slowly, then opened up the cover of the file, sliding two photographs across the table towards him. 'And the children?'

He looked down at the photographs and then slowly looked up, smile almost sympathetic. 'Unfortunately, I don't have children.' He cocked his head to one side.

'Is it possible you've gotten me confused with someone else?'

You know, Elliott had said to me one day – perhaps a month after the arrest of Kyle Lynch, Jackson Wolf – he always did love you. His little baby sister. You said psychopaths, that they can't love. Only Kyle, he did, you know. He worshipped you. Elliott had looked at me, gaze heavy. You said there was a time discrepancy? Six weeks between the murders and your discovery in Madison. I think he tried to keep you. Kyle. He would have been cocky enough, confident that he could raise a baby just as well as anyone else. Only kids, they're exhausting, and a teenage boy on the run ... you can see how that would get old fast. Elliott had looked at me, sadly. I don't know if that helps any, to know that. But ... maybe there is something human underneath there.

A commotion sounded to the right of the courtroom, a door swinging open, the jury.

'All rise.'

In the scrape of chairs on the floor, the rustle of clothing, I sought out Kyle. He stood in a perfectly fitted suit, looking every inch the college professor, his head bowed. Respectful. Weighed down by all that had befallen him.

'Six hours,' muttered Gina. 'They've been out for six hours. Is that good?'

I shrugged, my gaze shifting now to the jury, face after face, their jaws set, a sense of righteous determination hanging over them. 'Alice,' I murmured.

Detective Alice Parr leaned closer to me, shifting to

accommodate the mound of her pregnant belly, her hands roaming across it, again and again, a diamond wedding set catching the light of the courtroom.

'I think we could be in trouble,' I said, quietly.

Alice tugged her gaze away from the jury towards me, and I saw her eyes, wide with fear. Beyond her, Addie and Gray and Drew, looking desperately uncomfortable in a too-big suit.

'Please be seated.'

Alice tucked her arm through mine. 'No,' she said, trying to convince me and herself both. 'It'll be okay.'

It's death by a thousand cuts, the prosecutor had said. We go after him for your mother. It's the strongest in terms of the circumstantial evidence. And if that fails, then we go after him for Elizabeth.

But my gaze flew back to the jury, to the young woman right at the end, to the way her gaze returned, again and again, to my brother at the defence table.

'What you have to realise,' the defence lawyer had said, 'is that this is not the first time someone had entered the home of Nora Fisher. Approximately eight weeks before the murder, a burglary took place. Only it was interrupted, the culprits never caught.'

The murder of my mother, that was, sadly of course, the tragic consequence of the burglars returning, trying their luck again. After all, there was nothing connecting his client, Mr Kyle Lynch, to the scene. No DNA. No fingerprints. No, this was a case of overzealous prosecution, an innocent man, harangued within an inch of his life.

And the rest? The deaths, the cons, the changing identities. Irrelevant, concluded the judge, inadmissible. It is and can only be about the death of Nora Fisher.

I watched as the court settled itself, as Kyle slowly and carefully wiped a tear from his eye, and I dissociated myself from all that I knew, and I looked at my brother like I had never seen him before. And what I saw there was a grief-stricken man of middling age, weighed down by all of the tragedy that had befallen him. And I wanted to scream out to the jury, Don't look at him, don't listen to him. He is conning you.

Alice's hand clutched at my left, Gina my right. A year and a half, there or thereabouts. A year and a half of searching. Of coming home from work and of, night after night, trawling through NamUs, so that in the end my dreams became a never-ending series of facial reconstructions and unclaimed bodies. A year and a half of searching for a dead wife, two dead children, babies who had once existed and who were once loved.

Because there was little else I could do for them now. Only find them and return to them the identities that they had lost.

The jury foreperson stood. A woman in her late middle age, white-blonde hair cut into a long bob. Her voice shook as she spoke, as she affirmed that they had reached a verdict, that, yes, it had been unanimous.

'And what is your verdict?'

'Not guilty.'

Time stopped. My lungs clogged with concrete. Addie letting loose a low wail and Alice's hands flying to her mouth like she needs to hold back a scream. And Kyle, hugging his attorney, crying, looking to the jury, his hands clasped together. Thank you, he mouthed to them.

And then he was hustled from the courtroom, attorneys surrounding him, out past where I sat, and I felt a movement beside me, Alice lunging, like, pregnant or not, she's going to launch herself across the seats and rip his head off, and so I flung my arms out, wrapping her up in a clumsy embrace, the warm weight of her belly against me. And I whispered into her ear, 'No. We're not done, remember?'

And she pulled back, tugging her phone from her pocket, a low constant hum from her. 'Fuck, fuck, fuck.'

I turned to watch him, to see if my brother had left behind a look for me, but there was nothing, only the back of his head and the swinging shut of the door.

'Gabriel,' Alice barked. 'They fucking let him off. You have to arrest him on the Elizabeth Barrow case. Now.' She hung up. 'Gabriel is right outside with Ontario PD. They're going to pick him straight up.' Her hands flapped, shooing Gina and me out into the aisle. 'Hurry.'

Only, when you're six months pregnant, hurry isn't what hurry was, and by the time we were clear, the courtroom was all but empty.

'Fuck,' shouted Alice.

'Rosa?' Gina had stopped at the end of the bench, was crouching down to the floor. 'You see this?' She straightened, handed me an envelope that had been

393

dropped to the ground, my name neatly printed across the front of it, and my stomach lurched. I took it from her, hands shaking, and eased the flap of it open, sliding out the single sheet of paper inside.

Rosa,
Take care of yourself. I'll be sure to tell the kids all about their aunt.
Your loving brother.

The ground buckled beneath me.

'They're alive,' I breathed. 'The children are alive.'

Epilogue

Beth sat cross-legged, morning grass cool beneath her bare legs, a mug of milky coffee cradled in her hands. The sun had begun to crest the horizon, washing the Hohe Munde with light and staining the mountain's snow-topped peak a gentle orange. An eagle circled, somewhere off in the distance, and her gaze followed it in its lazy loops, and Beth allowed herself to breathe out slowly.

'Just think about today,' she murmured to herself. 'Only today.'

A shriek of laughter, punching through the early-morning Alpine quiet and sending a flock of starlings spiralling from the surrounding trees, and Beth smiled, the very motion of it driving away the fear. For the moment at least. She shifted her focus to the end of the garden, where the hedges encircled the vivid green grass, and where the children practised their dance, some traditional thing they had picked up in school. Although it seemed likely that tradition would be hard-pushed to recognise the version she was watching.

She watched as her daughter spiralled, pirouetted, seemed like all she would need was a gust of wind to sweep down the mountainside and she would be lifted up, would join the eagle riding on those thermals. Her son, features still baby-fat full, trailed along behind his sister, awkward hands mimicking her moves, his face split into a watermelon-wide smile.

Her daughter. Her son.

How long had they been that to her?

Not since she met them, because back then it had felt to her that she was an alien, landing on an unfamiliar planet, dropped into the heart of this family, everything unfamiliar and ill at ease. The sticky hands making her shudder, the loud voices making her brain clang against the inside of her skull.

She had never wanted children. That, at least, was the story she had told herself, a balm to protect against her body's rebellion, her fibroid-encrusted uterus. Whatever. Didn't want kids anyway.

And then there was him, and there was them, and then everything changed.

'Mama!' Her daughter's voice rang across the garden, bell-clear. 'He's not doing it right. He's being ... *dumm*.'

Beth raised the cup to her lips, allowing herself a moment with the heat of the coffee, the sweet, the trickling warmth, before she answered. 'Play nicely together, you two. And if he isn't doing it right, then teach him. Yes?'

She had never wanted children. That had been the lie she had told herself, at any rate. And now look at her, her heart taken from her body and split into two and placed into the billowing figures of a girl and a boy.

'That's better,' she called. 'Nice job.'

It always surprised her, the calmness of her voice, how little of the ever-present fear managed to escape with the words. A blessing, and a curse also. If you look like you're in control, then the world assumes that you are. And they leave you to get on with it.

She set down her mug amongst the blades of grass, picked up her phone and set her thumb on the email inbox, the fear grinding in her stomach as the world stilled, the moment stretching out into forever.

No new emails.

Beth shook her head. Same story. Different day.

It had been nineteen months and three days. Nineteen months and three days with each morning bringing with it the fresh realisation that he was gone. The family of four, cut down to three. Nineteen months and three days.

There should be a word, something that described that exquisite state of limbo, of loss and waiting, of love and loneliness. She cast her mind through her German, half sure that there would be something there. The Germans had words for everything.

Beth ran her fingers through the cool grass, twisting a blade up into a spiral and then releasing it to unfurl and blend in the wind.

Maybe tomorrow, she told herself. Maybe he will come home tomorrow.

Author's Note

It is rare that I get to speak to you directly. But, whilst this is a real treat, I'm not here simply to pass the time of day with you. *The Devil You Know* is one of those books that didn't turn out quite like I thought it would, and because of that, I thought that maybe an explanation may help.

Alert readers will have noticed that this is the second of my books to feature Jackson Wolf. If you didn't notice this, don't be alarmed. I frequently forget the names of my children, so I have zero expectations that anyone will remember the names in books released a year apart. Where was I ... oh yes, Jackson Wolf. Wolf was the starting point for me in this series of books. The stories of three women, each complete in and of themselves, but connected by their association to a single man. Whilst each of these books will expand a little on the story of Wolf, there is no order to them, which means you can read any – or all – of them in whatever manner pleases you. Because in each of the books, there is a woman. There is Alice and Rosa and Beth. And these women have stories of their own to tell. If you do, however, decide to join me in my tale of all three of these women, you will find an overarching story. That of Jackson Wolf.

Now to this particular book. I have two major passions in my life – storytelling and psychology. And music. And chocolate. And sometimes my dog, when he's not being a goober. I digress … My psychology has, since the start of my writing career, fuelled my storytelling, helping me to build characters and to understand their world and their responses to the often terrible situations in which they find themselves. In *The Devil You Know*, however, I have taken this a step further. I needed to understand – who was Jackson Wolf? What drove him? And, understanding all that, how would he then behave, react to and understand the world around him? I spent months – literally months, just ask my poor patient editor – immersed in the latest psychological research to help me understand just what I was dealing with here. And, throughout *The Devil You Know*, I have shared what I have learned with you. You don't have to be a psychology nut like me to read this book. But, for those of you who do have an interest, I hope that what I have learned will help you gain a deeper understanding of the world of the con and of a man like Jackson Wolf. All of the psychology information throughout is based on academic research in peer reviewed journals and is correct to the best of our knowledge to date.

That's it. That's all I have to say. Other than thank you for picking up *The Devil You Know* and I very much hope that it brings you pleasure.

Best wishes
Emma Kavanagh

Acknowledgements

No book is ever achieved alone. And this one is no exception.

As always, I would like to thank the wonderful Camilla Wray. Whose brilliance and insight and generosity of spirit make all things possible. Both my career and my life would be far poorer without you in it, my lovely friend.

Thank you to the ever-fabulous Sheila David, and to all the brilliant team at Darley Anderson.

To the team at Orion, whose warmth and enthusiasm truly make this a job that I feel deeply privileged to have, thank you for all that you do. And particularly the incredible Fran Pathak. Working with you is an utter joy.

To my author friends, too many to name. You hold my hand, you keep me sane - or you attempt to, at the very least. Thank you for being always in my corner.

I also need to, rather unusually, thank two of the characters in my book. The name of Rosa Fisher was kindly donated by a lovely young lady who won a draw at the Harrogate book festival. I very much hope that my Rosa Fisher does you credit. Thank you also to

Anne Martin, who became a character in this book in support of With Music In Mind.

To my family and friends, thank you for supporting me on this often crazy journey.

Finally, to my incredible boys, Daniel and Joseph, who make me proud enough to burst. And to Matthew, whose mere presence is enough to make all things well again. I love you all.

Credits

Emma Kavanagh and Orion Fiction would like to thank everyone at Orion who worked on the publication of *The Devil You Know* in the UK.

Editorial
Francesca Pathak
Lucy Frederick

Copy editor
Francine Brody

Proof reader
Jade Craddock

Audio
Paul Stark
Amber Bates

Contracts
Anne Goddard
Paul Bulos
Jake Alderson

Design
Debbie Holmes
Rachael Lancaster
Joanna Ridley
Nick May

Editorial Management
Charlie Panayiotou
Jane Hughes
Alice Davis

Finance
Jasdip Nandra
Afeera Ahmed
Elizabeth Beaumont
Sue Baker

For more about Jackson Wolf ...

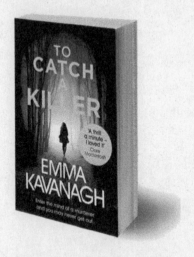

I've been watching you DS Alice Parr.
I saw you trying to save the poor young woman
you found in the park.
The woman I tried to kill.
I've been waiting for you to find her family.
To find someone who cares about her.
But you can't, can you?
You've never had a case like this.
I know everything about you.
You know nothing about me.
Even though I'm the man you're looking for.
And you will never catch me...

'What a rollercoaster ride! A thrill a minute – I loved it'
Clare Mackintosh